FOR MARY,
WITH MY DEAR LOVE

The sails of a square-rigged ship, hung out to dry in a calm.

1 Flying jib
2 Jib
3 Fore topmast staysail
4 Fore staysail
5 Foresail, or course
6 Fore topsail
7 Fore topgallant
8 Mainstaysail
9 Maintopmast staysail
10 Middle staysail
11 Main topgallant staysail

12 Mainsail, or course
13 Maintopsail
14 Main topgallant
15 Mizzen staysail
16 Mizzen topmast staysail
17 Mizzen topgallant staysail
18 Mizzen sail
19 Spanker
20 Mizzen topsail
21 Mizzen topgallant

Illustration source: Serres, Liber Nauticus.

AUTHOR'S NOTE

Those who have read any of the scores of books about Lord Cochrane, or the Earl of Dundonald as he became on his father's death, will remember that he was tried before Lord Ellenborough at the Guildhall for a fraud on the Stock Exchange and found guilty.

Lord Cochrane and his descendants always passionately maintained that he was *not* guilty and that Lord Ellenborough's conduct of the trial was grossly unfair; and most of his biographers, including Professor Christopher Lloyd, the best of them all, agree. Lord Ellenborough and his descendants, however, took the opposite view, and one of them set about refuting the publications of the tenth, eleventh and twelfth earls in a book devoted to the question. But he found that he was not competent to deal with the legal aspects and he handed over the task, together with his papers, to Mr

Attlay of Lincoln's Inn, a very able lawyer whose long, fully-documented and closely-reasoned book might shake all but the most determined of Lord Cochrane's supporters.

Yet the function of Mr Attlay's book, as far as this tale is concerned, was not to prove or disprove the guilt of either side but rather to show exactly how the trial proceeded, and this knowledge I have used, simplifying the complex legal issues, annihilating scores of witnesses, but carefully retaining the structure of the trial, together with its curious timetable. The reader may therefore accept the sequence of events, almost unbelievable to a modern ear, as quite authentic.

CHAPTER ONE

The West Indies squadron lay off Bridge-town, sheltered from the north-east trade-wind and basking in the brilliant sun. It was a diminished squadron, consisting of little more than the ancient *Irresistible*, wearing the flag of Sir William Pellew, red at the fore, and two or three battered, worn-out, under-manned sloops, together with a storeship and a transport; for all the seaworthy vessels were far away in the Atlantic or Caribbean, look-ing for the possible French or American men-of-war and the certain privateers, nu-merous, well-armed, well-handled, full of men, swift-sailing and eager for their prey, the English and allied merchant ships.

Yet although they were old, weather-worn and often iron-sick they were a pleasant sight lying there on the pure blue sea, as out-wardly trim as West Indies spit and polish could make them, with paint and putty dis-guising the wounds of age and their brightwork all ablaze; and although some of them had suffered so from fever in Jamaica and on the Spanish Main that they could scarcely muster hands enough to win their anchors, there were still plenty of men, both officers and foremast-jacks, who were intimately acquainted with the ship that was beating up against the steady breeze and with many of the people in her. She was the *Surprise*, a twenty-eight-gun frigate that had been sent to protect the British whalers in the South Seas from the *Norfolk*, an American man-of-war of roughly equal force. The *Surprise* was even older than the *Irresistible* — indeed she had been on her way to the breaker's yard when she was suddenly given the mission — but unlike her she was a sweet sailer, particularly on a bowline; and if she had not been towing a dismasted ship she would certainly have joined the squadron a little after dinner. As things were, however, it was doubtful whether she would be able to do so before the evening gun.

The Admiral was inclined to think that she might manage it; but then the Admiral was somewhat biased by his strong desire to know whether the *Surprise* had succeeded in her task, and whether the vessel she had in tow was a prize captured in his extensive waters or merely a distressed neutral or a

British whaler. In the first case Sir William would be entitled to a twelfth of her value and in the second to nothing whatsoever, not even to the pressing of a few seamen, for the South Sea whalers were protected. He was also influenced by his ardent wish for an evening's music. Sir William was a large bony old man with one forbidding eye and a rough, determined face; he looked very much the practical seaman and formal clothes sat awkwardly upon his powerful frame; but music meant a very great deal to him and it was generally known in the service that he never put to sea without at least a clavichord, and that his steward had been obliged to take tuning lessons in Portsmouth, Valletta, Cape Town and Madras. It was also known that the Admiral was fond of beautiful young men; but as this fondness was reasonably discreet, never leading to any disorder or open scandal, the service regarded it with tolerant amusement, much as it regarded his more openly-avowed but equally incongruous passion for Handel.

One of these beautiful young men, his flag-lieutenant, now stood by him on the poop, a young man who had begun life — naval life — as a reefer so horribly pimpled that he was known as Spotted Dick, but who with the clearing of his skin had suddenly blossomed into a sea-going Apollo: a sea-going Apollo perfectly unaware of his beauty however, attributing his position solely to his zeal and his perfectly genuine professional merits. The Admiral said, 'It may very well be a prize.' He gazed long through his telescope, and then referring to the captain of the *Surprise*, he added, 'After all, they call him Lucky Jack Aubrey, and I remember him coming into that damned long narrow harbour of Port Mahon with a train of captured merchantmen at his tail like Halley's comet. That was when Lord Keith had the Mediterranean command: Aubrey must have made him a small fortune at every cruise — a very fine eye for a prize, although . . . But I was forgetting: you sailed under him, did you not?'

'Oh yes, sir,' cried Apollo. 'Oh yes, indeed. He taught me all the mathematics I know, and he grounded us wonderfully well in seamanship. Never was such a seaman, sir: that is to say, among post-captains.' The Admiral smiled at the young man's enthusiasm, his flush of candid admiration, and as he trained his glass on the *Surprise* once more he said 'He is a tolerably good hand with a fiddle, too. We played together all through a long quarantine.'

But the flag-lieutenant's enthusiasm was not shared by everyone. Only a few feet below them, in his great cabin, the captain of the *Irresistible* explained to his wife that Jack Aubrey was not at all the thing. Nor was his ship. 'Those old twenty-eight-gun frigates should have been sent to the knacker's yard long ago — they belong to the last age, and are of no sort of use except to make us ridiculous when an American carrying forty-four guns takes one. They are both called frigates, and the landsman don't see the odds. "Oh my eye," he cries, "an American frigate has taken one of ours — the Navy is gone to the dogs — the Navy is no good any more." '

'It must be a great trial, my dear,' said his wife.

'Twenty-four pounders, and scantlings like a line-of-battle ship,' said Captain Goole, who had never been able to digest the American victories. 'And as for Aubrey, well, they call him Lucky Jack, and to be sure he did take a great many prizes in the Mediterranean — Keith favoured him outrageously — gave him cruise after cruise — many people resented it. And then again in the Indian Ocean, when the Mauritius was taken in the year nine. Or was it ten? But I have not heard of anything much since then.

No. It is my belief he overdid it — rode his luck to death. There is a tide in the affairs of men . . .' He hesitated.

'I dare say there is, my dear,' said his wife.

'I do beg, Harriet, that you will not incessantly interrupt every time I open my mouth,' cried Captain Goole. 'There, you have driven it out of my head again.'

'I am sorry, my dear,' said Mrs Goole, closing her eyes. She had come from Jamaica to recover from the fever and to escape being buried among the land-crabs; and sometimes she wondered whether it was a very clever thing to have done.

'However, what the proverb means is that you must make hay while the sun shines but not force things. The minute your luck begins to turn sullen you must strike your topgallantmasts down on deck directly, and take a reef in your topsails, and prepare to batten down your hatches and lie to under a storm staysail if it gets worse. But what did Jack Aubrey do? He cracked on as though his luck was going to last for ever. He must have made a mint of money in the Mauritius campaign, quite apart from the Med; but did he put it into copper-bottomed two-and-a-half per cent stock and live quietly on the interest? No, he did not. He pranced about, keeping a stable of race-horses and

16

entertaining like a lord-lieutenant and covering his wife with diamonds and taffeta mantuas . . .'

'Taffeta mantuas, Captain Goole?' cried his wife.

'Well, expensive garments. Paduasoy — Indian muslin — silk: all that kind of thing. And a fur pelisse.'

'How I should love some diamonds and a fur pelisse,' said Mrs Goole, but not aloud: and she conceived a rather favourable opinion of Captain Aubrey.

'Gambling, too,' said her husband. 'I have absolutely seen him lose a thousand guineas at a sitting in Willis's rooms. And then he tried to mend his fortunes by some crackpot scheme of getting silver out of the dross of an ancient lead-mine — trusted in some shady projector to carry it on while he was at sea. I hear he is in a very deep water now.'

'Poor Captain Aubrey,' murmured Mrs Goole.

'But the real trouble with Aubrey,' said the captain after a long pause during which he watched the distant frigate go about on to the larboard tack and head for Needham's Point, 'is that he cannot keep his breeches on.'

This seemed a very general failing in the Navy, for it was the character her husband gave to many, many of his fellow-officers; and in the first days of her marriage Mrs Goole had supposed that the fleet was largely manned by satyrs. Yet none had ever caused Mrs Goole the slightest uneasiness and as far as she was concerned they might all have been glued into their small-clothes. Her husband perceived her want of total conviction and went on, 'No, but I mean he goes beyond all measure: he is a rake, a whoremonger, a sad fellow. When we were midshipmen together in the *Resolution*, on the Cape station, he hid a black girl called Sally in the cable tiers — used to carry her most of his dinner — cried like a bull-calf when she was discovered and put over the side. The captain turned him before the mast: disrated him and turned him before the mast as a common seaman. But perhaps that was partly because of the tripe, too.'

'The tripe, my dear?'

'Yes. He stole most of the captain's dish of tripe by means of a system of hooks and tackles. We were on precious short commons in our mess, and the girl needed some too — famous tripe it was, famous tripe: I remember it now. So he was turned before the mast for the rest of the commission to learn him morals, and that is why I am senior to him. But it did not answer: presently he was at it again, in the Mediterranean this time, debauching a post-captain's wife when he was only a lieutenant, or a commander at the best.'

'Perhaps he has grown wiser with age and increasing responsibility,' suggested Mrs Goole. 'He is married now, I believe. I met a Mrs Aubrey at Lady Hood's, a very elegant, well-bred woman with a fine family of children.'

'Not a bit of it, not a bit of it,' cried Goole. 'The very last thing I heard of him was that he was careering about Valletta with a red-haired Italian woman. No, no, the leopard don't change his spots. Besides, his father is that mad rakish General Aubrey, the radical member that is always abusing the ministry, and this fellow is his father's son — he was always rash and foolhardy. And now he is going to dismast himself. See how he cracks on! He will certainly run straight on to the Needham's Point reef. He cannot possibly avoid it.'

This seemed to be the general opinion aboard the flagship, and talk died away entirely, to revive some minutes later in laughter and applause as the *Surprise*, racing towards destruction under a great spread of canvas, put her helm alee, hauled on an unseen spring leading from her larboard cathead to the towline, and spun about like a cutter.

'I have not seen that caper since I was a boy,' said the Admiral, thumping the rail with pleasure. 'Very prettily done. Though you have to be damned sure of your ship and your men to venture upon it, by God. Determined fellow: now he will come in easily on this leg. I am sure he is bringing a prize. Did you smoke the spring to his larboard cathead? Good afternoon to you, ma'am,' — this to Mrs Goole, whose husband had abandoned her for a hundred fathoms of decayed cablet — 'Did you smoke the spring to his larboard cathead? Richardson will explain it to you,' he said, making his rheumatic way down the steps to the quarterdeck.

'Well, ma'am,' said Richardson with a shy, particularly winning smile, 'it was not altogether unlike clubhauling, with the inertia of the tow taking the place of the pull of the lee-anchor . . .'

The manoeuvre was particularly appreciated by the watch below, plying spyglasses at the open gunports, and as the *Surprise* ran in on her last leg they exchanged tales about her — her extraordinary speed if handled right and her awkwardness if handled wrong — and about her present skipper. For with all his faults Jack Aubrey was one of the better-known fighting captains, and although few of the men had been shipmates with him many had friends who had been engaged in one or another of his actions. William Harris's cousin had served with him in his first and perhaps most spectacular battle, when, commanding a squat little fourteen-gun sloop, he boarded and took the Spanish *Cacafuego* of thirty-two, and now Harris told the tale again, with even greater relish than usual, the captain in question being visible to them all, a yellow-haired figure, tall and clear on his quarter-deck, just abaft the wheel.

'There's my brother Barret,' said Robert Bonden, sail-maker's mate, at another gun-port. 'Has been Captain Aubrey's coxswain this many a year. Thinks the world of him, though uncommon taut, and no women allowed.'

'There's Joe Noakes, bringing the red-hot poker for the salute,' said a coal-black seaman, having grasped the spyglass. 'He owes me two dollars and an almost new shore-going Jersey shirt, embroidered with the letter P.'

The smoke of the frigate's last saluting gun had hardly died away before her captain's gig splashed down and began pulling for the flagship in fine style. But half way across the roadstead the gig met the flotilla of bumboats bringing sixpenny whores out to the *Surprise*: it was a usual though not invariable practice — one that most captains liked on the grounds that it pleased the hands and kept them from sodomy, though others forbade it as bringing the pox and great quantities of illicit spirits aboard, which meant an endless sick-list, fighting, and drunken crime. Jack Aubrey was one of these. In general he loved tradition, but he thought discipline suffered too much from wholesale whoredom on board; and although he took no high moral stand on the matter he thoroughly disliked the sight of the brawling promiscuity of the lower deck of a newly-anchored man-of-war with some hundreds of men and women copulating, some in more or less screened hammocks, some in corners or behind guns, but most quite openly asprawl. His strong voice could now be heard, coming against the breeze, and the Irresistibles grinned.

'He's telling the bumboats to go and — themselves,' said Harris.

'Yes, but it's cruel hard for a young foremast jack as has been longing for it watch after watch,' observed Bonden, a goatish man, quite unlike his brother.

'Never you fret your heart about the young foremast jack, Bob Bonden,' said Harris. 'He will get what he wants as soon as he goes ashore. And at any rate he knew he was shipping with a taut skipper.'

'The taut skipper is going to get a surprise,' said Reuben Wilks, the lady of the gunroom, and he laughed, deeply though kindly amused.

'Along of the black parson?' said Bonden.

'The black parson will bring him up with a round turn, ha, ha,' said Wilks; and another man said 'Well, well, we are all human,' in the same tolerant, amiable tone. 'We all have our little misfortunes.'

'So that is Captain Aubrey,' said Mrs Goole, looking across the water. 'I had no idea he was so big. Pray, Mr Richardson, why is he calling out? Why is he sending the boats back?' The lady's parents had only recently married her to Captain Goole; they had told her that she would have a pension of ninety pounds a year if he was knocked on the head, but otherwise she knew very little about the Navy; and, having come out to the West Indies in a merchantman, nothing at all about this naval custom, for merchantmen had no time for such extravagances.

'Why, ma'am,' said Richardson, with a

blush, 'because they are filled with — how shall I put it? With ladies of pleasure.'

'But there are hundreds of them.'

'Yes, ma'am. There are usually one or two for every man.'

'Dear me,' said Mrs Goole, considering. 'And so Captain Aubrey disapproves of them. Is he very rigid and severe?'

'Well, he thinks they are bad for discipline; and he disapproves of them for the midshipmen, particularly for the squeakers — I mean the little fellows.'

'Do you mean that these — that these creatures could be allowed to corrupt mere boys?' cried Mrs Goole. 'Boys that their families have placed under the captain's particular care?'

'I believe it sometimes happens, ma'am,' said Richardson; and when Mrs Goole said 'I am sure Captain Goole would never allow it,' he returned no more than a civil, non-committal bow.

'So that is the fire-eating Captain Aubrey,' said Mr Waters, the flagship's surgeon, standing at the lee-rail of the quarterdeck with the Admiral's secretary. 'Well, I am glad to have seen him. But to tell you the truth I had rather see his medico.'

'Dr Maturin?'

'Yes, sir. Dr Stephen Maturin, whose

book on the diseases of seamen I showed you. I have a case that troubles me exceedingly, and I should like his opinion. You do not see him in the boat, I suppose?'

'I am not acquainted with the gentleman,' said Mr Stone, 'but I know he is much given to natural philosophy, and conceivably that is he, leaning over the back of the boat, with his face almost touching the water. I too should like to meet him.'

They both levelled their glasses, focusing them upon a small spare man on the far side of the coxswain. He had been called to order by his captain and now he was sitting up, settling his scrub wig on his head. He wore a plain blue coat, and as he glanced at the flagship before putting on his blue spectacles they noticed his curiously pale eyes. They both stared intently, the surgeon because he had a tumour in the side of his belly and because he most passionately longed for someone to tell him authoritatively that it was not malignant. Dr Maturin would answer perfectly: he was a physician with a high professional reputation, a man who preferred a life at sea, with all the possibilities it offered to a naturalist, to a lucrative practice in London or Dublin — or Barcelona, for that matter, since he was Catalan on his mother's side. Mr Stone was not so personally concerned, but even so he too studied Dr Maturin with close attention: as the Admiral's secretary he attended to all the squadron's confidential business, and he was aware that Dr Maturin was also an intelligence agent, though on a grander scale. Stone's work was mainly confined to the detection and frustration of small local betrayals and evasions of the laws against trading with the enemy, but it had brought him acquainted with members of other organizations having to do with secret service, not all of them discreet, and from these he gathered that some kind of silent, hidden war was slowly reaching its climax in Whitehall, that Sir Joseph Blaine, the head of naval intelligence, and his chief supporters, among whom Maturin might be numbered, were soon to overcome their unnamed opponents or be overcome by them. Stone loved intelligence work; he very much hoped to become a full member of one of the many bodies, naval, military and political, that operated behind the scenes with what secrecy they could manage in spite of the indiscretion, not to say the incurable loquacity of certain colleagues; and he therefore stared with intense curiosity at a man who was, according to his fragmentary, imprecise information, one of the Admiralty's most valued agents — stared until the quarterdeck filled with ceremonial Marines and the sound of bosun's pipes and the first lieutenant said 'Come, gentlemen, if you please. We must receive the Captain of *Surprise*.'

'The Captain of *Surprise*, sir, if you please,' said the secretary at the cabin door.

'Aubrey, I am delighted to see you,' cried the Admiral, striking a last chord and holding out his hand. 'Sit down and tell me how you have been doing. But first, what is that ship you are towing?'

'One of our whalers, sir, the *William Enderby* of London, recaptured off Bahia. She rolled her masts out in a dead calm just north of the line, she being so deep-laden and the swell so uncommon heavy.'

'Recaptured, so a lawful prize. And deep-laden, eh?'

'Yes, sir. The Americans put the catch of three other ships into her, burnt them and sent her home alone. The master of *Surprise*, who was a whaler in his time, reckons her at ninety-seven thousand dollars. A sad time we have had with her, both of us being so precious short of stores. We did rig jury-masts made out of various bits and pieces and made fast with our shoe-strings, but she lost them in last Sunday's blow.'

'Never mind,' said the Admiral, 'you have brought her in, and that is the main thing. Ninety-seven thousand dollars, ha, ha! You shall have everything you need in the way of stores: I shall give particular orders myself. Now give me some account of your voyage. Just the essentials to begin with.'

'Very good, sir. I was unable to come up with the *Norfolk* in the Atlantic as I had hoped, but south of Falkland's Islands I did at least recapture the packet she had taken, the *Danaë* . . .'

'I know you did. Your volunteer commander — what was his name?'

'Pullings, sir. Thomas Pullings.'

'Yes, Captain Pullings — brought her in for wood and water before carrying her home. He was in Plymouth before the end of the month — having been chased like smoke and oakum for three days and nights by a heavy privateer — an amazing rapid passage. But tell me, Aubrey, I heard there were two chests of gold aboard that packet, each as much as two men could lift. I suppose you did not recapture them too?'

'Oh dear me no, sir. The Americans had transferred every last penny to the *Norfolk* within an hour of taking her. We did recover some confidential papers, however.'

At this point there was a silence, a silence

that Captain Aubrey found exceedingly disagreeable. An untoward fall, the bursting open of a hidden brass box, had shown him that these papers were in fact money, a perfectly enormous sum of money, though in a less obvious form than coin; but this was unofficial knowledge, acquired only by accident, in his capacity as Maturin's friend, not his captain; and the real custodian of it was Stephen, whose superiors in the intelligence service had told him where to find the box and what to do with it. They had not told him why it was there, but no very great penetration was required to see that a sum of such extraordinary magnitude, in such an anonymous and negotiable form, must be intended for the subversion of a government at least. It was clearly something that Captain Aubrey could not speak about openly except in the improbable event of the Admiral's having been informed and of his giving a lead; but Jack hated this concealment — there was something sly, shifty and mean about it, together with an edge of very dangerous dishonesty — and he found the silence more and more oppressive until he saw that in fact it was caused by Sir William's private conversion of ninety-seven thousand dollars into pounds and his division of the answer by twelve: this with a piece of black pencil on the corner of a dispatch. 'Forgive me for a moment,' said the Admiral, looking up from his sum with a cheerful face. 'I must pump ship.'

The Admiral vanished into the quartergallery, and as Jack Aubrey waited he recalled the conversation he had had with Stephen while the *Surprise* was running in. By nature and profession Stephen was exceedingly close; they had never spoken about these bonds, obligations, bank-notes and so on until it became obvious that Jack would be summoned aboard the flagship in the next few hours, but then in the privacy of the frigate's stern-gallery, he said, 'Everyone has heard the couplet

In vain may heroes fight and patriots rave
If secret gold sap on from knave to knave

but how many know how it goes on?'

'Not I, for one,' said Jack, laughing heartily.

'Will I tell you, so?'

'Pray do,' said Jack.

Stephen held up a watch-bill by way of symbol, and with a significant look he continued,

'Blest paper credit! last and best supply!

That lends corruption lighter wings to fly!
A single leaf shall waft an army o'er
Or ship off senates to a distant shore.
Pregnant with thousands flits the scrap unseen
And silent sells a king, or buys a queen.'

'I wish someone would try to corrupt me,' said Jack. 'When I think of how my account with Hoares must stand at the present moment, I would ship any number of senates to a distant shore for five hundred pounds; and for another ten the whole board of Admiralty too.'

'I dare say you would,' said Stephen. 'But you take my meaning, do you not? Were I in your place I should glide over that unhappy brass box and its contents, with just a passing reference to *certain confidential papers* to salve your conscience. I will come with you, if I may, so that if the Admiral prove inquisitive, I may toss him off with a round turn.'

Jack looked at Stephen with affection: Dr Maturin could dash away in Latin and Greek, and as for modern languages, to Jack's certain knowledge he spoke half a dozen; yet he was quite incapable of mastering low English cant or slang or flash expressions, let alone the technical terms necessarily used aboard ship. Even now, he

31

suspected, Stephen had difficulty with starboard and larboard.

'The less said about these things the better,' added Stephen. 'I wish . . .' But here he stopped. He did not go on to say that he wished he had never seen these papers, had never had anything to do with them; but that was the case. Money, though obviously essential on occasion, usually had a bad effect on intelligence — for his part he had never touched a Brummagem farthing for his services — and money in such exorbitant, unnatural amounts might be very bad indeed, endangering all those who came into contact with it.

'I don't know how it is, Aubrey,' said the Admiral, coming back, 'but I seem to piss every glass these days. Perhaps it is anno Domini, and nothing to be done about it, but perhaps it is something that one of these new pills can set right. I should like to consult your surgeon while *Surprise* is refitting. I hear he is an eminent hand — was called in to the Duke of Clarence. But that to one side: carry on with your account, Aubrey.'

'Well, sir, not finding the *Norfolk* in the Atlantic I followed her round into the South Sea. No luck at Juan Fernandez, but a little later I had word of her playing Old Harry among our whalers along the coast of Chile and Peru and among the Galapagos. So I proceeded north, retaking one of her prizes on the way, and reached the islands a little after she had left; but there again I had fairly certain intelligence that she was bound for the Marquesas, where her commander meant to establish a colony as well as snapping up the half dozen whalers we had fishing in those waters. So I bore away westward, and to cut a long story short, after some weeks of sweet sailing, when we were right in her track — saw her beef-barrels floating — we had a most unholy blow, scudding under bare poles day after day, that we survived and she did not. We found her wrecked on the coral-reef of an uncharted island well to the east of the Marquesas; and not to trouble you with details, sir, we took her surviving people prisoner and proceeded to the Horn with the utmost dispatch.'

'Well done, Aubrey, very well done indeed. No glory, nor no cash from the *Norfolk*, I am afraid, it being an act of God that dished her; but dished she is, which is the main point, and I dare say you will get head-money for your prisoners. And then of course there are these charming prizes. No: a very satisfactory cruise, upon the whole. I congratulate you. Let us drink a glass of bottled ale: it is my own.'

'Very willingly, sir. But there is something I should tell you about the prisoners. From the beginning the captain of the *Norfolk* behaved very strangely; in the first place he said the war was over . . .'

'That's fair enough. A legitimate ruse de guerre.'

'Yes, but there were other things, together with a want of candour that I could not understand until I learnt that he was trying, naturally enough, to protect part of his crew; some of his men were deserters from the Navy and some had taken part in the *Hermione* . . .'

'The *Hermione*!' cried the Admiral, his face growing pale and wicked at the mention of that unhappy frigate and the still unhappier mutiny, when her crew murdered their inhuman captain and most of his officers and handed the ship over to the enemy on the Spanish Main. 'I lost a young cousin there, Drogo Montague's boy. They broke his arm and then fairly hacked him to pieces, only thirteen and as promising a youngster as you could wish, the damned cowardly villains.'

'We had a certain amount of trouble with them, sir, the ship having been blown off for a while; and some were obliged to be knocked on the head.'

'That saves us the trouble of hanging them. But you have some left, I trust?'

'Oh yes, sir. They are in the whaler, and if they might be taken off quite soon I should esteem it a kindness. We have never a boat to bless ourselves with, apart from my gig, and our few Marines are fairly worn to the bone with guarding them watch and watch.'

'They shall be clapped up directly,' cried the Admiral, pealing on his bell. 'Oh it will do my heart good to see 'em dingle-dangle at the yardarm, the carrion dogs. *Jason* should be in tomorrow and with you that will give us just enough post-captains for a court-martial.'

Jack's heart sank. He loathed a court-martial: he loathed a hanging even more. He also wanted to get away as soon as he had completed his water and taken in stores enough to carry him home, and from the obvious paucity of senior officers off Bridgetown he had thought he might be able to sail in two days' time. But it was no good protesting. The secretary and the flag-lieutenant were both in the cabin; orders were flying; and now the Admiral's steward brought in the bottled ale.

It was intolerably fizzy as well as luke-warm, but once his orders were given the

Admiral drank it down in great gulps, with evident pleasure; presently the savage expression faded from his grim old face. After a long pause in which the clump of Marines' boots could be heard, and the sound of boats shoving off, he said 'The last time I saw you, Aubrey, was when Dungannon gave us dinner in the *Defiance*, and afterwards we played that piece of Gluck's in D minor. I have hardly had any music since, apart from what I play for myself. They are a sad lot in the wardroom here: German flutes by the dozen and not a true note between 'em. Jew's harps are more their mark. And all the mids' voices broke long ago; in any case there's not one can tell a B from a bull's foot. I dare say it was much the same for you, in the South Sea?'

'No, sir, I was much luckier. My surgeon is a capital hand with a violoncello; we saw away together until all hours. And my chaplain has a very happy way of getting the hands to sing, particularly Arne and Handel. When I had *Worcester* in the Mediterranean some time ago he brought them to a most creditable version of the *Messiah*.'

'I wish I had heard it,' said the Admiral. He refilled Jack's glass and said, 'Your surgeon sounds a jewel.'

'He is my particular friend, sir: we have

sailed together these ten years and more.'

The Admiral nodded. 'Then I should be happy if you would bring him this evening. We might take a bit of supper together and have a little music; and if he don't dislike it, I should like to consult him. Yet perhaps that might be improper; I know these physical gentlemen have a strict etiquette among themselves.'

'I believe your surgeon would have to give his consent, sir. They probably know one another, however, and it would be no more than a formality; Maturin is aboard at this moment, and if you wish I will speak to him before I pay my call on Captain Goole.'

'You are going to wait on Goole, are you?' asked Sir William.

'Oh yes, sir: he is senior to me by a good six months.'

'Well, do not forget to wish him joy. He was married a little while ago: you would have thought him safe enough, at his age, but he is married, and has his wife aboard.'

'Lord!' cried Jack. 'I had no idea. I shall certainly give him joy — and he has her aboard?'

'Yes, a meagre yellow little woman, come from Kingston for a few weeks to recover from a fever.'

Jack's heart and mind were so filled with

thoughts of Sophie, his own wife, and with a boundless longing for her to be aboard that he missed the sense of the Admiral's words until he heard him say 'You will tip it the civil to them, Aubrey, when you run each of 'em to earth. These medicos are a stiff-necked, independent crew, and you must never cross them just before they dose you.'

'No, sir,' said Jack, 'I shall speak to them like a sucking dove.'

'Pig, Aubrey: sucking *pig*. Doves don't suck.'

'No, sir. I shall probably find them together, talking about medical matters.'

So indeed they were. Mr Waters was showing Dr Maturin some of his pictures of the most typical cases of leprosy and elephantiasis that he had met with on the island — remarkably well-drawn, well-coloured pictures — when Jack came in, delivered his message, took one glance at the paintings and hurried away to have a word with the Admiral's secretary before paying the necessary call on Captain Goole.

Mr Waters finished his description, returned his last example of Barbados leg to its folder, and said, 'I am sure you have observed that most medical men are hypochondriacs, Dr Maturin.' This, delivered with a painfully artificial smile, was clearly a prepared statement: Stephen made no reply, and the surgeon went on, 'I am no exception, and I wonder whether I too may importune you. I have a swelling here' — putting his hand to his side — 'that gives me some concern. I have no opinion at all of any of the surgeons on this station, least of all my assistants, and I should very much value your reflections upon its nature.'

'Captain Aubrey, sir, what may I have the pleasure of doing for you?' asked the secretary, smiling up at him.

'You would put me very much in your debt by producing a bag of mail for the *Surprise*,' said Jack. 'It is a great while since any of us has heard from home.'

'Mail for *Surprise*?' said Mr Stone doubtfully. 'I scarcely think — but I will ask my clerks. No, alas,' he said, coming back, 'I am very sorry to say that there is nothing for *Surprise*.'

'Oh well,' said Jack, forcing a smile, 'it don't signify. But perhaps you have some newspapers, that will give me an idea of how things stand in the world: for obviously you are much too busy with this damned court-martial to tell me the history of the last few months.'

'Not at all, not at all,' said Mr Stone. 'It will take me no time to tell you that things are going from bad to worse. Buonaparte is building ships in every dockyard, faster than ever; and faster than ever ours are wearing out, with perpetual blockade and perpetually keeping the sea. He has very good intelligence and he foments discord among the allies — not that they need much encouragement to hate and distrust one another, but it is wonderful how he touches on the very spot that hurts, almost as though he had someone listening behind the cabinet door, or under the council table. To be sure our armies make some progress in Spain; but the Spaniards . . . well, you know something of the Spaniards, sir, I believe. And in any event, it is doubtful that we can go on supporting all these people or even paying for our own part of the war. I have a brother in the City, and he tells me that the funds have never been so low, and that trade is at a stand: men walk about on Change with their hands in their pockets, looking glum: there is no gold to be had — you go to the bank to draw out some money, money that you deposited with them in guineas, and all they will give you is paper — and nearly all securities are a drug on the market: South Sea annuities at fifty-eight-and-a-half for example! Even East India stock is at a very shocking figure, and as for Exchequer bills

. . . There was a flurry of activity at the beginning of the year, with a rumour of peace causing prices to rise; but it died away when the rumour proved false, leaving the City more depressed than ever. The only thing that prospers is farming, with wheat at a hundred and twenty-five shillings the quarter, and land is not to be had for love or money; but at present, sir, a man with say five thousand pounds could buy stock, capital stock, that would have represented a handsome estate before the war. Here are some papers and magazines that will tell it all in greater detail; they will depress your spirits finely, I do assure you. Yes, Billings,' — this to a clerk — 'what is it?'

'Although there is no mail for Captain Aubrey, sir,' said Billings, 'Smallpiece says there was someone inquiring for him, a black man; and he conceives the black man might have a message at least, if not a letter.'

'Was he a slave?' asked Jack.

'Was he a slave?' called Billings, cocking his ear for the answer. Then, 'No, sir.'

'Was he a seaman?' asked Jack.

No, he was not; and when at last Smallpiece came sidling in, intensely, painfully shy and almost inarticulate, it appeared that the black man seemed to be an educated person — had first inquired for

Surprise in a general way among those that went ashore, when first the squadron came to Bridgetown, and then, since the frigate was reported in these waters, more particularly for Captain Aubrey.

'I know no educated black man,' said Jack, shaking his head. It was not impossible that a West Indian lawyer might employ a Negro clerk; and affairs being in so critical a state at home, it was not impossible that the clerk might wish to serve a writ on him. This could only be done on shore, however, and Jack instantly determined to remain aboard throughout his stay. He took the newspapers, thanked Mr Stone and his clerks, and returned to the quarterdeck. Here he found his midshipman, horribly shabby among all the snowy flagship youngsters, but obviously stuffing them up with prodigious tales of the Horn and the far South Sea, and to him he said, 'Mr Williamson, my compliments to Captain Goole and would it be convenient if I were to wait upon him in ten minutes.'

Mr Williamson brought back the answer that Captain Aubrey's visit would be convenient, and to this, on his own initiative, he added Captain Goole's best compliments. He would have made them respectful too, if a certain sense of the possible had not restrained him at the last moment; for he loved his Captain.

During this time Jack leant over the quarterdeck rail, by the starboard hances, in the easy way allowed to those of his rank, looking down into the waist and over the side. He had given his bargemen leave to come aboard and there was only the boat-keeper in the gig, talking eagerly to some unseen friend through an open port on the lower deck. There were several hands on the gangway and in the waist who stood facing aft and looking at him fixedly in the way peculiar to former shipmates who wished to be recognized, and again and again he broke off his small-talk with the first and flag lieutenants to call out 'Symonds, how do you do?' 'Maxwell, how are you coming along?' 'Himmelfahrt, there you are again, I see,' and each time the man concerned smiled and nodded, putting his knuckle to his forehead or pulling off his hat. Presently Barret Bonden and his Irresistible brother came up the forehatchway and he noticed that both of them looked at him not only with particular attention but also with that curious, slightly amused and even arch expression that he had seen, more or less clearly, on the faces of those men in the flagship who had sailed with him before. He could not make it out, but before he could really put his mind to the question his time was up and he walked aft to the captain's cabin.

Of his own free will Captain Goole would never have received Captain Aubrey. Midshipman Goole had behaved meanly, discreditably over that far-distant tripe; he had played a material though admittedly subordinate part in the theft, he had eaten as much as anyone in the berth; and on being hauled up before Captain Douglas he had blown the gaff — while utterly denying his share he had nevertheless turned informer. It was a pitiful performance and he had never forgiven Jack Aubrey. But he had no choice about seeing him; in the matter of formal calls the naval etiquette was perfectly rigid.

'I would not receive him, still less introduce him to you,' said Goole to his wife, 'if the rules of the service did not require it. He will be there directly, and he must stay for at least ten minutes. I shall not offer him anything to drink, however; and he will not take root. In any case he drinks far too much, like his friend Dundas — another man who cannot keep his breeches on, by the way — half a dozen natural children to my certain knowledge — birds of a feather, birds of a feather. It is the ruin of society.' A pause.

'You would never think so to look at him now, but Aubrey was once considered handsome; and it may be that which — hush, here he is.'

Jack had not forgotten Captain Douglas's tripe, nor the spectacular consequences of its theft — consequences that had seemed catastrophic at the time, although in fact he could scarcely have spent his time more profitably, since his half-year as a common seaman gave him an intimate, inside knowledge of the lower deck, its likes and dislikes, its beliefs and opinions, and of the true, unvarnished nature of its daily life — nor had he forgotten Goole. But he had forgotten the details of Goole's conduct, and although he remembered him as something of a scrub he bore him no ill-will; indeed, as he now walked into the cabin he was quite pleased to see such an old shipmate and he congratulated Goole on his marriage with perfect sincerity, smiling upon them both with an amiable candour that improved Mrs Goole's already favourable opinion of him. She did not find it at all surprising that he had been considered handsome; even now, although his scarred, weather-beaten countenance had nothing, but nothing, of the bloom of youth and although he weighed too much, he was not ill-looking; he had a certain massive, leonine style, and he fairly towered over Goole, who had no style of any kind; and his blue eyes, all the bluer in his mahogany face, had the good-natured expression of one who is willing to be pleased with his company.

'I am a great friend to marriage, ma'am,' he was saying.

'Indeed, sir?' she replied; and then, feeling that something more was called for, 'I believe I had the pleasure of meeting Mrs Aubrey just before I left England, at Lady Hood's.'

'Oh, how was she?' cried Jack, his face lighting up with extraordinary pleasure.

'I hope she was the same lady, sir,' said Mrs Goole hesitantly. 'Tall, with golden hair done up so, grey eyes and a wonderful complexion; a blue tabby gown with long sleeves gathered here —'

'Really, Mrs Goole,' said her husband.

'That is Sophie for sure,' said Jack. 'It is an age since I had any word from home, being the far side of the Horn — would give the world to hear from her — pray tell me just how she looked — what she said — I suppose none of the children were there?'

'Only a little boy, a fine little boy, but Mrs Aubrey was telling Admiral Sawyer about her daughters' chickenpox, now so far behind them that she had allowed Captain

Dundas to take them a-sailing in his cutter.'

'Bless them' cried Jack, sitting down beside her; and they engaged in a close conversation on the subject of chickenpox, its harmless and even beneficent nature, the necessity for passing through such things at an early age, together with considerations on the croup, measles, thrush, and redgum, until the flagship's bell reminded him that he must return to the *Surprise* for his fiddle.

The diseases that Dr Maturin and Mr Waters discussed were of quite a different order of gravity, but at last Stephen stood up, turned down the cuffs of his coat, and said, 'I believe I may venture to assert, though with all the inevitable reserves, of course, that it is not malignant, and that we are in the presence not of the tumour you mentioned, still less of a metastasis — God between us and evil — but of a splanchnic teratoma. It is awkwardly situated however and must be removed at once.'

'Certainly, dear colleague,' said Waters, fairly glowing with relief. 'At once. How grateful I am for your opinion!'

'I never much care for opening a belly,' observed Stephen, looking at the belly in question with an objective, considering eye, rather like a butcher deciding upon his cut. 'And of course in such a position I should require intelligent assistance. Are your mates competent?'

'They are reckless drunken empirical sots, the pair of them, the merest illiterate sawbones. I should be most reluctant to have either of them lay a hand on me.'

Stephen considered for a while: it was difficult enough in all conscience to love one's fellow men by land, let alone cooped up in the same ship with no possibility of escape from daily contact, or even to remain on civil terms; and clearly Waters had not accomplished this necessary naval feat. He said, 'I have no mate myself. The gunner, running mad, murdered him off the coast of Chile. But our chaplain, Mr Martin, has a considerable knowledge of physic and surgery; he is an eminent naturalist and we have dissected a great many bodies together, both warm-blooded and cold; but as far as I can recall he has not seen the opening of a living human abdomen and I am sure it would give him pleasure. If you wish, I will ask him to attend. In any case I must return to the ship for my violoncello.'

Stephen mounted the *Irresistible*'s various ladders, losing his way once or twice but emerging at last into the brilliant light of the quarterdeck. He stood blinking for a while, and then, putting on his blue spectacles, he

48

saw that the larboard side of the ship was crowded with bumboats and returning liberty-men. The flag-lieutenant was lean- ing over the rail, chewing a piece of sugar-cane and bargaining for a basket of limes, a basket of guavas, and an enormous pineapple; when these had been hoisted aboard Stephen said to him, 'William Richardson, joy, will you tell me where the Captain is, now?'

'Why, Doctor, he went back to the ship just after five bells.'

'Five bells,' repeated Stephen. 'Sure, he said something about five bells. I shall be reproved for unpunctuality again. Oh, oh. What shall I do?'

'Do not let it prey on your mind, sir,' said Richardson. 'I will pull you over in the jollyboat; it is no great way, and I should like to see some of my old shipmates again. Captain Pullings told me that Mowett was your premier now. Lord! Only think of old Mowett as a first lieutenant! But, sir, you are not the only one to be asking after Captain Aubrey. There is a person just come aboard again on the same errand — there he is,' he added, nodding along the larboard gangway to where a tall young black man stood among a group of hands. Stephen recognized them all as men he had sailed with in former commissions, most of them Irish, all of them Catholics, and he observed that they were looking at him with curiously amused expressions while at the same time they gently, respectfully urged the tall young black man to go aft; and before Stephen had time to call out a greeting — before he could decide between 'Ho, shipfellows' and 'Avast, messmates' — the young man began walking towards the quarterdeck. He was dressed in a plain snuff-coloured suit of clothes, heavy square-toed shoes and a broad-brimmed hat; he had something of the air of a Quaker or a seminarist, but of an uncommonly powerful, athletic seminarist, like those from the western parts of Ireland who might be seen walking about the streets of Salamanca; and it was in the very tones of an Irish seminarist that he now addressed Stephen, taking off his hat as he did so. 'Dr Maturin, sir, I believe?'

'The same, sir,' said Stephen, returning his salute. 'The same, at your service.' He spoke a little at random, for the bare-headed young man standing there in the full sun before him was the spit, the counterpart, the image of Jack Aubrey with some twenty years and several stone taken off, done in shining ebony. It made no odds that the young man's hair was a tight cap of black curls rather than Jack's long yellow locks, nor that his nose had no Roman bridge; his whole essence, his person, his carriage was the same, and even the particular tilt of his head as he now leant towards Stephen with a modest, deferential look. 'Pray sir, let us put on our hats, for all love, against the power of the sun,' said Stephen. 'I understand you have business with Captain Aubrey?'

'I have, sir, and they are after telling me you would know might I see him at all. I hear no boats are allowed by his ship, but it is the way I have a letter for him from Mrs Aubrey.'

'Is that right?' said Stephen. 'Then come with me till I bring you where he is. Mr Richardson, you will not object to another passenger? We might take turns with plying the oars, the weight being greater.'

The pull across was comparatively silent: Richardson was busy with his sculls; the black man had the gift, so rare in the young, of being quiet without awkwardness; and Stephen was much taken up with this transposition of his most intimate friend; however, he did say 'I trust, sir, that you left Mrs Aubrey quite well?'

'As well, sir, as ever her friends could desire,' said the young man, with that sudden flashing smile possible only to those with brilliant white teeth and a jet-black face.

'I wish you may be right, my young friend,' said Stephen inwardly. He knew Sophie very well; he loved her very dearly; but he knew that she was quick and perceptive and somewhat more subject to jealousy and its attendant miseries than was quite consistent with happiness. And without being a prude she was also perfectly virtuous, naturally virtuous, without the least self-constraint.

The young man was not unexpected in the *Surprise*; the rumour of his presence had spread to every member of the ship's company except her Captain and he came aboard into an atmosphere of kindly, decently-veiled but intense curiosity.

'Will you wait here now while I see is the Captain at leisure?' said Stephen. 'Mr Rowan will no doubt show you the various ropes for a moment.'

'Jack,' he said, walking into the cabin. 'Listen, now. I have strange news: there was a fine truthful young black man aboard the Admiral inquiring for you, told me he had a message from Sophie, so I have brought him along.'

'From Sophie?' cried Jack.

Stephen nodded and said in a low voice,

'Brother, forgive me, but you may be surprised by the messenger. Do not be disconcerted. Will I bring him in?'

'Oh yes, of course.'

'Good afternoon to you, sir,' said the young man in a deep, somewhat tremulous voice as he held out a letter. 'When I was in England Mrs Aubrey desired me to give you this, or to leave it in good hands were I gone before your ship came by.'

'I am very much obliged to you indeed, sir,' said Jack, shaking him warmly by the hand. 'Pray sit down. Killick, Killick there. Rouse out a bottle of madeira and the Sunday cake. I am truly sorry not to be able to entertain you better, sir — I am engaged to the Admiral this evening — but perhaps you could dine with me tomorrow?'

Killick had of course been listening behind the door and he was prepared for this: he and his black mate Tom Burgess came in at once, making a reasonably courtly train, as like a land-going butler and footman as they could manage; but Tom's desire to get a really good view of the visitor, who sat facing away from him, was so violent that they fell foul of one another just as the wine was pouring. When the 'God-damned lubbers' had withdrawn, crestfallen, and they were alone again Jack looked keenly at the young man's face — it was strangely familiar: surely he must have seen him before. 'Forgive me,' he said, breaking the seal, 'I will just glance into this to see whether there is anything urgent.' There was not. This was the third copy of a letter sent to the ports where the *Surprise* might touch on her homeward voyage: it spoke of the progress of Jack's plantations, the slow indeterminate stagnation of the legal proceedings, and the chickenpox, then at its height; and at the bottom of the page a hurried postscript said that Sophie would entrust this to Mr Illegible, who was bound for the West Indies and who had been so kind as to call on her.

He looked up, and again this uneasy sense of familiarity struck him; but he said, 'It was exceedingly kind of you to bring me this letter. I hope you left everyone at Ashgrove Cottage quite well?'

'Mrs Aubrey told me the children were taken with the chickenpox, and she was concerned for them, sure; but a gentleman that was sitting by whose name I did not catch said there was no danger at all, at all.'

'I do not believe my wife quite caught your name either, sir,' said Jack. 'At all events I cannot make out what she writes.'

'My name is Panda, sir, Samuel Panda,

and my mother was Sally Mputa. Since I was going to England with the Fathers she desired me to give you these,' — holding out a package — 'and that is how I came to go to Ashgrove Cottage, hoping to find you there.'

'God's my life,' said Jack, and after a moment he slowly began to open the package. It contained a sperm-whale's tooth upon which he had laboriously engraved HMS *Resolution* under close-reefed topsails when he was a very young man, younger even than the tall youth facing him; it also contained a small bundle of feathers and elephant's hair bound together with a strip of leopard's skin.

'That is a charm to keep you from drowning,' observed Samuel Panda.

'How kind,' said Jack automatically. They looked at one another with a naked searching, eager on the one side, astonished on the other. There were few mirrors hanging in Jack's part of the ship — only a little shaving-glass in his sleeping-cabin — but the extraordinarily elaborate and ingenious piece of furniture that Stephen's wife Diana had given him and that was chiefly used as a music-stand had a large one inside the lid. Jack opened it and they stood there side by side, each comparing, each silently, intently, looking for himself in the other.

'I am astonished,' said Jack at last. 'I had no idea, no idea in the world . . .' He sat down again. 'I hope your mother is well?'

'Very well indeed, sir, I thank you. She prepares African medicines in the hospital at Lourenço Marques, which some patients prefer.'

Neither spoke until Jack said 'God's my life' again, turning the whale tooth in his hand. Few things at sea could amaze him and he had suffered some shrewd blows without discomposure, but now his youth coming so vividly to life took him wholly aback.

'Will I tell you how I come to be here, sir?' asked the young man out of the silence, in his deep, gentle voice.

'Do, by all means. Yes, pray do,' said Jack.

'We removed to Lourenço Marques about the time I was born — my mother came from Nwandwe, no great way off — and there it was that the Fathers took me in when I was a little small boy, and very sickly, it appears. My mother was married to an ancient Zulu witch-doctor at the time — a heathen, of course — so they brought me up and educated me.'

'Bless them,' said Jack. 'But is not Lourenço Marques on Delagoa Bay — is it not Portuguese?'

'It *is* Portuguese, sir, but Irish entirely. That is to say, the Mission came from the County Roscommon itself; and it was Father Power and Father Birmingham took me to England with them, where I hoped I should find you, and so on to the Indies.'

'Well, Sam,' said Jack, 'You are very welcome, I am sure. And now you have found me, what can I do for you? Had it been earlier, as I could have wished, it would have been easier; but as I said, I had not the least notion . . . It is too late for the Navy, of course, and in any event . . . yet stay, have you ever thought of being a captain's clerk? It can lead to a purser's berth, and the life itself is very agreeable; I have known many a captain's clerk take charge of a boat in a cutting-out expedition . . .'

He spoke at some length, and with considerable warmth, of the pleasures of a life at sea; but after a while he thought he detected a look of affectionate amusement in Sam's eye, a discreet and perfectly respectful look, but enough to cut off his flow.

'You are very kind, sir,' said Sam, 'and truly benevolent; but I am not come to ask for anything at all, apart from your good word and the blessing.'

'Of course that you have — bless you, Sam — but I should like something more substantial, to help you to live. Yet perhaps I mistake — perhaps you have a capital place, perhaps these gentlemen employ you?'

'They do not, sir. Sure, I attend them, in duty bound too, particularly Father Power and he lame of a foot; but it is the Mission sustains me.'

'Sam, do not tell me you are a Papist,' cried Jack.

'I am sorry to disappoint you, sir,' said Sam, smiling, 'but a Papist I am, and so much so that I hope in time to be a priest if ever I can have a dispensation. At present I am only in minor orders.'

'Well,' said Jack, recollecting himself, 'one of my best friends is a Catholic. Dr Maturin — you met him.'

'The learned man of the world he is, I am sure,' said Sam, with a bow.

'But tell me, Sam,' said Jack, 'what are you doing at present? What are your plans?'

'Why, sir, as soon as the ship comes, the Fathers sail for the Mission's house in the Brazils. They take me with them, although I am not ordained, because I speak the Portuguese and because I am black; it is thought I will be more acceptable to the Negro slaves.'

'I am sure you will,' said Jack. 'That is . . . I am sure I shall be able to say that one of my best friends is not only Catholic but black into the bargain — why, Stephen, what's amiss?'

'I am sorry to burst in upon you, but your signal is flying aboard the Admiral. Mowett is deeply disturbed at the possibility of lateness. The gig is alongside and my 'cello is already in it. I say my 'cello is already in the gig.'

Jack checked a blasphemous cry, caught up his violin and said 'Come along with us, Sam. The gig will pull you ashore and take you off again tomorrow, if you choose to see the ship and dine with me and Dr Maturin.'

CHAPTER TWO

The caravel *Nossa Senhora das Necessidades*, a very old-fashioned square-sterned vessel, was taking advantage of the inshore breeze to approach Needham's Point; but unhappily she was doing so on the starboard tack and the moment she crossed the line of white water separating the local breeze from the trade-wind she was brought by the lee — the north-easter laid her right over and the Caribbean sea gushed in through her scuppers.

'Let all go with a run, you infernal lubbers,' cried Jack.

'There is Sam pulling on a rope,' said Stephen, who had the telescope.

'It is the wrong one,' said Jack, wringing his powerful hands.

But right or wrong the caravel somehow recovered, somehow heaved herself up, all her sails flapping wildly, and the mariners could be seen running about embracing and congratulating one another and the good

60

Fathers before they cautiously paid off, brought the steady trade a little abaft the larboard beam, and vanished behind the headland.

'Thank God,' said Jack. 'Now they will not have to rise sheet or tack until they reach Para: they may even arrive without the loss of a soul. Lord, Stephen, I have never seen such a piece of seamanship nor such an example of divine intervention. That horrible old tub should never have reached Bridgetown in the first place; and she would certainly have foundered with all hands just now but for the grace of God. Only an uninterrupted series of miracles can have kept her afloat these last sixty or seventy years. Yet even so I could wish he had sailed in something that did not call for guardian angels working double tides, watch and watch.'

'He is a fine young man,' observed Stephen.

'Ain't he?' said Jack. 'How I hope young George will be such another. It did my heart good to hear you and him prattling away in Latin, fourteen to the dozen: though I noticed that Parson Martin did not seem to follow him quite so well.'

'That was because poor Martin uses the English pronunciation.'

'What is wrong with the English pronunciation?' asked Jack, displeased.

'Nothing at all, I am sure, except that no other nation understands it.'

'I should think not,' said Jack. And then, 'Do you know, he can reach lower F without straining or losing volume? A voice like an organ.'

'Of course I do. I was there: it was I who asked him to give us the Salve Regina an octave below. It made the table tremble again.'

'So it did, ha, ha, ha! Still, I could wish he were not black.'

'There is nothing wrong with being black, brother. The Queen of Sheba was black, and a fine shining black too, I am sure. Caspar, one of the Three Kings, was black. Saint Augustine, Bishop of Hippo, was an African: and he too had a son born out of wedlock, as no doubt you will recall. Furthermore, once you are accustomed to black skins, yellowish-white bodies seem unformed and indeed repulsive, as I remember very well in the Great South Sea.'

'And I do wish — forgive me, Stephen — that he were not a Roman. I do not mean this as a fling at you; I do not mean it from the religious point of view — oh no, it is not at all impossible that he should be saved. No. I mean because of the feeling against them in England. You remember the

Gordon riots, and all the tales about the Jesuits being behind the King's madness and many other things. By the way, Stephen, those Fathers were not Jesuits, I suppose? I did not like to ask straight out.'

'Of course not, Jack. They were suppressed long ago. Clement XIV put them down in the seventies, and a very good day's work he did. Sure, they have been trying to creep back on one legalistic pretext or another and I dare say they will soon make a sad nuisance of themselves again, turning out atheists from their schools by the score; but these gentlemen had nothing to do with them, near or far.'

'Well, I am glad of it. But what I really mean is, if he had been white and a Protestant, he might have been an admiral — he might have hoisted his flag! A fellow with his parts, quick, cheerful, lively, resourceful, modest, and good company, was all cut out to be a sailor; given the least hint of a chance he would have distinguished himself, and in a bloody war and a sickly season he could not have missed of promotion — he might have ended wearing the union flag at the maintopgallant, an Admiral of the Fleet!'

'But being black and a Catholic he may become an African bishop, like St Augustine, and wear a mitre and carry a crook: indeed, he may even become the Bishop of Rome, the Sovereign Pontiff, and don the triple tiara. Then again, Jack, you are to consider that in being a papisher he is only following the example of all his English ancestors from the time Irish missionaries taught them their letters and the difference between right and wrong until the days of Henry VIII of glorious memory, only a few generations ago.'

Jack did not seem altogether satisfied. After a moment he said 'I must be going aboard the flag. This damned court-martial begins sitting at ten.'

'So must I,' said Stephen. 'I have a patient to attend.'

As they walked to the landing-place Jack said, 'But I am glad to hear what you tell about your saint, however.'

'He is your saint too, you know. St Augustine is acknowledged by even the most recent sects: he is, after all, one of the Fathers of the Church.'

'So much the better. If a saint and a Father of the Church can — can have an irregular connexion, why, that is a comfort to a man.'

'So it is too; though I believe he was not a practising saint at the time.'

64

Jack walked on in silence and then said, 'There was one thing I had wanted to ask Sam, but somehow I could not get it out. Somehow I could not say "Sam, did you mention your reason for wishing to see me at Ashgrove Cottage?" '

'He did not,' said Stephen. 'I am as certain as though I had been there. He is a dear, open, candid young man, but he is no fool. No fool at all; and he would never sow trouble.'

'Yet even so, I am afraid Sophie must have smoked it, looking at his face, black though it is, bless him. You did so right away, or you would never have told me not to be dismayed.'

'There is a very striking resemblance, it must be confessed.'

'Do you think, Stephen,' asked Jack in a somewhat hesitant voice, 'do you think it would answer, was one to mention St Augustine to Sophie? She is a great one for church. And she is much opposed to irregularities of that kind, you know. She could hardly be brought to love . . .' Here guardian angels stepped in again, one with a gag — for the name Diana had actually formed in his gullet: Diana, Sophie's cousin and Stephen's wife, who had been very irregular indeed on occasion — and the other with an inspiration, so that almost without a pause he went on '. . . could hardly be brought to love Heneage Dundas, because of his tribe of little bastards, until I told her he had saved me from a watery grave when we were boys.'

'Sure, it could do no harm,' said Stephen. More he could not say, because they were at the hard where the men-of-wars' boats landed and here was Bonden with the frigate's fine new barge, for the Admiral had kept his word and the *Surprise* was being handsomely supplied. She had already completed her water, bread, beef, and most of her firewood, and that afternoon the powder-hoy was to come out to fill her magazines: Mowett, her first lieutenant, and Adams, her purser, and all her people had been kept exceedingly busy, yet even so they had found time to beautify the barge, and the bargemen had spent their watches below beautifying themselves, or at least their clothes. Many captains liked their bargemen to wear uniform clothes, sometimes corresponding to the name of the ship — those of the *Emerald*, for example, wore bright green shirts; those of the *Niger* were all black; those of the *Argo* carried a swab dyed yellow — sometimes to the captain's private fancy: but Jack would have nothing to do with such capers and he issued no orders on the subject. His bargemen however took it upon themselves to dress all alike; it was their obvious duty to do the ship outstanding credit — by no means easy in the West Indies, the home of spit and polish, outward show and brilliantly white sepulchres — and they felt that in the present circumstances this was best done by wearing a very broad-brimmed sennit hat tilted far back, a three-foot ribbon embroidered *HMS Surprise* floating free from round its crown, a snowy shirt, equally brilliant trousers, very tight round the middle, very loose below and piped at the seams with blue and red, a newly-plaited pigtail down to the waist (eked out with tow if Nature had been near with the hair), a black Barcelona handkerchief knotted loosely round their necks and very small pumps with genteel bows on their huge feet, splayed by so much running about on deck without shoes. In this rig they could decently ferry their Captain across to the *Irresistible* for the court-martial, a full-dress affair, but they could not jump out on to the filthy hard without endangering the effect; they had therefore hired four little Barbadian boys to run out the gang-board and shove the boat off. It was only a short gang-board, but the bargemen had all sailed with

Dr Maturin for a number of years and they all knew what he was capable of in the way of plunging off ladders, out of stern-windows, and over the edges of quays, and they all craned round to watch his cautious unsteady advance over the mud. It was not that they feared for his life on this occasion, the sea being so shallow, but at low tide the water was horribly unclean, and floundering about in it he might splash their clothes. Besides, on being rescued he would certainly drip on them. In any case, he was not a fit companion for their skipper that particular morning: Captain Aubrey was resplendent in blue and gold; a Lloyd's presentation sword hung at his side and the Nile medal from the fourth buttonhole of his coat, while the chelengk, a Turkish decoration in the form of a diamond aigrette, sparkled in his best gold-laced hat, worn nobly athwartships like Nelson's; he had washed and shaved (a daily custom with him, even in very heavy weather), and his hair, having been rigorously brushed, clubbed, and fastened with a broad black band behind, was now exactly powdered. Dr Maturin, on the other hand, had certainly not shaved and had probably not felt the need to wash; he was wearing his breeches unbuckled at the knee, odd stockings, and a wicked old coat that his servant had twice endeavoured to throw away; and he had put altogether too much reliance on his scrub-wig to give him a civilized appearance.

'Perhaps, sir,' said Bonden, 'the Doctor might like to go back to the ship in a Moses. There is one putting off for the barky with vegetables this minute.' He nodded towards the basket-like flat-bottomed craft on the edge of the man-of-war's hard, a much steadier, more suitable conveyance.

'Nonsense,' said Stephen, stepping on to the gangboard. 'I am going to the *Irresistible*. They receive me in this — this shaloop, this embarkation, like a dog in a game of skittles,' he muttered in a discontented tone, creeping on. A slight tremor from a distant wave traversed the plank; he staggered, uttering a faint shriek, but Jack pinned his elbows from behind, ran him up, over the gunwale and into the boat, where powerful hands passed him aft like a parcel to the stern-sheets.

The same powerful hands propelled him up the flagship's accommodation-ladder, adjuring him to watch his step, to mind out, and to clap on with both hands. Jack, duly piped aboard, had already been received with full ceremony and carried aft; and by the time Stephen reached the quarterdeck he was no longer to be seen. Mr Butcher, lately the surgeon of the *Norfolk* and now a prisoner of war, was there however and to him Stephen said 'Good day to you now, Mr Butcher; how very kind of you to come. I am much indebted to you.' Butcher was a man of unusually wide experience and although he was not particularly learned nor, outside his profession, particularly wise, he also possessed a gift for diagnosis and prognosis that Stephen had rarely seen equalled.

'Not at all,' he said, 'I am only too happy to repay some small part of your kindness to poor Captain Palmer.' He took snuff, and observed, 'Mr Martin is already gone below.'

'Perhaps we should join him,' said Stephen.

'I guess we should,' said Butcher. 'But before we go, allow me to ask you why you operated here, rather than sending the patient to hospital? In Jamaica, with its miasmas and yellow jack, I should understand it, but in so healthy an island as Barbados . . .'

'The truth of the matter is that he is a little difficult, and he has fallen out with almost all his medical colleagues, including those belonging to the hospital.'

'Oh, in that case I understand his reluctance. Besides, although a hospital is far more convenient for operating, surviving is quite another matter: for my part I had rather be at sea. I have known a whole ward of amputations die in a week, whereas several of the men who had to be kept aboard for want of room lived on. Some are living yet.'

The patient did not seem particularly difficult. He thanked Mr Butcher for his visit, congratulated him on his coming release — the Swedish ship that was to convey the American officers home on parole had dropped anchor that morning — and sent messages to friends in Boston. But he felt that the question of his survival had been raised and he was acutely aware of Butcher's impartial judging eye upon him; he felt that the eye condemned him and he talked faster and faster to prove that the eye was mistaken, that he was quite well, that this issue from his wound and the slight recurrence of fever was of no importance. 'Laudable pus,' he said, searching their faces. 'Nothing but laudable pus. I have seen it a thousand times.'

'Well, sir?' asked Stephen, when they were on the quarterdeck again.

'Well, sir,' said Butcher, 'there is sepsis, as you know very well; but as for the turn it will take . . .' He imitated the motion of an uncertain balance with his hands, and added 'If there were some triumph, or if he had sudden good news it might turn the scale; but as things stand perhaps it would be wise to prepare for an unfavourable termination. I do not suppose you mean to attempt any heroic remedies?'

'I do not. It is a frail constitution there, much fretted with acrimony and discontent and domestic misfortune. Let us go and look at Captain Palmer.'

By this time the court-martial had decided against the request of three of the prisoners to have their cases tried separately; the charges against each had been read with all the necessary but wearisome legal repetition; and the machine that would grind slowly on until they were hanged by the neck was now in full motion.

There had been little dispute about identity. The description of all the *Hermione* mutineers had been circulated to every naval station: 'George Norris, gunner's mate, aged 28 years, five feet eight inches, sallow complexion, long black hair, slender build, has lost the use of the upper joint to his forefinger of the right hand, tattooed with a star under his left breast and a garter round his right leg with the motto *Honi soit qui mal y pense*. Has been wounded in one of his arms with a musket-ball.' 'John Pope, armourer, aged 40 years, five feet six inches, fair complexion, grey hair, strong made, much pitted with smallpox, a heart tattooed on his right arm.' 'William Strachey, aged 17 years, five feet three inches, fair complexion, long dark hair, strong made, has got his name tattooed on his right arm, dated 12 December.' There was no arguing with such evidence and although a few men asserted that they had shipped under a purser's name to avoid debt or a bastardy order and that an indictment using a pseudonym was invalid, this carried no weight, a naval court-martial having no use for quibbles that might have answered at the Old Bailey; and most of the accused acknowledged their identity. But so far none had acknowledged his guilt: the blame lay elsewhere, they said, and some of them did not scruple to say just where it lay, and to name the active mutineers. At present Aaron Mitchell was arguing passionately that as a boy of sixteen he could not have held out against the violent fury of two hundred men — that it would have been death to oppose them, and utterly useless — that he had wholly abominated the handing-over of the ship to the Spaniards, but that he was wholly powerless to prevent it.

There was a good deal of truth in what he said, thought Jack: it would have called for extraordinary moral strength and courage in a young fellow to withstand the determination of full-grown men, some of them fierce and bloody-minded brutes, who had been goaded beyond all endurance. Beyond all limits: Hugh Pigot, with the enormous powers of the captain of a man-of-war, had turned the *Hermione* into a hell afloat. The evening before the mutiny, the crew were reefing topsails: he roared out that the last man off the mizentopsail yard was to be flogged. Pigot's floggings were so dreaded that the two hands farthest out, at the weather and lee earings, on the yardarm itself, leapt over the inner men to reach the backstays or shrouds, their downward path, missed their hold and fell to the quarterdeck. When Pigot was told by those who picked them up that they were dead he replied 'Throw the lubbers overboard.'

Yes, but most unhappily Mitchell's was the usual line of defence, and every repetition weakened it disastrously. For the fact remained that the mutineers killed not only Pigot but also the first, second and third lieutenants, the purser, the surgeon, the captain's clerk, the Marine officer, the bosun, and the young midshipman, Sir William's cousin; and the ship had been handed over to the enemy. The surviving carpenter and gunner spoke of no seaman being shouted at or hustled or wounded, far less killed, for opposing the mutineers. Yet man after man said that he had had nothing to do with it, that he had been overborne, that he had begged them for God's sake to consider what they were about, but in vain. Some of the more articulate spoke surprisingly well; some others were of the familiar sea-lawyer kind who used legal terms and harried the witnesses, telling them to remember they were on oath and that perjury was death in this world and hell everlasting in the next; but most, intimidated by their surroundings and dispirited by their long imprisonment, made little more than dull, mechanical, obstinate denials, denials of everything. Yet they nearly all stood up for themselves; they nearly all tried to defend their lives with what skill and intelligence they possessed, although they must have known that there was very little hope.

In fact there was none. The court was dead against them and the case had been decided long before ever the sitting began. Quite apart from the abhorrence that this particular mutiny aroused, the evidence against the men was overwhelming; and to make doubly sure two of them had been allowed to turn informer and peach on the rest, their lives being promised them. Yet still the men resisted, struggling in the midst of accusations and counter-accusations, as though the court's decision could really be affected by what they did.

Jack listened to them with a grave, attentive expression, his spirits sinking steadily as the hours passed by. On his left hand sat Captain Goole, the president of the court, and on his right a grey-headed commander; beyond Goole there was Berry of the *Jason* and beyond him a young man named Painter, recently promoted commander and given the *Victor* sloop. They sat, a solid bench of blue and gold, all with much the same grave, self-contained look, and before them, at a table covered with papers, Stone, the deputy judge-advocate, helped by his clerks, directed the game. For a game it was, an odious game; and like most games it had intricate rules, one of which was that the accused should be allowed to have their say, should be allowed to cross-question the witnesses and address the court, so that the performance should have all the appearance of a fair, impartial trial. There was something very deeply unpleasant in playing a part in this solemn farce, something horribly indecent about being in the judgment seat and watching the others in their hopeless struggle. Jack could not lay his hand on his heart and swear that in young Mitchell's place he would have risked his life for the infamous Pigot: there were probably several men who had in fact been swept along in terrified neutrality, but it was utterly impossible to say who they were, and in any case those who had turned King's evidence swore that there was not one of the accused who had not taken up arms. How he wished he had knocked them all on the head in hot blood: how he wished that his duty did not require him to sit here in righteous squalor.

Not that the squalor was all on the safe, well-dressed, well-fed side of the table either; the thin, prison-hulk-pale, dirty, ragged, long-haired, unshaved prisoners, grotesque in front of their immaculate scarlet guard of Marines, had now in many cases abandoned themselves to naked lying and to throwing the blame wherever they thought it might stick. Of course it was infinitely more understandable on that side of the room, but that made it none the prettier. Jack had seen the strong mutual loyalty of seamen break down before now. He had seen men in overcrowded boats pulling away from a sinking ship thrust their swimming shipmates back and even cut off their fingers as they clung to the gunwale. This was much the same kind of spectacle.

By the time the court adjourned for a late dinner his spirits were very low indeed, all the more so because it was now apparent that the trial was going to last some time.

Stephen Maturin's were not much higher. Captain Palmer of the *Norfolk* had been suffering from a quartan ague and melancholia ever since the far South Sea: and since Butcher's medicine-chest had gone down with the ship, Stephen had prescribed for him, at first with considerable success. The ague and its sequelae had slowly yielded to Jesuits' bark and sassafras, but since their eastward rounding of the Horn the melancholia had grown steadily worse.

'He will cut his throat if he is not watched,' observed Butcher as they walked away.

'I am afraid so,' said Stephen. 'Yet the tincture of laudanum seemed to be having a radical effect. How I wish I could come at the leaves of coca, the Peruvian shrub. That would stir the desponding wretched mind far beyond our milk-and-water hellebore.'

Here they were interrupted by the coming

of the boat, and Stephen returned to the *Surprise.* Her captain had come aboard without ceremony, hooking on to the larboard chains only a few minutes before, and he gave Stephen a hand over the side.

'Have you had dinner?' he asked, for the gunroom hour was long passed.

'Dinner? Perhaps not,' said Stephen. 'No, I have certainly not had dinner.'

'Then come and take a bite with me: though God knows,' he added, leading the way into the cabin, 'there is nothing like a court-martial for cutting one's appetite.'

'It wants seventeen minutes of the hour, sir,' said Killick, with a surly look, as though he had been found in fault. 'Which you said four o'clock, it being a court-martial day.'

'Never mind,' said Jack. 'Tell the cook to stir his stumps, and bring some sherry while we are waiting.'

They did not have to wait long. Jack's cook was from the East Indies; he was accustomed to be flayed if he did not feed his employers promptly, and before the second glass of sherry was out a fish soup filled the cabin with the scent of saffron, lobster, crab, bonito, mussels, clams, and a wide variety of small coral fishes — fishes, that is to say, from the coral reef.

It was a splendid soup, one that they

would ordinarily have taken up to the last drop; but this time they sent it away almost untouched. 'Did you ask the Admiral about Mr Barrow and Mr Wray?' asked Stephen, when the steak and kidney pudding had been set on the table.

'Yes, I did,' said Jack, 'and he told me that the position was unchanged.'

'Thank you for remembering,' said Stephen, pushing the soft white crust with a spoon. 'I wish this pudding may be cooked.' He expressed no opinion about the news, but in fact he was rather pleased. Although the ailing Mr Barrow was still nominally the Second Secretary of the Admiralty his work had been done for some considerable time by Andrew Wray, a youngish well-connected man who had gained a reputation for ability at the Treasury. Stephen had met him long before Wray had anything to do with the Navy — he was an acquaintance of Jack's — but he had come to know him well only when Wray, as acting Second Secretary, came out to Malta to deal with corruption in the dockyard and a much more serious affair of treachery in the island's administration, in which some highly-placed man seemed to be giving one of the French intelligence services secret information of the first importance. Yet it was not this that had brought them together; at the time it had seemed to Stephen that Wray, a newcomer to this highly-specialized and very dangerous work, did not enjoy the full confidence of Stephen's own chief, Sir Joseph Blame, the head of naval intelligence, who naturally enough preferred his agents to give proof of their powers and above all of their discretion before entrusting them with the lives of a whole network of men. These reticences were very usual in intelligence and counter-espionage, where a man might be admitted to the hall, but might wait there five years before reaching the inner closet. So although Stephen and Wray were on friendly terms and although they listened to music and played cards together — extraordinarily unfortunate cards for Wray, who now owed Stephen a small fortune, and not so small either — Stephen had not seen fit to speak of his own work in the Mediterranean or to mention his connection with Sir Joseph until the very last moment, when he had no choice about it. Quite independently he had identified the traitor and his French colleague, yet no sooner did he possess this precious information than he was obliged to leave the island. He therefore sent posthaste to Wray, who was in Sicily, telling him everything he knew (and thereby of course revealing his own identity) so that Wray might wipe out the whole organization. Unhappily, although the traitor had been seized, the chief French agent had escaped, perhaps because of Wray's inexperience. Stephen heard of all this in Gibraltar, just before setting off on the voyage that took him to the South Seas; and although he did not see Wray, who was returning to England overland, he took advantage of Wray's offer to carry a letter home. In undermining the French intelligence agents in Malta Stephen had made use of a very good-looking Italian lady; he had often been seen with her, and she had sailed with him in the *Surprise* as far as Gibraltar. It was generally supposed that she was his mistress. Word of all this had reached Diana, an unusually passionate, impulsive woman; she had written to him in unusually passionate, impulsive terms and his letter was designed to do away with her resentment of what she saw not as immoral conduct (she had no particular objection to immoral conduct) but as an intolerable public affront. Most unhappily his letter, in the nature of things, could not be wholly candid; it could not tell the whole truth, and he relied upon Wray's spoken word, or rather his tone of voice, to convey the essential underlying truth that he could not write.

He also wanted to hear every last detail of the Maltese plot and the facts behind the traitor's curious suicide, and these would be much more valuable coming straight from Wray than filtered through Mr Barrow, that inexhaustible bag of foolish self-complacent words, or even through Sir Joseph; for although Sir Joseph (for whom Stephen had collected a large number of beetles and some butterflies) was ten times the size of Wray, a man of great sagacity and immense experience, he had not been there, on the spot, in Malta. Besides, even if Wray was not in Sir Joseph's class he was still sharp, quick, perceptive and clever. Perhaps rather too clever: certainly too much given to high living and playing for high stakes. Stephen did not dislike him; he had found Wray something of a bore towards the end of his stay in Valletta, when he would insist on playing cards, losing steadily more and more until at last he was unable to pay and was obliged to ask for Stephen's forbearance, but Stephen did like his deep love for music and the way he had brought about (or at least brought out) the promotion of Tom Pullings, Jack Aubrey's first lieutenant, in spite of a rather ugly disagreement between Aubrey and Wray some years before — a disagreement whose exact details were unknown to Stephen but one that might have left ill-feeling in a malignant mind. As for Wray's promises about helping Jack to a heavy frigate on the North American station and Pullings to a sea-going command by way of gratitude for this forbearance, Stephen was not so simple as to look upon them as wholly binding contracts; but even so they were as well to have.

Simplicity was not perhaps one of Stephen's most outstanding characteristics; yet his mind was not wholly free of it and he had never even suspected the possibility of Wray's being a French agent. Nor, it must be confessed, had the even less simple Sir Joseph, whose only objection to Wray was his unsuitability, his inexperience and his want of discretion. Neither Stephen nor Sir Joseph could conceive the possibility of any French intelligence organization recruiting an expensive, gambling, fashionable, unreliable, loquacious rake, however sharp and clever.

Nor did either of them conceive that Wray and his more intelligent and powerful but less showy friend Ledward (also a besotted admirer of Buonaparte) were in fact behind the obscure movement in Whitehall that was tending to discredit Sir Joseph and his allies, and to displace him in favour of the comparative nonentity Barrow, who could easily be manipulated even if he did return to effective office, a movement that would, if it were successful, give Wray and Ledward access to that curious body, so rarefied as to be almost ghostly, known simply as the Committee, which took cognizance, at the highest level, of the activities of all the various British and allied intelligence services.

And to crown all, in their short acquaintance Stephen had not perceived that Wray did in fact possess a malignant, revengeful mind. He hated Jack Aubrey for that distant quarrel and he had done him all the harm he could in the Admiralty. He did not hate Stephen except as Jack's friend and as an agent who had undone many of his French colleagues, but if he could bring the occasion about he would certainly deliver him up to the other side.

'I shall be glad to see him again,' said Stephen. 'Apart from anything else he owes me a vast great heap of money, so he does.'

'Who does?' asked Jack, for several minutes and a pound of steak and kidney pudding lay between his answer and Stephen's remark, and pudding under a tropical sun had a more muffling effect on the mind than it had south of the Horn. 'Wray,' said Stephen, and as he spoke the *Surprise* hailed an approaching boat. In the confused bellowing that followed the hail they distinctly heard the word 'letter'.

'Killick,' said Jack, 'jump up on deck and see whether any mail has arrived.'

They both of them waited, their forks poised and motionless. Stephen was exceedingly anxious to learn the effect of his first letter to Diana and of those he had sent her from Brazil and the far South Atlantic, and Jack longed to know just what Sophie had to say about Samuel's visit — he was deeply uneasy.

'No, sir,' said Killick returning. 'It was only a letter for Mr Mowett from Captain Pullings, just the one. The Swede spoke a ship he was passenger in and they lay to for half a glass, passing the time of day; and Captain Pullings, he dashed off this letter. To Mr Mowett. But the Swede says he is going back by way of England once he has dropped the Americans, and if we have any mail, would be happy.'

'Would it be worthwhile writing, at all?' asked Stephen.

'I doubt it,' said Jack, whose book-long serial letter to Sophie had come to an abrupt halt the day Sam arrived. 'We are little more than a thousand leagues from home, and we are likely to be there first — the Swede is only a highsterned cat, you know. Not that I look forward to it very much,' he added in an undertone; and then, 'Killick, ask Mr Mowett whether he would like to take coffee with us.'

The first lieutenant appeared at the same time as the fragrant pot, and his face fairly lit the cabin. Even at ordinary times it was a pleasant young open face, quite agreeable to see, but now it fairly radiated delight and they both smiled in spite of their gloom. 'Why, James Mowett, my dear,' said Stephen, 'what's to do?'

'My poems are to be published, sir. They are to be printed in a book.' He laughed aloud in pure delight.

'Well, I give you joy, I am sure,' said Jack, shaking his hand. 'Killick, Killick there. Rouse out a bottle of right Nantz.'

'Which I'm getting it, ain't I?' said Killick, but not very loud: he had heard, of course, and although it was not often that sea-officers brought out a volume of poetry he knew just how the fact should be celebrated.

Old Tom Pullings, it seemed, had been entrusted with the manuscript, and dear old Tom Pullings had found a most capital publisher, a splendid cove that meant to bring it out on the first of June, the Glorious First of June. This open-handed, gentlemanly cove loved poetry and loved the Navy, and had made a most amazingly handsome offer: Mowett was only to pay the cost of printing and paper and advertising and a small fee for seeing the book through the press, and he should have half the profits! The cove had said that Murray's, a house of much less standing than his, had sold five editions of Byron's book in nine months, and Byron's book was not nearly so long: Tom had closed with the offer at once, seizing upon it like a flowing tide. The cove thought the book, set in pica, would make a very neat royal octavo, at half a guinea in boards. He was to have the copyright, of course, and welcome to it, and the refusal of all Mowett's subsequent works on the same terms.

'What is pica?' asked Jack.

'God knows, sir,' said Mowett, laughing very cheerfully. 'I mean to ask Mr Martin. He knows all about books.'

'Let us ask him to share the ship's triumph and tell us about the technicalities of publication,' said Stephen.

When he was an unbeneficed clergyman Martin had indeed spent some lean, anxious and extraordinarily laborious years among the booksellers as a translator, compiler and even as a corrector of the press; he knew a good deal about the Trade and he instantly perceived that Mowett's cove had a somewhat more pronounced resemblance to Barabbas than most. But after no more than a moment's gravity he joined in the general congratulation and then told them (not without a certain satisfaction, having suffered much from cat-harpins and nether dog-pawls) that pica was the type that gave you six ems to the inch, and that all books, folio, quarto, octavo, duodecimo or even less, took their dimensions from the original sheets, folded twice, four times, eight times and so on, as the case might be, the original sheets having themselves various sizes and names, as foolscap, crown, quad crown, double quad crown, post, demy, royal and many more. Then he told them about the appalling difficulties of distribution, the impenetrable mystery of why some books were bought and others not, and the part played by the reviewers, whom he described as a mixture of gentlemen of letters, ruffians, and old shuffling bribed sots.

At one time it seemed that the subject could never be exhausted, but Mowett was a well-bred soul; he checked himself in the midst of conjectures about the title-page — would *By an Officer of Rank* stun the critics into respect, or would *By J. M., of the Royal Navy* look better? — and said 'Of course, sir, Tom sends you his best respects — love to all the gunroom too — and bids me tell you he had a most astonishing passage home, chased like smoke and oakum by the heaviest, fastest privateer he had ever seen, so that although the *Danaë* was a flyer — which we knew very well, ha, ha, ha! — he was forced to crack on most amazingly. Bonnets, drabblers, save-alls — the whole shooting-match — but even so he would have been caught if the privateer had not split her foresail in a late evening gust.'

'That must be the *Spartan*,' said Jack. 'The Admiral was telling me about her: a joint French and American venture that specializes in West Indiamen. If they are outward bound she takes them in to New Bedford and if they are going home with sugar she runs the blockade, loading it into chasse-marées off the French coast. Her usual cruising-ground is the windward of the Azores.'

'Yes, sir. That was where she took the *Danaë* in chase. And Tom says she was most diabolically cunning — so like a Portuguese man-of-war, trim, ensign, uniforms, signals and all that he let her come almost within gunshot before he smoked the cheat and bore away. Very like a man-of-war indeed.'

'But is not a privateer a man-of-war?' asked Stephen.

Jack and Mowett pursed their lips and looked disapproving. 'Why,' said Jack after a moment, 'I suppose strictly speaking you could call them men-of-war, private men-of-war; but no one ever does.'

'Some say letters of marque,' observed Mowett. 'It sounds a little better.'

'I know nothing whatsoever about privateers,' said Martin.

'Why,' said Jack, 'they are vessels armed and fitted out to cruise against the enemy, often by merchants and shipowners that cannot carry on their trade because of the war; and the Admiralty gives them letters of marque and reprisal. They are allowed to capture ships of the enemy nation named in their commission, and if the ships are condemned as lawful prize then they have them, just as we do. They have head-money too, like the Navy: five pounds for every man aboard the enemy at the beginning of the action.'

'So it is very much like the Navy altogether, except that the King does not have to provide the boat — the ship, I mean.'

'Oh no,' said Jack. 'It is quite different.'

'It is not at all the same,' said Mowett.

'I have often heard privateers referred to with strong reprobation,' remarked Ste-

91

phen. 'As, "Dog of a privateer, go your ways." It is certainly a term of reproach.'

'Forgive me if I am obtuse,' said Martin, 'but if both public and private ships of war attack the enemy under licence from Government, making legal prize of his merchantmen and distressing his trade, I cannot see the distinction.'

'Oh, it is not at all the same,' said Jack.

'No, no,' said Mowett. 'It is quite different.'

'You are to consider, my dear sir,' said Stephen, 'that the privateer is primarily concerned with gain; he lives on captured merchantmen. Whereas the gentlemen of the Royal Navy live chiefly on glory, and fairly scorn a prize.'

Both Jack and Mowett laughed, but not quite so heartily as Martin and Stephen, who had seen the gentlemen of the Navy in pursuit of a flying merchantman, their eyes starting from their heads and every nerve and sinew twanging-tight, and Jack said, 'No, sir, but in all sober earnest we do endeavour to make prize of the enemy's men-of-war first, and sometimes we succeed, at the cost of tolerably hard knocks. And that is more than can be said for the common privateer, who as the Doctor says is primarily concerned with pewter, with gain. Indeed, some of them are so concerned with it that they overstep the mark between privateering and piracy. That is what has given them such a bad name: that and the kind of men they ship, particularly the inshore privateers, who merely want a swarm of determined ruffians to board and overwhelm the trader's crew.'

'When I was last in London, I heard a statistical gentleman set the number of privateersmen at fifty thousand,' remarked Stephen.

'You astonish me,' said Martin. 'That is a third of all our seamen and Marines.'

Jack however had been following his own line of thought and now he said, 'Yet you are not to suppose that they are all tarred with the same feathers. Most privateers are very fine vessels, built for speed of course, and well manned, often with prime seamen; and their officers are sometimes perfectly respectable. Many an unemployed lieutenant has taken command of a privateer, rather than rot on the beach. There was one I knew, William Foster, such a good fellow — we were shipmates in *Euryalus* — he had one. You remember, Mowett: we spoke him in the chops of the Channel and he begged us not to take any of his men. And he very nearly made his fortune, taking a Hamburger fairly bursting with spices and silk; but he always was an unlucky wight and on some legal quibble or other the prize-court refused to condemn her.'

'Lord, sir,' cried Mowett. 'I do beg your pardon, but Pullings' letter quite deprived me of my wits and I completely forgot to beg you to honour the gunroom with your presence tomorrow. We are giving the American officers a farewell dinner: that is to say, those of them that are fit.'

'It is very kind in you, Mowett,' said Jack, 'but I am afraid the court may not adjourn until three or even later. It would never do to keep your guests slavering until then. Let me take a quick bite aboard the flag and join you for pudding. I should be sorry not to pay them every proper attention.'

The court did not in fact rise until past four, having packed a great deal of business into the day, but as the barge carried Captain Aubrey and Dr Maturin back to the *Surprise* it was clear to them that the gunroom's farewell dinner was still in progress. It was also clear to them that this was a very cheerful gathering, with a great deal of laughter and song, and both men realized that they would have to change their grave and even sombre faces. The trial alone had been enough to make Jack sombre, in all conscience, particularly as it seemed that late tomorrow, a Saturday, they might start passing sentence: and there was only one sentence that could be passed. But after the adjournment Goole had said, 'We have done a good day's work, gentlemen. The Admiral hopes that we may finish tomorrow, so that if there should be any sentences he may confirm them directly and have them carried out the next day.'

'But the next day would be Sunday,' cried the young commander, who knew very well that every man before the court would be found guilty and sentenced to death.

'That is the whole point,' said Goole. 'A Sunday hanging is most uncommon. Was we to finish sentencing on Monday, a Tuesday execution would be commonplace in comparison, although there are so many to be hanged. And if he stood them over till the next Sunday it would not have the same effect at all.'

And shortly after the rising of the court Mr Stone said to Stephen, whom he found on the deserted poop after a prolonged medical session first with the Admiral and then with the now delirious Mr Waters, 'Oh Dr Maturin, I have a piece of news that will interest Captain Aubrey — you know how these odd scraps of information reach the C-in-C's secretariat. My informant, a thoroughly reliable source, tells me that the *Spartan* sailed from New Bedford on a cruise, victualled for three months, five days ago.' He said this with a slightly knowing, confidential air and he clearly wished it to be understood that he had to do with intelligence-work, that *he too* had to do with intelligence-work and would not be averse to a little comfortable chat on the subject.

Stephen repelled the advance with impenetrable reserve and stupidity, and he was certain that Stone would never take such a foolish and improper liberty with him again. But he was equally certain that his double character was known or at least suspected in places where he had thought himself safe, and that with each fresh spread of this knowledge his usefulness and his safety diminished.

'Here you are, sir!' they cried as the Captain of *Surprise* came in, bending under the gunroom beams as he had bent this many a year and wearing a pretty good party-face. 'Here you are, sir, and very welcome too.' Mowett placed his chair for him and he sat there at the long table opposite Butcher, the guest of honour on Mowett's right. It was a familiar sight, this long low crowded gun-room, the diners packed four on a side and one at each end and as many servants moving about or standing behind their chairs, just as Killick had now moved to stand behind Jack's and big Padeen Colman, stooping low, behind Stephen's. The atmosphere was familiar too: the *Surprise* had always been a hospitable ship and there was a rosy, loquacious cheerfulness in the room that even the arrival of a post-captain could scarcely damp.

'We have kept back the pudding for you, sir,' said Mowett, 'and meanwhile Mr Butcher has been asking us riddles, some of them most amazingly clever. The present one, that we cannot find out, is *What is never out of fashion?*'

Jack tried to think of something witty to say, but wit was not at his command so soon after trying men for their lives and he sat there shaking his head, looking interested and amiable. Various suggestions came from up and down the table, but never the right answer. 'No, gentlemen,' said Butcher, 'you will never guess it, though yours is quite a manly service. What is never out of fashion is *the getting of bastards,* ha, ha, ha!'

In the split second before he began his laugh, rather heartier than the occasion required, Jack saw the eyes of all his officers instantly turn upon him: they expressed concern and support and all hands followed his lead with a violence that gratified Butcher and astonished the tall American midshipman, who had been exposed to the surgeon's riddles for ten thousand miles and who had thought them sad stuff even at the first hearing. Encouraged, Butcher now asked 'What did the fellow say who ran his nose against the door in the dark, although he had his arms stretched out?' but the entrance of the pudding put an end to the conundrum. It was Jack's favourite, a noble great spotted dog, the first really succulent, palely-gleaming suet pudding he had seen since they came north of Capricorn; yet he would have given a five-pound note to slip his piece through the scuttle or even, veiled in a handkerchief, into his pocket. It called for an iron determination to get the whole mass down under the approving eye of Mowett, who had saved him the particularly glutinous end, and of the gunroom steward, who had supervised the cooking.

Fortunately soon after this the cloth was drawn and the toasts began. Among others they drank *Wives and sweethearts* and although the usual facetious murmurs of *and may they never meet* were heard all round the table it was remarkable that hardly a man, on this last leg of their voyage, was unaffected. Vinous sentiment might have played some part in this but it certainly did not in every case; Jack, for example, had drunk nothing at all and yet he was so moved by a sudden diamond-sharp vision of his home — by this vision, coming on top of his horrible day, and by the thoughts that crowded into his head — that the only way he could think of to do his convivial duty by the gun-room and its guests was to drink to them each in turn. This he did not by order of seniority but counter-clockwise: 'Mr Mowett, a glass of wine with you, sir, and to the Muses. — Mr Butcher, I drink to you sir, and to the shores of the Potomac.' Allen, the grey-headed master of the *Surprise*, was a splendid seaman, but in formal gatherings he was usually so shy, ill-at-ease and constrained that it was no kindness to address him; but this afternoon he was bright pink with pleasure, and he replied to Jack's proposal by bowing low, filling a bumper and draining it with the hearty words 'And my dear love to you, sir.' Beyond Allen sat Honey, a master's mate whom Jack had appointed acting-lieutenant, and when Honey had finished explaining the English peerage to his right-hand neighbour, Jack called down the table and drank with him. Then, when the decanter came full circle he said to the neighbour in question, 'Mr Winthrop, sir, let us drink to the ladies of Boston.' Adams the purser came next, a cheerful man, now in full glow from having his pork, beef, bread, candles, tobacco, spirits and slops aboard and exactly booked; but when he poured his wine Jack cried 'Come, sir, I see some of the Almighty's daylight in that glass, which is close on high treason. Let it be abolished.' Much the same could have been said for Martin's modest toast, but Jack had too much respect for the cloth to point it out; and having emptied his own glass he poured another, saying 'Killick, take this to Mr Maitland,' — the other acting-lieutenant, who had the deck — 'and say I drink to him.' Then came Howard, the Marine officer, whose face was as red as his coat and whose body was scarcely capable of taking another drop of wine, though his spirit was clearly willing. And lastly there was Jack's left-hand neighbour: 'Dr Maturin, a glass of wine with you.'

The table was in a general din with three separate animated conversations going on at once, and both Mowett and Mr Allen had to rouse Stephen from his reverie (an unhappy reverie, alas) to make him understand the

Captain's proposal. 'A glass of wine? He wishes to drink a glass of wine with me? By all means. Your very good health, sir, and may no new thing arise. God send us luck on our voyage.' It was clear from his tone that he thought luck would be needed, and this might have cast a chill on the party had not the Marine officer chosen the same moment for gliding under the table, a smooth plunge into smiling, speechless coma.

A little after this farewells began, and presently the Americans were rowed back to their empty, echoing whaler, there to pack for their homeward voyage in the Swedish cartel.

In the cabin, as they were preparing their instruments for another evening with the Admiral, Jack said, 'It is great nonsense to say that wine changes your mood. I drank clean round the table, and yet I am as melancholy as a gib cat and as sober as a judge.'

'Are you in fact quite sober, Jack?'

'Oh, I may slur my notes a little more than usual in a quick passage, but my mind is stone cold sober. For example, there is not the slightest danger of my wrecking my career just for the pleasure of telling that old hound what I think of his Sunday hanging.'

'Your wits are unaffected, I find. Then listen, Jack: the secretary made a most improper and foolish communication to me this afternoon, from which it appears that the *Spartan,* the corsair that pursued Tom Pullings, sailed from New Bedford five days ago. No doubt the Admiral will tell you in due course, but it might be as well for you to know it now.'

'Sailed? The Devil she has,' said Jack, a dark gleam coming over his face. 'Then I may be able to cook two geese with one — I may both get out of this damnable hanging and have a chance of nobbling the privateer. Killick, Killick there. Pass the word for Mr Mowett. Mr Mowett, there is a possibility that we may be able to slip away on tomorrow's tide rather than wait until next week. The ship is ready to sail, I believe?'

'All except one last Moses of rum and two of sugar, sir, and some firewood.'

'Then once they are aboard, let there be a reasonable number of liberty-men tonight and tomorrow till noon. But there must be enough perfectly sober hands to carry us out with credit in the event of our sailing on the evening tide. So unless there are orders to the contrary you will stand by to weigh the moment my barge shoves off tomorrow. There will be at least one stone-cold sober watch to make sail and cat the anchors; and there will be no women on board whatsoever, no women at all. I cannot be sure of it, of course, but I hope the proceedings will be over before the turn of the tide.'

'It would be most improper in me to try to influence the proceedings of a court-martial in any way whatsoever,' said the Admiral at the end of their first trio, while sheet-music and little Barbados buns were being handed round. 'But I do hope you gentlemen will be able to make up your minds one way or another tomorrow. If the trial has to be adjourned until next week a great deal of the effect will be lost.'

'Yes, sir,' said Jack. 'I hope so too — I very much look forward to an early end, because with your leave I should like to sail on the evening tide. Mr Stone tells me the *Spartan* privateer sailed from New Bedford five days ago, and it seems to me that with a fair wind I might find her this side of the Azores; though of course there would not be a moment to lose.'

'I wish you may find her, with all my heart. The privateers are ruining this island — the planters are continually making representations to the Governor and me — and she is the worst of them all. But did Stone also tell you she has shipped forty-two-pounder carronades? I have been hoping to send *Harrier* and *Diligence* after her, but I can never spare both of them at the same time and neither is strong enough to tackle her alone: even you may find you have caught a Tartar, if you come up with her. A forty-two pound ball makes an ugly great hole in scantlings like yours. I beg your pardon, Doctor. Here are we tarpaulins talking shop and keeping you from your music. Pray forgive me, and let us set about the Dittersdorff.'

The Dittersdorff was a charming piece. It played on in their heads as they rowed through the warm moonlight and the lapping sea back to the *Surprise*, and it was still playing in Jack's inward ear as he stood on his quarterdeck, waiting to step into his barge the next morning. But it was cut short by the sight of a hoist running up to the flagship's peak. 'Do you know what that is?' he asked his youngsters, six boys gathered there to take part in the ceremony of piping the side — six boys he had taken aboard as children; and even now they were little more. 'No, sir,' said two breaking, unsteady voices and four clear trebles. 'No, sir: we have never seen it before.'

'You are an unobservant set of lubbers,' said Jack. 'You saw it yesterday and you saw it the day before, and a damned unpleasant sight it is. Union at the peak, a court-martial. Mr Boyle, tell the Doctor if he is not here in five seconds he will miss the boat. Mr Mowett, it would be as well to let Jemmy Bungs go ashore and pick up some old knocked-down slack-casks, enough to give the appearance of a deck-cargo, and about fifty yards of that scrim they use for lining sugar-barrels. He may spend ten pounds.'

Stephen came running with a piece of toast in his hand and hurried down into the barge; Jack followed him, in greater state, to the howl of pipes; and as the barge shoved off he said to himself 'I hope to God this is the last time: it will be a horrible session.'

It was the last time; and it was a horrible session, even more horrible than he had expected. When the court was cleared after the prisoners' last vain and generally irrelevant but sometimes extremely painful statements, the five members considered their verdict, the youngest, Painter, giving his opinion first. He had never sat on a court-martial before and the thought of judging a man's life away troubled him extremely. He turned the matter this way and that, but Stone and Goole dealt with his scruples in a calm, practical, businesslike manner; indeed, as the law stood he had no real choice, and when it came to the formal voting he said 'Guilty' to each name, though in a most hesitant and reluctant voice. Stone, the judge-advocate for the time being, bent to his table, writing fast and fair: 'find the charges proved . . . adjudge them and each of them to suffer death by being hanged by the neck on board such of His Majesty's ship or ships, at such time or times and at such place or places . . .' He looked over his paper with a keen, objective eye, nodded, and passed it to the members for their signature: it was an ugly document to put one's name to, and none of the captains relished it, not even Goole. Even less did they relish the next stage, when the prisoners were brought back, and when the bystanders had been silenced so that nothing but ship-sounds and a remote cry of 'Sweepers, sweepers aft, d'ye hear me there?' could be heard, the judge-advocate read his paper out in a strong, impassive voice, so that through all the legal forms and repetitions each man heard his sentence loud and clear.

It was an ugly business, and after taking a curt, barely civil leave of Goole and the others Jack walked out on deck. On the poop the yeoman of signals was folding up the court-martial flag, and looking with half-closed shielded eyes over the blazing sunlit water Jack saw that the *Surprise* was already moving across to her windward an-

106

chor, the fife shrilling loud upon her capstan as it turned.

Stephen Maturin was waiting for him at the head of the accommodation-ladder with a face as grave and heavy as his own. As Jack approached he said to Mr Waters' older assistant, 'Three drops each hour, and if possible continue the bark tomorrow,' and walked silently down into the barge.

'Larboard,' said Jack to Bonden, and the moment the boat reached the ship he sprang up the side, glanced fore and aft, saw that everything was in train, and said, 'Mr Mowett: to flag, *Request permission to part company.*'

CHAPTER THREE

If it had not been for the prospect of meeting with a French or American sloop, corvette or frigate, or with a privateer, this last leg of their journey would have been a sad one, for it was indeed a last leg, a run that would probably take the *Surprise* to the breaker's yard. Her officers and men, a particularly united crew, might say with perfect truth that well handled she was still one of the fastest of her class in the Navy, that her timbers were remarkably sound, and that she was a healthy as well as a happy and weatherly ship; but the fact remained that since she was built in the seventeen eighties frigates had grown very much larger and they had taken to carrying very much heavier guns. The *Surprise* had been left behind, and she could no more set about a modern American than she could attack a line-of-battle ship. There were still a few Frenchmen she could meet on reasonable terms, but they rarely left port, and the only real likelihood of an engagement, as far as national navies were concerned, was with a sloop or a corvette; there was no glory in taking a sloop or corvette, however, only disgrace in failing to do so, and the *Surprise* pinned her hopes mainly on the privateers that did so harasss the British and even the neutral trade between the old world and the new, and above all on the notorious *Spartan*. Of course there was no immortal glory in taking even an unusually heavy and powerful privateer either, but it would be a creditable thing, a thoroughly creditable thing; and if no more splendid opponent offered, then it would round off the commission handsomely. Besides, although no ship of war, public or private, could compare with a fat merchantman in the article of vulgar tangible profit, the *Spartan* would still be a far from negligible prize: she was remarkably fast, recently built in an excellent yard, and if she were not too much knocked about the Admiralty would certainly buy her into the service; then again there was head-money, five quid a knob, and the *Spartan* was said to carry a numerous crew.

They looked out for her, therefore, with more than usual zeal; and they did so in spite of the fact that many of them felt the luck had gone out of the ship. Or if not out of her then out of her captain, which was much the same thing. The belief was strongest among those who had been fishermen or whalers, for time and again they had seen that of two skippers with equal experience and skill, fishing the same waters with the same equipment, one would come home with full holds and the other would not. It was a question of the man's luck, a quality or rather an influence that sometimes set all one way, for good or bad, and sometimes shifted like a tide, but a tide whose ebb and flow obeyed laws that no ordinary men could see. The whalers held most to this belief, but it was also quite strong in a number of others, including some who had served longest in the frigate and who were most attached to her captain — hands who had been man-of-war's men from the beginning. There were varying creeds and some important differences of detailed belief, but broadly speaking luck and unluck were held to have little or nothing to do with virtue or vice, amiability or its reverse. Luck was not a matter of deserts. It was a free gift, like beauty in a very young woman, independent of the person it adorned; though just as beauty could be spoilt by frizzed hair and the like so ill-luck could certainly be provoked by given forms of conduct such as wanton pride, boasting of success, or an impious disregard for custom. Carrying parsons for example was unlucky, and yet here was Mr Martin. Reverend Martin was a good, kindly gent, not at all proud, nor above lending the Doctor a hand in the sick-bay or writing an official letter for a man or learning the boys to read; but he *was* a parson and there was no denying it. White-handled knives were notoriously unfortunate, and so were cats; yet the voyage had started with both aboard. But such things as these and even graver offences against the old ways of the sea were nothing, nothing at all, in comparison with shipping a Jonah, and a Jonah had been shipped at Gibraltar in the person of Mr Hollom, a thirty-five-year-old master's mate. It might have been supposed that the Jonah's death would have removed the misfortune, but not at all, for a downright curse had fallen on the ship when Homer, the gunner, first killed Hollom and Mrs Homer, they being lovers, on Juan Fernandez, and then hanged himself in his cabin some days later, off the coast of Chile. Some held that the curse had been lifted when the gunner was launched over the side sewed into his hammock with two round-shot at his feet; others did not. To the objection that the *Surprise* had made a number of

recaptures Plaice, the oldest and most respected of the prophets of woe, said Yes,
but recaptures, though welcome, were not
as who should say prizes, and anyhow the
last was taken just inside Admiral Pellew's
command, which instantly made the poor
unfortunate barky and her poor unfortunate
Captain eight thousand dollars the poorer.
Eight thousand bleeding dollars! The mind
could hardly conceive of such a sum. If that
was not a curse, Joseph Plaice would like to
know just what a curse was meant to be.
Then again, the Doctor, who had never
been known to miss his stroke with a knife,
saw or trepanning-iron — and here Plaice
tapped his skull, where a three-shilling
piece, hammered into a dome, covered the
neat hole Stephen had made on the outward
voyage — had almost certainly lost his last
patient, the surgeon of the *Irresistible*, which
not only upset him cruel but was clear proof
of a curse: and if proof were wanting they
only had to look a little farther aft. What but
a most uncommon curse could have brought
the Captain's misfortune walking into Ashgrove Cottage itself with the Missus there
and perhaps Mother Williams too?

Much of the talk about luck and the frigate's loss of it had been general, with people
airing their views in the galley during the

first or middle watch after they had been mustered, or in the tops, or quietly on the forecastle during a make and mend; but this particular conversation was confined to men who had served with Jack from his earliest command and who had followed him ashore during the peace and the days when he had no ship. As well-to-do bachelors Jack Aubrey and Stephen Maturin had staffed Melbury Lodge entirely with seamen, and after Jack's marriage Preserved Killick, his steward, Barret Bonden, his coxswain, Joseph Plaice, Bonden's cousin, and two or three more had moved on with him; they knew exactly what Ashgrove Cottage meant, having swabbed its floors, painted its woodwork and polished its brass as though it were a ship. And of course they knew the entire family, from Mrs Williams, the Captain's mother-in-law, to George, the youngest of his children; but in this context what Ashgrove Cottage meant for all of them, as it did for Jack himself, was Sophia Aubrey.

All the men liked her very much indeed; but above all they respected her to an almost religious degree. Sophie was indeed truly respectable, kind and good-looking — much more than good-looking — but since they had never come into close contact with women both amiable and respectable before, they may have set her on an even higher level than was quite right, there being something almost awful in such superiority. They also knew that she was her mother's daughter (improbable though it seemed) and that Mrs Williams, a short thick dark-haired red-faced passionate woman, was a Tartar, one of those who had made virtue singularly unattractive. Suspected peculation, absence without leave or fancied disrespect would rouse her to a volume of sound that seemed to mark the utmost limits of the female voice; but this was an illusion, for once unchastity in man or woman came to her attention these bounds were left far, far behind, the remote babbling of some distant brook. To be sure, Sophie never scolded, roared or bawled — no hard words, no turning out of doors, no assurances of eternal damnation — but she was her mother's daughter in this (though in this alone), that she would have no truck, no truck whatsoever with anything in the roving line. The getting of bastards might be fashionable, but it would not do for Mrs Aubrey.

'Aye,' said Bonden, 'it was a most unlucky stroke, by God. She could not have mistook that figurehead, though coloured somewhat dark. A damned unlucky stroke. You would think you might step aside, like, just once in a while, without having it thrown in your face twenty years later. A damned unlucky stroke. But that don't mean there is a curse on the ship. No. It only means the Captain's luck is out for the moment.'

'You may say what you like, Barret Bonden,' said Plaice, 'but I'm older than you, and I say this here barky's got what we call a . . .'

'Easy, Joe,' said Killick. 'Naming calls, you know.'

'What?' asked Joe Plaice, who was rather deaf.

'Naming calls, Joe,' said Killick, laying his finger to his lips.

'Oh,' said Plaice, recollecting himself. 'That's right, mate.'

Yet although Plaice and some others like him were determined to be apprehensive and although everybody knew that the gunner's ghost haunted the frigate's wake, the majority were neither consistent nor glum. They reconciled the irreconcilable perhaps even more easily than landsmen; and in a ship that could not come to good they looked out very eagerly for her next victim, her next success.

Eagerly and cheerfully, for although they

were, as Plaice pointed out, eight thousand dollars the poorer because of the Admiral's share of the last recapture, there were still the earlier ships, untainted by that vile twelfth, and there were after all the remaining eleven twelfths of the last; so that even allowing for the proctors' swingeing fees and the other legal expenses it was reckoned that each single-share man would have fifty-three pounds thirteen and eightpence prize-money and an able seaman (nearly all the Surprises were rated able) half as much again, a very charming sum indeed. Yet this did not prevent them from longing for more, much more: the general wish was to have enough money to set up a public house, but in practice scarcely a man was not willing to settle for an additional ten dollars or so, laid down on the capstan-head, with which to kick up Bob's a-dying if they touched at Fayal or anywhere else in the Azores.

The Azores however were a great way off, and with the curiously unseasonable, baffling light airs and calms that met the *Surprise* a few days out of Bridgetown, they seemed determined to remain there. For once in his naval career Captain Aubrey did not try to fly in the face of nature: in the light airs he certainly spread noble pyramids of canvas, from skyscrapers to water-sails, but he did not wet them with engine and buckets to gain a few yards in the hour, nor did he lower down the boats to tow the ship during the dead calms. The frigate proceeded soberly north-eastward, or as nearly north-eastward as the breezes would allow, and her captain soberly walked his quarter-deck, fore and aft, fore and aft, seventeen paces from the windward hances to the taff-rail, turn and back again, almost exactly a hundred turns to the mile. To and fro, passing the hen-coops abaft the wheel and the contemplative goat Aspasia, who had lain on this deck in bitter cold and furious wind and who now basked in the sunlight, her eyes closed, her beard nodding. Sometimes he paced off the distance between Portsmouth and Ashgrove Cottage, imagining the white road, the open country and then the woods; but much more often he pondered anxiously about his complex affairs, legal and financial, and about Sophie's probable attitude towards him now that she had seen Sam. As for the legal side of matters, there was little point in puzzling until he had seen his lawyers; with no word from home he had no more basis for an opinion now than he had had at the beginning of the voyage. As for the financial side, these prizes would bring him in about ten thousand pounds, for which he was most profoundly grateful. It was nothing like enough to clear him of debt if things had gone against him, but it did give him room, plenty of room, to turn around. And as for Sophie, on his more sanguine days he said that she had not the least cause to cut up rough; in those far-off times he had never even seen her, much less made any promise of fidelity. She had no right to complain whatsoever. These anxious reflections about Sophie always rose up through his thoughts about mortgages and the law, when indeed they did not precede them; for not only was Jack most sincerely attached to his wife, but like his shipmates he found a thoroughly virtuous woman an intimidating object. Just how intimidating might have been calculated from the number of times he repeated the statement about her total lack of grievance, which was sometimes accompanied by the words 'Perhaps she may even have liked him.' And as for Mrs Williams, if once she piped up he would simply desire her never to mention the matter again: he would speak very firmly indeed, as to a defaulter, otherwise there would be no peace in the house at all.

Yet these early golden almost windless

days were not all passed in anxious thought: very far from it. There were mornings when the ship would lie there mirrored in a perfectly unmoving glossy sea, her sails drooping, heavy with dew, and he would dive from the rail, shattering the reflexion and swimming out and away beyond the incessant necessary din of two hundred men hurrying about their duties or eating their breakfast. There he would float with an infinity of pure sea on either hand and the whole hemisphere of sky above, already full of light; and then the sun would heave up on the eastern rim, turning the sails a brilliant white in quick succession, changing the sea to still another nameless blue, and filling his heart with joy.

And there were many other things that gave him intense satisfaction. Although the Sargasso Sea lay rather more eastward than usual that year, they did pass very slowly through its western tip a little north of the tropic line, and it was wonderfully pleasant to see Stephen and Martin scrabbling about among the mats of weed and its denizens, paddled about in the jolly-boat by the infinitely patient Bonden: pleasanter still to see their shining faces as they came aboard grasping their improbable collections.

He was pleased with his young gentlemen

too. Circumstances had compelled him, much against his will, to take no less than six squeakers, some of them first-voyagers, of no use to man or beast. But he always had been a conscientious captain, and these being all sons of sea-officers he had determined to do his best for them: he had not only shipped a schoolmaster, but he had made sure that his schoolmaster, who was also the chaplain, could teach them Latin and Greek. He had suffered much from his own lack of education and he wished these boys to be literate creatures, to whom the difference between an ablative absolute and a prolative infinitive was as evident as that between a ship and a brig; he therefore supported Mr Martin's efforts with encouragement of his own, sometimes delivered with the victim seized to a gun, his bottom bare, but more often taking the form of sumptuous breakfasts in the Captain's cabin or suet puddings sent below. The results were not perhaps quite all that might have been hoped for, since practical seamanship in often trying conditions had to take precedence, and it did not seem probable that a Bentley or a Porson would burst upon an astonished world from the midshipmen's berth in HMS *Surprise*; yet even so Jack could truthfully swear that the frigate had the most accomplished berth in the entire service. Often during the middle watch he would come on deck and call the reefer on duty over to join his pacing, desiring him at the same time to decline a Latin noun or conjugate a verb in Greek.

'They are decent youngsters,' he said. 'They are reasonably well based in simple navigation, and they have a tolerable notion of seamanship, particularly Calamy and Williamson, who are such old hands. And with all this Latin and Greek — why, their own families would hardly recognize them.' This was no doubt true, for in addition to the Latin and Greek they had learnt much about the nature of the high southern latitudes, extreme cold, short commons, and the early stages of scurvy. In the course of learning Boyle had had three ribs stove in; Calamy had gone bald, and although he now had some downy hair it was not very beautiful; Williamson had lost some toes and the tips of both ears from frost-bite; Howard seemed permanently stunted, and want of teeth made him look very old, while Blakeney and Webber had suddenly shot up, all awkwardness, ankles, wrists and broken voices. They were also familiar with violent death, adultery and self-murder; but the knowledge did not seem to oppress them;

they remained vapid, cheerful, very apt to race about the higher rigging like apes at play, to lie late in bed in the morning, and to neglect their duty at the least hint of fun elsewhere.

He had another cause for satisfaction in the frigate's stores, so handsomely replenished in Bridgetown by the Admiral's direct, insistent order. He and the bosun and the carpenter had had to ponder so heavily over the use of a few fathoms of cordage or a couple of deals for so long that it was a sensuous delight to move about among the bales, coils and casks, smelling pitch, paint, new rope and sailcloth and freshly-sawn wood. He had also laid in supplies of his own, so that he was able to return to his round of dinners, inviting his officers with a certain style in the traditional way: he liked all his officers, and he revered the traditions of the service.

But his cause for satisfaction was of course his ship. It seemed to him that she had never sailed so sweetly, and that her people had never worked so well and heartily together. He knew that this was almost certainly the last leg of her last voyage, but he had known that she was mortal for a great while now and the knowledge had become a kind of quiet heartbreak, always in the background, so that at present he took very particular notice of her excellence and of each day he passed on her.

Each day had its own character; it could not be otherwise at sea; but during this early calm progress before the frigate picked up the westerlies they were wonderfully alike. The immemorial sequence of cleaning the upper decks in the earliest morning, pumping ship, piping up hammocks, piping hands to breakfast, cleaning the maindeck, piping to the various morning exercises, the solemn observation of noon, hands piped to dinner, grog piped up, the officers drummed to the gunroom dinner, the afternoon occupations, hands piped to supper, more grog, then quarters, with the thundrous great guns flashing and roaring in the twilight — the immemorial sequence, punctuated by bells, was so quickly and firmly restored that it might never have been broken. This was the sort of sailing everybody was used to, and now that the Agent Victualler in Bridgetown had done his duty by them this was the diet that everybody was used to as well; there were no more dolphin sausages served out to confound the mind and the calendar, no more imperfectly smoked penguins, but the regular and natural succession of salt pork, dried peas, salt beef, more dried peas, more salt pork; so that the days, though so much alike, could be told apart in a moment from the smell of the galley coppers.

It all gave a pleasant illusion of eternity, this quiet sailing under a perfect sky towards a horizon perpetually five miles ahead, never nearer; but at the same time every man aboard, apart from the Gibraltar lunatics and one homegrown innocent called Henry, knew that there was no permanence about it at all. For one thing, the paying-off pennant was already being prepared, a splendid silk streamer the length of the ship and more that was to be hoisted the day she went out of commission and all her people, paid at last, changed from members of a tight-knit community to solitary individuals. For another, since everybody was determined that if the barky were to be laid up in ordinary or if she were to go to the breaker's yard, then she should go in style, they spent a great deal of their time beautifying her. She had been much battered south of the Horn, and all that Mr Mowett had screwed out of the Bridgetown yard and all that he had bought out of his own pocket — best gold leaf and two pots of vermilion — would hardly be enough to bring her to full perfection.

Given the *Surprise*'s very high standards and her first lieutenant's love of perfection the prettying and the pennant would in any case have been difficult and time-consuming; they were rendered very much more so by the frigate's deck-cargo and side-cloths. These were designed to give her the appearance of a merchantman, and the first was made up of empty casks that could eventually be knocked down and used for firewood, while the second were long strips of cloth painted with the likeness of gunports and fastened along the frigate's sides, covering her real gunports and giving a fine impression of falsity, particularly when they rippled in the breeze.

The Surprises had long been used to their Captain's ways and they took great delight in this disguise; there was something piratical about it and something of the biter bit (or to be bit) that pleased their very souls; and although the *Spartan*, a far-ranging privateer, could scarcely be expected for several hundred miles they worked double-tides on the painted portlids, going over them again and again to get them just wrong, just a little too large and out of true, so that a sharp, predatory eye should pride itself on seeing through the deceit and close without hesitation. Nor did they make the least objection to striking down the deck-cargo in order to make a clean sweep fore and aft every evening for quarters.

This was Jack's favourite time of the day, and the time when he was proudest of his ship and her people. He had always been a great believer in gunnery, and at great cost in time, spirit and private powder he had trained his gun-crews to something very near the highest pitch of efficiency their instruments allowed.

At different times the *Surprise* had been armed in different ways. At one point she had carried almost nothing but carronades, short, light guns that shot a very heavy ball for a very small charge of powder, so that with her twenty-four thirty-two-pounders and her eight eighteen-pounders she could throw a broadside of no less than 456 pounds, more than the gundeck of a line-of-battle ship. But she could not throw them very far nor very accurately, and although these carronades, these smashers as they were called, were wonderfully effective at close quarters so long as they did not over-turn or set the ship's sides on fire because of their shortness, Jack did not think much of them for blue-water sailing. At close quarters he preferred boarding to battering, and at a distance he preferred the fine-work of exact, very carefully aimed gunfire in rippling broadsides. At present the frigate carried twenty-two twelve-pounders on her maindeck and two beautiful brass long nines, Captain Aubrey's private property, the gift of a grateful Turk, that might be fitted in the chase-ports below or that might, in suitable weather, take the place of the two forecastle carronades. She possessed six twenty-four-pounder carronades, but since they tended to oppress her in heavy seas they were often struck down into the hold; and in any case it was the cannon, the real guns, that Jack Aubrey loved. With them he could only command a broadside of 141 pounds, but he knew very well that even a hundredweight of iron hitting a ship in the right place could wound her terribly, and like a fair number of other commanders — his friend Philip Broke, for example — he was convinced of the truth of Collingwood's dictum 'If a ship can fire three well-directed broadsides in five minutes, no enemy can resist them.'

By dint of long, arduous and costly training he had brought this figure down to three broadsides in three minutes ten seconds. The training was costly in the most obvious sense, for in this matter as in many others the Admiralty did not see eye to eye with Captain Aubrey and the regulations allowed him only a pitiful amount of powder apart from that blazed away in action; all the rest had to be supplied by him, and at the present rate a broadside cost close on a guinea.

For some little time after they had left the last of the sargasso weed astern, the evening exercise had consisted of no more than dumb show, of heaving the great guns in and out and going through the motions of firing them; but Thursday was Sophie's birthday, and her husband meant to make the heavens ring by way of celebrating it. Furthermore the conditions were almost ideal — a topgallant breeze in the south-west, an easy, moderate swell — and he hoped the ship might beat her record.

Like most records it had something artificial about it. Long before the drum beat for quarters the men knew that they were going to fire in earnest, since they had heard the Captain tell the first lieutenant to have a raft and three beef-barrels and a red flag prepared; yet although there was nothing spontaneous or unexpected about the simulated battle they took their attempt upon the record very seriously. The crew of the brass chasers, for example, spent a good deal of their watch below in going over the nine-pound balls with a hammer, removing irregularities; for these long, accurate guns had very little windage, and they called for glass-smooth round-shot. Once the preliminaries were over — once the drum had beat, once the disguise had been cleared away, once all the cabin bulkheads had been knocked down so that there should be a clean sweep fore and aft, with the decks wetted and sanded, damp fearnought screens over the hatchways to the magazine, and all hands at their action stations, the pigtailed members of the gun-crews (and that was most of them, the *Surprise* following the old days) doubled their queues and tied them short: some took off their shirts, and many knotted a handkerchief round their foreheads against the sweat. They stood easy, each in a place he knew intimately well, with his own particular tackle-fall, rammer, sponge, powder-horn, wad, handspike, crow or round-shot just at hand, the lieutenants behind their divisions and the midshipmen behind their groups of guns, and they watched the blue cutter towing the raft away over the sea. The breeze hummed gently through the rigging; smoke from the slow-match in the tubs wafted here and there about the deck.

In the silence Jack's words to the master

were heard clearly on the forecastle. 'Mr Allen, we will haul our wind two points, if you please. Mr Calamy, jump down to the orlop and ask the Doctor, with my compliments, for the loan of his watch.'

The *Surprise* turned to larboard; the cutter reappeared, casting off her tow: tension mounted, and the men spat on their hands or hitched their trousers. Then came the ritual words: 'Silence fore and aft. Cast loose your guns. Level your guns. Out tompions. Run out your guns.' And here there was a universal roar as eighteen tons of metal were heaved out as fast as they could go. 'Prime. Fire from forward as they bear.'

The target was bobbing out there on the flashing sea, well beyond the accurate reach of carronades. Bonden, the captain of number two, the starboard chaser, crouched over his piece, glaring along the barrel: the elevation was right, but to point it true he made little jerks of his head to the men with the crow on one side and the handspike on the other, they standing with their backs to the ship's side to heave the ton and a half of brass a trifle one way or another. The long brass gun in the broad bow-port could be trained very far forward, and presently Bonden had the target full over his dispart sight; but he was as eager as his Captain to beat the record and he would not fire until the number four gun on his right, *Wilful Murder* by name, should also have it clear. Unbreathing moments, two heaves of the long slow swell, and then the murmur from *Wilful Murder*. 'Whenever you like, mate.' Bonden reached out his hand for the glowing match and clapped the pink end down on the touch-hole, arching his body to let the instantly recoiling gun shoot inboard under him. They were scarcely aware of the enormous ringing crack and the jet of flame, the flying bits of wad, the smoke and the twang of the breeching: they took them for granted as they held the gun firm, sponged it, rammed the cartridge home, the ball and the wad, and ran the piece up again with a satisfying thump — took them as much for granted as the deeper report of number four, instantly followed by *Towser*, number six, and so on in double quick time to twenty-two and twenty-four, *Jumping Billy* and *True Blue*, which were in Jack's sleeping-place and great cabin respectively, or as the dense white smoke that eddied in the breeze; but their motions, though extremely rapid, exact and powerful, were so nearly automatic that most of the crew had time to see the flight of their ball and the fountain of water as it pitched just under the target. 'A hairsbreadth, a hairsbreadth . . .' muttered Bonden, bent over the reloaded, pointed gun; and then he whipped the glowing match across.

On the quarterdeck Jack stood holding Stephen's watch — a fine Breguet with a centre seconds hand — and he craned to rise above the smoke of the present broadside. The first had covered the target with white water, not a single ball badly astray: this one was even better, sending two of the barrels and most of the raft into the air. 'Well done, well done, by God,' he cried, very nearly pounding the watch to pieces on the rail. He checked himself and passed it to Calamy, his aide-de-camp. 'Note the very second twenty-four has fired,' he said and skipped from a carronade-slide into the lower shrouds to see the fall of the next discharge. The broadside began as the ship rose under him almost to the height of the roll and it reached twenty-four before she had heeled back half a strake, a long roaring peal, a bank of smoke pierced through with lightning stabs, and beyond it all the flight of the shot, as pretty a grouping as he had ever seen, all close together, all well pitched up, leaving nothing of the target whatsoever. He jumped down on to the deck and looked at Calamy, who replied with a grin, 'Three minutes and eight seconds, sir, if you please.'

Jack laughed with pleasure. 'We have done it,' he said. 'Yet what I really value is the accuracy. Any fool can bang off quick, but this was deadly, deadly.' He walked along the line of guns and their jolly, sweating crews, particularly commending the captains of *Viper, Mad Anthony, Bulldog* and *Nancy's Fancy* for their briskness, but warning them that if they grew any brisker it would be a simultaneous discharge — the guns would all go off together — and that would never do. Her timbers would not stand it now. They would fall apart, and he had far rather they stayed together, in case they should see this heavy privateer, the *Spartan*.

They saw her three times. A little before dawn no more than three days after this out-standing exercise, Mr Honey, the officer of the watch, sent a lookout to the masthead as usual, this being the very best time for finding an enemy close at hand, stronger or weaker as the case might be. It had been a thick, murky night, and there were still veils of mist turning and drifting on the breeze when the man hailed the deck — a sail, a sail to leeward.

'Where away?' called Honey, who could

see nothing from the deck.

'Right on our beam, sir,' came the answer. 'But I can't make her out any more. A ship, I think. Maybe a long mile away.'

'She is the *Spartan* for sure,' said Awkward Davies to his mate over the enormous padded stone called a bear they were scouring the deck with. 'You can take my word for it: John Larkin has seen the *Spartan*. John Larkin has always been the lucky cove.'

Honey sent his midshipman to tell Mowett; and Jack, stirring in his cot, heard an elderly Italian seaman just by the skylight say to another, 'John Larkin, im see *Spartano*.'

By the time Jack reached the deck Mowett, still in his nightshirt, had descended billowing from the top, and he said with a beaming face, 'Sir, I was just about to send to ask permission to alter course and make sail. There is a sail to leeward, and Larkin thinks it might be the privateer.'

'Ha, ha,' said several of the men on the gangway, their swabs idle in their hands.

'Very well, Mr Mowett,' said Jack. 'Alter course by all means. And perhaps at the same time you might induce the watch to do a little towards preddying the deck. The King does not pay them for their beauty alone, and it would be a pity to speak this privateer, if privateer she be, in such a state of unspeakable squalor — to be seen, even by foreigners, looking like Sodom and Gomorrah.'

Privateer she was, but she was not the *Spartan*. Indeed she was not a foreigner at all, but the *Prudence*, a twelve-gun brig out of Kingston. As soon as the sun had burnt off the haze she backed her foretopsail and lay to; and when the *Surprise* was within hailing distance her master came across with her papers.

He ran up the side and saluted the quarterdeck Navy-fashion, a man in a plain blue coat about Jack's age. He was obviously ill at ease and at first Jack put this down to his anxiety about having his men pressed, but it persisted even after Jack had remarked that he had no need of any more hands, and when some time had passed Jack perceived that it arose from a fear of being recognized and of not being acknowledged.

'I had no idea I had ever seen him at first,' he said, when he and Stephen were tuning their strings that evening. 'No notion at all, until he threw out a hint about "recognizing the old *Surprise* with her thirty-six-gun ship's mainmast right away", and then I smoked it: he was the same Ellis that had commanded the *Hind*, eighteen, a King's ship, and I had seen him half a dozen times at the Cape. This is a sad come-down for him, of course, rather as it was for the men I spoke of when we were telling Parson Martin about privateers. Though in this case I am afraid there was a court-martial: I forget the details — something to do with bills drawn on the Navy Board, I believe: not very pretty. But we got along famously, once I had recollected who he was, and he told me a good deal about the *Spartan*. We are not likely to see her this side of the Azores, I fear.'

'Mr Allen's duty, sir,' said the dwarvish Howard, hurrying in, 'and there are the lights of four sail of ships, three points on the starboard bow.'

Howard's want of teeth made him hard to understand, but in time his message came through and Jack said, 'Yes, those are the West Indiamen the privateer was speaking of. Let them be given two blue lights and a windward gun.'

The gun went off, and it could be heard being made fast again; but still Jack sat on, his fiddle drooping in his hand.

'You are in a fine study, brother,' said Stephen, not unkindly, when he had been waiting a very long while.

'Lord, yes,' cried Jack. 'I do beg your pardon. It is that I was just wondering whether the infernal ptarmigan was there when Sam called at Ashgrove Cottage: not that it really signifies, however.'

'Certainly not.' Stephen played a phrase: Jack replied with a variation, and so they handed it to and fro, playing sometimes separately, sometimes together, hunting it through a great number of forms until the pattern worked out in a fine satisfying close with both in unison; and at this point their toasted cheese came in.

'In England, I find,' said Stephen after a while, 'cranes are called herons; and there are many other differences. As an Englishman, pray how would you define a ptarmigan, now?'

'Why, ptarmigans are those contentious froward cross overbearing women you come across only too often. Lady Bates is one; so is Mrs Miller. They are called after Mahomet's wife, I believe; or at least that was what my old father told me when I was a boy.'

Had General Aubrey confined himself to etymology, however bold, he would have done his son no harm; but he had seen fit to go into politics as an opposition member for various rotten boroughs, and since he was a

137

man of weak understanding but inexhaustible energy his perpetual vehement harrying of the ministry had made even his Tory connexions objects of dislike or suspicion. He was now associated with the least reputable members of the Radical movement, not because he wished to see the slightest reform of parliament or anything else, but because in his folly he still imagined that the ministry would give him some plum, such as a colonial governorship, to shut his mouth. He also thought that some of his Radical friends were devilish clever money-making fellows; and he was intensely eager, indeed avid, for wealth.

Stephen had met Jack's father — a really dangerous parent — and the wish that the General might choke to death on his next bite fleeted through his mind, but he passed the toasted cheese in silence, and soon after they played a very gentle lament he had learnt in the City of Cork from Hempson, the great harper of the world, when he was a hundred and four.

The second *Spartan* they saw was in fact just this side of the Azores, plum to windward, within a hundred miles of the place where she had taken Pullings and the *Danaë* in chase; and just as Pullings had said in his letter, she was so like a Portuguese man-of-war that at a mile even an old experienced hand would have sworn she was all she seemed. Everything was right: colours, officers' uniforms, even the gilded crucifix catching the sun on the quarterdeck.

The old experienced hand would still have sworn it at half a mile: and Captain Aubrey and Mr Allen, who had been standing there side by side with their telescopes fixed on the approaching ship while the keen smell of slow-match wafted about them and hands stood by to cast off the cloths masking the loaded guns, turned to one another with the same expression of dawning comprehension, surprise, disappointment, and relief.

'Thank God we never fired, sir,' said the master.

Jack nodded, and cried, 'Dowse the match, there; dowse the match. Mr Mowett, pennant and colours.' The Portuguese hail came across the water, somewhat testy, and he went on 'Mr Allen, pray reply,' — for the master was fluent in Portuguese — 'and ask the captain to dine with me.'

The Portuguese captain would not dine, but he did accept Jack's apologies and explanation with a good grace. They split a bottle of capital white port in his cabin, and Jack learnt that although there were two

American privateers in the harbour of Fayal, neither was the *Spartan*, nor anything like her size. She had been seen in these waters, but the Portuguese thought she had probably borne away for the Guinea coast, unless conceivably she was lying far to the eastward 'looking out for some of your fat West Indiamen with the full moon to chase them in' he said with a chuckle, for he loved a prize as much as any man living.

The full moon was indeed no great way off, and its increase tended to swallow the wind, so that by the time the *Surprise* saw her third *Spartan*, well to the east of Terceira, the Atlantic looked as harmless as the Serpentine, ruffled here and there with light airs and varying breezes. She appeared as ships so often did, from a morning bank of haze: she was lying there to the northward, hull up from the quarterdeck, on the frigate's starboard bow and she too was on the larboard tack. At first she met with little credit. The starboard watch, red legged from cleaning the decks with water that was now quite cold, were sick of this here so-called privateer, sick of this goddam deck-cargo and these bloody side-cloths. It was far too late to come across any *Spartan* now, and they wanted their breakfast.

Jack, staring out over the sea from the

maintop, was much of their opinion, but he did think it worthwhile to call down that hammocks were not to be piped up and that the watch below was to stay there until further orders.

As the light strengthened he was glad he had done so. His very recent experience of a Portuguese man-of-war made the *Spartan*'s disguise — for this was the true, the genuine privateer — less convincing; and in any case the ship over there answered exactly to Pullings' description. A tall ship with massive spars, no doubt very fast indeed, and capable of throwing a shockingly heavy broadside, at least at close quarters. On seeing the *Surprise* she had at once clapped her helm a-lee, and this seemed to Jack profoundly significant, since it would in time give her the weather-gage. A real Portuguese, with no more than a discretionary duty to inspect, would not go to so much trouble — would not undertake a move which at this distance and in these light airs could come to good only after hours of careful manoeuvring.

Jack steered a corresponding course, and as he took his breakfast in the top he watched her with unremitting attention. By his last cup of coffee he was perfectly convinced of her identity, and his conviction had communicated itself to the crew. From time to time he sent still more men below, so as to reduce his visible crew as nearly to the size of a merchantman's as he could: a difficult task, since at the same time he needed enough hands to make sail and brace round the heavy yards as quickly as the privateer, which, he saw, was very well manned indeed.

The larboard watch, at first delighted with the idea of the starbowlins doing all the cold wet work on deck while they lay like lords in their hammocks, soon became uneasy: then, as more starbowlins were sent below, almost desperate. On the lower deck there were of course no ports nor even scuttles and they were obliged to rely on reports delivered down the forehatchway by their happier companions.

Ships in the Royal Navy differed enormously in the matter of discipline. There were some in which two men could hardly be seen talking together quietly without being put down as malcontents, perhaps potential mutineers, and reported by the master-at-arms. The *Surprise* was nothing remotely like any of those unhappy vessels, but even so prolonged conversation on duty was not encouraged, especially at a time when exceedingly delicate operations were in hand. The accounts that came down the hatchway were therefore sparse and fragmentary; but uttered by seamen for seamen they gave the broad picture quite accurately.

The two ships lay north and south of one another, and although there were odd cat's paws and small local breezes from other quarters the undoubted general movement of the air was from the westward; and there were signs that in time, perhaps tomorrow, it might freshen. The aim of each captain was to get the weather-gage, that is to say to gain a position westward of the other so that he might come down with the breeze on his best point of sailing and force the engagement at the moment and in the conditions most favourable for himself rather than undertake a long and perhaps inconclusive windward chase, with the continual possibility of having an important spar knocked away by gunfire or carried away by the breeze. But each wished his manoeuvre to seem unstudied, a natural part of his ordinary, peaceful voyage, so that his unsuspecting, unhurrying adversary should let himself be outstripped, thinking no harm.

This added a fresh dimension to the snail-paced but strenuous race to windward, in which every vagrant puff had to be wooed and embraced by all the canvas that could be spread, but it was one that set the *Surprise* at a disadvantage to begin with, since in her character as a prudent merchantman she had no royal masts above her stump topgallants, and they could hardly be sent up man-of-war fashion without exciting suspicion; nor could royals, skysails, moonsails, stargazers and other flying-kites, all very useful in these mere zephyrs, where the higher air moved somewhat faster than that just over the sea.

The masts and yards were sent up in time and the lofty sails were set upon them, but in the meanwhile the *Spartan,* profiting by a north-western slant of wind, had come half a mile closer.

This did not suit Jack's book at all. He did not want his ship or his people to be wounded or killed for the sake of a privateer: what he hoped to do was to gain a decided advantage in beating up to the west and then, with the *Spartan* under his lee and well within reach of his long guns, to throw off his disguise, send a shot across her bows and await her surrender. If it did not come directly, then a couple of broadsides should certainly bring it. But if this present advance went on the privateer would be laying him aboard and there would be a general mêlée, the *Spartan*'s forty-two-pound carronades coming into play, with the ship being hurt and a great many people wounded.

Looking very keenly at the cat's paw travelling over the smooth surface and bearing the *Spartan* with it, Jack leaned over the top-rim and called down his orders. The *Surprise* turned gently to starboard, glided across towards the *Spartan*, to within random shot, picked up the cat's paw as it left her and went about, staying with a smooth perfection. For ten or fifteen minutes the *Surprise* ran fast enough to make the water ripple along her side, leaving the *Spartan* with all her sails limp, barely capable of steering.

By the time the breeze left the frigate too the balance had been restored. This was reported to the men below, and Faster Doudle, an old and knowing hand, observed that now they could settle down to a luffing-match in peace: the skipper need fear no one in a luffing-match, and as for sailing on a bowline, the barky had no equal — she would eat the wind out of anything afloat by the end of the day.

It was a luffing-match, certainly, with each ship trimming its sails with infinite attention and sailing wonderfully close to what wind there was, with bowlines twanging taught; but it was also much more, with each ship moving from her windward line, sometimes perilously far, in search of one of the vagrant breezes that passed across the sea, often under the fat cushions of cloud. And then there were the moves intended to deceive, such as paying off to gather impetus, putting the helm a-lee, with hands at their stations for going about, and even letting the headsails shiver as though the ship were on the very point of tacking, but then flatting in the jib and foretopmast staysail, falling off and carrying on as before — the intention being that the other ship, carrying out the same manoeuvre, should either hang in stays on seeing her error and so lose time, or go about briskly and lose still more time getting back on to the original tack.

By the late afternoon — a hot, damp, oppressive afternoon — each captain had a distinct notion of his opponent's capabilities. It was clear to Jack that the other fellow was a thorough seaman, cunning, devious, and up to every kind of duplicity, and that his ship, at least in light airs, was almost a match for the *Surprise*. Almost, but not quite, for when the sun began to sink towards the horizon, swallowing even the lightest airs so that the sea was glass from rim to rim, the *Surprise* had gained perhaps a quarter of a mile of windward distance and Jack felt reasonably confident that if the breeze revived with the setting of the sun, which was probable, he could increase this lead by the amount required to cover the mile or so separating them (for they had been sailing on parallel tacks until the wind fell quite away), place the *Spartan* directly under his lee, and so call upon her to surrender. But for this the breeze had to revive, and although the *Surprise*'s people, starting with her Captain, whistled and scratched backstays, never a breath did they raise. Nothing whatsoever broke the surface of the sea, not the heave of a distant whale, nor a flight of flying-fish (though half a dozen had been picked up on the gangway yesterday evening), nor the slightest ripple of a moving air; and the ships lay there motionless, both with their heads to the north, the *Surprise* looking at the *Spartan*'s larboard quarter.

'You might ask the Doctor and Mr Martin whether they would like to see a perfect clock-calm,' said Jack to his coxswain, who was in the maintop with him. 'Perhaps *their* whistling might do something to change it.'

When Bonden came back he found some difficulty in delivering his message. Both gents, it seeeemed, were profiting by this splendid freedom from motion to spread their important collections of Brazilian and Polynesian coleoptera out in the gunroom. Bonden had unfortunately trodden upon some and swept others to the ground as he recoiled; the gents had answered rather testy, even the chaplain: they would whistle if so required, and would even scratch a backstay like idolatrous heathens if the implement were pointed out, but unless the Captain absolutely desired it they begged to be excused — they had far rather not leave their beetles now.

'Well,' began Jack, smiling, 'it was only a . . .' He broke off and clapped his telescope to his eye. 'They are hooking yards and stays to lower boats,' he said, and a few moments later the *Spartan*'s yawl splashed down, picked up a line from the bows and towed the ship's head round until she was broadside on to the *Surprise*. After a careful pause she fired one of her heavy carronades: Jack saw the captain point the gun, at full elevation, and pull the lanyard. The ball grazed the smooth surface and came skipping over the sea towards the *Surprise* in great leaps; it kept a wonderfully true line, but the range was too great and the ball sank at the tenth rebound, a little after the sound of its firing had reached the ship. It was clear that the privateer's captain was still convinced of the frigate's innocence, and that he meant to finish things out of hand, in case the coming breeze should enable her to work still farther to windward. He meant first to intimidate her with this heavy ball and then to overcome her by towing his ship within killing range and boarding with his boats — the others were ready for lowering.

'All hands,' called Jack in a strong but not unexpected voice, and the seamen below rushed up from their odious leisure. This was followed by a quick succession of orders, and Martin said to Stephen, 'How they do run about, to be sure. What are those little groups beyond the teapot?'

'They are duplicates for Sir Joseph Blaine.'

'You have mentioned Sir Joseph before, but I do not believe you have ever told me who he is,' said Martin, looking a little jealously at a Dynastes imperator of which he had only two examples.

'His daily bread is Whitehall,' said Stephen, 'but his delight is entomology, and he has a fine cabinet of rarities. He was one of the vice-presidents of the Entomological Association last year: I will introduce you when next we are in town. I trust I shall see him quite soon after landing. Amen, amen,

amen,' he said privately with some warmth, for that vile brass box and its monstrous uneasy wealth preyed upon his waking and his sleeping mind.

'Casks over the side,' called Jack. 'Cast off the side-cloths. Mr Mowett, when is that boat going to be hoisted out?'

'Directly sir, directly,' cried Mowett from the gangway. But for once the ship's efficiency failed her. The pin of a block had broken; the tackle was hopelessly jammed, and in spite of the bosun's furious efforts the boat hung dismally from a single ring until the second cutter was bundled unceremoniously over the quarter. In the meantime, and to his intense vexation, Jack saw the farther sea, the northern sea, ruffling with a breeze coming fast from the west. It reached the *Spartan* and, filled with suspicion, she swung round to bring it on to her larboard quarter, veering the yawl astern as she moved away eastward, faster and faster, her people bracing round the yards with extraordinary activity.

'Maintop, colours and the short pennant,' cried Jack. 'Master Gunner, put me a ball across her bows: and another through her mainsail if that don't stop her.'

In the present position the starboard chaser was the only gun that could bear, but in any case Jack would not have used his broadside to begin with. Quite apart from killing people unnecessarily, he had no wish to maul the privateer and then spend days knotting and splicing. If she did not strike and lie to, however, he would have to do so; and all that was needed for the murderous discharge was swinging the ship six points, a simple matter in a sea as smooth as silk.

A simple matter, but for Awkward Davies. The blue cutter had been launched over the side by main force and had shipped a great deal of water in the process, but the crew took no notice of the bath they sat in and pulled furiously ahead to pick up the towline. Davies, at stroke oar, caught it: the cutter pulled on a few strokes to take in the slack, and then Davies stood up. His dark, fierce, brutal face was set, a line of white showed between his lips and his eyes were ablaze; taking no notice of Howard's squeaking orders he set his foot on the gunwale and gave an enormous heave. The boat instantly tilted, filled and sank.

Few of the cutter's crew could swim and the situation was complicated by other people, also unable to swim, plunging in after them. By the time they had all been brought aboard, some of them pretty far gone, and by the time the ship had at last been swung round, the *Spartan* was a great way off. She had seen the horrid accuracy of the chaser, she had seen the long row of unmasked guns and the sudden swarm of men about her decks; she did not mean to wait for any further proof and she was already rigging out her weather studdingsail booms.

'Fire high,' said Jack, dripping on to his quarterdeck — he had fished out the wretched Davies, as well as little Howard, for the third or even fourth time in their long acquaintance — 'Fire high, and let the smoke clear between each shot.'

No. The broadside speckled the sea in the *Spartan*'s wake, short and poorly grouped.

'House your guns,' he said, and they did so, looking at him nervously. But this was no time for recrimination with the *Spartan* already making better than five knots — a cable's length farther away every minute — and the breeze, the true, the steady breeze this time, spreading south to reach the *Surprise*. He studied the course of the wind with the keenest attention, unaware of the towel, the dry shirt and coat that Killick held out, mute for once, and he called 'Man the fore clew-garnets.'

His mind was wholly concerned with making up these lost miles, for not only had the *Spartan* gained this flying start, but all the *Surprise*'s former gain was now so much handicap. The first high gusts reached the frigate's royals and skysails: she swung round: she gathered steerage-way, and as the sun went down, turning her nascent wake blood-red, he began to make sail. Hitherto she had been beating up, with an array of sharply-braced square sails and staysails reaching almost to the sky; now she was to have the breeze on her quarter, or very near, and he set studdingsails aloft and alow, with a ringtail to the driver, bonnets, of course, and save-alls under the studding-sails and even the driver-boom, brought the foretack to the cathead with a passaree, cast off the maintack and hauled the weather-clew of the maincourse to the yard.

All the hands, from the miserable Davies to the wholly irreproachable Bonden, seemed to be suffering from a sense of collective guilt, and his cold, impersonal, objective orders, with never an oath or a hasty word, designed solely to get the last ounce of thrust out of the breeze, quite daunted them. They hurried about in dead silence, with anxious faces; and when he ordered the fire-engine into the tops so that the sails, being wetted, might draw better, they pumped with such force that the jet reached beyond the royals, which ordinarily called for buckets, sent up with a whip.

In the darkening twilight he concentrated all his powers on the exact trim of sails and braces and presently the ship began to speak: her cutwater split a distinct bow-wave and innumerable small bubbles ran down her side with a continuous hiss, while the slightly increasing wind hummed and sang in the rigging. The moon rose directly ahead, and in her path he saw the *Spartan*, a magnificent wide-winged spread of canvas, like a distant bird; a distant bird, but no more distant than she had been a little while ago. She was no longer obviously gaining.

He loosened his very strong grip of the fife-rail, yawned from hunger, and glanced fore and aft. Over to leeward he was aware of Stephen and Martin smiling at him, as though willing to be spoken to.

'You are too late for the clock-calm,' he said, remembering that he had sent to them long ago. 'There is a light air from the west at present, and with any luck it may grow into a breeze.'

'We are sorry about the calm,' said Stephen, 'but we thought you might like to view our beetles. They are now fully set out for the first time, a most gratifying sight, covering the entire table and the floor. It cannot last however, the gentlemen of the gunroom being so impatient for their supper.'

'That would give me great pleasure,' said Jack, with a last searching look under the mainsail to the fully-drawing forecourse. 'And if the gunroom — after the bugs, of course — would invite me to take a bite of bread and cheese, how happy I should be. Mr Mowett, pray have the hands piped to supper at last, watch by watch, and tell Killick to rouse me up an elbow-chair, my broad night-glass and a boat-cloak. The dew is falling, so the engine may leave off.'

In this chair, wrapped in his cloak, he spent the long moonlit night, rising at every bell to walk along the gangway to the fore-castle and out along the bowsprit to peer at the *Spartan* with his night-glass between the spritsail course and its topsail. She was maintaining her lead, possibly increasing it, and she was obviously a flyer, commanded by a very able man; but Jack had the feeling that she would not be so happy in heavy weather, and if only the west wind would come on to blow as it sometimes did in these waters, he believed the *Surprise* would close with her. Apart from anything else he had a way of enabling her to bear an extraordinary press of sail, particularly with the wind abaft the beam: he sent light hawsers and cablets to the mastheads, and although they made the ship look barbarously ugly they did keep her masts standing, where in another ship with the same thrust acting on her they would have carried away, shrouds, back-stays, preventer-backstays and all.

The moon sailed across the pure sky, and the pale stars in their due sequence; the ship followed her nightly routine with the same kind of ordered regularity. The log was heaved — five knots to five knots two fathoms, no more — the log-board marked by the glow of the binnacle — the depth of water in the well reported — the glass was turned, the bell struck, the helm relieved, and all round the ship the lookouts cried 'All's well'.

At four bells in the middle watch the breeze hauled a little forward, so that Jack filled the mainsail, but apart from that both ships raced over the sea with never a change, as though they were running in a timeless dream.

A little before dawn, with the moon right low astern, Mars blazing in the east, and the head-pump already setting the forecastle awash for the swabbers, the sharp scent of coffee pierced through his reflexions. He walked into his lit cabin, and with half-closed eyes he looked at the quicksilver in the glass: it had not actually gone down, but the top of the column was concave rather than the other way about — there was at least a reasonable hope of wind. Killick brought him the pot and some very old rye bread toasted and asked in a subdued, dutiful tone whether there was anything else he would like. 'Not for the moment,' said Jack. 'I suppose the Doctor is not about?'

'Oh no, sir.' Stephen was a bad sleeper, but he disapproved of the habitual use of soporifics on medical and moral grounds and he usually delayed the taking of his pill or draught until two in the morning, so that he was rarely to be seen before eight or nine o'clock.

'When he is up, say that I should be happy to see him and Mr Martin to dinner, wind and weather permitting. And pass the word for the officer of the watch.' 'Mr Allen,' he said to that officer, 'I shall turn in for a few hours, but I am to be called at the slightest change, either in the weather or the chase.'

A few hours, he said, and they carefully refrained from any noise abaft the mizenmast, cleaning the deck only with silent swabs; but at the changing of the watch there he was, stalking forward to stare at the chase in the brilliant morning. She was almost exactly the same, only sunlit rather than moonlit; she had perhaps drawn a little

ahead, but she had not altered her sails —
there was indeed very little she could add —
and, what was more important, she had not
deviated half a degree from her course,
northeast by east.

The night's chase had been dreamlike; the
day's was scarcely less so, for although there
was the prevailing sense of urgency and even
crisis and although there was the engine in
the tops, squirting with all its might, while
the brass long nines stood ready on the forecastle, trained right forward, with their gar-
lands of smooth shot beside them, there was
remarkably little to do. With the perfect
steadiness of the breeze, it was like rolling
down the trades to the Cape, never touching
sheet or brace for days and even weeks on
end; but whereas in the trades there was always cleaning, painting ship, washing
clothes, making and mending, and the many
forms of exercise, to say nothing of church
and divisions, here nothing was appropriate
but the making of wads and the chipping of
roundshot. And so to the click-click of fifty
or sixty hammers the *Surprise* ran on, going
as fast as the most careful attention to brace
and helm could drive her, pursuing a chase
that lay perpetually half way to a horizon
that perpetually receded before them both.

It was to the distant accompaniment of

this sound that Jack and his guests ate their dinner. Shaved and shining after a cat-nap, Jack was in fine form; yesterday's intense frustration belonged to history; he had not felt so well or so alive since the horrible days of the court-martial, and he enjoyed his company. Neither Stephen nor Martin was a sailor nor indeed anything remotely like a sailor; neither believed in the sacred majesty of a post-captain and both talked quite freely — a great relief. Furthermore, the glass was sinking, a sure sign of wind; and throughout the meal the steady chipping of shot told him that all was well on deck. A chase in sight, his ship in perfect order, and a blow coming on: this was real sailoring — this was why men went to sea. It is true that the chaplain's presence was usually something of a constraint upon him, and that since the appearance of Sam his troubled conscience had made Jack almost mealy-mouthed when they conversed; but today an abundance of vitality thrust conscience to one side and they talked away in a very pleasant manner. He told them that he was now quite sure the privateer was running for Brest, which was one of her home ports; that he hoped they might come up with her long before Ushant and its tangle of inshore reefs and islands; but there was no certainty of it at all. The chase had shown no signs of distress; she had not started her water over the side still less her boats and guns. But from the look in his bright-blue, cheerfully predatory eye both his listeners concluded that his unspoken mind was less reserved, less cautious towards fate. Martin said he supposed that the engine, pumping with such force upon the sails, striking them from behind, as it were, must urge the boat along, and so increase its speed.

'There cannot be the least doubt of it,' said Stephen.

'*When virtue spooms before a prosperous gale*
My heaving wishes help to fill the sail

says Dryden, that prince of poets, and the dear knows we spoom in the most virtuous manner. I suggest we all go and blow into the mainsail; or that some blow while others tie a rope to the back of the ship and pull forwards as hard as ever can be, ha, ha, ha!' He cackled for a short while at his own wit, and in doing so (the exercise being unusual with him) choked on a crumb. When he recovered he found that Martin was telling Jack about the miseries of authors: Dryden had died in poverty — Spenser was poorer still — Agrippa ended his days in the workhouse. He might have gone on at very great length, for the material was not wanting, but that Mowett sent to report the appearance of a parcel of bankers on the starboard bow. They were of no great consequence from the warlike point of view, being fishermen from Biscay and the north of Portugal on their way to fish for cod on the Newfoundland banks, but even a single sail in mid-ocean was something of an event; Jack had often travelled five thousand miles in quite frequented sea-lanes without seeing another ship, and when dinner was over he suggested that they should take their coffee on to the forecastle to look at the spectacle.

Killick could not actually forbid the move, but with a pinched and shrewish look he poured the guests' coffee into villainous little tin mugs: he knew what they were capable of, if entrusted with porcelain, and he was quite right — each mug was dented when it came back, and the captain of the head had to deplore a trail of dark brown drops the whole length of his snowy deck. It was not that the wind had yet increased, but during dinner the beginning of a swell from the south had reached these waters, and the *Surprise*'s skittish roll almost always caught them on the wrong foot.

By the time they reached the forecastle

the foremost vessels of the straggling fleet of bankers was right ahead of the *Spartan* and in one view the eye could embrace the picture of peaceful, if rather slow and slovenly industry, and of striving war — of one set of ships creeping in a formless, talkative heap north-westward, while the other raced through them, running east with the utmost efficiency as fast as ever they could move, wholly taken up with mutual violence.

An hour or so later the Biscayans had vanished over the edge of the world, taking all philosophical reflections with them, and Stephen and Martin had retired below, but Jack Aubrey was still there on the forecastle, considering the chase, the frigate's magnificent spread of canvas, and the weather. He was also a little uneasy about her trim: she might be a trifle by the stern, and he was afraid she would resent it, if a full gale were to come on.

'Mr Mowett,' he said, returning aft, 'I believe we may ship rolling-tackles, strike the carronades down into the hold, and make ready to start maybe ten tons of water from the aftermost casks. And pray ask the bosun to have cablets and the like ready to his hand, in case it should come on to blow — the glass is sinking. I am just going to show the youngsters how to find whether the chase is gaining or not with a sextant and then I shall turn in for a while.'

It was as well that he did, for with the rising of the moon the wind increased, blowing straight into her round, foolish face and across the growing swell. By the time he came on deck Mowett had already taken in the lower studdingsails, and as the night wore on more and more canvas came off until she was under little more than close-reefed fore and main topsails, reefed courses and trysails, yet each time the reefer of the watch cast the log he reported with mounting glee, 'Six and a half knots, if you please, sir. — Seven knots two fathoms. — Almost eight knots. — Eight knots and three fathoms. — Nine knots. — Ten knots! Oh sir, she's doing ten knots!'

With the courses reefed Jack could see his quarry from the quarterdeck, see her plain in the bright moon, for though the wind was in the west, backing a little south, there were few clouds in the sky, and those few were thin racing diaphanous veils, no more. The sea, though not yet really heavy — short and choppy rather than Atlantic-rough — had a torn white surface, and the *Spartan* showed up strangely black, even when the moon was well down the western sky and far astern. She had much the same sail as the *Surprise*, and though twice she tried a foretopgallant, each time she took it in.

From time to time Jack took the wheel. At this kind of speed the complex vibrations reaching him through the spokes, the heave of the wheel itself, and the creak of the raw-hide tiller-ropes told him a great deal about the ship: whether she was being overpressed or whether she would bear a reef shaking out, even an inner jib hauled half way up. He spoke little to the succession of officers who took the watch, Maitland, Honey and the master, yet even so the night seemed short. At first dawn he took his first breakfast: the barometer had continued its steady fall and although this could not yet be called a hard gale it was certainly a stiff one, and likely to grow stiffer; he decided to have his cablets sent up to the mastheads in good time, as soon as hammocks were piped up and he had both watches on deck.

'I beg pardon, sir,' said Mowett in the doorway, 'but the privateer has taken a leaf out of our book and she has sent hawsers aloft.'

'Has she?' cried Jack. 'Oh, the wicked dog. Come, have a cup of coffee to keep your spirits up, Mowett; then we shall go on deck, where virtue spooms before the goddam gale, and our heaving wishes will help to fill the sail, ha, ha, ha! That is Dryden, you know.'

On deck he found that the privateer had indeed forestalled him in fortifying her masts and was now outstripping him in speed. With her full topsails she was already making something like eleven knots or even more to the *Surprise*'s ten, and she was throwing a spectacular bow-wave as she did so, clearly to be seen some three miles away. 'All hands,' called Jack, and down below came the cry 'Rouse out, you sleepers. Rise and shine, there, rise and shine. Heave ho, heave ho, lash up and stow.'

This sending up of hawsers and cablets was a simple, even an obvious idea, and Jack had often wondered why so very few commanders resorted to it in heavy weather; but it was also time-consuming, and before the very powerful extra supports were made fast and heaved taut aboard the *Surprise* the *Spartan* had gained horribly. She was now hull-down except on the top of the roll, tearing along under an extraordinary press of sail. 'If a banker crossed her hawse at this moment,' reflected Jack, with his glass trained on her, 'she would sheer clean through.'

He sent the hands to breakfast watch by watch and began cautiously packing on, sail by sail. The ship's speed mounted; the whole sound, the whole vast chord of her motion changed, rising through two whole tones; and out of the corner of his busy eye he noticed all the reefers and many of the larboard watch along the weather rail and gangway, eating their biscuit and grinning with delight at the flying, swooping speed.

But he also noticed, and this was much more to the immediate point, that the wind was strengthening and backing farther still. This continued throughout the forenoon watch, and as the gale became more distinctly a south-wester so it brought racing cloud low across the sea. The dawn itself had been grey, but now really thick and dirty weather threatened, and although the *Surprise* had regained one of her lost miles by the end of the watch — she was indeed the faster ship in a heavy sea — Jack was very much afraid that if he did not come up with the *Spartan* before nightfall he would lose her in the murk.

Furthermore, as the wind backed so it blew in the same direction as the growing swell, and the seas grew heavier by far. Both wind and swell were right aft by the time the gunroom sat down to dinner with their guests, Captain Aubrey and Mr Midshipman Howard, and the ship was pitching through forty-one degrees. All those present had known a good deal worse far south of the Horn, but even so it took away from the splendour of the feast. The gunroom had meant to regale their Captain on fresh turtle to begin with and then a variety of other delights, but the early extinction of the galley fires, put out as soon as the men's salt beef had been boiled, had reduced them to a cold, or sometimes luke-warm, collation; however, it included soused pig's face, one of Jack's favourite dishes, and treacle pudding, which he always said ate better if it did not scald your gullet.

'You were speaking of the miseries of authors,' said Stephen across the table to Martin, 'but neither of us thought to mention poor Adanson. Do you know, sir,' — addressing himself to Jack — 'that Michael Adanson, the ingenious author of the *Familles naturelles des Plantes*, to which we all of us owe so much, submitted twenty-seven large manuscript volumes relating to the natural classification of all known beings and substances, together with a hundred and fifty — I repeat, a hundred and fifty — others containing forty thousand species arranged alphabetically, and a completely separate vocabulary containing two hundred thousand words, and they explained, as well as detached memoirs and forty thousand figures and thirty thousand specimens of the three kingdoms of nature. He presented them, I say, to the Academy of Sciences in Paris, and they were received with the utmost applause and respect. Yet when this great man, after whom Linnaeus himself named the baobab tree Adansonia digitata, was invited to become a member of the *Institut* a little before I had the honour of addressing it, he did not possess a whole shirt nor yet an untorn pair of breeches in which he could attend, still less a coat, God rest his soul.'

'That was very bad, I am sure,' said Jack.

'And I might have remembered Robert Heron,' said Martin, 'the author of *The Comforts of Life*, which he composed in Newgate, and many another more learned work. I wrote out his appeal to the Literary Fund, his hand being then too weak, and in it he truthfully stated that he worked from twelve to sixteen hours a day. When the physicians examined him they found him totally incapacitated by what they termed the indiscreet exertion of his mind in protracted and incessant literary labours.'

Jack's attention was, as to three parts, elsewhere, for the altered motion of the deck under his feet and the wine in his glass told him that the wind was backing farther still, backing fast with some nasty flaws and gusts; several of the miseries and calamities of authors therefore escaped him, but he returned in time to hear Stephen say, 'Smollett observed that had his friends told him what to expect in the capacity of an author "I should in all probability have spared myself the incredible labour and chagrin that I have undergone." '

'Think of Chatterton,' cried Martin.

'Nay, think of Ovid on the dank and fetid shores of the old cold Black Sea:

Omnia perdidimus, tantummodo vita relicta est,
Praebeat ut sensum materiamque mali.'

'Yet perhaps, gentlemen,' said Mowett, beaming on them, 'there may be *some* happy authors.'

Both Martin and Stephen looked extremely doubtful, but before either could reply a fierce, savage, triumphant roar broke out overhead, drowning the powerful voice of the wind and the sea and just preceding the appearance of Calamy in his streaming tarpaulin jacket, reporting that the chase had split her foresail.

So she had, and although she set her close-reefed foretopsail in the most seamanlike fashion, the *Surprise* gained more than a mile before she was running at anything near her former pace.

Jack and Mowett stood there on the forecastle, studying the *Spartan*. 'I wonder, I wonder,' murmured Jack: if he could gain five or six hundred yards more he could fire his chaser with some hope of cutting up her rigging, knocking away a spar, or at least holing her drum-tight canvas: with that done he should certainly be able to lay her aboard before dark. The *Surprise* was now rolling heavily as well as pitching, but she carried her weather chaser so much the higher, and with very good gunners dangerous fire would still be possible for a while. A veil of small rain swept between them and the *Spartan* vanished. 'I believe she will wear it,' he said. 'Let the reefs be shaken out of the maintopsail. And tell the gunner to stand by to try for the range.'

A solid packet of water sweeping from aft soaked him as he hurried, bent low, along the gangway, but he hardly noticed it: the air was full of flying spindrift, and it looked as though they were in for a thoroughly dirty night. He had already shifted sail for the shift of wind, and she had a fine press of canvas: as the reefs came out of the maintopsail she heeled still farther, so that the deck sloped another five degrees, and his hand automatically reached out for the backstay: there was a pure keen delight in this flying speed, the rushing air, and the taste of sea in his mouth. He was not the only one to appreciate it, either: the four men at the wheel and the quartermaster at the con had the same expression of grave pleasure; and when two bells in the first dog-watch struck a few moments later the midshipman who heaved the log reported 'Eleven and a half knots exactly, sir, if you please,' with a look of perfect bliss. And certainly although the difference between two knots and three was neither here nor there, at this pace even half a knot more made an immense change in the feeling of speed: it was also very hard to attain. But two bells already: that meant there was precious little daylight left; it would be a damned near-run thing, if indeed it could be done at all. And now in his glass he saw the *Spartan* starting her water over the side, two thick jets of it flying to leeward, relieving her of many tons.

Right forward, just as the ship was reaching the height of her rise, the gunner let fly. At almost the same moment an extraordinarily violent gust split the *Surprise*'s maintopsail.

The men leapt to the sheets, halliards, buntlines and clewlines and the moment he gave the order the flapping, cracking, streaming sailcloth was gathered into the top, there to be mastered, unbent and sent down — they laid aloft as though they were on a millpond with never a breeze at all. At the same time the bosun, the sailmaker and their mates were rousing out a number two canvas topsail and manhandling the awkward, unwieldy mass up through the fore hatchway.

It was a most uncommonly rapid, skilful, efficient, seamanlike operation, almost without words, certainly without loud, harsh, angry words, and in the midst of his intense frustration Jack was aware of it: but rapid though it was it still took time, and there was the *Spartan* fleeting away into the thick grey weather ahead. The sun, such as it was, would soon be gone; the moon would not rise until the changing of the watch, and little light would she give even then.

His only hope was to crack on. The gale, now stronger still, came roaring in just before the quarter, the *Surprise*'s favourite point of sailing, and he was almost sure that the gust that had wrecked the topsail marked the end of the wind's backing. He was almost sure that it would now blow steadily, though very hard.

He might be wrong; the wish might be father to the thought; but whether or no it was his only chance. On the other hand, was he going to run the ship on to the rocks of Ushant? He had not been able to fix his position at noon, and at this pace they must have run off a great deal of the distance. But then with singular clarity his mind presented him with a dead reckoning since the last observation; they were closing with the land, yet even at this rate they could not raise it before midnight. With his eye fixed on the faint and dwindling privateer far over the white-torn sea he cried 'Fore topgallant-sail.'

It was only a comparatively small sail, but its sheeting home and hoisting fairly made the frigate stagger; its force came on to her just as she was reaching the crest of a wave and she changed step like a horse on the point of shying. Once she had recovered her smooth swooping pace Jack stepped forward, laid his hand on the cablet sustaining the foremast, nodded, and called 'Maintopgallant. Cheerly, now.'

She was already under single-reefed topsails, and these two, so high, added immensely to their thrust. She was clearly gaining on the *Spartan*. But she was not gaining fast enough. At this rate the *Spartan* would run into the safety of darkness before she could be laid aboard: and now there was no possibility of distant gunfire for anything but a ship of the line — both swell and speed were now so much greater that green seas swept the forecastle every other heave.

'Lifelines fore and aft,' said Jack. 'What?'

'Come on now, come on, sir,' cried Killick in a very angry whine. 'Ain't I called out fifty times? Come into the cabin.' His indignation gave him such moral superiority that Jack followed him, stripped off his sopping coat and shirt and put on dry, with tarpaulin hat and jacket over all. Returning, he took Honey's speaking-trumpet and roared, 'Stand by for the studdingsails.'

The men stood by, of course, but they looked aft and they looked at one another with significant expressions; this was cracking on indeed.

Yet even foretopmast and lower studdingsails did not satisfy him. Although the *Surprise* was now making very close on thirteen knots, with her larboard cathead well under water and her lee rail hardly to be seen for the rushing foam, while her bow-wave flung the spray a good twenty yards and her deck sloped at thirty-five degrees, he still called for the spritsail course. It was an odd, rather old-fashioned sail, slung under the bowsprit and masking the chasers, but it had the advantage of reefing diagonally, so that its leeward corner was hitched up out of the sea and its windward half gave just that additional impulse Jack longed for.

Both ships had their battle-lanterns lit between decks by now, and both raced on through the rain and the spin-drift in a dim glow. But when the *Spartan* began throwing her guns overboard bright orange squares appeared as her ports opened, opened again and again, for her leeward guns had to be manhandled across to be heaved out on the windward side, a shocking task in such a sea. Her boats were jettisoned too, lightening her still more; but for all that the *Surprise* was now running a full knot faster than the chase and Jack felt confident that he should have her if only he could keep her in sight for half an hour. Yet there was murk ahead, and frequent squalls, the certainty of an impenetrable night. He sent the sharpest eyes in the ship into the foretop and stood at the weather rail, as tense as he had ever been, watching the *Spartan*, her white wake, the suffused light from her stern-window, and the low dark cloud sweeping up from the south-south-west. Five minutes. Her last two guns went over. Ten minutes more at this same tearing pace or even faster and she was not a quarter of a mile ahead; but nor was the dark broad squall. She faded, faded, and suddenly she dowsed all her lights, disappearing entirely. For a moment her wake could still be seen, and then that too was gone. The rain swept in, flat on the driving gale.

'She's hauled her wind,' roared the foretop; and the squall parting, there she was again, the faintest unlit ghost in the dimness, five points off her course. 'I have her now,' said Jack. But now the squall clearing farther still showed a great ship nearer by far, a three-decker wearing an admiral's top-lantern, and more ships beyond her. And as the three-decker fired, sending a ball across the *Surprise*'s forefoot, Jack realized that he was in the midst of the Channel fleet, and that the *Spartan* had slipped through them for Brest, unseen in the squall. He shot up into the wind, lowering his topsails on the cap, and made the private signal, together with his number and the words *Enemy in the east-north-east*.

The three-decker replied *'Captain repair aboard flag,'* and carried on her course.

Jack had read the signal before it was reported to him. He looked at the greyness where the *Spartan* had been. He looked at the mountainous sea between him and the flagship — a pull of half a mile into the teeth of the gale — and caught Mowett's shocked and anxious eye. He opened his mouth, but discipline was too strong, too deep-rooted, and he shut it again.

'Your barge, sir?' asked Mowett.

'No,' said Jack. 'The blue cutter. She is more seaworthy. She may swim.'

CHAPTER FOUR

'Sweetheart,' wrote Jack Aubrey to his wife, dating his letter from the Crown, 'The last farewells are over and the Surprises are a ship's company no more, but only two or three straggling bands of sailormen making holiday on shore: I can hear the forecastle division, the oldest soberest seamen in the ship, kicking up Bob's a-dying, a prodigious great din three streets away, at the Duncan's Head; but most of the rest are already speechless. Saying goodbye to so many old shipmates was painful, as you may imagine, and I should be tolerably low in my spirits, were it not for the thought that I shall be seeing you and the children in a few days' time. Not quite as soon as I could wish, because as we were lying here at single anchor, waiting for our signal and the tide, the Lisbon packet came tearing out under a press of sail in that showing-away fashion that packets have — anything for speed — and instead of shaving

178

our stern close, absolutely ran into it. We screeched, of course, and fended her off with swabs and anything that came to hand, but even so she did so much damage that I have been kept busy having it put right ever since. I have not even had time to tell you of my meeting with the Admiral. I came aboard him after as disagreeable a pull as any I can remember and without asking me how I did or whether I should like to shift my clothes or even dry my face he told me I was a reckless mad lunatic, rushing into the midst of a fleet at that wild pace with studdingsails aloft and alow and why had I not saluted the flag? Could not I see it? Could not I see a three-decker, forsooth? Had I no lookout? Were lookouts no longer sent to the masthead in the modern Navy? "There were two, my lord," said I, but in a very meek, submissive tone. Then, said he, they were both to be flogged, with one dozen strokes from me and another dozen from him; and as for me, I might consider myself reprimanded, severely reprimanded. "And as for this alleged priva-teer," he went on, "I dare say it was only some trumpery merchantman; you young fellows are always whoring after merchant-men. The moment you are given a command you go whoring after merchantmen — after prizes. I have seen it time, time and again, and the fleet left without frigates. But since you are here, you might as well make yourself useful to your King and country." I was rather pleased with the "young fellows", but less so when it appeared that my usefulness might take the form of leading an attack by fireships on the harbour of Bainville, which I happen to know uncommonly well. I do not like fireships: the plan seemed to me ill-conceived, with not nearly enough attention paid to the coast batteries and the very strong run of the tide, and with little likelihood of the fireships' crews being able to get away. No one who has been in a fireship can expect any quarter: if he is taken he is either knocked on the head directly or put up against a wall and shot a little later; that is why they are always manned with volunteers. I am sure that all the Surprises would have volunteered, but I very much disliked the idea of their being captured and I was just as pleased when it was represented that if I were given the command it would mean my being put over the heads of several men senior to me on the post-captains' list. At the council the point was made several times with great eagerness and warmth and those who made it said that Lord Keith had preferred me again and again in the Mediterranean, while even these last few months I have been given a cruise that many frigate-captains would have given their eye-teeth for and that had no doubt brought me in great wealth (how I wish it had). True, I have spent less time on shore than most men, and few have had such luck; but I was surprised to find how much jealousy it had caused. I had no idea I had so many enemies, or at least ill-wishers, in the service. But, however, the scheme was dropped, and my usefulness came down to conveying the Admiral's sister to Falmouth. She had been ordered to sea by her physicians for a shortness of breath; but as Stephen observed, the cruise had very nearly cured her of every disease in Buchan's *Domestic Medicine* by cutting off her breath entirely: the poor lady was sea-sick from the first word to the last, and was grown quite pitifully thin and yellow.

'Stephen himself left for town this morning, treating himself to a chaise so that he could set Parson Martin down somewhere far off the main road. I wish I could give you a better report of him. He seems anxious and unhappy. At first I thought he might be worrying about money, but not at all — our agent has been as brisk as a bee with having our prizes condemned and paid for. Besides, when he told me of his godfather's death he observed that he had inherited from him; I do not suppose it is anything out of the way, but Stephen has always been content with very little. I am afraid he grieves for the old gentleman, but even more than that I believe he is most painfully anxious about Diana. I have never seen him so uneasy in his mind.' Jack thought of telling Sophie the rumours about Stephen's infidelity that had been current in the Mediterranean, but after a moment he shook his head and went on,

'I shall be sending you Killick, Bonden and perhaps Plaice with most of my dunnage by the slow coach, which leaves tomorrow: I shall have to stay a little longer, to make sure of leaving the ship as I could wish (there is some hope of her going into ordinary rather than to the breakers) and to see some inquisitive gentlemen from the Admiralty and Navy Board; yet even so I may be in town as soon as Stephen, or even sooner, if this sweet south-wester holds. Harry Tennant has *Despatch*, and he promises me a lift. She is acting as the cartel for the moment — you remember the cartel, that brought us back from our captivity in France? and she is very fast sailing large, though a slug on a bowline. It will only be touch and away at Calais, and then from Dover the London mail will whirl me up. I shall have to see the lawyers first to find how things stand — a proper flat I should look, was I to post down to Ashgrove and instantly be arrested for debt, if any of the cases have been decided against us. And for the same reason, since the ship's arrival will have been reported in the papers these many days past, I shall stay at the Grapes, and not come down till Sunday; but if you would like me to bring anything down, please write to me at the club; they are more used to letters there, and will not tidy them away among the dish-covers.' The Bunch of Grapes was a small, comfortable, old-fashioned inn that lay within the liberties of the Savoy, so its customers were out of reach of their creditors all the week, as they were throughout the kingdom on Sundays. Jack had spent a considerable time here, ever since he had grown rich enough to be a worthwhile prey for land-sharks, and Stephen kept a room all the year round, as a base, retaining it even after his marriage with Diana, they being an odd, semi-detached couple.

'But I believe I may say that Sunday is certain — as certain as anything can be, that has to do with the sea — and I cannot tell you how I long for it. After so long a time we shall have so very, very many things to say to one another.' He stood up and walked over to the window: it commanded a fine view of

Telegraph Hill, where the vanes of the semaphore were in continual motion, information travelling to London and back at an extraordinary pace. The Admiralty would have known of the *Surprise*'s arrival the very day she made her number, far out in the offing; and by now, perhaps, they would have made up their minds what to do with her. But he hoped that she might be laid up in ordinary, in reserve, rather than be sold out of the service: so long as she was whole there was hope.

'She would make a perfect cartel, for example,' he reflected on Tuesday, sitting alone in the great cabin of the *Despatch* as she ran fast up the Channel with the wind at west-south-west. 'Far, far better than this wallowing tub. She has everything to recommend her, beauty, speed, grace; at ten miles you cannot mistake her. Such waste — the pity of it all. But if I go on like this, battering my head against a brick wall, I shall go out of my mind — run melancholy mad.'

He did go on thinking about her however, and the more objective part of his mind offered the reflexion that although there was something to be said for speed, recognizability was no virtue in a cartel, or at least not in the particular cartels that plied between France and England this war. Since Buonaparte had decreed that there should be no exchange of prisoners these were scarcely cartels at all in the usual sense; nor had they much evident reason for existing. Yet to and fro they went, sometimes carrying envoys from one side or another with proposals or counterproposals, sometimes eminent natural philosophers such as Sir Humphry Davy or Dr Maturin, invited to address one or another of the academies in Paris or the *Institut* itself, sometimes objects to do with science or natural history captured by the Royal Navy and sent back by the Royal Society, to whom the Admiralty submitted them, and sometimes (though far more rarely) specimens travelling the other way, but always carrying the newspapers from either side and elegantly dressed dolls to show London just how fashions were developing in France. Discretion was their prime virtue, and on occasion their passengers spent the voyage in different cabins, being landed separately by night. This time the *Despatch*, met by a pilot-boat in Calais road, lay at an empty wharf until four in the morning, when Jack, dozing in a hammock slung in Tennant's dining-cabin, heard three sets of people come aboard at half-hour intervals.

He was reasonably familiar with the ways

of a cartel, because he and Stephen had travelled in the *Despatch*'s predecessor on one of the rare occasions when the convention was abused: they had been prisoners in France and Talleyrand had engineered their escape so that Stephen, whom he knew to be an intelligence-agent, might take his private proposals for betraying Buonaparte to the English government and the French court in exile at Hartwell. He was therefore not at all surprised when Tennant asked him to stay below while the other passengers disembarked in a secluded part of Dover harbour, far from the traffic of the port — far too from the customs office, through which Jack would have to pass. It did not matter as far as duty was concerned, since his valise had nothing customable in it, but it did mean that the people before him would probably take up all the places on the London coach, both inside and out, and possibly all the post-chaises too: in the present decayed state of the town there were very few.

'Come and have dinner with me at the Ship,' said Jack, as the *Despatch* tied up at the customs wharf and sent a brow across. 'Prodgers has a damned good table d'hôte.'

'Thankee, Jack,' said Tennant, 'but I must run straight up to Harwich on this tide.'

Jack was not altogether sorry for it. Harry Tennant was a prime fish, but he would go on and on about the *Surprise*'s miserable fate — doomed to be firewood — no hope of reprieve in these cases — oh the cruel waste — the dispersal of such a fine ship's company — Jack's officers probably on the beach for good — never get another ship — Tennant's uncle Coleman fit to hang himself when his *Phoebe* went to the knacker's yard — it certainly hastened his death.

'Carry your bag for you, sir?' piped a voice at his elbow, and looking down he saw to his astonishment not a little confident black-guard barefoot boy of the usual knowing kind but a nervous little girl in a pinafore, her face blushing under its dirt. 'Very well,' he said. 'To the Ship. You take one handle and I will take the other. Clap on tight, now.'

She clapped on with both hands, he lengthened his arm and bent his knees, and so they made their uneasy way up through the town. Her name was Margaret, she said; her brother Abel usually carried the gentlemen's bags, but a horse trod on his foot last Friday; the other great boys were quite kind, and would let her have his place till he was better. At the Ship he gave her a shilling, and her face dropped. 'That's a shilling,' he said. 'Han't you ever seen a shilling?' She shook her head. 'It's twelve pennies,' he said, looking at his change. 'You know what a tizzy is, I dare say?'

'Oh yes. Everybody knows what a tizzy is,' said Margaret rather scornfully.

'Well, here are two of 'em. Because twice six is twelve, do you see.'

The child yielded up the unknown shilling, solemnly received the familiar sixpences one after another, and all at once her face beamed out like the sun coming from behind a cloud.

Jack walked into the dining-room: he was sharp-set, being used to the old-fashioned naval meal-times, but a waiter said 'Not for half an hour yet, sir. Would you like something to drink in the snug while you are waiting?'

'Well,' said Jack, 'I should like a pint of sherry, but let me have it here, by the fire, and then I shall not lose a minute when dinner is put on the table. I am so sharp-set I could eat an ox. But first, can you get me a place on the London coach, inside or out?'

'Oh no, sir. They was all took half an hour ago.'

'What about a post-chaise, then?'

'Why, sir, what with things being so slack, we don't do 'em any more. But Jacob here,' nodding towards the only bearded waiter

Jack had ever seen in a Christian country, 'will step across to the Union or the Royal, and see what they have in their yards: he has already been there for another gent.'

'Aye, pray let him do that,' said Jack, 'and he shall have half a crown for his pains.'

'On reflexion,' he said to himself, drinking a first contemplative glass of sherry, 'he is not quite a waiter, either. He is no doubt an hostler that helps in the dining-room from time to time; and is therefore entitled to a beard.'

Dinner came in at last, immediately pursued by a troop of hungry gentlemen; the first of these, a lean, clever-looking man in a fine black coat with gold buttons, took a chair next to Jack and at once troubled him for the bread; he began to eat it with something as near avidity as good manners would allow, but said no more: a reserved gentleman, perhaps a chancery lawyer with a pretty good practice, or something of that kind. On the other side of the table sat a middle-aged merchant with his broad-brimmed hat squarely on his head who eyed Jack first through his spectacles and then without them until he had finished the broth and herb-pudding with which the meal began and then said 'Friend, hast ever a leathern convenience?'

'I am sorry, sir,' said Jack, 'but I do not even know what a leathern convenience is.'

'Why, I thought thee was a Friend, from thy dress, with no sinful pride.' Jack was indeed dressed very simply — his civilian clothes had suffered cruelly under both tropics and even more between them — but he had not supposed he was quite so sinless as to be remarked upon. 'A leathern convenience,' went on the merchant, 'is what the profane call a machine drawn by an horse: a chaise.'

'Well, sir,' said Jack, 'I have no convenience yet, but I hope to have one soon.'

The hope was scarcely uttered before it was dashed. The bearded servant, passing a dish of parsnips between Jack and his black-coated neighbour, said to the latter, 'The Royal's shay will be waiting for you after dinner, sir, in our yard, just behind.' And to Jack, 'I'm sorry, sir, but that was the last one. There ain't another in the town.' Yet even while he was speaking, the Quaker's neighbour, a flash, auctioneer-looking fellow, cried 'That's all goddam humbug, Jacob. I spoke for the Royal's shay first. It's mine.'

'I think not,' said Jack's neighbour coldly. 'I have already paid for the first stage.'

'Nonsense,' said the flash-looking fellow.

'It's mine, I tell you. And what's more,' — addressing the Quaker — 'I'll give you a lift, old Square-toes.' He started up and hurried out of the room, calling 'Jacob, Jacob!'

This made something of a scene, and people stared, but with the eager satisfaction of hunger up and down the table and the inn-keeper's steady carving, sending along more beef, more mutton, more roast pork with a little crackling, calm soon returned, and with it more rational, connected thought. There were few men who relished wit more than Jack Aubrey, either in himself or others, and he was turning parsnips, butter and soft words over in his mind in the hope that something brilliant might come of it when his neighbour addressed him again. 'I am sorry you are disappointed of your chaise, sir; but if you choose to share mine, you are very welcome. I am going to London. May I trouble you for the butter?'

'You are very kind indeed, sir,' said Jack. 'I should be most uncommon obliged — particularly wish to be in London today. Allow me to pour you a glass of wine.'

They naturally fell into conversation: it was a conversation of no very great importance, bearing chiefly on the weather, the strong likelihood of rain later in the day, the appetite engendered by sea-air, and the difference between the true Dover sole and upstarts from the German Ocean, but it was pleasant, harmless and friendly. It nevertheless succeeded in angering the spectacled man, who directed indignant looks across the table and left them at the time of cheese, beating his chair upon the floor in a very marked manner and stalking off to join the flash cove in the doorway.

'I am afraid we have displeased the Quaker,' observed Jack.

'I do not believe he is a Quaker at all,' said Black Coat quietly after a pause in which some of their neighbours farther down the table also left. 'I know many respectable people — Gurneys and Harwoods — who are Friends. They behave like reasonable beings, not like characters on the provincial stage. Those peculiarities of dress and language are quite exploded among them, I understand; they have been laid aside these fifty years and more.'

'But why should he wish to pass for a Quaker?' asked Jack.

'Why, indeed? Conceivably to profit from their reputation for honesty and plain-dealing. But the heart of man is unsearchable,' said Black Coat with a smile, picking up a leather folder that leaned against his chair, 'and perhaps he is only pursuing some illicit amour, or escaping from his creditors. Now, sir, if you will forgive me, I shall collect my bag.'

'But will you not stay for the coffee?' cried Jack, who had ordered a pot.

'Alas, I dare not,' said Black Coat. 'It disagrees with me. But do not hurry, I beg. My inner man is already somewhat disturbed, and I shall retire for longer than it will take you to drink two or even three pots of coffee. Let us meet at the chaise in say a quarter of an hour. It will be in that deserted-looking yard behind the kitchen, where the Ship used to keep its carriages.'

In fourteen minutes Jack Aubrey walked into the yard, carrying his valise. Even before he turned the corner he heard a strange bawling, wrangling din, and the moment he reached the gateway he saw the Quaker and the flash cove grappling with his friend, while the little post-boy clung to the horses' heads, rising clear from the ground at every plunge and shouting as loud as his faint breathless treble would allow. The flash cove had knocked Black Coat's hat down over his eyes and was busy throttling him: the Quaker, giving awkward kicks whenever he could, was tugging at the leather case that Black Coat clung to with all his might.

Jack might be slow conceiving a joke but he was exceedingly brisk in action. He ran at top speed from the gateway, launched his sixteen stone in a flying leap upon the flash cove's back, cracked his head upon the cobbles and sprang up to deal with the Quaker. But the Quaker, surprisingly nimble for his years and bulk, was already flying fast, and Black Coat, extricating himself from his hat, caught Jack's arm and cried 'Let him go, let him go, if you please. Pray let him go. And this drunken ruffian too,' — for the flash cove was getting to his knees. 'I am infinitely obliged to you sir, but pray let there be no scandal, no outcry, no noise.' People from the Ship's kitchen were at last beginning to congregate and stare.

'No constable?' asked Jack.

'Oh no, no: let us have no public notice of any kind, I beg,' said Black Coat very earnestly. 'Pray let us get in. You are not hurt? You have your baggage. Let us get in at once.'

For some time, indeed until the post-chaise was out of Dover and well on the open London road, Black Coat dusted his clothes, rearranged his cravat, and smoothed the papers in his wrenched and battered case. He was clearly very much shaken, although in reply to Jack's inquiries he said he was 'only a little bruised and scraped — nothing in comparison of a fall from a horse.' But a little past Buckland, with the horses going easy and the chaise running smoothly along, he said, 'I am infinitely obliged to you, sir. Infinitely obliged, not only for your rescuing me and my possessions from those scoundrels but also for letting the matter drop. If the constable had been called, we must have been delayed; and far worse than that, there must have been a great deal of troublesome noise, a scandal. In my position I cannot afford the least breath of scandal or public notice.'

'To be sure, scandal is a damned unpleasant thing,' said Jack. 'But I wish we had tossed them into the horse-pond.'

There was a silence, and after a while Black Coat said 'I owe you an explanation.'

'Not at all,' said Jack.

The other bowed and went on, 'I am just returned from a confidential mission to the Continent, and those fellows were waiting for me. I noticed the ruffian with the Belcher neckerchief on the ship — wondered how he came to be there — and regretted having been obliged to leave my servant in Paris with my principal, a stout, courageous young man, my gamekeeper's son. The foolery about the chaise was a mere blind, to give their attack some countenance: they were not after the chaise, nor were they after my property, my watch and what little money I carry. No, sir, they were after the information, the news, that I carry here,' — laying his hand on the leather case — 'News that would be worth a mint of money, in certain hands.'

'Good news, I trust?' said Jack, looking out of the window at a handsome young woman, pink with exercise, cantering along the broad verge, followed by a groom.

'Pretty good, sir, I believe: at least, many people will think so,' said Black Coat, smiling; but then, perhaps feeling that he had been indiscreet, he coughed, and said 'Here is the rain we were speaking of.'

They changed horses at Canterbury, and when Jack tried to pay for them or at least for his share, Black Coat was immovable: No, no, it would not do; he must beg to be excused. He could not allow his preserver to put his hand in his pocket; in any event the cost would be the same whether Jack were there or not; and to end with a knock-down argument, Government was paying. When they moved off again he suggested that unless Jack had any objection they should sup at Sittingbourne. 'Many an excellent meal have I had at the Rose,' he said, 'and they have a Chambolle-Musigny of ninety-two which is one of the finest wines I have ever drunk. Then again, we shall be served by the daughter of the house, a young person I delight to contemplate. I am no satyr, but I do find that pretty creatures about one add much to the pleasure of life. By the way,' he said after a pause, 'it is rather absurd, but I do not believe I have introduced myself: my name is Ellis Palmer, very much at your service.'

'How do you do, sir?' said Jack, shaking his hand. 'Mine is John Aubrey.'

'Aubrey,' said Palmer meditatively. 'That is a name which has been much in my mind recently, in connexion with chelonians. May I ask whether you are any kin to the famous Mr Aubrey of Testudo aubreii, that most splendid of the tortoise kind?'

'I suppose I am, in a way,' said Jack, with something as near to a coy simper as his deeply tanned, battle-scarred, weather-beaten face could manage. 'Indeed, the creature was called after me: not that I had any hand in the matter, however. I mean, its discovery was no merit of mine.'

'Good Heavens!' cried Palmer. 'Then you must be Captain Aubrey, of the Navy; and you must necessarily know Dr Maturin.'

'He is my particular friend,' said Jack. 'We

have sailed together these many years, during this war and the last. Do you know him?'

'I have never had the honour of being introduced to him, but I have studied all his valuable works — his non-medical works, that is to say, for I am only a naturalist, and a mere dilettante at that; parliamentary drafting is my occupation — I have heard him read papers at the Royal Society, when a member has taken me there, and I was present when he addressed the *Institut* in Paris.'

'Was you, though?' said Jack. From this and some other things that had been let drop it was now pretty clear to him that Palmer was one of those emissaries who went to and fro, the men for whom the cartel ships really continued to exist.

'Indeed I was. His subject was the solitaire, as of course you must know very well: I was unable to catch all he said — the hall was rather large — but afterwards I read the account in the published minutes with the greatest profit and enjoyment. Such a range of inquiry, such erudition, such illuminating comparisons, such flashes of wit! It must be a privilege to know such a man.'

They talked of Stephen until they reached Sittingbourne, and they talked of him during their admirable supper. 'I wish he were with us now,' said Jack, looking at the candle through his burgundy. 'He loves good wine even more than I do; and this is a truly noble year.'

'So he adds that virtue to all the rest: I am delighted to hear it. He sounds the best and happiest of men. My dear,' — this to the rose-like daughter of the house — 'I believe we could do with another bottle.'

Jack might have replied that Stephen lacked a sense of time and of discipline, and that he was capable of giving a sharp answer, but he did not: he said 'And as you observed just now, he is amazing witty on occasion. I heard him say the best thing I ever heard in my life, straight off, taking it on the half-volley, no clearing the decks and beating to action. I wish I may get it right this time, but sometimes I blunder, it being so damned subtle; and it is never quite so droll when it was to be put right and explained. First I must observe that in the Navy we have two short watches of only two hours apiece, called the first and the last dog-watches. Now it so happened that on the Toulon blockade there was a civilian aboard who did not understand our ways, and at dinner one day he asked "Why *dog* watches?" We explained that they shifted the times of duty, so that the starbowlins should have the graveyard watch one night and the larbowlins the next; but that was not what he meant. "But why *dog?*" says he, "Why should short watches be *dog* watches?" And there we were, all at a stand, unable to tell, until Maturin piped up, "Why, don't you see sir? It is because they are curtailed." We did not smoke it quite at once, but then it flashed upon us — *cur-tailed,* do you see?'

It now flashed upon Palmer, and although he was not ordinarily a laughing man he burst out with such a peal that it brought the lovely young woman in, amazed, with the corkscrew in her hand.

They lingered long over their walnuts, and once or twice Palmer began to speak in an unusually grave tone but then changed his mind. It was not until they were on the road again, with the carriage-lights boring into the darkness ahead and the rain drumming on the roof, giving a fine enclosed sense of privacy, that he brought out what was in his mind. 'I have been wondering, Captain Aubrey, I have been wondering just how I might express my gratitude.' Jack uttered the customary protests, but Palmer went on, 'And it occurs to me that although on the one hand a present of money to a gentleman in your position would clearly be unthinkable, even if it amounted to a very considerable sum, yet on the other, a piece of information that would lead to the acquisition of the same amount, or indeed more, might prove acceptable.'

'A kindly thought,' said Jack, smiling in the darkness.

'It is certainly kindly meant,' said Palmer. 'But I must confess that it depends on the possession of a certain amount of money in the first place, or of friends who will advance it, or of credit with an agent or a banker, which is much the same thing; for to the rich shall be given, you know, and only to the rich.'

'I should not describe myself as rich,' said Jack, 'but for the moment I should not describe myself as destitute either.' His mind searched among the race-meetings for the kind of horse that Palmer was about to recommend, and he was wholly taken aback when he heard the words, spoken very seriously, 'As I dare say you are aware, negotiations to end the war have been going on for some time: that is why my principal and I have been to Paris. They have succeeded. Peace will be signed in the next few days.'

'Good Lord above!' cried Jack.

'Yes, indeed,' said Palmer. 'And of course there are an infinity of reflexions to be made. But what is to my immediate purpose is that as soon as the news is made public, Government stock and a large variety of commercial shares will rise enormously, some of them cent per cent.'

'Good Lord above,' said Jack again.

'A man who bought now,' said Palmer, 'would make a very great deal of money before next settling-day; he might borrow or pledge his credit or make time-bargains with absolute confidence.'

'But is it not wrong to buy in such circumstances?' asked Jack.

'Oh dear me no,' said Palmer, laughing. 'That is how fortunes are made in the City. It is not wrong either legally or morally. If you knew for certain that a given horse was going to win a race, it might be said that it was wrong to bet on it, because you would be taking money away from the other man. But when stocks and shares rise, and you profit by the rise, you are not taking money away from anyone: it is the country's or the company's wealth that increases, and you profit by the increase, harming no one at all. Of course it cannot be done on a very large scale, for fear of disturbing the money-market. Are you acquainted with the money-market, sir?'

'Not I,' said Jack.

'I have studied it closely for many years, and I do assure you that upon occasion it is as nervous, irrational, and skittish as a foolish woman, given to the vapours. Disturbance upsets it for a long while, which has a very bad effect on the country's credit. In cases of this kind, therefore, Government limits the information to a small number of people, all of them men who can be relied upon to act with discretion, and not to exaggerate.'

'What would exaggeration amount to?'

'Anything much exceeding fifty thousand in omnium, in Government stock, would probably be frowned upon. Investment in commercial shares could of course be spread out and therefore disturb the market less, but even there I do not think much larger dealings would be approved.'

'There is little danger of my being thought indiscreet,' said Jack, laughing; and then, much more earnestly, 'I am most uncommonly obliged to you, sir. It so happens that I do have a certain amount of prize-money in hand, and like most men I should be happy to see it increase. May I speak of all this to Maturin?'

'Why, as to that,' said Palmer, 'I am afraid it would not quite do, the information being so very strictly confidential. For the same reason, if you do decide to buy, you should not do so through one person but through several — your agent, say, your banker, and a couple of stockbrokers. The market is very sensitive to sudden purchases in a time of general morosity, above all purchases by a single individual. On the other hand you could urge Dr Maturin, and perhaps one or at the most two other particular friends, to buy in moderation: you could urge it very strongly, though without citing any authority nor of course betraying my confidence. Does Dr Maturin understand the stock-exchange?'

'I very much doubt it.'

'Yet so philosophic a mind might well contemplate the City, and observe the conflict of greed and fear in the minds of its inhabitants, symbolized by the Stock Exchange quotations; but at all events perhaps he might care for a list of the securities most likely to appreciate, or rather likely to appreciate most. I should very much like to mark my esteem for him; although only at such a distance. You might even find it useful yourself: it is the fruit of much study.'

The list was still in Jack's pocket when he walked into his club the next day, but by now it was ticked, crossed off, scored through, and heavily annotated.

'Good afternoon, Tom,' he said to the hall-porter. 'Are there any letters for me?'

'Good afternoon, sir,' said Tom, looking at his rack. 'No, sir; I am sorry, never a one.'

'Well, well,' said Jack, 'I suppose there has not been time. Have you seen Dr Maturin?'

'Dr Maturin? Oh no, sir: I never even knew he was in England.'

Jack walked upstairs. He was feeling cheerful, but very, very tired: light in heart, heavy in body. The night, most of it taken up with talking hard in the post-chaise, had not been restful; walking on paved, unyielding streets after so long at sea was physically exhausting; and the emotions of the night and day were more wearing still. His first call had been at his lawyers'. Here he had learnt that none of the cases had been decided one way or another; that everything was much as he had left it, except that the opinion of two eminent counsel on the first had been obtained, neither of them altogether unfavourable, and perhaps the case might come on early next term. This did at least mean that he could walk about without being arrested for debt and carried off to a sponging-house, so he went straight to his prize-agent, where he spent a busy morning, more fruitful than he had expected in the article of Adriatic captures, now made so long ago that he had almost forgotten their names, and then to his bank, where he had a singularly flattering compliment paid to him. He passed some time with one of the younger partners, and as they were coming down stairs together he observed that he must also call on the cashier — he had little money on him. Mr Hoare stepped behind the counter and said 'This is Captain Aubrey of the Navy; I believe we may manage gold for him.' Almost everybody had had to be content with notes these many years past, but Jack left the bank with twenty-five guineas, a comfortable weight in his pocket, a feeling of real, solid wealth. Then, having eaten in a chophouse, he walked to two different stockbrokers, his own and his father's: the second he had not met before and he regretted the acquaintance as soon as it was made. Mr Shape had all the bouncing easiness and confidence of a City man of the third rate; he was not a regular stockbroker, not a member of the Exchange, but an outside dealer, and even for one as little used to business as Jack his establishment gave off an indefinable air of malpractice. However, he meant to be friendly and he told Jack that General Aubrey was in town, that he had seen him only a few days since, and that the old gentleman was 'as spry as ever'. Shape would also very much have liked to know just why these securities were being bought and he threw out a good many hints; but when he was confronted with a scrub Jack could look tolerably forbidding, and Shape's confidence did not extend to the direct question.

After this rather unpleasant interlude Jack took a coach back to Whitehall. He nodded to the Admiralty, that fount of intense joy and deep distress, and walked through St James's Park and to his club. He was fond of London and he liked his walk, but now he was quite done up. He called for a tankard of champagne and sat with it in an easy chair by a window overlooking the street. Within him the spring of life began to flow again, lapping gently over his bruised heels and blistered feet; and cheerfulness, even the ebullience of the early morning, rose even faster as he reflected upon the immense amount of business he had accomplished that day. Presently he would gather himself together, rise up and go to the Grapes; there he might possibly find a letter from Sophie and perhaps run into Stephen. At least he would have word of him.

He smiled; and the smile was wiped from his face by the approach of Edward Parker, a former shipmate. He had nothing whatsoever against Edward Parker, but he did not want any man to commiserate with him about the *Surprise*. However, there was a way of dealing with the situation: Parker was a pretty good seaman, brave and successful; he belonged to a well-known naval family and he was sure of continuous employment and eventually of a flag; furthermore he was slim, handsome, and much caressed by women; but he valued himself only on two qualities that he did not possess: the ability to ride a horse like the cove in the poem, and to drink any man under the table.

'Oh, Aubrey,' cried he, 'how very sorry I am to hear about *Surprise*.'

'Never mind,' said Jack. 'This is St Groper's day, the patron of topers: no tears on St Groper's day. William, a tankard of the same for Captain Parker.' The club had particularly elegant silver tankards and this one looked finer than usual as it came frosted all over on a shining salver. 'St Groper,' said Jack, 'and his immortal memory in one heroic swig. Waste not a drop.'

Parker did manfully, but he weighed nine stone against Jack's sixteen, and he had not tramped about London all day. Although he himself proposed the second can, it was his undoing: after sitting with a fixed, artificial smile on his pale face for some minutes he made a barely coherent excuse and hurried from the room.

Jack settled back in his chair and contemplated the evening tide in St James's Street. There had been a long-lasting levee at the palace, and quantities of unusually gorgeous officers were to be seen, scarlet and gold, gleaming with silver and steel and plumed like Agamemnon, hurrying anxiously towards Piccadilly for fear of the coming shower. The more provident had servants with umbrellas, and some, tucking up their swords, dashed with jangling spurs into one or another of the clubs along the street. There were several, and almost immediately opposite Jack's window stood Button's, to which General Aubrey belonged. Jack was also a member, but he hardly ever went there, not caring much for his company, which consisted of exceedingly rich men — it had more dukes than any other — and a fair number of blackguards, sometimes of excellent family.

Once the officers had reached shelter, civilians took over the street again, and Jack observed with regret that the fine coloured coats of his youth were losing more and more ground to black, which, though well enough in particular cases, gave the far pavement a mourning air. To be sure, bottle-green, claret-coloured, and bright blue did appear now and then, but the far side of the street was not the flower-garden that once it had been. And pantaloons were almost universal among the young.

A good many acquaintances passed by. Blenkinsop of the Foreign Office, looking superior. Waddon, a Hampshire neighbour and an excellent creature but now very far from happy on the back of a recently-purchased horse that advanced sideways down towards the clock-tower, foaming and farting; and as soon as the half-hour struck the animal (a light chestnut gelding) uttered a kind of scream and rushed into the narrow alley by Lock's. He saw Waddon emerge, looking sullen, having apparently abandoned the animal. He saw Wray of the Admiralty and another man whose name he could not recall walk into Button's, both in black; more black coats followed them; then came the old familiar bright blue, and without much surprise Jack recognized his father.

At one time it must have been possible to love General Aubrey, since he had married a thoroughly amiable woman, Jack's mother;

but for the last twenty years and more even his dogs had felt no affection for him. His mind was almost wholly taken up with the notion of gaining money by some expedient or other; at one time he had felled all the timber on their land, although the trees were not even half mature, thus doing Jack a sad ill-turn at almost no profit to himself; and he now associated with some very odd creatures on the fringes of banking, insurance and property development. He had also blasted Jack's chance of inheriting an impoverished but reparable estate by marrying his dairymaid, at the cost of a swingeing settlement, and by begetting another son.

Yet Jack had a strong sense of filial piety and he had written a note in which he urged his father to put every penny he could into the securities on Palmer's list, saying that his recommendations could not be explained and must remain secret. He had meant to hand this letter in, no more: but now, seeing that tall bony figure grasp the railings to heave himself up the steps he said 'Damn it, he *is* my father, after all. I shall go and ask him how he does.' 'If you do,' replied his somewhat clouded intelligence, 'you will have to deal with questions.' 'Not at all,' he said, 'I have only to say that I am bound to silence — have given my word — for him to understand,' and finishing his wine he walked across the street.

'Well, Jack, how beest?' cried the General, recognizing him. 'Have you been away?'

'Yes, sir. I have been in the Pacific.'

'And now you are back. Capital, capital.' The General seemed quite pleased. 'I dare say Sophie was glad to see you,' he said, pleased with himself again for having remembered her name, so pleased that he asked Jack what he would take.

'That is very kind of you, sir, but I have just had three cans of champagne over the way, on a pretty nearly empty stomach, and I can distinctly feel it. But perhaps I might have some coffee.'

'Nonsense,' cried his father. 'Don't you be a goddam milksop. Good wine never did a man any harm. We will stick with the champagne.'

While the first glasses were going down Jack made civil inquiries about his step-mother and her son. 'A couple of silly bitches, both on 'em, perpetually lamenting,' replied the General. He poured more wine and then after a pause he said again, 'But I dare say Sophie was glad to see you.'

'I hope she will be,' said Jack, 'but I have not been home yet. Capital wine, sir: fruitier than ours. No, I have not been home: the cartel landed me at Dover and I thought it better to come through London first.'

'I remember that young whoremaster of a lieutenant of yours had the cartel ship at one time. What was his name?'

'Babbington, sir. Now it is Harry Tennant.'

'Harbrook's son? Well, so Harry Tennant has the cartel ship, has he?'

'Yes, sir,' said Jack, wishing he had never mentioned the wretched tub; he had forgotten how his father loved to pick upon some little often irrelevant piece of information and worry it to death. 'May we go and sit in a quiet corner of the south room? I have something very important to tell you about buying stock.'

'The Devil you have?' said the General, looking at him keenly. 'Come along, then, and bring your wine. But you must talk quick. I have some people coming. Where did you get that horrible coat?' he asked, leading the way. 'I wish you may not have been robbing a scarecrow.'

In the south room Jack said to himself 'I had better not talk much.' He sat at a writing-table and quickly copied out the essence of his letter. 'There, sir,' he said, giving the list to his father. 'I do most earnestly urge you to place every penny you can spare in these,' and in the clearest terms he could devise he stated the anonymous, entirely confidential nature of his information. He said that he could answer no questions, and emphasized the fact that he had pledged his word that the knowledge should not go beyond two of his closest friends. His honour was immediately concerned.

The General watched him with shrewd, searching eyes until he had finished, then opened his mouth to speak; but before any word came out a footman hurried in to say that his guests had arrived.

'Stay there, Jack,' said the General, putting down his empty glass. A few minutes later he brought three men into the room. With a sinking heart Jack saw that one of them was his father's stockbroker and the other two were showily dressed citizens of the kind he saw only too often whenever he went down to his boyhood home: he remembered that when his father wished to impress associates of this kind he would bring them here and show them a duke or two.

'This is my son,' cried the General, 'though you would not expect it from his age: I first married very young, very young indeed. He is a post-captain in the Navy, and he is just home from the seas. Landed at Dover from the cartel but yesterday and he is already advising his old father about investments, ha, ha, ha! James, a magnum of this same wine.'

'The Captain and I are old friends,' said the stockbroker, patting Jack's reluctant shoulder. 'And I can tell you, General, he understands investment very well.'

'So you came on the cartel boat, sir,' said one of the others. 'Then perhaps you can tell us the latest news from Paris. Lord, suppose Napoleon was really dead! Lord, suppose the war was to come to an end! Only think!'

'The cartel?' said the stockbroker, who had missed the first mention of it.

'Understands investment?' said the General, and they both looked at Jack.

The wine came in: the cork flew off: 'I always say there's nothing like sham,' said one of the General's guests.

Jack sat there, drinking glass for glass and evading questions, until the bottle was out. On being called upon for his opinion about the progress of the war and its probable duration he uttered a fine series of platitudes: he heard himself doing so at a slight distance, not without satisfaction. But when his father suggested that they should all go to Vauxhall he absolutely declined: filial piety had its limits — they had been far surpassed — and he possessed a perfect excuse — 'I am not really dressed for town,' he said, 'let alone for Vauxhall in decent company.'

'Perhaps not,' said one of the simpler, more drunken, more highly decorated guests. 'But everybody makes excuses for our gallant tars. Do come. I'll stand treat. It will be such fun. Only think!'

'Thank you for my wine, sir,' said Jack to his father. 'Gentlemen, good night.' He bowed, and with his eye fixed sternly upon the door he steered straight for the open space, upright, rigid, never breathing, and never deviating an inch from his course.

CHAPTER FIVE

Stephen Maturin turned from the Strand down into the liberties of the Savoy. It was a familiar path, so familiar that of their own accord his feet avoided the worst chasms in the paving, the iron grid that before now had given beneath his modest weight, plunging him down a coal-hole, and the filthy gutter; and this was just as well, since his mind was far away: he was, as Jack had observed, intensely anxious about Diana, so anxious and apprehensive that he was going to the Grapes in order to change and be shaved before presenting himself at Half-Moon Street and in order to have news of her, since she would surely have passed by — she and Mrs Broad, the landlady, were great friends, and both paid too much attention to his linen.

His mind was far away, and the shock was therefore all the greater when, having turned the corner to the inn, he looked up and saw nothing but a blackened hole railed off from the street, with rain-water shining in its cellars, a few charred beams showing where the floors had been, and grass and ferns growing in the niches that had once been cupboards.

The dwelling-houses on either hand seemed untouched; so were the shops on the Westminster side of the street, untouched and busy, with people hurrying up and down as though the horrible sight were commonplace. He crossed, to check his bearings and make doubly sure that this was indeed the shell of the Grapes and not some spatial illusion; and as he stood there he felt a gentle pressure on the back of his leg. Turning, he saw a large rough ugly yard-dog bowing and waving his tail; his lips were writhed back in a grin that might express pleasure or extreme rage, and Stephen instantly recognized the butcher's mongrel. He was not a promiscuous dog; he belonged firmly to the butcher; but he and Stephen had always passed the time of day, and there was a steady, long-standing affection between the two.

'Why, if it ain't the Doctor,' said the butcher. 'I thought it must be you, as soon as I see him bowing and scraping like a French Punch and Judy. You are looking at the poor old Grapes, I do suppose.'

The fire had happened about the time the *Surprise* left Gibraltar: nobody had been hurt, but the insurance company disputed the claim and Mrs Broad could not rebuild until they paid up; in the meantime she had gone down to her friends in Essex, sadly missed by the whole neighbourhood. 'Every time I look across the way,' said the butcher, pointing with his knife, 'I feel the Liberty has a wound in it.'

A wound, and a strangely unexpected one, thought Stephen, walking north. He had had no idea how much that quiet haven meant to him; there were also some fairly important collections he had left there, mostly of birds' skins, many books . . . The immeasurably greater wound, 'Mrs Maturin does not live here any more,' delivered at the Half-Moon Street house lacked that sudden staggering quality and for the moment it shocked him less.

He walked steadily towards St James's Street, saying 'I shall most deliberately feel nothing until I have some confirmation: there are a thousand possible explanations.'

Jack's club was not the kind of place that Stephen would have joined of his own accord, but Diana had made a point of it; she had made many of her friends as well as Jack support his candidature, and he had been a member for some time now.

'Good morning, sir,' said the hall porter. 'I have some letters for you, and a uniform-case.'

'Thank you,' said Stephen, taking the letters. The only one of consequence was on top and he broke the seal as he walked up the stairs. It began

> *Why should a foolish marriage vow,*
> *Which long ago was made,*
> *Oblige us to each other now,*
> *When passion is decayed?*

Between this and the last paragraph came a close-packed section, much underlined and not clearly legible in this light. The lines of the last paragraph were spaced wider; it was written more calmly and with a different pen, and it said 'Your best uniform came just after you had left, so rather than leave it at the Grapes, where the *mice* and *moths* swarm prodigiously in spite of all good Mrs Broad can do, I shall send it to the club. And Stephen, I do beg you will remember to put on a *warm flannel undershirt* and *drawers* when you are in England: you will find some *on top* of the uniform and some *underneath* it.'

These words he had absorbed before he

reached the landing. He put the letter into his pocket, walked into the empty library, and looked through the others. One was a request for a loan by return of messenger; there were two invitations to dinners long since digested, and two communications about the Manx shearwater. He read them attentively and then returned to Diana's letter: he must have known, she said, that when he paraded his redheaded lady up and down the Mediterranean, without the least disguise, she would resent it as an open, direct insult. She did not speak of the moral side of things — that was not her style and anyway prating about morality could safely be left to others — but she must own that she had never expected Stephen to do so illbred a thing; or having done it in a fit of folly, not to justify himself, at least by a story that she could decently pretend to believe. Here Stephen looked sharply for the date of the letter: there was none. Any woman of spirit would resent it. Even Lady Nelson, a far, far meeker woman than Diana, had resented it, although there had been the decent veil of Sir William. She was obliged to confess that with all Stephen's faults she had never, never expected him to behave like a scrub. She knew very well that ordinary men did so when *passion was decayed,* but she had never looked upon Stephen as an ordinary man. She would never, never forget his kindness to her, and no amount of resentment would do away with her friendship; yet she was glad, yes so glad, that they had never been married in a Christian or a Roman Catholic church. Then, clearly after a pause and with this second pen, but he was never to think unkindly of her: and after that the postscript about the shirts.

He would no more have thought unkindly of her than he would of a falcon that had flown free, imagining some injury — he had known very proud, high-tempered falcons, passionately attached and passionately offended — but he was wounded to the heart, and he grieved. At first with a generalized grief that included his own desolate loss, so intensely that he clasped his hands and rocked to and fro, then more particularly for her. He had known her a great while, but of all the wild flings, of all the coups de tête he had seen her make, this was the most disastrous. She had run off with Jagiello, a Lithuanian officer in the Swedish service who had long and quite openly admired her. But Jagiello was an ass: a tall, beautiful, golden-haired ass, adored by young women and liked by men for his cheerful candour and simplicity, but a hopelessly volatile ass, incapable of resisting temptation and perpetually surrounded by it, being rich as well as absurdly handsome. He was much younger than Diana; and constancy was not to be looked for. Marriage was impossible, because whatever she might suppose the ceremony Stephen and Diana had passed through aboard HMS *Oedipus* was legally binding. An active social life was as necessary to her as meat and drink, and he had no reason to suppose that Swedish society would be particularly kind to an unmarried foreign woman whose only protector was a young and foolish Hussar. The thought of her fate in five years or even less made his heart sick. All he could find by way of light in all this darkness was the reflexion that at least she was independent: she did not have to rely on any man's generosity. Yet even this was not certain: at one time she had had great quantities of money, but whether she had invested enough of it to be assured of a reasonable income for the rest of her life he did not know. It was probable, however, since she had a most capable adviser in her friend the banker Nathan, a man whom Stephen also liked. 'I shall ask Nathan,' he said; and moving in his chair he felt the rim of that damned brass box against his hip. It was strapped to his side by a long

223

surgical bandage — before now he had left compromising, confidential papers in the pocket of a coach — and he must deal with it at once.

He reflected. The cold process of thought was a precious relief after all this turmoil of feeling, of passionate inward ejaculations, barely coherent protests against the injustice of it all, and repetitions of her name: he stood up, walked over to a desk and wrote *Dr Maturin presents his compliments, and would be happy to wait on Sir Joseph Blaine as soon as it may be convenient.* He was surprised to find his hand so unsteady that the words were scarcely to be read. He copied it out again with particular care and carried it down to be delivered not to the Admiralty but to Sir Joseph's private house in Shepherd Market.

'Why, Stephen, there you are,' cried Jack, walking in at this point. 'How glad I am to see you. Ain't it a damned thing about the poor dear old Grapes? But at least no one was hurt. Come upstairs: I have something very important to tell you.'

'Have any of the cases been decided?' asked Stephen.

'No, no, it is not that. Nothing has stirred in the legal way. This is quite different — you will be amazed.'

The library was still empty. Stephen, sitting with his back to the window, watched the play of expression on Jack's face, turned full to the light and alive with pleasure at the thought of making his friend's fortune. 'But the point is,' said Jack in conclusion, 'that the investments have to be made within the next few days. That is why I was so very glad to run into you just now. I was on the point of going round to Half-Moon Street to bring you this list, in case you might have been there.'

A message for Dr Maturin came in on a salver. 'Forgive me, Jack,' said Stephen. Turning to the window, he read that Sir Joseph would be more than happy to see Dr Maturin at any time after half past six o'clock; and turning back into the room he saw Jack looking at him with great concern.

'Are you taken poorly, Stephen?' he asked. 'Sit down and let me fetch you a glass of brandy.'

'Listen, Jack,' said Stephen, 'Diana has gone off to live in Sweden.' There was an embarrassed silence. Jack at once saw that Jagiello was concerned but he could not in decency seem to understand and there appeared to be no remark he could possibly offer. Stephen went on, 'She thought Laura Fielding was my mistress, and that publicly parading her up and down the Mediterranean was a deliberate or at least a callous affront. Tell me, did it have that appearance? Did I seem to be Laura's lover?'

'I believe people generally thought — it looked rather as though . . .'

'And yet I explained it as fully as I could,' said Stephen, almost to himself. He stared at the clock, but although the hands were clear enough he could not make out the time: his mind was wholly taken up with the question *Did she go before or after Wray brought her my letter? That is a point I must determine.* 'What's o'clock?' he asked.

'Half past five,' said Jack.

'I shall not catch him at the Admiralty,' reflected Stephen. 'I shall call at his house, so. It is quite near Nathan's. I shall have time for both if I hurry.' He said 'Jack, my best thanks for your advice about stocks and shares; I am deeply sensible of your kindness. Tell me, my dear, are you fully committed?' Jack nodded. 'Then there is no point in my asking what inquiries you made about your informant.'

'Oh, he is all right. He knew you — he knew about Testudo aubreii.'

'Indeed?' Stephen stood there considering for a moment. There was no way in which the man could gain by deceiving Jack;

and if the informant was himself mistaken Jack would still possess the securities, losing no more than the brokerage. 'I must leave you,' he said. 'I have some calls to make.'

'You are coming down to Ashgrove, of course,' said Jack. 'Sophie will be so happy to see you. I had thought of Sunday, because of the bums, but now we could go down tomorrow, if you would like it.'

'I doubt I shall be free until Tuesday,' said Stephen.

'I had just as soon stay a little longer,' said Jack. 'Let us say Tuesday, then.'

The first of these calls was unsuccessful. Stephen sent in his name, but after a few minutes he learnt that Mr Wray was not at home. 'I had almost forgotten,' he observed, walking off into the drizzle, 'he owes me a very great deal of money. My coming may be mighty inconvenient.'

The second was no more fortunate. Indeed it was hardly made at all. Well before he reached the door it occurred to Stephen that Nathan, like all their acquaintance in London, must be aware of the separation and that as Diana's confidential adviser he would think it improper to speak of her affairs. Stephen did ring the bell, but he was just as glad when he heard that Mr Nathan was not in the way. Nathan's younger brother Meyer was there, however, and in the hall itself; and when Stephen absolutely refused to have a coach or a chair called for him against the increasing rain, Meyer pressed an umbrella into his hands, a very powerful gingham and whalebone affair. It was under this spreading shelter that Stephen made his way through the hurrying, jostling crowds to the baggage office, for he had made the last part of his journey in a coach. Here the road was particularly deep in semi-liquid mud, horse-dung, and general filth and the crossing-sweeper hurried in front of him, clearing a Red Sea passage with his active broom. On the far pavement he cried 'Don't forget the sweeper, your honour.'

Stephen plunged his hand first into one coat pocket, then into the other. 'I am sorry, child,' he said, 'but the wicked dogs have not left me a penny piece, nor a handkerchief. I am afraid I have no money on me.'

'Did your mother never tell you to keep your wipe and your pewter in your breeches?' asked the little boy, frowning. 'Whoreson old bumpkin,' he added as an afterthought, from some little distance. 'Whoreson old cuckold.'

In the stage-coach office Stephen took a parcel from his sea-chest, gave directions for the delivery of the rest of his baggage, and made his difficult way to Shepherd Market, carrying the parcel and at the same time managing the broad, heavy umbrella in the increasing wind. The umbrella was a mark of the younger Nathan's sympathy: Stephen had instantly perceived the more than usually grave, attentive expression, the considerate tone, and in his present excoriated state it seemed to him that it resembled most forms of commiseration: useless, embarrassing, cumbersome and painful.

'I hope Sir Joseph will not feel obliged to condole,' he said, approaching the door. 'I do not think I can bear any more. Sure, the social contract requires some expression of concern; but not now, oh Lord, not now.'

He need not have feared for Sir Joseph. Nothing could have been kinder than his welcome, yet there was not the least hint of uneasy awareness or woundingly particular consideration for a great while. It was not until they had dealt with the obvious preliminaries about the voyage and had exchanged a great deal of gossip to do with other entomologists and the proceedings of the Royal Society that Stephen asked particularly after Sir Joseph's health: he asked as a physician, having prescribed for him — the trouble had been a want of sexual vigour, which assumed a certain importance in view of Blaine's intended marriage, and Stephen wished to know how his physic had answered. 'It answered in a most surprising and gratifying manner, I thank you,' said Sir Joseph. 'Priapus would himself have been put to the blush. But I laid it aside. I reflected upon matrimony, and although I found a great deal to be said for it in theory, when I looked attentively among my friends I found that the practice did not seem to produce much happiness. Scarcely a single pair did I find who appeared really suited to please one another for more than a few months; after a year or so contention, striving for moral advantage, differences of temper, education, taste, appetite and a hundred other things led to bickering, uneasiness, indifference, downright dislike or even worse. Few of my friends can be said to be happily married, and in some cases . . .' He broke off, evidently regretting his words, and returned to the contemplation of the beetles that Stephen had brought him from Brazil and the Great South Sea. After some talk of insects he added, 'Besides, in your private ear I will confess that I heard the lady refer to me as "my old beau". *Old* I could bear; but there is something strangely chilling and smart and provincial about *beau*. Then again, marriage and intelligence make awkward yoke-fellows: not that I am much concerned with intelligence any more, however.'

'Are you not?' said Stephen, looking into his face.

'No,' said Blaine, 'I am not. You will recall that I sent you a somewhat cryptic warning of squalls — of troubled waters — of dark obscure currents — when you were in Gibraltar. Well now, almost everything I forecast has come about. Just let me have a word with Mrs Barlow about our supper, and when we have eaten it I will tell you in more detail.'

'First may I beg you to lend me a handkerchief? My pocket was picked as I was going to the White Horse.'

'I hope you did not lose much?'

'Fourpence and a spotted handkerchief, and a mighty dose of self-esteem. I had thought myself a match for a common pickpocket. It is true I was struggling with a cumbrous great umbrella at the time, but that is a poor excuse. My pocket picked clean, as though I were just off the mountain or the bog, for shame.'

It was a lobster of moderate size that they ate for their supper, followed by a boned capon in a pie and then by a rice pudding, a dish they were both very fond of: but Sir Joseph only toyed with his, and when they carried their wine into the library he said 'Your having your pocket picked like a countryman brings my own mishap so clearly to my mind that it quite takes my appetite away. I am older than you, Maturin, I have had even more experience, and yet I have been done brown; and what angers me even more is that I no more know who roasted me than you know who picked your pocket.'

He gave Stephen a circumstantial account of the changes that had come about in naval intelligence. Sir Joseph still had a high-sounding title, but in the course of one of those silent Whitehall struggles that turn ministries upside-down he had been deprived of almost all real power: he still represented the Admiralty at the meetings of the Committee for the moment, but he had nothing to do with the day to day business of the department. Last January his horse had fallen with him on an icy road in the country: it had meant no more than a fortnight in bed, but that was fourteen days too long — there had been three important meetings at which his opponents carried all before them and when he crept back he found the organization wholly recast. By now nearly all his friends had been removed or sent to obscure positions far away, and those who remained could hope for no countenance or advancement. Their clerks were taken from them, their rooms were given to others, and they were lodged in mean holes and corners to induce them to resign, and the least slip of some remote agent was seized upon to discredit them. It was the same with those outside the administration. 'Invaluable colleagues have been treated with disrespect and have withdrawn in disgust. When you call at the Admiralty, do not be surprised if they ask you to give up your key to the private door. The pretext will no doubt be that the locks are being changed.' Sir Joseph himself would have resigned months ago if this had been an ordinary department and if he had not had some hopes of reversing the situation in the end. 'I cannot tell you, Maturin,' he said, 'how passionately I long to put things right again, and I shall hold on, in spite of all affronts, in order to do so.'

'When you speak of your opponents, do you have them clearly in your eye?' asked Stephen.

'No, I do not, and that is what makes me so uneasy. Barrow is back as second secretary, as I dare say you know, and we have never liked one another; indeed I might say that since the Wilson affair we have lived in a perpetual reciprocation of malevolence. He is an immensely laborious, immensely diligent man, devoted to form and detail, and respectful of rank to a servile degree; he is widely ignorant and he is quite incapable of taking a broad, intelligent view of any given situation; but having risen from a humble situation by his own efforts he has an extraordinarily high opinion of his abilities, and at first I thought that this reorganization was simply an attempt on his part to gain more power, particularly as he has kept Wray, an ambitious young man, as his chief adviser. But that is not the explanation. He is a little man and his idea of a famous victory is six extra clerks and a Turkey carpet. It is true that Wray, though flighty, paederastical and unsound, is very, very much cleverer, but now that I have seen how things are handled and the amount of influence, particularly Treasury influence, that has been brought to bear, it seems to me that the whole thing is far beyond their scope. It seems to me that some Macchiavel, possibly in the Treasury, possibly in the Cabinet Office, is manipulating them; but who he is or what his aim may be I cannot tell. There are times when I feel that the ordinary insatiable appetite for power, patronage, and having one's own way explains it all; and there are times when I fancy I smell if not a rat, then a pretty sinister mouse. However, I shall say no more about that, even to you, until I have something a little more solid than these impressions. A disappointed, angry man is very apt to exaggerate the wickedness of his opponents. But they must not think that by depriving me of the C and F reports and of contact with the agents in the field, they are cutting me off entirely. A man in my position has many old and tried friends in the other intelligence services, and with their help I do not despair of getting to the bottom of the matter.'

'I am very much concerned at what you tell me,' said Stephen. 'Very much concerned indeed.' And after a pause, 'Listen, Blaine. Before we left Gibraltar the Admiral's secretary sent for me: his orders were to tell me the Government had sent a Mr Cunningham to the Spanish South American colonies in the packet *Danaë* with a large sum of money in gold. It was now feared that she might be taken by the American frigate we were being sent to deal with. If we met the *Danaë* in the Atlantic I was to leave Mr Cunningham his gold but I was to remove a very much larger sum that had been concealed in his cabin without his knowledge. The American did in fact take the *Danaë*, but we recaptured her this side of the Horn. I considered that my instructions required me to look for this larger sum, and I found it: it was contained in a small brass box that is now attached to my person. Jack Aubrey sent the *Danaë* home under Captain Pullings, but since it was not improbable that she should be taken yet again I thought proper to keep this box aboard a man-of-war, as being less liable to capture. Yet several aspects of the matter made me uneasy in mind: the seal on the box broke when it fell from its hiding-place; the eventualities foreseen in my instructions did not include the packet's recapture and it might be said that I had exceeded my authority; the sum that Jack Aubrey and I — for he had helped me to follow the nautical directions — picked up from the cabin floor was very great indeed, far, far greater than I cared to be answerable for or indeed associated with; and I had had your letter speaking of the troubled, murky atmosphere in Whitehall. However, we put it all back in the brass box, sealed the lid again, using my watch-key, and here it is.' He tapped his side.

'Have you seen Barrow or Wray?' asked Sir Joseph.

'I have not. I did call on Wray at his house, but he was not at home and in any event that was about another matter entirely.' A spasm of pain crossed his usually impassive face and for a moment he hung his head. 'No. From the first I had no intention of going to the Admiralty until I had seen you unofficially and had asked your advice: now I am doubly glad of it.'

'Is it indeed a very great sum?'

'You shall see.' Stephen stood up, took off his coat and waistcoat, tucked up his shirt and unwound the bandage. Once again the brass box fell unexpectedly; once again it burst open; and once again the amount astonished those who picked it up.

'No, no,' said Sir Joseph. 'This is nothing to do with us. This is nothing to do with naval intelligence. This exceeds the whole department's budget. This is something on quite another scale. This represents the subversion of a realm.'

'I had not remembered it as so much,' said Stephen. 'I doubt I made the addition at the time: my mind was much taken up by my patients.' He waved a sheaf of bills and said *'In vain may heroes fight and patriots rave, If secret gold sap on from knave to knave,* at least in this amount.'

'Heavens,' said Sir Joseph, still busily

creeping about the floor, 'were I as good at the mathematics as your friend Aubrey — and I remember the paper he read to the Royal Society on a new way of calculating the occultation of stars made my head ache — I could reckon the number of men required to carry this sum in gold. And a small brass box will hold it all! Oh the convenience of paper money and the draft on a discreet banking house, made out to bearer! Do you remember how your couplet goes on?' he asked, getting up with creaking knees.

'Pray remind me,' said Stephen, who was very fond of Blaine.

'Blest paper credit,' said Sir Joseph, emphasizing the *paper* and raising one finger,

'Blest paper credit! last and best supply!
That lends corruption lighter wings to fly!
A single leaf shall waft an army o'er
Or ship off senates to a distant shore.
Pregnant with thousands flits the scrap unseen
And silent sells a king, or buys a queen.'

'Pregnant with thousands, yes indeed,' said Stephen. 'The question is, what am I to do with my pregnant scraps?'

'It appears to me that the first thing to do is to make an inventory,' said Sir Joseph.

'Let us put them into some kind of order, and then if you will read out the bare names, dates and figures I will write them down.'

The inventory took some time and at the end of each page they paused for a glass of port. During one of these pauses Sir Joseph remarked 'To begin with, Barrow was positively obsequious to me; then he learnt that I too was the son of a labouring man and he despised me straight away. Wray is well-connected, and I believe it is that, quite as much as his cleverness, which makes Barrow value him.'

'Will I seal it again?' asked Stephen, when the list was finished and the box was full.

'You might as well,' said Sir Joseph. 'I do not believe there is a piece of string in the house; I tried to put up a parcel not long since, but with no success.'

'And is it Barrow I will give it to, or Wray? And will I desire them to give me a receipt?' asked Stephen: a great mental and spiritual fatigue had come over him and all he wanted was to be told what to do.

'You should say you wish to see me, and when they tell you I am not there you should ask for Wray, since it was with him that you were last in contact. As for a receipt . . . No. I think a certain sancta simplicitas is in order here — a placid handing-over of this enormous fortune without any question of quittance or formal acknowledgement. In any event a receipt would be pointless, since if there is bad faith they can always say there was more in the box in the first place, before the seal was broke. It would be as pointless as this inventory, which has no legal force or validity whatsoever. But I do not have to tell you, Maturin, that in intelligence we do not always regard the law very closely.' He passed the wax and held the candle while Stephen sealed the box and went on, 'This war has caused the most enormous pouring-out of public funds, and peculation has kept pace. A great deal of money passes through various hands in the Admiralty and some of them are tolerably retentive. When Mr Croker took over as First Secretary — I believe you were abroad at the time: oh yes, you were a great way off — he instantly looked into the affairs of Roger Horehound, Jolly Roger as we used to call him, and found that he had taken no less than two hundred thousand pounds. Not that that was in our department however: as you know the First Secretary has virtually nothing to do with intelligence — until recently it was entirely my concern. Jolly Roger's goose was cooked, but there are people cleverer and more cautious than

Roger, and it has sometimes appeared to me that this taking-over of our department may well have greed as its motive, or one of its motives; it is a department in which expenditure cannot be closely controlled and in which large sums pass from hand to hand. If that is the case, and I am more and more persuaded of it, then the people concerned will surely cling to some of this superabundance,' — nodding towards the brass box. 'Not Barrow, for although I find him singularly unlovable I am perfectly certain that he is honest, rigidly honest: but he is a fool. The people concerned, I say, will cling . . . the temptation is very great . . . But it so happens that I am very well with the Nathans and their cousins — they have supported us nobly in this war — and as soon as any one of these bills is negotiated I shall know of it and what is more important I shall know just who my enemies are.' He made some remarks about the money-market to which Stephen paid little attention and then observed, with a chuckle, 'Such an elegant little trap; if it had not existed I should have had to invent it. But should I ever have had such a happy thought? I doubt it. Tell me, my dear Maturin, does anyone know that you were coming to see me?'

'No one. Except conceivably the porter at my club, who saw to the delivery of my note.'

'What is your club?'

'Black's.'

'It is mine too. I did not know you were a member.'

'I rarely go.'

'It would be wiser for us to meet there. And Maturin, it would also be wise to armour yourself. I may of course be quite mistaken about the bad faith I referred to just now, but it can do no harm to suppose I am right. You are in a vulnerable position. May I suggest that you let it be seen that you are not defenceless, not without allies, and that you cannot be treated as a man of no account might be treated — overwhelmed, put down, made to bear the blame? Will you not go to the birthday levee, for example? The Duke of Clarence will be there, and many of your grander friends.'

'I might,' said Stephen, with no conviction. He stood up to take leave, putting the brass box in his pocket. Weariness had quite dulled his mind.

'And lastly may I suggest,' said Blaine in a low, hesitant voice, 'may I suggest that if a mission across the Channel is proposed, you should refuse it?' Stephen looked up, fully alive again. 'No, no, I do not mean that,' cried Sir Joseph, seeing the shocked, startled question in his face. 'I only mean loose talk and inefficiency: anything more sinister would be only the most extreme hypothesis. But in your particular case I prefer the precautions to be extreme. Come. I will see you home. The streets are far from safe at night. Though indeed,' he added, 'it might save a world of trouble, were your pocket to be quietly picked again.'

In the morning, a bright clear morning so far, though to a sailor's eye 'there was foul weather breeding there in the east-north-east', Jack and Stephen walked through the park to the Admiralty. Captain Aubrey, paying an official call, was in uniform: Dr Maturin, as a civil adviser, was in a decent snuff-coloured coat with cloth-covered buttons. They were shown into the waiting-room where Jack had spent so many hours of his life, and there they found a dozen officers already installed. Most were lieutenants and commanders, of course, they being the most numerous class; but so many of these had been passed over for promotion that Jack found several contemporaries among them. Indeed, there was one lieutenant who had been second of the *Resolu-*

tion when he was a midshipman in her, and they were deep in recollections of her after-hold when a clerk came to tell Jack that the First Lord was now at leisure.

In his curiously frigid and inhuman way the First Lord was happy to welcome Captain Aubrey home and to say that the Board, on hearing his dispatch read by Mr Croker, had been glad to learn that the expedition to the South Sea was satisfactorily accomplished and the *Surprise* brought home in such good condition. He regretted having to tell Aubrey that there was no suitable command vacant for him at the moment, but his name should certainly be borne in mind for the next eligible ship: he regretted still more having to say that the Board had decided to sell the *Surprise* out of the service, because he knew how attached sailors became to their vessels.

'Yes, indeed, my lord,' said Jack. 'Never was a ship like *Surprise*: I have known her, man and boy, these twenty years, and we all loved her very dearly. But I trust I may be able to buy her: she is not likely to fetch a mint of money, I suppose.'

'Let us hope for at least a moderate amount, for the sake of the naval estimates,' said Melville, looking sharply at Jack Aubrey. Sea-officers quite often primed themselves with brandy, rum, or even gin for an interview at the Admiralty; but this was not the case with Jack. His lack of protest at the news (news whose bite was quite removed by his knowledge of the coming peace, when the frigate's occupation would be gone), his whole attitude and the look on his face was caused by the cheerfulness at the idea of being rich again, of seeing Sophie within the next few days, and of telling her that their anxieties were at an end.

'Finally, my lord,' said Jack, standing up when the conversation drew to a close, 'may I put in a word for Thomas Pullings, a very fine seaman, a commander, at present unemployed? He brought the *Danaë* home as a volunteer.'

'I will bear him in mind,' said Melville. 'But as you know Whitehall is lined with commanders who are very fine seamen and who would be glad of a sloop.' He walked to the door with Jack and just before he opened it Jack said 'Now that our official interview is over, may I ask how Heneage does?'

Heneage Dundas was Melville's younger brother and the mention of his name brought a disapproving look. 'Heneage is down at Portsmouth, seeing to the fitting-out of *Eurydice* for the North American station: he should sail within the month, and the sooner the better. I do wish, Aubrey, that as a friend you could make him see how very much his irregularities are disapproved by the world in general. On Saturday still another bastard was laid at his door. It is a disgrace to himself, to his family, and even to his friends.'

In quite another part of the building Stephen was still waiting. He had asked for Sir Joseph and had been led to the obscure regions in the back: there he had been told that Sir Joseph was not available. 'In that case I should like to see Mr Wray,' he said, and they showed him to a small, blind, almost naked room. In order to get at least some sleep the night before he had taken his usual opiate, the alcoholic tincture of laudanum, and its calm, grey influence was upon him still, at least physically; furthermore the whole matter of this brass box had lost its importance, and so long as he could be cleanly rid of it he did not care. What really concerned him in this interview was learning just when Wray had given his letter to Diana.

Stephen therefore waited with never a restless movement, his mind swimming deep beneath the surface. Yet even he had his limits and when the clock striking the hour pierced through his thoughts he realized that he was being treated with disrespect. He waited until the quarter sounded and then he walked out, through a large office filled with startled clerks and so down two corridors to the main waiting-room, where Jack had stayed for him. There he left a note to the effect that his business with Sir Joseph or Mr Wray had been connected with the packet *Danaë* and that he would look in tomorrow at eleven in the morning. 'Come,' he said to Jack, 'let us walk about until some respectable house will give us a meal. Do you know of any that opens early?'

'Fladong's is used to naval people,' said Jack. 'When I was a young fellow, and happened to be in funds, they would feed me at two o'clock.'

Fladong's was still used to naval people, and it fed them not indeed at two o'clock, but at a strangely early hour for London. When they had finished Stephen said 'Bear with me, Jack, while I step round to Upper Grosvenor Street. I wish to call on Wray, who will be thinking of his dinner now. It is merely to make an appointment.'

'If you mean to call on Wray,' said Jack some minutes later, nodding towards the park end of the street, 'you have a very fair chance of finding him at home.'

'What eyes you have, brother,' said Stephen. 'I should not have distinguished him from here without a glass. Listen, now: unless you choose to come with me, take a pair of turns about the square till I rejoin you.'

'Very well,' said Jack, 'but then I really must go back and change into civilian clothes. It is not at all the thing to walk about like a goddam lobster.'

They separated. Stephen walked along, rang the bell, sent in his name, heard that Mr Wray was not at home, and returned to the square.

'I hope you found him in?' said Jack.

Stephen might have replied that on the contrary he had found him out, but he lacked the spirit and only replied 'The poor man owes me a terrible great card-debt, and believes I mean to dun him for it. In fact all I want is a simple date about another matter. Not that the money would be unwelcome either: sure, I risked my own and would have paid it had I lost.'

And when Jack came downstairs, wearing his scarecrow coat and drab pantaloons for the concert of ancient music they were about to attend, Stephen said 'My dear, forgive me if I rat on you for Tuesday. I must attend the birthday levee, I find.' He might have added 'for I shall not see Wray at the Admiralty tomorrow either' if such a remark had not been contrary to both his innate and his acquired habits of reticence.

He did not see Wray tomorrow; and in a way he was just as glad. He was not at all in form that day and the idea of having to put up with Wray's pitying face, his decently but not entirely concealed civil triumph, set a fire of anger burning in his heart. Several times as he came down Whitehall to keep his appointment he was jostled and each time he repaid the shove with interest, a rare thing with him, since he usually avoided physical contact and kept his emotions under very strict control. He was shown into a rather grand room that might have been Wray's; it had a fine blaze in the bright hearth and a considerable expanse of carpet, but behind the spacious desk and the silver standish he saw a middle-sized dry man, dressed in glossy black, with an immense starched white neckcloth and an uncommon amount of powder on his hair, the very type of superior official. The habitual expression of his face was authoritarian and discontented but at present there was a certain nervousness upon it too. He presented himself as Mr Lewis, acting for the head of the department, and by way of establishing a moral superiority right away he observed that Dr Maturin was ten minutes late. It was now more than ten minutes past eleven o'clock.

'That is possible,' said Stephen. 'Are you aware that I was kept waiting over an hour yesterday, without any sort of explanation or apology?'

'It is regretted that you were kept waiting, but the Second Secretary's deputy, the deputy to the Second Secretary of the Admiralty, cannot be expected to receive all and sundry the moment they choose to walk in.'

'All and sundry,' said Stephen, getting up and walking over to the fire. 'All and sundry,' he repeated, taking up the poker to make a better draught in the middle.

Lewis watched him with intense displeasure, but having consulted the notes on the desk he made an effort to be civil. 'All and sundry is not quite the expression, however, as I see you have a key to the private door. I am directed to ask all holders to deliver up their keys, as the locks are being changed. Have you yours with you?'

'I have not.'

'Then perhaps you will have the goodness to bring it or send it this afternoon. Now, sir, you wish to speak to me about the *Danaë*.'

'Are you aware that I was desired to remove certain papers from her, in the event of a meeting in the Atlantic?'

'I have all the details here,' said Lewis, touching a folder bound with red tape and speaking in a particularly irritating tone of official, omniscient superiority. It was instantly apparent to Stephen that the man was lying, that he knew nothing about intelligence and next to nothing about the present affair — the file was ludicrously thin. He was an administrative person called in merely to hear what Dr Maturin had to say. Nevertheless Stephen went on, 'The meeting took place and the papers were removed. In the circumstances I did not see fit to send them home by the recaptured packet.' Stephen returned to his seat.

'Did you at once inform the proper authorities?'

'I did not.'

'You landed in England on the seventeenth; why did you not inform them then?'

'Let us understand one another, Mr Lewis. Your inquiry is not a question but a form of reproof; and I am not come here to be reproved.'

'If you are come here with the notion of some additional grant, let me tell you that your superiors —'

'Christ's blood in heaven, you ignorant incompetent whey-faced nestlecock,' said

Stephen in a low venomous tone, leaning forward, 'do you think I am a hired spy, an informer? That I have a master, a pay-master, for God's love?' To all his present bitterness there was added the spectacle of an efficient intelligence-service threatening ruin, and his own dedicated, highly-skilled form of warfare gone. 'You little silly man,' he said.

Lewis strained back in his chair, looking shocked and stupid: the look on Stephen's face appalled him. He said 'Calm yourself, my dear sir, calm yourself.'

Stephen's hand shot across the desk, seized Lewis's nose, shook it so furiously from side to side so fast that the hair-powder flew, then wrung it left and right, right and left; he flung the standish into the fire, wiped his bloody hand on Lewis's neck-cloth, said 'If you wish to find me, sir, I am at Black's,' and walked out.

At Black's itself he saw Sir Joseph making his slow way up the stairs. 'How happy I am to see you, Blaine,' he said. 'Shall we take a dish of tea in the writing-room?'

'A dish of tea would make me glad and fain,' said Sir Joseph. 'Or at least, fairly glad and fain.' At this time of the day there was no one in the writing-room, and he closed all the windows directly: he hated a draught.

'Have you seen how shares are rising?' he asked, letting himself heavily down in his chair.

'I have not,' said Stephen. 'Listen, do you know an animal called Lewis in the Admiralty?'

'Oh yes. He was called in from the Treasury after the death of Mr Smith, who was reorganizing the accountancy. He is rectitude itself, and the letter of the law; a fount of platitude, and a very great affliction at a dinner-party.'

'Would he be a fighting man, at all? I was led to pull him by the nose just now, and I told him where he might find me, if he chose to have satisfaction.'

'No, no. Oh no. He would be far more likely to have you taken up and sworn to keep the peace; but in the present case that would never be allowed. No. Good heavens no. But I am glad to hear what you tell me, about pulling his nose.'

'And I am glad to hear your opinion. Had he been a man of blood I should have had to beg my friend to remain, and he is so longing to be away to his wife it is pitiful to see.'

Later that day he said to Jack, 'I do beg, my dear, that you will go down to Ashgrove by this evening's coach. I have an entomological and a chirurgical meeting tomorrow

'— we shall see nothing of one another — and then I shall turn in before ten to be in form for the levee.'

'Well, if you insist,' said Jack. 'But you must give me your word to follow as soon as it is over.'

'As soon as ever I can.'

'Sophie will be so pleased,' said Jack; and then, unable to keep back a great smile, 'Have you seen the papers today?'

'I shall read them before going to sleep,' said Stephen, moving towards his room. 'God bless, now, and give my dear love to Sophie.'

'You will be amazed,' called Jack up the stairs. 'And this is only the beginning, ha, ha, ha!'

The birthday levee was a crowded affair. Mr Harrington kissed hands as Governor of Bermuda and Sir John Hollis as Principal Secretary and many gentlemen attended to share their triumph and to contemplate the faces of their disappointed rivals. As well as these there was of course the brilliant spectrum of officers — the particoloured Scots were particularly admired — people from the various ministries in their comparatively subfusc court dress, and civilians of all sorts, the levee being a wonderful place for discreet contacts, for the gathering of information, and for learning just how influence and favour waxed or waned. Stephen and Sir Joseph exchanged bows at a distance, but did not speak: Stephen also saw him bow to Wray, who was standing by a short, wooden-faced man who was obviously unused to his sword. 'It will have him down before the end of the day,' observed Stephen. 'I suppose he is Mr Barrow.' This notion was strengthened by the man's ill-bred jerk in reply to Sir Joseph's salute, and Stephen reflected for some little while on the exact degree of calculated incivility allowed in a well-bred man. The example of Talleyrand's exquisitely-dosed insolence came to his mind, but before he could recall more than half a dozen examples a general movement at the top of the room broke in upon his thoughts. The various ceremonies were over; the new Petty Bag had received his staff and the Clerk of the Hanaper his fee. All those present formed the usual circle and the Regent, followed by some of his brothers, began his progress. He might lack elegance of form, conduct and constancy, but no one could deny him the regal quality of remembering names: he recognized almost every other face and made some amiable, generally appropriate remark. He did not speak to Stephen, but his brother the Duke of Clarence did so for him, calling out in his quarterdeck voice, 'Why, there you are, Maturin! Are you back?'

'I am, sir,' said Stephen.

'So you are, so you are. We must have a word when 'tis all over, hey, hey?' He was wearing an admiral's uniform, wearing it with much more right than most royals, and he was particularly attentive to the sea-officers attending. Stephen heard him greet Heneage Dundas with a fine roar as he passed down the line. The house of Hanover was not Stephen's favourite family, and he disapproved of almost all he knew of the Duke; but there was a remainder that he could not help liking — a simplicity, direct-ness and at times a generosity that he had no doubt learnt in the Navy. Stephen had been called in when the Duke was dangerously ill: the patient thought it was Stephen's treat-ment that had cured him (a naval doctor must necessarily have a better under-standing of naval officers' diseases than a ci-vilian) and he was quite touchingly grateful; they had seen a good deal of one another during his convalescence, and since Ste-phen was used to dealing with rough, self-willed, boisterous, domineering patients, and since he added a good deal of natural authority to that of a physician, they got along well enough.

Now, when 'twas all over and people were moving about, greeting their friends and seeing who would be civil to whom, he came across, took Stephen by the elbow and said 'Well, and how are you coming along, eh? eh? And how is Aubrey? I am so sorry to learn about *Surprise* — the sweetest sailer on a bowline, and in capital order — but she is old, Maturin, old; it is a question of anno Domini, like the rest of us. Do you know, I am nearly fifty! Ain't it shocking? What a crowd! You would say Common Hard on a Saturday evening. Half the Admiralty must be here. There's Croker, the new secretary. Do you know him?'

'We met in Ireland long ago, sir. He was at Trinity College.'

'Oh? Then I shan't call him over. Anyway,' — in a low voice — 'he's no friend of mine. And there's the Second Secretary. You know him too, I dare say? But no, I don't suppose you do. He is not an Irishman, and anyhow the Sick and Hurt people are more in your way.' He beckoned and Barrow came hurrying over with a look of devotion on his face. 'So you are back among us, Barrow?' said the Duke in a voice attuned to the imperfect hearing of a former invalid, and in an aside to Stephen, 'He was ill for a great while.' Then to Barrow again, 'Here is Dr Maturin. He would have set you on your feet in a trice. I *advise* you to ask his *advice* next time you are seized with the marthambles.'

Barrow said that he should certainly do so, if Dr Maturin would allow it, that he was much honoured, that he would always remember his Royal Highness's condescension, and he would have gone on in this strain for some time if the Duke had not cried 'What a' God's name is that uniform? The bottle-green — no, the *waistcoat*-green coat with a scarlet cape? Go and ask him, Barrow.' Shortly after this a passing admiral caught the Duke's eye and he quitted Stephen, giving him a friendly shake of the hand. He was succeeded by Heneage Dundas, who seemed very pleased with himself for an illegitimate father, though he cursed his ill-luck at missing Jack Aubrey. They quickly exchanged their gossip and news and then he had to tear himself away — he was posting down to Portsmouth directly — had only come up to see someone, that is to say, a young person, and must get back to his ship — if Maturin had any commissions for North America or if Dundas could be of any service whatsoever, a line to

Eurydice would command him.

'A line to Eurydice,' said Stephen, with the bitterest sudden pang.

'Cousin Stephen,' said a voice at his side after Dundas had gone, and it was Thaddeus himself in a fine red coat. True to the ancient Irish way, Stephen's Fitzgerald cousins had never taken much notice of his bastardy, and now Thaddeus led him over to three more of them, all soldiers, one in the English, one in the Austrian, and one (like Stephen's father) in the Spanish service; they gave him news of Pamela, Lord Edward's widow, and their kindness and the sound of their familiar voices did his heart good. When they had passed on he moved to some more acquaintance and some more quite surprising, interesting gossip; then he walked down to a place near the door from where he could survey the room and make sure that the main reason for his presence did not escape. He had been aware that Wray or Barrow were watching him much of the time; now he did the same by them, and presently Wray, feeling his cold gaze upon him, left his friends and came over with outstretched hand and a creditable appearance of friendly confusion.

'My dear Maturin,' he cried, 'I owe you ten thousand apologies.' In a low voice he explained that he no longer had anything to do with American intelligence — that was in other hands — a reorganization was in course — Stephen's long wait had been a mere muddling of messages, gross inefficiency rather than gross impoliteness — and could Maturin dine on Friday? Some interesting people were coming, and Fanny would be so pleased to see him. While he was speaking Stephen observed that his nails were bitten to the quick and that there was a flush of eczema on the back of his hands and under the powder on his forehead. Although he spoke well it was clear that he was under great nervous tension and Stephen was reminded of the reports he had just been hearing, reports to the effect that the great fortune Wray had married in the person of Admiral Harte's daughter Fanny had proved to be tied up to the lady and her offspring with preternatural skill; that the couple did not agree — never had agreed — that Wray's personal income was by no means adequate to his train of life, above all not to his almost nightly losses at Button's, and that yesterday he had been carried home drunk.

'You are very good,' said Stephen, 'but I am afraid I am engaged on Friday. Yet there are some matters that I should like to talk to you about and that cannot be discussed here. We will go to your house, if you please.'

'Very well,' said Wray, with a forced smile, and they made their way through the press. As they crossed the Green Park he gave Stephen a pretty clear account of the sequence of events in Malta, and Stephen listened attentively, though with not a tithe of the zeal he would have felt a few days before: not a hundredth part. Wray blamed himself exceedingly for the escape of Lesueur, the chief French agent in the island; but at least the organization had been destroyed and no information had been conveyed from Valletta to Paris since then. 'The trouble was that I was horribly out of order,' said Wray. 'I still am. I wish you would prescribe for my poor liquescent belly,' he said with a smile, opening the door of his house. 'Pray walk in.'

'I should prescribe for your mind, my friend, if I prescribed at all,' said Stephen inwardly. 'That is the peccant part. But if I were to give you the tincture of laudanum, the physic that would best suit your case, you would become addicted within the month, a mere opium-eater. Addicted, as I believe you are already to the bottle.'

They went upstairs to Wray's library and

there, Stephen having refused wine, cake, sherbet, biscuits, tea, Wray said, not without embarrassment, that he hoped Maturin would not think he was avoiding him or trying to get out of the debt he owed. He freely owned the debt and thankfully acknowledged Maturin's forbearance during this long period; but he was ashamed to say that he must still beg for a little more time. By the end of the month he would be in funds and they would square accounts at last. In the meantime Wray would give him a note of hand. He hoped this delay might not be too inconvenient.

After a slight and disagreeable pause Stephen agreed, and from this point of advantage he said, fixing Wray with his pale eye and defying him to show the least awareness of his condition, 'When last we corresponded, in Gibraltar, you were kind enough to suggest taking a letter to my wife, since you were travelling overland. Pray just when did she receive it?'

'I am very sorry to say I cannot tell,' said Wray, looking down. 'When I reached London I went round to Half-Moon Street at once, but the servant told me his mistress was gone abroad. He added that he had instructions to forward letters, so I put it into his hands.'

'I am obliged to you, sir,' said Stephen, and he took his leave. If he had seen Wray watching him from behind the lace curtain, grinning and jigging on one leg and making the sign of the cuckold's horns with his fingers he would quite certainly have turned and killed him with his court sword, for this was a very cruel blow. It meant that Diana had not waited for any explanation, however halting and imperfect, but had condemned him unheard; and this showed a much harder, far less affectionate woman than the Diana he had known or had thought he knew — a mythical person, no doubt created by himself. It had of course been evident from her letter, which made no reference to his; but he had not chosen to see the evidence and now that it was absolutely forced upon his sight it made his eyes sting and tingle again. And deprived of his myth he felt extraordinarily lonely.

'Sir! Oh sir!' called the porter as he turned in at Black's after a walk that had taken him right across the park to Kensington and beyond, far into the night, and then down by the river at low tide. 'This was brought by special messenger, and I was not to fail to give it you the moment you came in.'

'Thankee, Charles,' said Stephen. He noticed the black Admiralty seal on the letter, put it in his pocket and walked upstairs. As he hoped he should, he found Sir Joseph in the library, reading Buffon. 'Sad stuff, Maturin, sad stuff,' he said aloud, for once again they were alone in the room. 'There never was a Frenchman sound on bones apart from Cuvier.' He put the book down with a disapproving air and then said 'I was very glad to see you at the levee, and I was very glad Clarence was so civil. Barrow was suitably impressed — he fairly dotes upon that prince, although he knows he is not well-seen at the Admiralty: knows it as well as anyone, and better than most. He seems incapable of realizing that some royals are far more royal than others. An odd contradiction. Still, it does mean that if you call again you will not be treated rudely. Will you call again, do you suppose?'

'Sure I must, unless I am to send the damned box by a common porter. This is probably an invitation.' He held up the letter, opened it and said 'So it is. Mr B infinitely regrets — most lamentable misunderstanding — would be most gratified — presumes to suggest — but any other hour at Dr M's convenience.'

'Yes,' said Sir Joseph, 'it is inevitable that you should go.' A pause. 'By the way, I picked up a little news of your brass box. It was a Cabinet Office affair, of course — FitzMaurice and his friends — and the Navy was only the carrier, with no knowledge of the contents. The "much larger sum" that you were told about was either a conjecture of Pocock's part or a monstrous Foreign Office indiscretion that should never have been passed on. I dare say most well-informed people have heard of it by now, at least in general terms. Oh Lord, pray send us a few public servants who know what discretion means! Tell me, Maturin, are you looking in at the Royal Society tonight?'

'Not I. I walked a great way after an unpleasant visit; I missed my dinner, and I am entirely destroyed.'

'Certainly you look quite fagged out. Might not supper set you up? Something light, like a boiled fowl with oyster sauce? I should very much like you to meet a colleague from the Horse Guards, an uncommonly intelligent engineer. I have been consulting him and several other friends in an unofficial way, as I told you, and they agree that my mouse is perhaps beginning to assume the form of a rat.'

'Sir Joseph,' said Stephen, 'forgive me, but tonight I should not turn in my chair if it assumed the form of a two-horned rhinoceros. Buonaparte may come over in his flat-bottomed boats and welcome, as far as I am concerned.'

'You had much better eat a boiled fowl with me,' said Blaine. 'A boiled fowl with oyster sauce, and a bottle of sound claret. Maturin, is the name Ovart at all familiar to you?'

'Ovart? I doubt I have ever heard it,' said Stephen, gaping with hunger and fatigue. He said goodnight and walked slowly off to bed.

There was little spring in him the next morning either, although a blackbird from the Green Park had perched on the parapet outside his window, singing away with effortless perfection. At breakfast an aged member told him that it was a fine morning, and that the news was more encouraging; it seemed that there was the possibility of a peace before long.

'So much the better,' said Stephen. 'With the people who run the country at present we cannot carry on the war very much longer.'

'Very true,' said the aged member, shaking his head. Then he asked whether Stephen were going to Newgate for the executions. No, said Stephen, he was going to the Admiralty. Did they hang people there?

asked the aged member eagerly, and when he was told that they did not he shook his head again, observing that for his part he never missed a hanging — two eminent bankers guilty of forgery were to be strung up today among the ordinary people — the Stock Exchange would spare neither father nor mother, wife nor child when it came to that sort of thing — did Stephen remember Parson Dodd? — never missed a hanging, and when he was a boy he would often walk to Tyburn with his aunts, following the cart all the way along past St Sepulchre's to Tyburn itself: it used to be called Deadly Never Green in those days.

At the Admiralty a clerk was waiting on the steps for Dr Maturin and he was shown straight into Mr Barrow's room. Stephen was a little surprised to see Wray there too, but it did not matter: so long as he could deliver his infernal box into responsible hands he was content.

Mr Barrow thanked him profusely for coming and repeated that he could not adequately express his regret for the recent misunderstanding. He explained just how it came about that Mr Lewis had been left in ignorance of the nature of Stephen's invaluable and of course entirely honorary, gratuitous, voluntary services. 'I am afraid he must have been sadly offensive, sir?'

'He was offensive, sir,' said Stephen, 'and I told him of it.'

'He is still away from the office, but as soon as he is better he shall wait upon you and tender his apologies.'

'Never in life, not at all, not at all. I would not require that of him. In any case I was too hasty. He spoke in ignorance.'

'He was as ignorant of your quality as he was ignorant of the nature of the papers in question. Indeed, as far as they are concerned I could not have enlightened him, since officially even I know nothing. But I may tell you in confidence, Doctor, that we have heard of a brass box, and we understand that the Foreign Office and the Treasury were most exceedingly concerned at having *to write it off,* as the commercial gentry say.'

'This will dispel your ignorance,' said Stephen, taking the box from an inner pocket and putting it down on the desk.

'What a curious seal,' said Barrow in the tense silence.

'It is my watch-key,' said Stephen. 'The seal was broken in the first place — the box fell and burst open — and I sealed it again to keep it shut. As you see,' he said, breaking the wax, 'the lid springs up for a nothing.'

Barrow had an inquisitive nature and he looked eagerly at the papers on top; but then his countenance changed; he looked first startled and then indignant. He pushed the box from him as though it were something dangerous. He began to say something in an angry, disclaiming tone, coughed and changed it to the words 'It is enormous.'

'It is what we heard about,' said Wray. He flicked through the rest of the sheaf, saying 'Do not be uneasy. I will deal with this. Ledward and I will see to it all.'

'The sooner it is out of our hands the better,' said Barrow. 'What a responsibility, what a responsibility! Pray let it be locked up at once.' After a while he recovered himself enough to say to Stephen, 'It must have weighed upon you in the most dreadful manner. And I suppose you could not share your anxiety? I suppose no one saw these — these papers but you?'

'Never a Christian soul,' said Stephen. 'Are such secrets to be shared?'

Wray came back, and there was a silence, broken by occasional exclamations, until Barrow said uneasily 'Even now, I believe we should really have no *official* knowledge of the matter. So perhaps we may now move on to the second part of our intended conversation. The fact is, sir, it has been suggested that you might be induced . . . Mr Wray, pray tell Dr Maturin of the suggestion that was made.'

'Our agent in Lorient, Madame de La Feuillade, whom you know,' said Wray, 'has been arrested; and since she not only sends information from there but also forwards her sister's from Brest, her absence is most unfortunate. She has not been taken up for helping us, however, but for evading her taxes. She is being detained at Nantes, and Hérold, who brought the news, states that the examining magistrate can certainly be persuaded to dismiss the case if the proper means are used. In view of Madame de La Feuillade's position the affair obviously calls for exceptional tact and ability and a fair amount of money. It was hoped that Dr Maturin might provide the one, while the department provided the other. There are a certain number of vessels that carry brandy and wine from Nantes to England under licence from the admiral commanding the Channel Fleet: we use four of them regularly and they are thoroughly reliable; so the passage to and fro could easily be arranged at any time that may prove convenient.'

'I see, I see,' said Stephen, looking at them with a considering eye. But what in fact did he see, and what did he merely imagine?

And how remarkable it was, to feel the old eagerness coming to life in his heart, although only that morning he had regarded the whole service with frigid indifference. 'I see that the matter calls for some consideration, and since I go down to the country tomorrow I shall have peace and leisure for reflecting upon it. From what I know of Madame de La Feuillade, her imprisonment on such a charge will not be very arduous nor her interrogation very severe.'

CHAPTER SIX

The Portsmouth night coach was an almost entirely naval concern, apart from the horses and one of the inside passengers, an elderly lady; the coachman had been in Lord Rodney's household, the guard was a former Marine, and all the passengers belonged to the present Navy in one way or another.

When the stars were beginning to fade in the east, the machine ran past some dim houses and a church on the right-hand side of the road and the elderly lady said, 'It will be Petersfield in a few minutes: how I hope I have forgot nothing.' She counted her parcels over again and then said to Stephen, 'So I am not to buy, sir? That is your firm opinion?'

'Madam,' replied Stephen, 'I repeat that I know nothing of the Stock Exchange: I could not readily distinguish between a bull and a bear. I only say that if your friends' advice is based upon their persuasion that peace is to be concluded within the next few days, then you should perhaps reflect that they may be mistaken.'

'And yet they are very knowing, well-informed gentlemen: and then you too, sir, you may be mistaken, may you not?'

'To be sure, ma'am. I am as fallible as my neighbour — perhaps even more so, indeed.'

The guard blew a fine blast, imitated by most of the younger outside passengers, for whom an English spring night on the top of a coach was nothing in comparison with a night on the billows off Brest.

'Then that is settled,' said the lady. 'I shall certainly not buy. How glad I am that I asked your opinion. Thank you, sir.'

The coach wheeled into the yard of the Crown to change horses, and when the passengers who had been stretching their legs during the operation came aboard again Stephen said to the coachman 'You will never forget to set me down at Buriton, I am sure; and if you could do so at the little small ale-house rather than the cross-roads it would save me the weary walk. Here is a three-shilling piece.'

'Thank you, my lord,' said the coachman. 'The ale-house it is.'

'I am convinced you were right, sir, in advising the gentlewoman not to buy,' said one of the insides, an accountant at the Dockyard, when Petersfield was behind them. 'It does not appear to me that there is any real likelihood of peace at present.'

'I should think not,' said a tall awkward midshipman, who had spent much of the night kicking the other passengers, not from vice or wantonness but because every time he went to sleep his long legs gave convulsive jerks, entirely of their own accord. 'I should think not. I passed for lieutenant only last week, and a peace now would be monstrous unjust. It would mean . . .' At this point he became aware that he was prating to his elders, a practice discouraged in the service; he fell silent, and pretended to be absorbed in the first red streaks of sunrise far ahead.

'Two years ago, yes,' said the accountant, taking no notice of him, 'but not now, with the continental allies crumbling like dust and so much of our time and treasure taken up with this miserable, unnecessary, unnatural war with America. No, sir, I believe the rumours the gentlewoman's friends had heard were merely flim-flam put about by evil-disposed men that wish to profit by the rise.' He went on to explain just why he thought Napoleon would never desire a negotiated peace at this juncture, and he was still speaking when the coach slowed to a halt and the guard cried 'All for the Jericho ale-house, gentlemen, if you please. Good fare for man and beast. Prime brandy, right old Nantz straight from the smuggler, and capital water straight from the well — never mixed except by accident, ha, ha, ha!'

A few minutes later Stephen was standing there with his baggage by the side of the road while the dim coach disappeared in a dust-cloud of its own making and a long trail of early-morning rooks passed overhead. Presently the door of the ale-house opened and an amiable slut appeared, her hair done up in little rags, very like a Hottentot's, and her garment held close at the neck with one hand. 'Good morning, now, Mrs Comfort,' said Stephen. 'In time pray let the boy put these things behind the bar till I send for them. I mean to walk to Ashgrove over the fields.'

'You will find the Captain there, with some saucy foremast jacks and that wicked old Killick. But won't you step in, sir, and take a little something? It's a long, long way, after a night in the coach.'

Stephen knew that the Jericho could run to nothing more than tea or small beer, both equally repugnant to him in the morning; he thanked her, and said he believed he should wait until he had walked up an appetite; and when asked whether it would be that wicked old Killick who came in the cart for his portmanteau he said he would make a point of asking the Captain to send him.

For the first mile his road was a lane between high banks and hedges, with woods on the left hand and fields on the right — well-sprung wheat and hay — and the banks were starred all along with primroses, while the hedges had scores of very small cheerful talkative early birds, particularly goldfinches in their most brilliant plumage; and in the hay a corncrake was already calling. Then when the flat land began to rise and fall this lane branched out into two paths, the one carrying on over a broad pasture — a single piece of fifty or even sixty acres with some colts in it — and the other, now little more than a trace, leading down among the trees. Stephen followed the second; it was steep going, encumbered with brambles and dead bracken on the edge of the wood and farther down with fallen branches and a dead tree or two, but near the bottom he came to a ruined keeper's cottage standing on a grassy plat, its turf kept short by the rabbits that fled away at his approach. The cottage had lost its roof long since and it was filled tight with lilac, not yet in bloom, while nettle and elder had overwhelmed the outbuilding behind; but there was still a stone bench by the door, and Stephen sat upon it, leaning against the wall. Down here in the hollow the night had not yet yielded, and there was still a green twilight. An ancient wood: the slope was too great and the ground too broken for it ever to have been cut or tended and the trees were still part of the primaeval forest; vast shapeless oaks, often hollow and useless for timber, held out their arms and their young fresh green leaves almost to the middle of the clearing, held them out with never a tremor, for down here the air was so still that gossamer floated with no perceptible movement at all. Still and silent: although far-off blackbirds could be heard away on the edge of the wood and although the stream at the bottom murmured perpetually the combe was filled with a living silence.

On the far side, high on the bank of the stream, there was a badger's holt. Some years ago Stephen had watched a family of fox-cubs playing there, but now it seemed to him that the badgers were back: fresh earth had been flung out, and even from the bench he could distinguish a well-trodden path. 'Perhaps I shall see one,' he said; and after a while his mind drifted away and away, running through a Gloria he and Jack had heard in London, a very elaborate Gloria by Frescobaldi. 'But perhaps it is too late,' he went on, when the Gloria was ended and the light had grown stronger, a brighter green, almost the full light of dawn. Yet scarcely were these words formed in his mind before he heard a strong rustling, sweeping bumping sound, and a beautifully striped badger came into sight on the other side of the brook, walking backwards with a load of bedding under its chin. It was an old fat badger, and it grumbled and cursed all the way. The last uphill stretch was particularly difficult, with the burden catching in hazel or thorn on either side and leaving long wisps, and just before the entrance the badger lifted its head and looked round, as though to say 'Oh it is so *bloody* awkward.' Then, having breathed, it took a fresh grip on the bundle, and with a final oath vanished backwards into the holt.

'Why do I feel such an intense pleasure, such an intense satisfaction?' asked Stephen. For some time he searched for a convincing reply, but finding none he observed 'The fact is that I do.' He sat on as the sun's rays came slowly down through the trees, lower and lower, and when the lowest reached a branch not far above him it caught a dewdrop poised upon a leaf. The drop instantly blazed crimson, and a slight movement of his head made it show all the colours of the spectrum with extraordinary purity, from a red almost too deep to be seen through all the others to the ultimate violet and back again. Some minutes later a cock pheasant's explosive call broke the silence and the spell and he stood up.

At the edge of the wood the blackbirds were louder still, and they had been joined by blackcaps, thrushes, larks, monotonous pigeons, and a number of birds that should never have sung at all. His way now led him through ordinary country, field after field, eventually reaching Jack's woods, where the honey buzzards had once nested. But it was ordinary country raised to the highest power: the mounting sun shone through a faint veil with never a hint of glare, giving the colours a freshness and an intensity Stephen had never seen equalled. The green world and the gentle, pure blue sky might just have been created; and as the day warmed a hundred scents drifted through the air.

'Returning thanks at any length is virtually impossible,' he reflected, sitting on a stile and watching two hares at play, sitting up and fibing at one another, then leaping and running and leaping again. 'How few manage even five phrases with any effect. And how intolerable are most dedications too, even the best. Perhaps the endless repetition of flat, formal praise' — for the Gloria was still running in his head — 'is an attempt at overcoming this, an attempt at expressing gratitude by another means. I shall put this thought to Jack,' he said, having considered for a moment. The hares raced away out of sight and he walked on, singing in a harsh undertone 'Quoniam tu solus sanctus, tu solus Dominus, tu solus altissimus' until a cuckoo called away on his left hand: cuckoo, cuckoo, loud and clear, followed by a cackling laugh and answered by a fainter cuckoo, cuckoo, cuckoo far over on the right.

His happiness sank at once and he walked on with his head bowed and his hands clasped behind his back. He was now close to Jack's land: one more field and a lane and then the Ashgrove woods began, on poor spewy ground, with the vile lead-mines and their ancient heaps of spoil among them: then came Jack's plantations, dwarvish still and much gnawed by rabbits, hares, deer, and a large variety of caterpillars, and at last the cottage came in sight. By now the day had woken up entirely to ordinary life; the silence had long since gone and even if no cuckoo had called cuckold there would still have been nothing left of that feeling of imminent miracle; it was now no more than an exceptionally pleasant, summery day in spring.

He was approaching the house from the back and he saw it to no great advantage. Jack had bought the place when he was poor and he had enlarged it when he was rich; the result was an inharmonious jumble, with few of the advantages of a house and none of what meagre conveniences a cottage might have to offer. But at least it had glorious stables. Not only did Jack Aubrey love hunting the fox, but he was persuaded that he was as good a judge of horseflesh as any man in the Navy List, and when he came home from the Mauritius campaign deep-laden with prize-money he laid out a noble yard with a double coach-house and accommodation for hacks and hunters on one side and a range of loose-boxes to house the beginnings of a racing-stable on the other, with tack-rooms at the short ends, forming an elegant quadrangle of rosy brick trimmed with Portland stone and crowned by a tower with a blue-dialled clock in it.

Stephen was not surprised to find the

greater part shut up, since the hunters and the running-horses had disappeared as soon as Jack's misfortunes began, but the absence of any other creatures, of the cart and the low-slung gig in which Sophie went abroad was harder to understand. So, when he came to it by way of the kitchen-garden, was the silence of the house. Jack had three children and a mother-in-law, and silence was unnatural: yet never a sound emerged from the doors or windows, and an uneasiness came upon him, an uneasiness strengthened by the fact that all the doors and all the windows were open, and not only open but partly dismantled, which gave the house a blind, ravaged, gap-toothed, desolate air. The silence also reeked of turpentine, conceivably used as a disinfectant. He had known plagues in which entire households were struck down overnight: the cholera morbus, too. 'God between us and evil,' he muttered.

A cheer from far away changed the current of his mind, and some moments later this was followed by the peculiarly English sound of a bat striking a ball and then by further cries. He passed quickly through what Jack called the rose-garden — lucus a non lucendo — through the shrubbery to the edge of the hill and there below him on a broad meadow was a game of cricket all laid out, the fielders in their places, keenly attentive to the bowler as he went through his motions, the sound of the stroke again, the batsmen twinkling between the wickets, fielders darting for the ball, tossing it in, and then the whole pattern taking shape again, a formal dance, white shirts on the green.

He walked down the slope, and as he came nearer he recognized the players, or at least all the batting side, and some of their opponents. Plaice and Bonden were in and Captain Babbington, formerly one of Jack's midshipmen, then one of his lieutenants and now commander of the *Tartarus* sloop of eighteen guns, was bowling to his old shipmates as though he meant to carry their legs away as well as their stumps. For his part Plaice was content to stop every straight ball and leave the rest alone, but Bonden had his eye well in and he hit almost everything with equal fury. He had scored fourteen runs off the present over, and now the last ball came down, pitched rather short and outside the off stump: he gave it an almighty blow, but he had misjudged the rise, and instead of skimming over the fielders' heads the ball rose in a most surprising way, like a mortar bomb or a rocket, vanishing almost entirely.

Three fielders ran in Stephen's direction, all gazing up and spreading their hands, while others called 'Heads, heads!' or 'Stand from under'. Stephen's mind was far away: he had noticed neither the stroke nor the flight of the ball, but one of the few things he had learnt at sea — learnt painfully and thoroughly — was that *Stand from under* usually preceded, but only just preceded, a downpour of boiling pitch, or the fall of a very heavy block, or that of a needle-pointed marline-spike, and he hurried anxiously away, crouching, with his hands protecting his head, an unlucky move that brought him into collision with one fielder who was running backwards and with another already poised where the ball was about to come down. They fell in a confused heap from which he was extracted amidst cries of 'It's the Doctor,' 'Are you hurt, sir?' and 'Why can't you look where you are a-coming to, you clumsy ox?' — this to the *Tartarus*'s yeoman of the sheets, who had held the catch in spite of everything and who rose through the welter of limbs, triumphantly holding it up.

'Well, Stephen,' said Jack, leading him to the refreshment cart, after he had been brushed down and put to rights, with his wig set straight on his head, 'so you have come down by the night coach, I find: how glad I am you found a place. I did not look to see you till tomorrow, or I should have left a note. You must have been quite amazed to find the house all ahoo. Will you take a can of beer, or should you prefer cold punch?'

'Would there be any coffee, at all? I missed my breakfast.'

'Missed your breakfast? God's my life, how very shocking. Let us walk up and brew a pot — there are five wickets to fall, and Plaice and Killick will stick there like limpets: we have plenty of time.'

'Where is Sophie?' asked Stephen.

'She is not here!' cried Jack. 'She is away, gone to Ireland with the children and her mother — Frances is having a baby. Ain't it amazing? I looked pretty blank when I reached the house and found no family at all, I can tell you. Nobody, and even old Bray down at the ale-house, toping. She had no idea we were in this hemisphere, even, but she is leaving the children and posting back directly: with any luck we shall see her on Tuesday, or even Monday.'

'I hope so, indeed.'

'Lord, Stephen, how I look forward to it,' said Jack, laughing at the prospect; and then after they had been walking for a few moments, 'But in the meanwhile, here we are all a-high-lone, a parcel of poor miserable bachelors. Luckily the *Tartarus* is in, to keep up our spirits, and there are so many old Surprises here and in Pompey that by including the youngsters and even your Padeen, God help us, we were able to get up a team to play them, although Mowett and Pullings had to go up to town to see the publisher — you only just missed them, which was a great pity, for two men in a higher state of nervous tremor I have never seen, and they would have profited from one of your comfortable slime-draughts. Still, a team we have, and the Goat and Compasses is going to send our dinner out to the field; you would not believe how well the Goat cooks venison — it eats as tender as veal. Look, Stephen, you see this corner of the wood and the shrubbery? I mean to cut the ground right back so that the new wing shall have a terrace and a fine stretch of grass. A lawn, if you understand me. I have always wanted a lawn; and perhaps I might be luckier with grass than with flowers.'

'So there is to be a new wing?'

'Oh Lord yes! We were most horribly cramped, you know; and with three children and a mother-in-law who often comes to stay it was like living in a cutter, all hugger-mugger, cheek by jowl, fourteen inches to a hammock, no more. And Sophie said that without more cupboards, she really could not go on. There is Dray, turning into the yard. The gig, there! The gig ahoy! I sent him into Portsmouth for the newspapers.'

The gig wheeled about. 'How are we doing, sir?' cried the one-legged seaman as he drove in across the sacred gravel and handed out *The Times*, touching his forehead to Stephen with the other hand.

'Forty-eight for five,' said Jack. 'We shall wipe *Tartarus*'s eye, with any luck. Cut along down: I will put the gig away.'

Dray fastened his wooden stump, unshipped for the drive, and pegged away down the slope as fast as ever he could go; for although his playing days were over, he was a most ardent critic. The gig itself scarcely needed putting away. It was attached to a very short-legged, short-sighted, deaf, meek animal of uncertain age carefully chosen for Sophie, who feared and disliked horses, as well she might, having been made to ride an iron-mouthed biter when she was far too young and having seen various hunters break her husband's ribs and collarbones, while the running-horses might have run off with her daughters' portions, had the capital not been tied up. The present animal, Moses, walked quietly towards the yard, peering in its purblind way at Jack as he unfolded *The Times* to reach the financial page. Still reading, Jack opened the door of a palatial loose-box: Stephen cast off the gig, Moses walked in, lay down, uttered a deep sigh, and closed his eyes.

'It is even better than I had thought,' said Jack, and his shining face was younger by a good ten years. 'How I hope you profited by what I said.'

'Sure, I took notice of your advice,' replied Stephen, with no particular emphasis, and Jack knew that he should learn no more.

'We shall certainly have a really spacious terrace, perhaps with fountains. And there is a good deal to be said for a billiard-room too, on days when it is raining very hard,' said Jack. He led the way to the kitchen, opened the door of the little stove and plied the bellows till the charcoal glowed almost white. 'You must forgive the smell of paint,' he said, fetching down the coffee-mill, 'we laid on the first coat yesterday.' The rest of his words were drowned by the sound of grinding.

They drank their grateful brew outside, walking up and down in the pure soft air while Stephen (an abstemious soul) ate two thin biscuits. When the pot was drunk, Jack cocked his ear to a roaring from the cricket-field. 'Perhaps we had better be going down again,' he said; and on the way, looking back in the narrow path, he said with a singularly sweet smile, 'Did I tell you I mean to buy *Surprise*? She can moor in a private ordinary at Porchester.'

'Heavens, Jack! Is not this a very onerous undertaking? I seem to remember that Government gave twenty thousand pounds for the *Chesapeake*.'

'Yes, but that was mostly to encourage others to go and do likewise. Selling out of the service is another thing. I doubt *Surprise* will fetch anything like so much.'

'How does one set about buying a ship?'

'You have to be there yourself, with cash in hand — well hit, sir, well hit.' Honey, a very dangerous cross-bat smiter, had struck the ball in a high arc towards the approaching waggon from the Goat and Compasses, a waggon bearing the cricketers' dinner and drawn very deliberately by a pair of cows.

Honey dealt with the next ball in much the same way, but a cunning Tartarus, the ship's corporal and up to any guardo move, had lingered there: he caught the ball — Honey was out, the innings was over, and in an excess of gaiety the men unharnessed the cows and ran the waggon at breakneck pace to their respective captains.

'Padeen, now,' said Stephen in Irish to his servant, a huge, gentle Munsterman with a great stutter and small knowledge of any other language, 'and did you score a run, at all?'

'I believe I did, sir dear; but then I ran back, and will it ever be counted to me, who can tell?'

'Who indeed?' said Stephen, who had played the game once, in the Spice Islands, but who had never quite mastered the finer points; nor, for that matter, the coarser ones either.

'Will your honour explain the Saxon game perhaps?'

'I might,' said Stephen. 'When the venison pasty and sure it is the venison pasty of the world is finished I will ask the little captain to tell me its whole nature, he having played for the Gentlemen of Hampshire; and you are to understand that what Thomond is to the hurling, so Hampshire is to the cricket.'

The little captain was Babbington, and he certainly knew a great deal about the game; but rarely, rarely would his shipmates, his former shipmates, his superior officer or his subordinates allow him to finish a sentence of his explanation. The seven pasties, the ten apple pies, the unlimited bread and cheese, and the four kegs of beer might have been expected to have a deadening effect, but no: every man there present and even some of the beardless miscellaneous such as youngsters and Marine Society boys had particular views on the origins of cricket, on what constituted fair bowling, on the number of stumps in their grandfather's time, and the best way of using a bat; and one of Babbington's own midshipmen quarrelled with his definition of a wide. Nobody contradicted Captain Aubrey, who in any case had gone to sleep leaning against the wheel of the cart with his hat over his face, but they wrangled so pertinaciously among themselves that Babbington invited Stephen to walk round the field to be shown the positions of square leg, long-stop, and mid on.

He soon dismissed the remaining points of fielding and observed that tomorrow he hoped to show Stephen the difference between a slow, dead wicket and one upon which the ball would really turn.

'You will never play all this afternoon and all tomorrow too, for God's love?' cried Stephen, shocked out of civility by the thought of such insufferable tedium drawn out to such unconscionable length.

'Oh yes. It would have been a three-day match, only with Mrs Aubrey coming home, the house must be turned out, swabbed and flogged dry, and the paintwork touched up: still, with the long evenings I dare say we shall each have our two innings. But sir,' said Babbington after a silence, and in quite a different tone, 'one of the many reasons I was so glad to hear from the Captain that you was coming down was that I wanted to ask your advice.'

'Ah?' said Stephen. In former times this had usually meant a question of a medical nature (his companions had once persuaded the very young and costive Babbington that he was going to have a baby) or a request for the loan of sums varying from sixpence to as much as half a guinea; but that was long ago, and now Babbington had a considerable estate, which included a parliamentary borough as rotten as a borough could well be; and it was no longer probable that he should think himself pregnant.

'Well, the fact of the matter is, sir,' said Babbington, 'and not to put too fine a point on it — I mean, it is better to be plain. I dare say you remember that Admiral Harte cut up uncommon rough when he found me — well, kissing his daughter?'

'I remember he made use of some illiberal expressions.'

'He did worse than that. He shut Fanny up, and he beat her when he found we corresponded. And then he married her to Andrew Wray, swearing she should never go to a play or a ball unless she consented and that anyhow I was pursuing the Governor's daughter in Antigua — it was notorious — it was common knowledge. But, however, not to put too fine a point upon it, the fact of the matter is, when I brought *Dryad* home — you remember *Dryad*, sir? Such a weatherly ship — we happened to meet at a ball, and we found that we were as fond of one another as ever: more so, if possible.'

'Listen, William my dear,' said Stephen, 'if you wish me to advise you to commit adultery . . .'

'No, no, sir,' cried Babbington, smiling. 'No, I don't need any advice about adultery. My point is this — but perhaps I should explain the position. I dare say you knew the Admiral was uncommon rich? And everyone said what a prodigious heiress Fanny would be and what a fine match for Wray. But what they did not know was that he can scarcely get at a penny without her consent. And they don't agree — never have — how could they agree? As different as chalk and cheese. He is a wretched scrub of a fellow that drinks too much and cannot hold his wine, and he beats her: he told her openly he had only married her for her money. It seems he is in debt up to the ears: the bailiffs are often in the house, and they have to be staved off by one shift or another.'

'My visit must have been mighty importunate,' reflected Stephen.

'But I am not to be blackguarding the man,' said Babbington. 'My point is this: you saw a good deal of him in Malta, and you see farther through a brick wall than most people, so which do you think the wisest thing to do? There is the idea of making over some share of Fanny's fortune, on the understanding that they keep up the appearance of being married but in fact each go their own way; but I am told that no contract to that effect would be binding and he would have to be trusted. And then there is the idea of bolting and letting him sue me for crim con — for damages for criminal conversation.'

'Sir, sir,' cried a youngster, running up behind them, 'the Captain is awake, and asks do you choose to start your innings now, since there will be so much to do Saturday?'

'I shall come at once,' said Babbington, and in a low voice to Stephen, 'Will you turn it over in your mind, sir, and tell me what you think?'

Although he knew that in cases of this kind any advice that did not exactly agree with the wishes of those concerned was always useless and often offensive Stephen did turn it over in his mind all through that interminable afternoon while the Tartaruses built up their score, mostly in singles and byes. Their captain of the forecastle faced the bowling first, a square, middle-aged seaman who had been at the siege of Gibraltar in his youth and who had never forgotten the value of dogged resistance; neither he nor the carpenter was there for frivolous amusement and they fairly broke the hearts of the bowlers, who sent down fast straight balls, fast balls well outside the wicket, tempting lobs and cunning twisters, all in vain until the declining sun, shining in Gibraltar's eye, caused him to miss a despairing full toss directed at his middle stump.

The next day's play was somewhat less rigid, with the Tartaruses leaving Jack's team two hundred and fifty-five to get before owl-hoot and the Surprises beating the ball about the field in a brisk, seamanlike fashion, but by now it was too late: as far as Stephen was concerned cricket was marked down for ever as an intolerably insipid pastime, decorative enough for half an hour, perhaps, but not to be compared with hurling for speed, skill, grace of movement, and dramatic fire.

This second day, however, was enlivened by the coming of Martin, thin and dusty with having walked from Fareham to Portsmouth and then from Portsmouth to Ashgrove. On leaving the *Surprise* for the village where lived the young lady he wished to marry he had forgotten that he needed Captain Aubrey's certificate of good conduct and moral behaviour before he could draw his pay, and Captain Aubrey, so rarely carrying a chaplain, had forgotten it too. Yet the money was most urgently required. 'You cannot conceive, my dear Maturin,' said Martin, reclining in a hammock-chair at the edge of the field with a glass of brandy and ginger ale on the grass beside him and his certificate glowing in his lap, 'or perhaps you can, but I could not, having always lived in lodgings — you cannot conceive what it costs to set up house. We are only to have a cottage, quite close to her father's rectory so that she shall not be lonely when I am at sea, yet also conveniently near one of the best places for thick-kneed plover you can imagine; but furnishing it with the simplest necessities — Heavens above! The outlay in patty-pans, andirons, market-place delf and common green-handled knives alone is enough to make a man turn pale; to say nothing of brooms, pails, and washing tubs. It is a very grave responsibility: I feel it much.'

Stephen had already welcomed Martin, had led him up to the house for food and wine, and had given him joy of his approaching marriage; now, having listened to the exorbitant price of coppers, cheese-graters and a number of other domestic objects for a long while he said 'Should you like to see a lesser pettichaps on her nest, not half a mile from here?'

'To tell you the truth, Maturin, on a perfect vernal day like this, I find nothing so pleasant as sitting on a comfortable chair in the sun, with green, green grass stretching away, the sound of bat and ball, and the sight of cricketers. Particularly such cricketers as these: did you see how Maitland glanced that ball away to leg? A very pretty stroke. Do not you find watching good cricket restful, absorbing, a balm to the anxious, harassed mind?'

'I do not. It seems to me, saving your presence, unspeakably tedious.'

'Perhaps some of the finer shades may escape you. Well played, sir! Oh very well played indeed. That was as pretty a late cut as ever I have seen — how they run, ha, ha — he was very nearly run out — see how the bails fly! But he was just within his ground. It is years since I have seen such a serious game of cricket.'

'This one is serious enough, for all love. Nay, funereal.'

'You know Sir Joseph Banks, of course?'

'The Great Cham of Botany? Sure I know him, since he is the president of the Royal Society.'

'He was at the same school as I, though of an earlier generation; he often came down to watch us, and once he told me that cricket was played regularly in Heaven; and that, from a man with his attainments, is surely a recommendation.'

'I must draw what comfort I can from the doctrine of Limbo.'

'Butterfingers,' cried Martin as mid-on dropped a catch and fumbled for the ball behind him. The batsman beckoned for the run: mid-on whipped round and threw down the wicket with diabolic force and speed. 'Oh the dog' said Martin, 'oh the artful hound,' and when the cheering, hooting, and calling out had stopped he went on, 'I was so very sorry to have missed

Mowett. This publisher wishes him to bring the book out by subscription and I had hoped to tell him something of the disadvantages of such a method; nothing can easily exceed the misery of going about among one's acquaintance with a subscription-list and desiring them to put down half a guinea. I wished to warn him against the man, too; he is tolerably notorious in Grub Street, I find, and I am afraid sailors ashore are not always as cautious as they should be, considering the rapacious duplicity of certain landsmen.'

After some more considerations of this kind, Martin undertook to make Stephen love cricket by showing him the finer shades; but when, having endured ten overs more, Stephen found that there were still five men to go in and be got out, he observed that he had seen a wryneck over on the far side of the demesne, and he made no doubt it was still there. Yet even this would not move Martin, who said, 'A wryneck? Yes, they call him the cuckoo's mate in these parts, and the cuckoo is here. Dear me, yes. Hear them: three at least. Cuckoo, cuckoo. Oh word of fear, unpleasing to a married ear. Lord, and to think I shall be a husband in a fortnight's time! Pitch it up, man, pitch it up, or you will never get him out. Long hops are no good to man or beast.'

The afternoon was even more perfect than the morning, and Stephen spent much of it wandering in Jack's woods and meadows; he visited the lesser pettichaps and many another bright-eyed bird, including a hen-pheasant sitting hard, and a goshawk with a silver bell on her leg, perched on a branch, that looked at him doubtfully as he passed. He had plenty of time to reflect on Babbington's situation, and he did so; but to no purpose. In the evening, when as Martin had predicted the match ended in a draw, he said 'William, I am sorry to say I have nothing positive or even moderately intelligent to offer. It has of course occurred to you that an injured husband in the Admiralty itself is capable of hurting a sea-officer's career?'

'Yes, and I have weighed it pretty carefully; but, you know, my cousins and I can certainly rely on five and probably on seven votes in the Commons, and that is where support for the ministry really counts at present, rather than in the Lords. So I think that cancels out.'

'You know more about these things than I do, sure. The only other observation I have to offer is that it is probably unwise to trust any man you do not know very well, above all a man who dislikes you. I do not say this against Wray in particular; I only throw it out as a generality. A generality worthy of La Pallice, I must confess.'

'I was sure you would be in favour of our bolting,' cried Babbington, shaking his hand.

'I am nothing of the kind,' said Stephen.

'I always knew you were the best head-piece in the service, and I shall tell Fanny so when I bring *Tartarus* home.'

'She is on the Brest blockade, I collect?'

'Yes, and we sail on Monday, alas, unless there is some reprieve.'

'You will miss Sophie.'

'I am afraid so, more's the pity; but at least we shall be able to lend a hand in getting the place ready for her.'

Stephen had seen Captain Aubrey, his officers and men getting their ship ready for an admiral's inspection, but he had not seen Jack preparing the house for the return of a dearly-loved, long-absent wife. It was an impressive sight, and all the more so because Jack was increasingly aware that Sophie might be very bitterly offended against him; he was nervous, apprehensive, deprecating.

In ships of the Royal Navy painting went on nearly all the time when the weather would allow it, while in those which made a clean sweep fore and aft at quarters, as did all Jack's commands, the carpenters, their crews, and the captain's joiners took it as a matter of course that all the bulkheads, all the internal walls, together with the accurately fitted doors and lockers, should be taken down every evening and put up again an hour or so later. Jack therefore had very highly skilled labour at his disposal, and not only his own people either but all the best Tartarians and two expert joiners from Portsmouth as well: and on Wednesday they had set about the house, removing every door, shutter and window, scraping them, rubbing them down, and laying on the first coat.

Now the second coat of a quick-drying naval paint could go on, followed by the massive cleaning of everything in sight, so that late on Sunday the principal rooms could be restored to use and the rest on Monday morning. Meanwhile hammocks had been slung in the loose-boxes and the coach-house filled with furniture.

'You will not mind turning out rather early tomorrow, Stephen?' said Jack that night. 'With a little extra time I believe we may take up the flag-stones in the hall, kitchen, scullery and pantry, and grind them to a good fresh white, squaring their angles and giving them a true surface. It was Babbington's idea. His captain of the hold was once a master stone-dresser, and he says all we need is a bear, a staging and half a bushel of Purbeck grit.'

Stephen had grown used to extreme discomfort at sea or in any other place where the Navy carried its Hebraic notions of ritual cleanliness, but never had he experienced anything to touch the desolation of Ashgrove Cottage shortly after the various working-parties had moved in at dawn. Now all the doors and windows were out, made fast by dowels to an ingenious system of lines in the stable-yard that allowed both sides the maximum of sun and air, and throughout the house there was the sound of sluicing water, violent scrubbings and thumping, and strong nautical cries which strengthened the impression that the place had been boarded and carried by storm. In spite of the celestial weather the cottage was like something between a manufactory, a water-works and a house of correction with the inmates put to hard labour, and Stephen was glad to get away from it, driving Martin to Portsmouth in the gig, there to take the Salisbury coach.

Once removed from cricket, Martin became a reasonable companion again, and they took particular delight in the whinchats and wheatears on Ports Down and in a middle-spotted woodpecker eating ants like its great green cousin, which neither had seen before; but once they were in the town the future husband tended to predominate. He drew a list from his pocket and said 'One conical gravy-strainer, one bottle-jack and crane, three iron spoons, one jelly-bag, indifferent big: you will not mind if we look into an ironmonger's, Maturin? Now that I am sure of my pay, I believe I may venture upon a *copper* gravy-strainer and a *brass* bottle-jack; but it is a consequential purchase, you know, and I should be most grateful for your advice.'

Stephen's advice on bottle-jacks was of no great value, but he gave it for rather more than half a wavering, undecided hour, he having a sincere regard for Martin. Yet well-founded though it was, his affection would not run to discussing the merits of different kinds of copper-bottomed tin-bodied well-kettles for an equal length of time; he left Martin with the ironmonger's kind and infinitely patient wife and stepped across the street to a silversmith's, where he bought a teapot, cream-jug and sugar-bowl as a wedding-present.

Returning with the parcel, he found

Martin now divided between two pewter freezing-pots of slightly different size and quality and said 'I beg you and your bride will accept these, with my love.'

'Oh,' said Martin, astonished. 'Oh, thank you very much. May I look?'

'You will never be able to do it up again pretty,' said Stephen.

'I will wrap it up for the gentleman,' said the ironmonger's wife eagerly.

'Upon my word, Maturin,' cried Martin, holding up the pot, 'this is extremely handsome in you — I take it very, very kindly — Polly will be so delighted. Bless you.'

'Now, sir, what are you thinking of?' said the silversmith angrily, running into the shop. 'If Bob had not seen you step into Mrs Westby's, what should I have looked like? Jack Pudding, that is what. Now, sir, just you count with me,' he went on emphatically, putting down the notes and coins he was carrying, one by one. 'And five is seventeen, which makes seventeen pound four and threepence change, sir, at your service,' he ended quite sharply, with a meaning look at Mrs Westby, who pursed her lips and shook her head.

Stephen put what face he could upon it, but this was not his day. The re-wrapping of the pot and the packing of the ironmongery took so long that they had to run furiously for the Salisbury coach, hallooing to make it pause; it did take Martin up, but as it bowled fast and faster still away, already somewhat late, Stephen noticed that the hand he was waving still held the medium-sized jelly-bag.

Slowly he and Moses made their way back to Ashgrove Cottage, and the evening light showed it even more ravaged than before, because by now the entire hall, kitchen, and all that lay beyond on the ground floor had been eviscerated. Where neat stone had been, the startled eye now saw dank malodorous earth, like a battle-field, with pools of water traversed by planks. The flags themselves were being ground on the staging in groups of six, with four powerful seamen heaving the double-weighted bear to and fro with a fifth standing on it, laughing, sprinkling Purbeck grit and directing the jet of water while two hundred years of patina ran away down a neat channel into Jack's asparagus bed. The whole garden was criss-crossed with planks over wet sailcloth, and great amorphous objects stood here and there in the twilight, veiled by still more sailcloth, this time dry.

'Oh Stephen,' cried Jack on seeing his disconsolate face, 'I cannot tell you how pleased I am with the flags. They have taken a little longer than I thought and I am afraid they may not all be finished tonight, but we have already floored part of the back scullery — come and see. There. Ain't that prime?'

'It is as neat as a chess-board,' said Stephen, raising his voice over the thunder of swabs flogging the boards dry overhead.

'Sophie will be amazed,' said Jack. 'Come and see the grinding-stage.'

Work on the grinding-stage had stopped, however: the four heavers stood with their ropes slack, the fifth man was fixed in mid-caper and his water dribbled idly as he too gaped at the post-chaise. Jack followed their gaze and his stern, impatient eye looked straight into Sophie's face. Her expression, incredulous, appalled, instantly changed to open delight.

He plucked her out, kissed her most heartily, and began to explain what they were at — everything shipshape tomorrow — paint dry — flags laid — they had found a disused well in the passage — how were the children? while at the same time in a rapid voice, the words bubbling over one another, she told him of her excellent crossing — nothing at all: slept all the way — obliging, civil people at the inns — kind postboys —

children and Mama all well — Frankie and her baby too — a boy — Mr Clotworthy delighted — how lovely to be home. She then recovered her wits and averting her eyes from the wreck of her house she shook Babbington's hand, embraced Stephen tenderly, greeted all the officers, young gentlemen and seamen she knew, and said she would not get in their way — would go and sort her baggage and draw breath in one of the loose-boxes: there was nothing she preferred to a really commodious loose-box.

It was in this loose-box, which had once sheltered Jezebel, Jack's candidate for the Oaks, that they ate their supper, lit by a stable-lantern. They had, if not a vast stretch of time, then at least a very great number of events to communicate, and they were rarely silent. One of the difficulties was to know just how much had already been told by letter — which letters had arrived and which had miscarried.

'The very last I had from you,' said Jack, and as he spoke he realized that he was running fast into uncharted shoaling water. However, there was no help for it now, and in a somewhat constrained voice he went on, looking at his plate, 'was in Barbados. A copy of one you sent to Jamaica too, I believe.'

'Oh yes,' cried Sophie. 'The one that kind, attentive young man offered to carry. And so he found you, then? I am so glad, my dear.' She looked at him, hesitated, and then flushing a little she went on, 'I thought him so particularly amiable, all one could wish in a young man, and very much hope he will give us a long visit as soon as ever his duties allow. I should very much like the children to know him.'

By eleven o'clock on Monday morning the last pieces of the disrupted pattern fell into place, and Ashgrove Cottage, new-painted, new-floored, its brass, glass, pump-handles and all metalwork gleaming with a somewhat aggressive naval cleanliness, looked very much as Jack had wished Sophie to see it when she arrived.

At noon Babbington's men were regaled with roast beef and plum duff, and then packed, reasonably sober, into two waggons to take the *Tartarus* to sea on the evening tide; and now Jack was leading Sophie about the wood beyond the shrubbery to show her the improvements he had in mind.

'This is the path that Stephen calls the boreen,' he observed. 'He has some very strange expressions, poor dear fellow. How I hope I did not offend him, by taking notice of his way of saying Cato: sometimes he is a little touchy.'

Stephen had driven in to Portsmouth on Sunday to hear Mass in a Romish chapel there, and he had not reappeared, only sending Padeen back with a message to the effect that he found himself obliged to go to London and begged to be excused.

'I am sure you did not, my dear,' said Sophie. She was morally certain that Stephen found her deeply affectionate sympathy more painful than any other, and she was wondering how this could be phrased or indeed whether it could be said at all when they saw Killick hurrying towards them from the house.

Killick was perfectly used to having the Captain pursued for debt and to foiling the bums, and there was a concerned, intelligent, knowing look on his face that instantly brought some of these episodes to mind.

'Is it the bailiffs?' asked Jack.

'It is a rum cully, sir,' said Killick, 'more like a gent. And sir,' he said in a low, anxious voice behind his hand, 'it's no good tipping them the go-by. There's a party of heavyweight coves each end of the lane and behind, and they look precious like Bow Street runners.'

'I will deal with him,' said Jack, smiling, and he walked into the house. There he found a calm, self-possessed man with a folded paper in his hand. 'Good day, sir,' he said. 'I am Captain Aubrey. What may I do for you?'

'Good day to you, sir,' replied the man. 'Might we step into a private room? I have been sent from London on a matter that affects you most particularly.'

'Very well,' said Jack, opening a door. 'Please to mind the paint-work. Now, sir, what is this matter you are speaking about?'

'I am concerned to say that it is a warrant for your arrest.'

'The Devil it is! At whose suit?'

'It is not an arrest for debt, sir. It is an arrest by warrant.'

'On what charge?' asked Jack, amazed.

'Conspiracy to defraud the Stock Exchange.'

'Oh, is that all?' said Jack with great relief. 'Good Lord, I can very easily explain my dealings with them.'

'I am sure you can, sir. But in the meanwhile I must ask you to come with me. I trust you will not make my duty more unpleasant than it has to be — I trust you will not oblige me to place a gentleman of your quality under restraint. If you will give me your word not to attempt an escape, I will delay the execution of this warrant for half

an hour so that you may make your arrangements. But then we must set off for London:
I have a carriage waiting at the door.'

CHAPTER SEVEN

'I wish I had better news for your return,' said Sir Joseph, 'but at times one's friends are sadly disappointing.'

'At others, however, they exert themselves to a degree that even the most sanguine could never expect,' said Stephen.

'Not at all, not at all,' said Sir Joseph, smiling and waving his hand. 'Yet the fact of the matter is that Holroyd will not appear for Captain Aubrey. I regret it extremely, for Holroyd is one of the few counsel who are well with Lord Quinborough, who is to conduct the trial: Quinborough would not bully him, as he bullies so many counsel, and he might even treat his client decently. Furthermore, Holroyd has an excellent way with a jury — everybody says he is the very man for the case. His refusal vexes me, I must admit, for I had not thought he could refuse my direct request, he being under some obligation to me. Indeed, he looked both shabby and mean when he said that he was not master of his time — that with the trial being hurried on so soon he could not do the defendant justice, being deeply engaged, and a variety of other shuffling excuses.'

'They did not convince you, I collect.'

'No, they did not; and until the afternoon I could not understand why he was making them. But then I dined at the Colebrooks', where I heard that one of the judges had died unexpectedly and that the choice of his successor was in the balance, with Holroyd and a couple of others as the most likely candidates. Since the ministry has set this whole unusually rapid and zealous prosecution on foot with the sole intention of damaging the Radical opposition — of destroying General Aubrey and his friends — Holroyd does not wish to indispose the Chancellor by appearing as the champion of the General's son at this decisive moment. Nor does he wish to indispose Lord Quinborough, who is as furiously anti-Radical as the Chancellor and who is also a member of the Cabinet: it is odd that a judge should be a member of the Cabinet.'

'Jack Aubrey is so far from being a Radical that he hates the name of even a moderate Whig,' said Stephen, who did not give a curse for the composition of the Cabinet. 'When he thinks of politics at all, which may happen twice a year, he is a high Tory.'

'But he can be shown to be the son of a Radical — a damned noisy Radical too, perpetually on his feet in the House, denouncing the ministry — the son of a Radical and at least in this instance the associate of Radicals: so it makes little odds what he may say once or twice a year.'

'Is there any news of the General?'

'He is said to have gone to ground in Scotland, but there is no certainty about it. Some people say he has shaved and hidden himself among the Repentant Magdalenes at Clapham.'

'Do not his parliamentary privileges cover him?'

'I know they cover practically everything except treason and felony, and I do not imagine rigging the market amounts to either; but I dare say he means to make assurance double sure, to lie low, risk nothing, and rely on his son and his friends to take all the blame. He is a horrible old man, you know.'

'I have met General Aubrey.'

'To go back to Holroyd: he did produce one piece of advice. Since the entire defence lies in identifying the man in the post-chaise who started the lie, he said we should apply to an independent thief-taker and he gave me the name of a man who had been useful to him in several cases, the best of his kind in London, often employed by the insurance companies. Since time presses, I took it upon myself to set him at work directly, although his fees are a guinea a day and coach-hire, and I have him in the kitchen at this moment. You would not object to seeing him?'

'Faith,' said Stephen, 'I have hob-nobbed with the hangman for the sake of an interesting corpse before this, and I am certainly not going to jib at a thief-taker.'

The thief-taker, whose name was Pratt, looked like a discreet tradesman of the middle sort, or possibly a lawyer's clerk; he was conscious of the general dislike for his calling, so close to that of the common informer, and he stood diffidently until he was asked to sit down. Sir Joseph told him that this gentleman was Captain Aubrey's particular friend, Dr Maturin, who had been obliged to attend a patient in the country: Pratt might speak quite openly in his presence.

'Well, sir,' said Pratt, 'I wish I had better news for you; I am morally certain how the case lies, but so far I have nothing that will stand up in a court of law. Of course the whole thing is a put-up job, as we say: that was clear from the moment I saw the Captain. Yet even so I made the necessary checks: I found there was no parliamentary draftsman by the name of Ellis Palmer or anything like it, nor any member of the learned societies except a Mr Elliott Palmer who is close on eighty years of age and confined to his house by gout. So when I had satisfied myself in London I went down to Dover. At the Ship they remembered the Quaker and the flash cove and the row about the post-chaise, but nobody had taken much notice of Mr Palmer; they did not remember having seen him before and they could not give me any clear, reliable description. Howsomever, I had better luck at Sittingbourne, where they recalled how particular he had been about his wine and where the daughter of the house said there was something odd about him, because although he had only been there once he talked and behaved like a man who had known the place for years. Her description matched the Captain's — it is very important to have at least two versions — and I came back to town with some notion of the kind of man I should look for and the kind of place where I might find him — an educated chap — person, I mean — perhaps connected with the bar or even the Church, perhaps an unfrocked parson — likely to frequent the better gambling places — and I travelled back in a chaise with the same post-boy that had driven the Captain and Mr P, dropping the Captain at his club and Mr P in Butcher Row. That is just after Hollywell Street, sir, towards the City.' This aside was for Stephen, who reflected 'My clothes were made in London, my half-boots also; I have not uttered five words, and I am tolerably good at preserving an impassive countenance; yet this man has detected that I am not a native. Either I have been flattering myself these many years, or he is exceptionally acute.' 'And then, sir,' Pratt went on, now addressing himself more to Sir Joseph, 'the post-boy, having seen his fare walk off northwards up Bell Yard, wheeled his chaise down Temple Lane, called a street boy to water his horses in Fountain Court, and went back to the mutton-pie shop on the corner by Temple Bar, where the hackney-coaches stand: it is open all night. He was standing there with some of the drivers he knew, eating his second pie, when he saw Mr P on the other pavement, walking very tired with his little portmanteau and papercase. Mr P crossed

Fleet Street, coming from north to south, you follow me, sir, and hailed the first coach. The post-boy did not hear where he went, but the next day I found the driver, who remembered having taken a gentleman from Temple Bar to Lyon's Inn very early in the morning. Lyon's Inn.' Pratt's eye rested on Stephen for a moment, but Stephen happened to know that obscure, out-of-the-way series of courtyards, once the haunt of Chancery lawyers, and he said 'I believe Mr Pratt began by observing that we have nothing yet in the way of legal proof — that we are not approaching a crisis, but rather reviewing the present position — so perhaps I will retire for a moment.' He smiled apologetically at Sir Joseph, adding 'I travelled all night.'

'Of course, of course,' cried Blaine. 'You know the way.'

Stephen knew the way. He also knew that a lamp was kept perpetually burning in Sir Joseph's dim, book-lined privy: he took a cigar from his case, broke it in two, lit one half at the lamp (he was no hand with a tinder-box) and sat there drawing the smoke in deep. Somewhere far below him in the house he heard the grinding of a coffee-mill, no doubt fixed to the kitchen wall from the way the vibration travelled, and he smiled: the present tobacco and the prospective coffee soothed at least the very top of his mind, that part which had been so harassed by an exceptionally disagreeable night's journey in a lurching coach with drunken fellow-travellers. The rest of it could not so easily be relieved: he knew little of the English law, but he was almost certain that Jack Aubrey was undone; he was intensely anxious about his friend Martin, upon whom he had operated, perhaps too late, for a badly strangulated hernia and whom he had left comfortable but still in grave danger; and then he had had a particularly trying time with Sophie when he called in at Ashgrove Cottage. He was very deeply attached to her, and she to him; but in this instance her tears, her unconcealed distress and her need for support were something of a disappointment. Of course, exhaustion from her long journey and the sudden overthrow of her happiness accounted for a great deal, but it seemed to him that Diana, or at least his idealized Diana, would have shown more courage, more fortitude, more manliness. Diana might well have used foul language, but surely he would never have heard the faintest echo of Mrs Williams from her. And surely Diana, having failed to bribe or bamboozle those sent to arrest her husband, would have followed him with a change of stockings and a couple of clean shirts in spite of his direct command, instead of wringing her hands. For a while he twisted the knife in his wound, thinking of Diana as a tigress; then, after a final draught that made his head swim, he threw his hissing stump away and walked downstairs.

'Mr Pratt,' he said as they sat drinking their coffee, 'you began by saying that as soon as you saw Captain Aubrey you were convinced that all this was a put-up job. May I ask what led you to this conclusion? Did he produce irrefragable arguments that I am unacquainted with?'

'No, sir, it was not so much what he said as the way he said it. He was so amused at the idea anyone should think him capable of inventing such a rigmarole — he had never heard of a time-bargain or selling forward until Palmer explained — he was sure Palmer would turn up — such a good fellow, and an excellent judge of wine — they would have such a laugh when it was all over. In my calling, sir, I have heard a good many denials and explanations, but never one like that. It would get him nowhere with a jury at the end of a long trial, with him bewildered in a court-room and badgered by the prosecution and maybe the judge — certainly the judge in this case — but man to man in that two-pair front at the Marshalsea — why, as the Romans say, you would give him the blessed sacrament without confession. In my line you get a nose for these things, and I had not listened to him five minutes, no nor two, before I knew he was as innocent as a babe unborn. But dear me, gentlemen, lambs to the slaughter ain't in it: I have rarely seen the like.'

'I dare say you have had a great deal of experience, Mr Pratt?'

'Well, yes, sir, I think I may say I have had as much or even more than most. I was born in Newgate, do you see, where my father was a turnkey, so I grew up among thieves. Thieves and their children were my companions and playmates and I came to know them very well. Some few were right bastards, particularly among the informers; but not many. Then my father moved on to the Clink and after that the King's Bench, so I made a good many more friends among the thieves and such south of the river and the low attorneys and gaolers and constables and ward officers, and it all came in very useful after I set up on my own, after a spell with the Bow Street runners.'

'Aye,' said Stephen. 'I am sure it would.'

'Now, sir,' said Pratt, putting down his

cup, 'perhaps I had better be getting back to Lyon's Inn. I must admit I thought I had run my man to earth, for although a great many people live there now, particularly in the back court, which is a regular warren, there could not be many that would match my description. He had to be about five foot seven, lean, bob-wig or his own hair powdered, fifty or thereabouts, a sharp of course.'

'What do you mean by a sharp?'

'I am sorry to talk low, sir: it is a cant word we use to mean a dishonest person. They reckon you are a flat if you don't snap up whatever offers: the world is divided into the sharps and the flats. Mr P was a sharp of course, because nobody but a sharp would have tried to conceal his tracks like that; and a genuine nob, or gentleman by birth. He could never have had dinner with Captain Aubrey and talked to him all night if he had only been one of the swell mob, dressed up for the part, or the Captain would have seen through him, simple though he — that is to say, the Captain would have seen through him for sure. So I thought I had my man: but I was wrong. He did not live there. He was either spoiling the scent again, which I doubt, or he had just called in to rest or leave a message. It was a cruel blow, but I am carrying on, talking to maid-servants and street boys and ticket-porters and scavengers and the like, as well as my other connections — I am carrying on at the inn, trying to find out who he called on and so work back to him. And I am looking elsewhere too, among the genuine nobs known to my friends who might be that way inclined. But, gentlemen,' said Pratt, looking from one to another, 'now that my first bit of luck turned out not to be so lucky after all — now that I did not manage to take it first bounce — I should not like to make any great promises. This here caper is not the low toby, nor the high toby, but the very tip-top or what you might call the celestial toby: these jobs — and I have seen a few insurance frauds and one rigging of the market on something like the same scale, prepared very careful and damn the expense — are always run by gentlemen who have just one confidential agent as you might call him that hires the underlings, always at two or three removes, and sees to all the details. Always at two or three removes: if I was to pick up the Quaker and the flash cove, who certainly belong to the race-course mob, they would be no use to us — they would have no idea of the men who were behind the dummy that recruited them. The confidential agent is the only one who can peach on his principals, and they take good care he does not do so by having a hanging felony to hold over his head: or by some surer way, if things begin to go a little wrong.' Stephen and Sir Joseph exchanged a covert glance; the practice was not unknown in intelligence. 'And this chap looks after himself in much the same fashion all the way down the line. I shall go on looking for Mr Palmer, of course, and I may find him; but even if I do, I doubt we shall learn anything about the men at the head of the affair.'

'From our point of view,' said Stephen, 'it is the finding of Palmer that is essential: and with the case coming on so soon, he must be found quickly. Listen, Mr Pratt, have you any reliable colleagues who could work with you, to save time? I will gladly pay them whatever fee you think right, and double yours, if we may have a word with Mr Palmer before the trial.'

'Why, sir, as to colleagues . . .' Pratt hesitated, rasping his bony jaw. 'Of course, it would save a mort of time, having Bill work south of the river,' he muttered, and aloud he said 'There is only Bill Hemmings and his brother I could work with really cordial. They were both at Bow Street with me. I will have a word with them and let you know.'

'Do that, if you please, Mr Pratt, and pray waste not a minute: there is not a moment to be lost. And remember, you may commit me to a handsome fee. Do not let a few score guineas stand in the way.'

'My dear Maturin,' said Blaine, when Pratt had left them, 'allow me to observe that if you make bargains like that, you will never be a rich man. It is fairly begging Bill Hemmings to fleece you.'

'It was thoughtless, sure,' said Stephen: then, with a wan smile, 'But as for never being a rich man, why, my dear Blaine, I am one already. My godfather made me his heir, God rest his soul. I never knew there was so much money in the world, so much money, that is to say, in a private person's hands. But this is between ourselves, I would not have it generally known.'

'When you speak of your godfather, I presume you refer to Don Ramón.'

'Don Ramón himself, bless him,' said Stephen. 'You will not mention it, however.'

'Of course not. An appearance of decent mediocrity is better by far — infinitely wiser from every point of view. But in this strict privacy, let me give you joy of your fortune.' They shook hands, and Sir Joseph said, 'If I do not mistake, Don Ramón must have been one of the richest men in Spain: perhaps you will endow a chair of comparative osteology.'

'I might too,' said Stephen. 'My thoughts have turned that way, when they have had time to turn at all.'

'Speaking of wealth,' said Sir Joseph, 'come into my study and see what Banks has sent me.' He led the way, opening the door with caution, for the entire room was crammed with case after case of botanical, entomological and mineral specimens, all balanced in tottering piles.

'God love us,' cried Stephen, seizing the dried skin of a Surinam toad, 'what splendour!'

'The beetles are beyond anything,' said Sir Joseph. 'I spent such a happy morning with them.'

'Where did all these beautiful things come from?'

'They are the collections made for the Jardin des Plantes by a number of agents, and they had reached the Channel before *Swiftsure* snapped them up: Admiralty passed them on to the Royal Society, and Banks is sending them to Cuvier by the next cartel, as he always does in these cases. He has just let me have the sight of them before they are packed.'

'If the gentlemen would like to eat their

dinner while it is hot,' said Sir Joseph's housekeeper in a carefully restrained voice, 'perhaps they will come now.'

'Heavens, Mrs Barlow,' said Sir Joseph, peering at the clock behind a heap of preserved serpents, 'I am afraid we are late.'

'Could we not eat it in our hand?' asked Stephen. 'Like a sandwich?'

'No, sir, you could not,' said Mrs Barlow. 'A soufflé is not a sandwich. Though it may be very like a pancake if you do not come directly.'

'People say unkind things about Lord Sandwich,' observed Stephen as they sat down, 'but I think mankind is very much in his debt for that genial invention: and in any event he was an excellent good friend to Banks.'

'People say unkind things about Banks, too. They say he is a tyrannical president of the Royal Society — that he does not esteem the mathematics as he should — everything for botany — would botanize on his mother's grave. Some of this is perhaps jealousy of his wealth, and certain it is that he can go off on expeditions that few other men could afford, employing capital artists to figure his discoveries and engraving them without regard for the expense.'

'Is he indeed very wealthy?'

'Oh dear me yes. When he inherited Revesby and the other estates, they brought in six thousand a year: wheat was just under a guinea a quarter in those days and now it is close on six pounds, so that even with income tax I dare say he was thirty thousand clear.'

'No more? Well, well. But I dare say a man can rub along on thirty thousand a year.'

'You may say what you like, Dr Croesus, but even this trifle gives him a weight and consequence that some people resent.' Sir Joseph refilled Stephen's glass, ate a large piece of pudding, and then, with a benevolent look, he said 'Tell me, Maturin, do you find wealth affect you?'

'When I remember it I do: and I find its effects almost entirely discreditable. I feel better than other men, superior to them, richer in every way — richer in wisdom, virtue, worth, knowledge, intelligence, understanding, common sense, in everything except perhaps beauty, God help us. In such a fit I might easily patronize Sir Joseph Banks: or Newton, if he happened to be at hand. But fortunately I do not often remember it, and when I do I rarely believe it entirely: penurious habits die hard, and I do not suppose I shall ever be such a heavy swell as those who were born to riches and who are wholly convinced both of their wealth and their merit.'

'Allow me to help you to a little more pudding.'

'With all my heart,' said Stephen, holding out his plate. 'How I wish Jack Aubrey were here: he takes a truly sinful pleasure in pudding, above all in this one. Would you think me very rude if I were to beg leave to carry mine into your study? I must be at the Marshalsea before six, and I should be very sorry not to see more of Cuvier's treasures before they are packed up. By the way, do you know where the Marshalsea is?'

'Oh yes. It is south of the river, on the Surrey side. The easiest way is to cross by London Bridge, carry on right down the Borough to Blackman Street, and then still on until you reach Dirty Lane, which is the fourth turning on your right hand. You cannot miss it.'

He repeated his direction and his remark at their parting; but he had mistaken his man. As Stephen had observed, penurious habits die hard, and instead of taking a chair or a coach he walked: when he arrived at the Surrey side he was unhappily inspired to ask the way to Dirty Lane rather than the perfectly obvious Marshalsea. A kindly native told him, and even set him on his way, assuring him that he should reach Dirty Lane if he followed his nose for another two minutes, no more: two minutes by the clock. So he did, too; but it was the wrong Dirty Lane, there being at least two in Southwark, and from this point he hurried along empty streets inhabited by strangers, often looking at his watch and proceeding at a gasping half-trot until he came to Melancholy Walk, where another, even kindlier native, speaking a dialect of which Stephen could catch only one word in three, told him that he was going directly away from the Marshalsea, that if he carried on in that direction he would eventually reach Lambeth and then Americay, that he had no doubt been taking the air in the Liberties, which included these here St George's Fields — pointing to a stretch of scrofulous earth with sparse weeds standing in it here and there — and had grown confused in his intellects; that he certainly wanted to get back to his kip before lock-up, and he had best be led there the quickest way, rather than be left to wander in the dusk 'for there were a great many forking thieves about in those parts, and a single gent might never be seen again: pork pies were assured of a ready sale in the Marshalsea and the King's Bench prison, no great way off; and the cost of the pastry was trifling, given the vicinity of the flour wharves down the way.'

In the event Stephen was only a few minutes late, and a number of small fees, amounting to no more than three times the coach-hire, brought him through the debtors' side to what might be considered the true heart of the prison, the building in which the sailors were confined: for the Marshalsea had always been the Navy's prison, and here those who escaped hanging for striking their superiors served their sentence, together with officers who had run their ship aground for want of attention, those whose accounts were hopelessly entangled and deficient, those who had been detected taking things from prizes before those prizes were legally condemned, those who had been fined for a number of offences and who could not pay, some who had run mad, and some who were guilty of contempt of any admiralty or vice-admiralty court, of the Lord Steward or of any such officers of the Board of Green Cloth as the Coroner of the Verge.

Captain Aubrey, therefore, though not perhaps in quite the company he would have chosen, was at least in nautical surroundings. Strong sea-going voices echoed from the narrow court below, where a party of officers were playing skittles, watched and encouraged by Killick from a little square window, only just large enough for his head, and Jack was obliged to call out quite loud to make himself heard. 'Killick, Killick, there. Bear a hand, bear a hand — there is someone at the door.' Captain Aubrey, being for the moment well supplied with money, had hired two rooms, and this being so, the turnkey knocked at the outer door, instead of walking straight in.

'Why, if it ain't the Doctor,' cried Killick, his face changing from the mean, pinched, suspicious expression it always wore when in contact with the law, to open pleasure. 'We have a surprise for you, sir.'

Mrs Aubrey was the surprise, and she ran out of the inner room dusting flour from her hands, wearing an apron, and looking more like a happy, rosy girl than was reasonable in a mother of three. She kissed him on both cheeks, stooping to do so, and with a particular look, a blush, and a squeeze of his hand conveyed to him that she was much ashamed of her recent weakness, that she should never behave so again, and that he was not to hold it against her.

'Come in, come in,' called Jack through the door. 'How glad I am to see you, Stephen; I was beginning to think you might be lost. Forgive me for not getting up: I dare not trust these to any hand but my own.' He was toasting sausages on a long fork made of twisted wire at a small, bright-glowing hearth. 'We shall be shipshape by Monday, I hope,' he went on, 'but at present we are a little on the primitive side.'

As far as Stephen could see they were tolerably shipshape already. The bare little rooms had been sanded and scrubbed; various neat lockers economized space; a complication of white cordage in the corner showed that a hanging chair, that most comfortable of seats, was being made; and hammocks lashed up with seven perfectly even turns and covered with a rug formed a not inelegant sofa. Jack Aubrey had spent most of his naval life in quarters very much more confined than this; he had also a good deal of experience of French and American prisons, to say nothing of English sponging houses, and it would have been a hard gaol indeed that found him at a loss. 'These are from a local man,' he said, turning the sausages on their fork, 'and they are famous. So are his pork pies: should you like a slice? It is already cut.'

'I believe not, thank you,' said Stephen, looking intently at the contents of the pie. 'I dined not long ago with a friend.'

'But tell me, Stephen,' said Jack in a much graver tone, 'how did you leave poor Martin?'

'I left him comfortable and in good hands — his bride to be is a most devoted nurse and he is attended by an intelligent apothecary — but I long for news of him: they have promised to send an express daily.'

They talked of Martin and their voyages together while Sophie went on with her apple tart. She was not a distinguished cook, but apple tart was one of the dishes she had succeeded with a little more often than not, and now, since Stephen was to sup with them, she decorated it with pastry shamrock leaves.

'If you please, sir,' said Killick, interrupting them, 'the young gentleman from the lawyers.'

Jack went into the next room, and returning some minutes later he said 'That was to tell me they have retained a Mr Lawrence. It was announced as a great piece of good news, and the young fellow seemed quite dashed when I did not cry out with delight. It appears that Mr Lawrence is a very clever lawyer indeed, and I suppose I should be glad; but upon my word I cannot see that I want a lawyer at all. We get along very well without counsel at courts-martial. And there are certainly no counsel present when defaulters are called to the quarterdeck and the grating is rigged; yet I believe justice is done. This affair is nothing like those miserable cases to do with the Ashgrove lead-mines, with innumerable obscure points of disputed contract and liability and interpretation that have to be dealt with by specialists; no, no, this is much more like a naval matter, and what I should like is simply to have my say, like a man called before his captain, and tell the judge and jury just what happened. Everyone agrees that there is nothing fairer than English justice, and if I tell them the plain truth I am sure I shall be believed. I shall say that I never conspired with anyone, and that if I followed Palmer's tip I did so with a perfectly innocent mind, as one might have followed a tip for the Derby. If that was wrong, I am perfectly willing to cancel all my time-bargains; but I have always understood that guilty intent was the essence of any crime. And if they confront me with any man who says that what I say is not true, why then, the court must decide which of us is to be believed — which is the more trustworthy — and I have not much fear of that. I have every confidence in the justice of my country,' said Jack, smiling at the pompous sound of his words.

'Have you ever been present at a trial?' asked Stephen.

'Courts-martial by the score, but never a civilian trial. All mine have taken place when I was away at sea.'

'I have listened to some, alas,' said Stephen, 'and I do assure you, brother, that the rules of the game, what constitutes evidence, the exits and entrances, and who is allowed to speak when, and what he may say, are infinitely more complex than they are in naval law. It is a game that has been going on for hundreds and hundreds of years, growing more tortuous with every generation, the rules multiplying, the precedents accumulating, equity interfering, statutes galore, and now it is such a black bitter tangle that a layman is perfectly helpless. I do beg you will attend to this eminent counsellor, and follow his advice.'

'Pray do, sweetheart,' said Sophie.

'Very well,' said Jack. 'I dare say the case needs one, just as sometimes a ship needs a pilot for what seems the simplest harbour.'

This was most decidedly Mr Lawrence's opinion. He was a tall, dark man who not only looked and sounded very well in court but who also had a reputation for defending his clients with the most dogged tenacity, rather as some medical men fight tooth and

337

nail for their patients' lives, making a great personal point of it. He was not one to stand on his dignity nor on legal etiquette and after the first meeting in his chambers with Jack's solicitors he often saw Stephen informally, all the more so since they took to one another at once. They had both been to Trinity College in Dublin, and although they had scarcely met there they had many acquaintances in common; they were both ardent champions of Catholic emancipation; and they both detested Lord Liverpool and most of his Cabinet colleagues. 'I do not think the ministry set this matter on foot,' said Lawrence. 'That would be too gross even for Sidmouth's myrmidons; but I am quite sure that they mean to take every possible advantage of the situation now that it has arisen, and I must tell you that if this Palmer is not produced — physically produced and identified as the man in the chaise, I mean, whether he denies the whole affair or not — then I fear for your friend.'

'For some time now we have had Pratt searching for him, as I told you,' said Stephen. 'And now there are several others. On Monday morning a man who had lost money to me at cards long ago sent me a draft on his banker, which pleased me, and on Monday afternoon I had an express from the country, telling me that a friend upon whom I had operated was quite recovered, was quite out of danger — a valued friend. So by way of a thank-offering I have put up this unexpected sum as a reward for the discovery of the man in the chaise.'

'A considerable sum, I collect, from your reference to several men?'

'I should be ashamed to tell you how much. We played piquet day after day in Malta, and throughout the whole period the law of averages was suspended in my favour; if he had a septieme I had a huitième, and so it went for the dear knows how many tedious sessions. He could not win at all, the creature. I did not scruple to accept his draft, however; and I find it concentrates my searchers' minds to a wonderful degree. I am to see Pratt this afternoon.'

'How I hope he has good news for you. The eagerness of this prosecution — the steady refusal of bail, the hurrying forward of the case so that it shall be heard by a furious Tory, a member of the Cabinet — is something rare in my experience; and unless we have something solid to go upon it is hard to see any line of defence that can withstand their attack.'

Stephen was drinking his after-dinner

coffee at Fladong's when he saw Pratt come in: the man looked pale, drawn, tired and discouraged. 'Here is a chair, Mr Pratt,' said Stephen. 'What will you take?'

'Thank you, sir,' said Pratt, letting himself down heavily. 'If I might have a glass of gin and water, cold, that would be prime. I believe we have found our man.' But there was no exultation in his tone nor on his face — his was not a triumphant look — and Stephen called for the gin before saying 'Will you go on, now, Mr Pratt?'

'It was Bill Hemmings' friend Josiah. He was going over the river corpses with the Southwark coroner's man and he came across one that fitted my description — right for age, height, hair and build, dressed genteel, and had not been in the water above a dozen tides. But what fixed Josiah in his mind was that the coroner's man, name of Body, William Body, whose wife works at Guy's, had got hold of a paper, a little hand-bill passed about the hospitals and police-offices and so on asking for information for just such a gentleman — a Mr Paul Ogle, it said, that was likely to have been taken ill — and anyone who brought news of his where-abouts to N. Bartlet of 3, Back Court, Lyon's Inn, should be rewarded for his trouble. Lyon's Inn, sir.'

'Just so, Mr Pratt.'

'I hurried round to 3, Back Court, in course, and in course I drew a blank again. N. Bartlet was gone and nobody knew where she was gone to. She was a whore, sir, and she was in the flogging line: a quiet, plain woman, no longer young; had not been in the court long, and kept herself to herself, but was well liked; and it seems that Mr Ogle was her sweetheart. She was in a sad way about him.'

'What are the chances of finding her?'

Pratt shook his head. 'Even if she could be found she would deny everything — refuse to speak. Otherwise she knows very well they would serve her out the same way they served Ogle.'

'True enough,' said Stephen. 'She would never stand up and swear to him in court. But this does not apply to the post-boys or the people of the inn at Sittingbourne. The young woman there took a good look at the man's face. She could identify him, which would at least be something. You said he had not been long in the water, I believe?'

'No more he had, sir, not above a dozen tides,' said Pratt. 'But —' he hesitated, '— there ain't no face.'

'I see,' said Stephen. 'You are sure of your identification, however?'

'Yes, sir, I am. I went over at once and picked him out among two score without being told,' said Pratt. 'You get the knack of these things with practice: but that would not answer for the young woman at the inn, nor it would not stand up in a court of law.'

'Well,' said Stephen, 'I will come and look at your cadaver. Perhaps it has some physical peculiarities that might be useful: I am, after all, a medical man.'

'Although I am a medical man,' said Stephen to Lawrence, 'I have not often seen a more saddening, shocking spectacle than the cellar where the river-dead are kept. In hard times they get as many as twenty a week, and now, with the coroner away . . . I examined the body — the keeper was most civil and obliging — but until we turned it over I found no particular marks by which a man could be recognized. On the back, however, there were the traces of habitual flagellation, and this I found perfectly convincing.'

'Certainly,' said Lawrence. 'It certainly reinforces *our* conviction, but I am afraid it would be useless or even damaging as evidence, even if it were admissible. Had we been able to find the living man and had we been able to look into his antecedents then he would have been an invaluable witness, however hostile; but a faceless corpse, identified by no more than hearsay, no, it will not do. No: I shall have to fall back on other lines of defence. You have great influence with him, Maturin: could not you and Mrs Aubrey persuade him to incriminate the General? Even just a very little?'

'I could not.'

'I was afraid you would say that. When I approached the subject at the Marshalsea he did not take it at all well. I am not an exceptionally timid man, I believe, but I felt extremely uneasy when he stood up, about seven foot tall and swelling with anger. And yet, you know, it was quite certainly that grasping old man and his stock-jobbing friends who bought and bought and then industriously spread the rumour of peace; it was they who sold out at the top of the market, not Captain Aubrey; and his dealings were trifling, compared with theirs. Most of their transactions would have been made through outside dealers, who are not under the control of the Stock Exchange committee, and they cannot be traced, but intelligent men in the City tell me they probably moved more than a million of money in the Funds alone. Captain Aubrey's business, on the other hand, was mostly conducted by regular brokers, and the committee have all the details.'

'In these matters he is not to be led,' said Stephen. 'Then again, he has a very high notion of English justice, and is persuaded that he has but to tell a plain, unvarnished, wholly truthful tale for the jury to acquit him. He has a reverence for judges, as part of the established order almost on a par with the Royal Navy or the Brigade of Guards or even perhaps the Anglican church.'

'But surely he has had some experience of the law, has he not?'

'Only of the interminable Chancery cases that you know about, and for him they do not represent the real law at all, but only the technical warfare of pettifogging attorneys. For him the law is something much simpler and more direct — the wise, impartial judge, the jury of decent, fair-minded men, with perhaps a few barristers to speak for the inarticulate and ask questions designed to bring out the truth, probing questions that he will be happy to answer.'

'Yes, so I had gathered. But he must know that he will not be allowed to speak — his solicitors must have told him the nature of a Guildhall trial?'

'He says it is all one. As an officer speaks up for a tongue-tied foremast hand, so counsel will speak for him: but he will be there — the judge and jury can look at him, and if counsel strays off course he can pull him up. He says he has every confidence in the justice of his country.'

'It would be a friendly act to bring him to a more earthly, mundane view of things. For I must tell you, Maturin, that with no Palmer I really fear for Captain Aubrey.'

'I have not had much more experience of these matters than Jack Aubrey. Tell me, now, how should I best blackguard the law?'

'You could not truthfully blackguard the law, which is the best law that any nation was ever blessed with,' said Lawrence, 'but you might point out that it is administered by human beings. Some of them, indeed, can scarcely claim so high a rank. You might remind him of the number of Lord Chancellors who have been dismissed for bribery and corruption; you might speak of notoriously political, cruel, and oppressive judges, like Jeffries or Page or I am sorry to say Lord Quinborough; and you might tell him that although the English bar shines in comparison with all others, it has some members who are perfectly unscrupulous, able and unscrupulous: they go for the verdict, and be damned to the means. Pearce, who leads for the prosecution, is just such a man. He gained a great reputation as a Treasury devil and now he has a most enviable practice. A very clever fellow indeed, quick to take advantage of every turn in a case, and when I contemplate my bout with him, Quinborough keeping the ring, why, I feel less sanguine than I could wish. And if the rumours of one of General Aubrey's stock-jobbing friends turning King's evidence are true, I do not feel sanguine at all.'

'I am concerned to hear it. May I ask what you consider the best line of defence?'

'If Captain Aubrey cannot be induced to incriminate the General, then I shall be reduced to abusing Pearce, discrediting his witnesses as much as possible, and playing on the feelings of the jury. I shall of course speak at length about Aubrey's distinguished record: no doubt he has been wounded?'

'Myself I have treated — let me see — oh, the dear knows how many sword-thrusts, bullet-wounds, great gashes made by flying splinters, and blows from falling blocks. Once I was within an ace of taking off his arm.'

'That will be useful. And I have no doubt that Mrs Aubrey will attend, looking beautiful. But the trouble is, a Guildhall jury is made up of City men, and broadly speaking, money is far more important in the City than sentiment, let alone patriotism; and then again, if I am compelled to call any witnesses — I shall try to avoid it, but witnesses may be forced upon me — then Pearce will have the right of reply, and he will have the last word with the jury. And whether or no, Lord Quinborough will of course sum up, probably at great and vehement length, and these merchants will retire with the impression of his words rather than mine. I dread the result. Pray do make this clear to Captain Aubrey: he will attend to you, as a friend for whom he has a great respect. And pray let him know that Pearce will rake up anything and everything that may be to his disadvantage, anything that may lower him and through him his friends and connexions, and that the prosecution will have all the resources at the ministry's command to help in the raking. Aubrey's name will be dragged in the mud. And it is most unfortunate that the man charged with him, the only important alleged conspirator who has not disappeared or whose dealings were not hidden ten deep behind men of straw, Cummings —'

One of the General's guests at Button's on that unhappy evening?'

'Yes, the buffoon Cummings: he has a

past made up of dubious joint-stock companies, fraudulent bankruptcy and many other
things, and of course this will come out,
spattering all his associates. Captain Aubrey
is in deep water, and his confidence is mis-
placed.'

'If the worst comes to the worst, what is
likely to happen to him?'

'A heavy fine for certain: perhaps the pillory, perhaps imprisonment. Perhaps both.'

'The pillory? Do you tell me so? The pillory for a naval officer?'

'Yes sir. It is quite a usual punishment in
the City for fraudulent dealings and so on.
And of course he would be dismissed the
service.'

'God between us and evil,' said Stephen.
He was moved beyond his usual calm and he
did not recover even the appearance of it
until he was walking up the steps of his
club.

'I am sorry to be late, Blaine,' he said, 'but
my interview with Lawrence lasted longer
than I had expected, and it was far, far more
distressing. Now that Palmer cannot possibly be brought forward, Lawrence has no
hope. He did not say so directly, but it was
evident. He has no real hope at all.'

'I do not suppose he has,' said Sir Joseph.
'Appearances are so very much against poor

Aubrey. If his worst enemy had contrived this scheme he could not have done him more harm.'

'You too think he will be condemned?'

'I should not go so far as that. But this is a political trial, with all the furious passion that implies: it is aimed against General Aubrey and his Radical friends, and so long as their reputations are blasted the rest does not signify. The end justifies the means in these matters. How Sidmouth and his people must have welcomed such an opportunity! Indeed, I am sometimes tempted to wonder whether some zealous follower may not have engineered it, anticipating their wishes and perhaps at the same time meaning to enrich himself. It is a specious theory, though I do not believe it.'

There was a silence, during which Stephen looked at the carpet and Sir Joseph contemplated his friend, whom he had never seen so perturbed.

'As I was coming here,' said Stephen at last, 'I reflected on what I should do in the event of a condemnation. Jack Aubrey, dismissed the service, would go stark mad on land; and I have no great wish to stay in England either. I therefore think of buying the *Surprise*, since Jack will no longer have the means of doing so, taking out letters of marque, manning her as a privateer and desiring him to take command. May I beg you to reflect upon this and give me your considered opinion tomorrow?'

'Certainly. On the face of it, I should say it is an excellent scheme. Several unemployed naval officers have turned privateer, continuing their war independently and sometimes causing havoc among the enemy's trade at great profit to themselves. You are away?'

'I must go to the Marshalsea: I am already late.'

'You must take a hackney-coach,' said Blaine, looking beyond Stephen at the clock. 'You must certainly take a hackney-coach, though even then you will have very little time before the gates are locked.'

'It is all one — there are beds to be had in the coffee-house on the debtors' side. God bless, now.'

'I shall tell Charles to fetch a coach,' Sir Joseph called after him as he ran up the stairs to his room.

The coach, an unusually rapid vehicle, took him the shortest way, by Westminster Bridge; but when it set him down at the gates of the prison the man said, 'Just five minutes to go before the lock is on. Should you like me to wait, sir?'

'Thank you,' said Stephen, 'but I believe I

shall stay the night.' And to himself 'God help me — I am far behind my hour — I shall be reproved.'

In the event, however, Jack was playing such an energetic, hard-fought game of fives in the courtyard that he had lost count of the time, and when the last point was over he turned his scarlet, streaming, beaming face to Stephen and said in a gasping voice, 'How glad I am to see you, Stephen,' without a hint of blame. 'Lord, I am out of form.'

'You were always grossly obese,' observed Stephen. 'Were you to walk ten miles a day, and eat half what you do in fact devour, with no butcher's meat and no malt liquors, you would be able to play at the hand-ball like a Christian rather than a galvanized manatee, or dugong. Mr Goodridge, how do you so, sir? I hope I see you well.' This to Jack's opponent, a former shipmate, the master of HMS *Polychrest* and a fine navigator, but one whose calculations had unfortunately convinced him that phoenixes and comets were one and the same thing — that the appearance of a phoenix, reported in the chronicles, was in fact the return of one or another of the various comets whose periods were either known or conjectured. He resented disagreement, and although in ordinary matters he was the kindest, gentlest of men, he was now confined for maltreating a rear-admiral of the blue: he had not actually struck Sir James, but he had bitten his remonstrating finger.

Upstairs, when Jack had changed his shirt and they were sitting by the fire, Stephen said 'Did I tell you of Lord Sheffield, Jack?'

'I believe you have mentioned him. In connexion with Gibbon, if I don't mistake.'

'The very man. He was Gibbon's particular friend. He inherited many of his papers, and he has passed me a very curious sheet expressing Gibbon's considered opinion of lawyers. It was intended to form part of the *Decline and Fall*, but it was withdrawn at a late stage of page-proof for fear of giving offence to his friends at the bar and on the bench. Will I read them to you?'

'If you please,' said Jack, and Sophie folded her hands in her lap, looking attentive.

Stephen drew a sheaf from his bosom: he unfolded it; his expression, formed for reading the grave, noble, rolling periods, changed to one of ordinary vexation, quite intense and human vexation. 'I have brought Huber on Bees,' he said. 'In my hurry I seized upon Huber. Yet I could have sworn that what lay there on the right of the pamphlets was Gibbon. How sorry I shall be if I have thrown Gibbon away, the rarity of the world and a jewel of balanced prose, taking him for a foolish little piece on Tar Water. And I did not commit much of it to memory. However, the gist of it was that the decline of the Empire —'

'There is the bell,' cried Sophie as a remote but insistent clangour reached them. 'Killick, Killick! We must go. Forgive me, Stephen dear.' She kissed them both, a rapid though most affectionate peck, and darted from the room, still calling 'Killick, Killick, there.'

'She and Killick are going down by the evening coach, so they must not be locked in,' said Jack. 'She wants to fetch some things from Ashgrove.'

'As for Gibbon, now,' said Stephen when they were settled by the fire again, 'I do remember the first lines. They ran "It is dangerous to entrust the conduct of nations to men who have learned from their profession to consider reason as the instrument of dispute, and to interpret the laws according to the dictates of private interest; and the mischief has been felt, even in countries where the practice of the bar may deserve to be considered as a liberal occupation." He thought — and he was a very intelligent

man, of prodigious reading — that the fall of
the Empire was caused at least in part by the
prevalence of lawyers. Men who are accustomed over a long series of years to supposing that whatever can somehow be
squared with the law is right — or if not
right then allowable — are not useful members of society; and when they reach positions of power in the state they are noxious.
They are people for whom ethics can be
summed up by the collected statutes. Tully,
for example, thought himself a good man,
though he openly boasted of having deceived the jury in the case of Cluentius; and
he was quite as willing to defend Catiline in
the first place as he was to attack him in the
second. It is all of a piece throughout: they
are men who tend to resign their own conscience to another's keeping, or to disregard it entirely. To the question "What are
your sentiments when you are asked to defend a man you know to be guilty?" many
will reply "I do not *know* him to be guilty
until the judge, who has heard both sides,
states that he is guilty." This miserable
sophistry, which disregards not only episte-
mology but also the intuitive perception
that informs all daily intercourse, is sometimes merely formular, yet I have known
men who have so prostituted their intelli-

gence that they believe it.'

'Oh come, Stephen. Surely saying that all lawyers are bad is about as wise as saying that all sailors are good, ain't it?'

'I do not say that all lawyers are bad, but I do maintain that the general tendency is bad: standing up in a court for whichever side has paid you, affecting warmth and conviction, and doing everything you can to win the case, whatever your private opinion may be, will soon dull any fine sense of honour. The mercenary soldier is not a valued creature, but at least he risks his life, whereas these men merely risk their next fee.'

'Certainly there are low attorneys and the like, that give the law a bad name, but I have met some very agreeable barristers, perfectly honourable men — several of the members of our club are at the bar. I do not know how it may be in Ireland or upon the Continent, but I think that upon the whole English lawyers are a perfectly honourable set of men. After all, everyone agrees that English justice is the best in the world.'

'The temptation is the same whatever the country: it is often to the lawyer's interest to make wrong seem right, and the more skilful he is the more often he succeeds. Judges are even more exposed to temptation, since they sit every day; though indeed it is a temptation of a different sort: they have enormous powers, and if they choose they may be cruel, oppressive, froward and perverse virtually without control — they may interrupt and bully, further their political views, and pervert the course of justice. I remember in India we met a Mr Law at the dinner the Company gave us, and the gentleman who made the introductions whispered me in a reverential tone that he was known as "the just judge". What an indictment of the bench, that one, one alone, among so many, should be so distinguished.'

'The judges are thought of as quite great men.'

'By those who do not know them. And not all judges, either. Think of Coke, who so cowardly attacked the defenceless Raleigh at his trial and who was dismissed when he was chief-justice; think of all the Lord Chancellors who have been turned away in contempt for corruption; think of the vile Judge Jeffries.'

'God's my life, Stephen, you are uncommon hard on lawyers. Surely there must be some good ones?'

'I dare say there are: I dare say there are some men who are immune to the debasing influence, just as there are some men who may walk about among those afflicted with the plague or indeed the present influenza without taking it; but I am not concerned with them. I am concerned with shaking your confidence in the perfect impartial justice of an English court of law, and to tell you that your judge and prosecutor are of the kind I have described. Lord Quinborough is a notoriously violent, overbearing, rude, ill-tempered man: he is also a member of the Cabinet, while your father and his friends are the most violent members of the opposition. Mr Pearce, who leads for the prosecution, is shrewd and clever, brilliant at cross-examination, much given to insulting witnesses so that they may lose their temper, conversant with every legal quirk and turn, a very quick-witted plausible scrub. I say all this so that you should not be quite certain that truth will prevail or that innocence is a certain shield, so that you should attend to Lawrence's advice, and so that you should at least allow him to hint that your father was something less than discreet.'

'Yes,' said Jack in a strong decided voice, 'you speak very much as a friend and I am most deeply beholden to you; but there is one thing you forget, and that is the jury. I do not know how it may be in Ireland or in foreign parts, but in England we have a jury: that is what makes our justice the best in the world. The lawyers may be as bad as you say, but it seems to me that if twelve ordinary men hear a plain truthful account they will believe it. And if by any wild chance they come down hard on me, why, I hope I can bear it. Tell me, Stephen, did you remember my fiddle-strings?'

'Oh, by my soul, Jack,' cried Stephen, clutching his pocket, 'I am afraid I forgot them entirely.'

CHAPTER EIGHT

For many years Stephen Maturin had kept a diary: but diary-writing was not really a suitable habit in an intelligence-agent, and although the code in which it was written had never yet been broken, the book had proved an embarrassment when he was taken prisoner by the Americans. Yet just as he had returned to opium when Diana disappeared from his life, so the returning urge to record, to communicate at least with his future self, overcame his scruples now and he indulged himself in the purchase of a comfortable green-bound quarto of blank pages that opened really flat; in this he confined himself to observations on medicine, natural philosophy and personal affairs, so that if by any remote chance the book should fall into an enemy's hands it would compromise no other agent or network but would rather tend to show that the writer had no concern with such matters. Yet what he did write was perfectly candid and sincere, being intended for his own eye alone; and it was written in the Catalan of his youth, as familiar to him as English and more so than the Irish of his childhood. Now, beginning a new page, he wrote 'I have committed two very grave and dangerous blunders these last days: God send I may not commit a third with this ship. The first was offering far too much money as a reward for Palmer. With such a sum at stake every thief-taker and writ-server and constable in London ran up and down day and night and of course word of it reached the principals, who at once knocked Palmer on the head, putting themselves out of danger and depriving Jack of his life-line. The second was my heavy-handed attempt at manipulating him. There has always been this difference of nationality between us and although it is nearly always far beneath the surface I fear I brought it up and well into sight by my foolish reiteration of *English* justice. He will not tolerate the least reflexion on his country, however justified, from a foreigner; and I am, after all, a foreigner. I should have known, from his tapping fingers and constrained expression, that he did not like the trend of my words, but I continued; and the only result is that he is now even more confirmed in his determination than he was before. I have not only done no good but I have done positive harm, and I dread the possibility of doing the same or even worse by buying the *Surprise*. However, in this case I do at least have the benefit of advising with an intelligent man who understands the matter through and through, with all its attendant circumstances, a man full of good will.'

He closed the book, looked at his watch, and nodded: five minutes to spare. He looked at his bottle of laudanum on the mantelshelf, a square pint-bottle from a spirit-case, and shook his head. 'Not until this evening,' he said: but the association of diary-writing (an evening occupation in general) and opium-taking was so strong that he turned back at the door, walked swiftly to his bedside table, took a wine-glass and filled it to the half-way mark from the square bottle. He drank the pleasant-smelling amber liquid in three small voluptuous gusts and walked downstairs as Sir Joseph came into the hall.

At this time of the afternoon there were few people in the club and they had the long front room commanding St James's Street entirely to themselves. 'Let us sit at the middle window and look down on mankind like a couple of Olympians,' said Blaine; and when they were settled, gazing out into the thin grey drizzle, he said, 'I have thought over your scheme, my dear Maturin, and on serious consideration I believe it to be a good one. I am making three assumptions: first, that you mean to buy the ship whatever the outcome of the trial: that is to say, whether she is needed for this purpose or not?'

'I do, too; for if Jack Aubrey is acquitted he will certainly take her off my hands, and if he is not, which God forbid, she represents at least a certain refuge. And then from a purely selfish point of view there are the great advantages that came into my mind when you were speaking of Sir Joseph Banks: I too should infinitely relish botanizing from a man-of-war, above all a man-of-war that I could persuade to stop if an important occasion demanded.'

'I say this because the sale is the day before the opening of the trial, and clearly you have to make your decision before you know the result. My second assumption is that in the present state of the department you do not contemplate any naval intelligence work.'

'None whatsoever. None until your confidence is restored: fully restored.'

'And lastly I am assuming that you have

the necessary funds in England, since ready money is always required in these transactions. If you have not . . .'

'I believe I have. Little do I know about the cost of buying and fitting-out a man-of-war, but there are three of these drafts on Threadneedle Street from the Bank of the Holy Ghost and of Commerce,' — passing one — 'and if they are not enough, why, more are to be had.'

'Heavens, Maturin,' said Sir Joseph, 'this alone would build, equip and man a new seventy-four, let alone buy a small old-fashioned frigate, third-hand and long past mark of mouth.'

'The *Surprise* sails with the most admirable celerity on a — with some particular arrangement of the bowlines; and one gets used to the smell and the want of space, the low ceilings and the confinement, downstairs.'

'She would make a splendid privateer; there are few merchantmen that could outrun or outgun her. But, you know, you must have letters of marque and reprisal — without them you are a mere pirate — and you must have letters against each particular state we are at war with. I had a friend who took a Dutchman at the beginning of the war, though he only had a commission against the French. A quick-witted King's ship met him, looked at his papers, seized his prize, and, height of misery, pressed half his men. However, I still have some influence in the remoter parts of the Admiralty, and you shall have letters against every nation under the sun this very afternoon. But as I was saying, the sale is fixed for the day before the beginning of the trial. How does that affect you?'

'Captain Pullings told me of it this morning. I have turned the matter over in my mind, and I think it better that I should go down. Travelling post I should be back early on the third day: Lawrence expects the trial to last three days. In principle he does not wish to call me as a witness — all my evidence about Aubrey's wounds is there in my official journals at the Sick and Hurt Office and on the tallies of my smart tickets — but if he should against all expectation need me, it would be on the third day. And I certainly have no wish to see Jack Aubrey baited, still less humiliated, in court. These are cases, I believe, when friends should be present only in the near-certainty of victory. Now reverting to Captain Pullings —'

'Thomas Pullings, Captain Aubrey's former first lieutenant, recently promoted commander?'

'Himself. Is he correct, will you tell me now, in supposing his chance of a ship is already very slight, and that if the decision goes against Jack Aubrey, then the chance will be slighter still?'

'I am afraid he is. A commander with no interest, identified with a post-captain who has, however unjustly, been disgraced, is almost certain to spend the rest of his life on shore, whatever his merits.'

'Then I need not scruple to accept his offer of accompanying me, seeing to the removal of the ship, and attending to her welfare?'

'No, you need not. What a very fortunate stroke, upon my word! I did have another man in the back of my mind to propose to you, since you would have to have a practical sailor upon the spot or be cheated right, left and centre, the ship pillaged, stripped of her copper and probably changed for a mud-scow. But Pullings would be far better, far better in every way.'

'Manning is another question that weighs upon my mind. Many captains of my acquaintance have gone to sea pitifully short-handed in spite of drafts from the receiving-ship, the activities of the impress-service and their own zealous press-gangs on land and sea. How then can we hope to find an adequate number of efficient mariners?'

'How indeed? It is a mystery to me, it is a mystery to those much more concerned with manning than myself; and yet the thing is done. Privateers are manned, and handsomely manned. By some obscure channel of communication or perhaps by instinct, the seamen, or many of them, become aware of the motions of those who mean to press them, and move secretly to small ports, where they join these private ships of war. There are between fifty and sixty thousand men belonging to them, probably the most intelligent of their amphibious kind, and I have no doubt that in the event of his needing them Captain Aubrey, lying in some discreet inlet, would have his pick. It is an interesting reflexion upon the civic sense, that its imperatives weaken according to the square of the distance from land, so that the mild fishermen of Dover, always willing to help the distressed merchantman, becomes the sea-wolf of the Caribbees, very like a pirate; and that he goes aboard a corsair knowing very well that this will happen.' Two members came in, sitting in the farther window-seat, and Sir Joseph said 'But these reflexions have occurred to you a dozen times. There is something else I wish to say to you, something far more interesting; and since the drizzle has stopped for the moment, we might take a turn in the Green Park. Have you stout shoes upon your feet? Charles will lend us an umbrella, in case the rain starts again.'

The rain did start again, and under that wonderfully private gentle drumming dome Sir Joseph said 'What I have to say is tentative and fragmentary and at present you have so much on your mind that I shall not trouble you with more than one or two observations. First I will remind you that when you first came back from the South Sea I told you that I smelt if not a rat behind the changes in our department then at least a mouse. But a true rat it was, Maturin; and it has grown to a monstrous size. What on the face of it was a commonplace though tolerably unscrupulous struggle for power and influence and patronage and a free hand with the secret-service money now seems to me and to some of my friends to have an air of treason. Not that the notion of fraud is absent: by no means. One of the obligations you recovered from the *Danaë* was proposed for negotiation in Stockholm a little while ago and then withdrawn. I will not go into the details, but it was a wonderful confirmation of my suspicions. Furthermore the transaction was attempted to be carried out in a way that eliminated you entirely.'

'So much the better.'

'I am glad of it too, because until that was wholly cleared up my friends could not go on to the next point: and by my friends I mean those gentlemen I have referred to before, who have to do with other intelligence-services. May I ask you how you would regard the independence of say Chile or Peru?'

'I should be wholly in favour of both. As you know, I have always looked upon the rule of the Castilian government in Catalonia as a tyranny only a little less odious than that of Buonaparte; and their record in South America is even worse — a heartless, stupid exploitation of the people and their countries, together with the most abhorrent form of slavery. The sooner the connexion is broken the better.'

'I thought you would say that. It is also the view of certain South American gentlemen — abolitionists, I may say — some of them of mixed Indian and Spanish blood, who are in London at present and who have approached the government for support.' They separated to avoid a puddle in the walk and when they came together again Sir Joseph said 'It will scarcely astonish you to learn that the administration would not be averse to seeing a number of independent countries in that part of the world, rather than a united and potentially dangerous empire. Obviously it could do nothing openly — could not possibly send a man-of-war to help any eventual insurgents, for example — but it might provide all kinds of discreet assistance — it might look with favour upon a wholly unofficial expedition. And although perhaps the time may not yet be quite ripe, it is not impossible that I may be asked to approach you on the subject. I perfectly see that it cannot arouse the same feelings in you as the independence of Catalonia; but when the proposition was floating in the air I reflected upon the opportunities — the wonderful combination of opportunities for a natural philosopher and, if I may say so, a natural liberator.'

'You are too kind by far. Though indeed, the opportunities would be very great, greater even than Humboldt's, and at any other time my heart would beat to quarters at the prospect; but just now . . .'

'Of course, of course. I meant only to make a vague general reference, to learn whether you would be opposed in principle or whether the two eventualities might possibly coincide. The rain is growing heavier. Shall we turn? In any event, we must dress within the next half hour, and it is very disagreeable, even dangerous, to pull on silk stockings over wet feet. They *must* have time to dry naturally; mere rubbing with a towel is never quite the same.'

'Why must I dress, for all love?'

'We are dining with Sir Joseph Banks in Soho Square, together with a dozen other gentlemen. Donovan will be there.'

'I shall rejoice of meeting Mr Donovan,' said Stephen, passing his hand over his forehead. As they parted he went on 'Will you indulge me in an indiscretion? The bill, now, that was attempted to be negotiated, sure it never came from the obvious source in the Admiralty?'

'No, no. Certainly not: I should have told you at once. Nathan has not yet traced all the stages of the proposition — for it was no more: the document never left England, and even the proposition was withdrawn, as though the proposer felt the risk too great. But a King's Messenger was concerned and it is clear that the initiative was taken by someone at a higher level and in a different ministry. I fear it will be exceedingly difficult to run the man to earth.'

Before leaving for his journey Stephen Maturin paid a last call on Lawrence, whom he found looking old, tired, and discontented. 'Really, Maturin,' he said, 'it is very difficult to help your friend. When I suggested that in view of the disagreeable nature of some of the evidence, he might prefer to stay away from the court, he at once replied, with a most offensively knowing expression, as though I could not be trusted to look after my client's interests, "that he preferred to see what was going on". It was all I could do not to take him up, and if we parted on civil terms, it was only because his lovely wife was there. Far lovelier than he deserves: and more intelligent.'

'You are to consider that I spent a considerable time undermining his confidence, not perhaps in the law, but in law-courts and lawyers.'

'But not in his own counsel, for Heaven's sake! That would be a criminal excess of zeal.' Lawrence turned aside and stifled a sneeze. 'Forgive me. Do you sometimes feel cursed snappish of a morning?'

'I feel cursed snappish on most mornings, but above all when I am sickening for a common cold, even more the Spanish influenza, God forbid. Will I feel your pulse, now?'

'No, no, I thank you. I passed by Paddy Quinn just now — he said it was nothing and gave me a bottle of physic. I had a late night — it is nothing.'

Stephen had no opinion of that vapouring quack, the cattle-thief Quinn, but a certain decency had to be preserved between physicians and he said no more.

Having blown his nose twice and searched among the papers on his desk, Lawrence asked, 'Who is this Mr Grant they mean to call? Mr Grant of the Navy?'

'He is an ancient lieutenant, superannuated by now I believe. Long ago he had some experience of the voyage to New Holland, or Australia, if you prefer, and so he was appointed to the *Leopard* when Jack Aubrey was ordered to take her there. But, however, on the way the horrible old *Leopard* struck a mountain of ice in the high southern latitudes: Mr Grant thought she would sink, and he went off with several like-minded men in a boat; Aubrey stayed with his ship, took her to a remote and I may add delectable island, repaired her and so carried her to her destination, our own Banks's well-named Botany Bay. Grant survived, but he was never promoted. This he attributes to Jack Aubrey's malignance, and he has written many scurrilous letters on the subject and even some pamphlets, accusing him of every kind of dishonesty. He is quite mad, poor man.'

'I see,' said Lawrence, and he made a note.

'You look grave.'

'Yes. Statements made against a man by his enemies always seem to have greater force than those made in favour by his friends; and God knows the prosecution seems to have scraped a great many together, and to have tampered with almost everyone who has ever met him. Surely it cannot be true that he is the father of a black Catholic priest?'

'The young man is not a priest. He is only in minor orders, and a bastard cannot go farther without a dispensation.'

'Exorcist or acolyte or priest, it is all one so long as he is a Papist. Imagine the effect on a rigidly Puritanical judge, who is at the same time a violent political opposer of Catholic emancipation and a slave-owner in the West Indies. Quinborough is a garrulous judge and he never spares the court his moral reflections on points of this kind: that is one of the things that I wanted to spare Aubrey when I suggested he should stay away.'

'Conceivably you mistake your man. From his jolly, rosy-gilled, well-fed appearance you would scarcely think so, but he is

in fact something of a Stoic. He admires fortitude beyond any other virtue and once he
is tied to the stake he feels he must go
through with it. But tell me, is it really possible that he should just absent himself from
court at his pleasure, without leave?'

'Why, of course it is. This is a Guildhall
trial.'

'No prisoner, and the sentence executed
upon a proxy, I dare say?'

'Surely Aubrey's solicitors must have
made it clear to the meanest understanding?
This is a misdemeanour removed into the
King's Bench, so naturally it has some anal-
ogies with civil proceedings and the defendants may appear by attorney rather than in
person. They only have to appear in person
some days after the verdict, to hear the sentence.'

'What could be more logical or evident?
You will not forget my shorthand report of
the proceedings, I beg?'

'I have already bespoken Tolland. What
now?' — this, testily, to a clerk.

'I ask pardon, sir,' said the clerk, holding
up a bottle and a spoon, 'but Dr Quinn said
every hour exactly.'

'May it profit you,' said Stephen, standing
up. 'There is also something to be said for
going to bed. You look destroyed entirely.'

'If I did not have to defend a wretched boy this afternoon I should certainly lie down. But he stole a five-guinea watch — caught in the act — and unless I can persuade the jury that it was worth less than twelve pence he will be sentenced to death. It is only the effects of a late night — it will pass off tomorrow. Besides, I have Quinn's draught.'

'Damn Quinn and his draught,' said Stephen to himself as his hackney-coach threaded through the heavy traffic in the Strand. 'If I could have given him a good comfortable dose of pulvis Doveri I should have felt no anxiety. Ten or even fifteen grains would have answered very well. Dover: Dr Thomas Dover: he too was a privateer's man. He sacked Guayaquil, if I do not mistake, which is no way for a medical man to behave; but then on the other hand he saved some two hundred of his men, and they stricken with the plague.' The top of his mind reflected upon that enterprising physician and corsair, while all the lower part turned the question of Jack's trial over and over again, with the same ignorant but boding anxiety.

At a wine-merchant's in St James's Street he sent a dozen of Hermitage to the Marshalsea, and at a grocer's in Piccadilly a great raised pie, a Stilton cheese, and some potted anchovies for relish; then he picked up Pullings at Fladong's and they drove to the Cross Keys, where a carriage had been booked.

'This is travelling in style,' said Pullings, looking out at the familiar Portsmouth road. 'I never was in a chaise and four but once, and that was when the Captain was carrying dispatches. I went along for the ride and the glory, and taking the whole journey we travelled at very near ten miles an hour; but then we never stopped for meals — ate bread and cheese in our hands — and the Captain leaned out of the window much of the way, encouraging the post-boys.'

'It is the only way I know of purchasing time,' said Stephen. 'We shall not stop for meals either. The only halts I have in mind at all are at Portsmouth to see Captain Dundas, for whom I carry a message, and possibly to look in on Mr Martin, if we have daylight by then. I had also thought of passing by Ashgrove to pick up Bonden and Padeen, but I question whether their weight and the consequent loss of speed is worth their help in moving the ship. What do you say?'

'They would be very valuable, sir. We are only likely to find a few slack-arsed longshoremen down there, and to carry the barky round to Shelmerston brisk we should have some right taut petty-officers. I am sure Captain Dundas would lend you one or two, and they could come on with Bonden by coach. We should not need them the first day. We could do business first, going post-haste, and they would follow us the next day, do you see?'

'That of course is the answer. Well done, Thomas Pullings. But tell me now, will you, just how disreputable is it, to go a-privateering? And which sounds least offensive to the naval ear, privateer or corsair?'

'They are both pretty low, but since that chap Mowett is always talking about — grandson of the Admiral —'

'Byron.'

'Aye, Byron — wrote his piece, I dare say some young fellows had rather be called corsair. But the Captain would certainly prefer the old-fashioned letter of marque. As for being disreputable, why, it has a bad name, to be sure, like sodomy; but I remember how you told the master of the *Defender* when he was going on about how they all ought to be burnt alive rather than just hanged — how you told him that there were many good, brave and gifted men among them. And so there are among privateers: some of their ships are run Navy-fashion, so you would hardly know the odds, but for no man-of-war's pennant and no regular uniforms.'

'But in general the word privateer is a reproach in the service, is it not? So do you think that commanding one would be very repugnant to Captain Aubrey? I mean, supposing he were cast out of the Navy.'

'He might find it hard in home waters, among those in the service that don't like him: and there are a good many jealous unofficerlike lubbers he has offended one way or another. Any jumped-up lieutenant commanding a cutter could order him to come aboard and show his papers, and maybe keep him waiting about on deck; any King's officer could press his men and ruin his voyage, if he fell unlucky; any ill-conditioned scrub with a commission might check him and he could not reply. But was he to go far foreign, Madagascar, say, or the Spanish Main, he would either be among friends or, if there were any awkward commanders on the nearest station, he could keep his distance. There is nothing in her class nor near it can catch *Surprise* when he is sailing her. And any rate, even in home waters it would be better than eating his heart out on shore.' They both looked absently out at the traffic for a while, and then

Pullings said in a low and almost secret voice, 'Doctor, how likely is it he will be — what shall I say — be undone?'

'My opinion is not worth the breath to utter it: nothing do I know of the law at all. But I do remember that the Bible likens human justice to a woman's unclean rag — quasi pannus menstruate — and I have little faith in truth as an immediate safeguard, in this world.'

'What I am so afraid of is that they may catch him on a false muster.'

'A false muster, Thomas?'

'It is when you put a friend's son's name down in your ship's books so as to gain him some sea-time, when in fact he is at home, still in petticoats or at school. Then when he comes to pass for lieutenant he can show certificates of having been at sea the full six years. Everyone does it — I could name half a dozen captains offhand — but if some ugly swab with a grudge swears to the fact, swears that the boy never appeared when all hands were piped for muster, why then you are dismissed the service, just as though it were a real false muster — I mean bearing men on your books that don't exist, merely to draw their wages and victuals.'

'Yet surely that is an entirely naval, maritime offence, is it not? Whereas this is a trial by land: a false muster could not affect the Stock Exchange.'

'I don't know, I'm sure. But Captain Dundas will tell us.'

Captain Dundas, however, was not to be seen on the *Eurydice*'s busy quarterdeck when Stephen went aboard her, and the officer of the watch was 'by no means sure he would be at leisure'.

'Perhaps you would be so good as to mention my name, however: Maturin, Dr Maturin.'

'Very well,' said the lieutenant coldly: he called a youngster and then walked off, leaving Dr Maturin by himself. The Navy, upon the whole, liked its visitors to be neat, trim, and reasonably well-dressed: Stephen had not shaved for some time; he had used his rolled-up coat as a pillow during the later part of the journey, and now it was strangely wrinkled and dusty; and his breeches were unbuckled at the knee. Yet none of this made any difference to Captain Dundas's welcome. He came hurrying out of his cabin, dressed in civilian clothes, and cried 'My dear Maturin, how happy I am I was delayed — another five minutes and I should have missed you — I am just off to town.' He led Stephen below, asked most anxiously after Jack Aubrey, and dismissed the notion of false muster as irrelevant: what did Maturin think of the case — was there any real danger from the civilian point of view?

'Looking at it from a distance I should have said there was none, but looking at counsel's face, and remembering what has happened in trials with a political side to them, I fear for the outcome. So much so that I am on my way to buy the *Surprise*.'

'Are you, by God?' cried Dundas, who instantly took the point. 'But, you know,' he said, looking doubtfully at Stephen, 'she is likely to fetch a pretty penny, an uncommon pretty penny, as a private man-of-war.'

'So I was told by a great man at the Admiralty; but even so I think it can be encompassed. Would it be possible for you to lend us an able hand or two, to help move her to Shelmerston? They could come down in the coach with Bonden and my servant, while Tom Pullings and I go ahead in the chaise and transact the business.'

'You shall have a party at once. The sale is tomorrow, I believe? Dear me, you have no time to spare. If you are to be there before nightfall you must be on your way directly. Let me pull you ashore. My barge is alongside, and as soon as I have given orders about your men we can shove off. You must not be late for the fair, whatever happens. How glad I am that you have Tom Pullings with you. Had you been alone I should certainly have accompanied you, by way of protection against the shoals and the sharks — ship-buying calls for expert knowledge, just like cutting off a leg — a pair of legs — and I have absolutely engaged to go up to town, to see the young person I was telling you about. I shall be at Durrant's —'

'Not at your brother's?'

'No. Melville and I ain't on speaking terms. You cannot abuse another man's children or their mother without expecting to be kicked. And I shall still be there when you come back. Pray let me know how things have gone, will you? You do not mean to be at the trial, I collect?'

'I do not, unless I am called as a witness on the third day.'

'No; no,' said Dundas, shaking his head. 'A great deal of muck-raking, no doubt. Perhaps I shall just lurk in a passage and come in to cheer at the end. You will not forget to give my very best wishes to Tom Pullings?'

For this purpose Stephen could not in fact have had a better ally than Tom Pullings. They came out of their inn as the sky cleared after a rainy night and walked down over the shining cobbles towards the quay, and time and again he responded to 'Captain Pullings, sir, good day to you,' or greetings of that kind; he was well known in the town and obviously respected, and Stephen observed that as the sea came nearer so Captain Pullings became more and more wholly adult. There was a brief lapse into the young fellow Stephen had known so long ago when they turned a corner and the long harbour came into sight, with the *Surprise* lying against the quay on the far side, lit by a clear sea-light and a high, gently dappled sky as though for her portrait. 'There she lays,' he cried. 'Oh there she lays! Ain't she the loveliest thing you ever saw?'

'She is, too,' said Stephen, for even to his profound ignorance she stood out among the common workaday vessels like a thoroughbred in a troop of carthorses.

But apart from that enthusiastic cry, the Pullings who guided him to the steps was a grave, obviously capable officer, possessed of great natural authority. His London diffidence had quite gone by the time they were sitting in the boat that was to carry them to the far side, and it was clear to Stephen that Tom could deal with any commander in the service, let alone a gathering of marine brokers, ship breakers, auctioneers and the like.

The frigate was quite unchanged, seen from the level of the sea, and even Dr Maturin would have recognized her towering mainmast with its particular rake, her fine entry and her flowing lines from a mile away or even more. But what a different state of things was seen when they came aboard! The familiar decks, the gunroom, the great cabin itself were full of merchants of one kind or another, and since they were also going to attend the sale of a captured American whaler they were all dressed in old and greasy clothes, which made their prying, evaluating, horse-coping motions even more offensive to the prejudiced observer. Several groups came up to Pullings and spoke to him in low confidential tones, proposing arrangements for various parts of the ship — arrangements to avoid undue competition — arrangements for the advantage of all concerned — and while he dealt with them in his cheerful, decided, competent way, Stephen lapsed into a reverie, his hand resting on his meagre belly in a somewhat Napoleonic attitude.

Beneath his hand, beneath his buff waistcoat and his shirt, lay a sheaf of crisp new Bank of England notes, a man-of-war in small compass straight from Threadneedle Street, and for a while he took a certain remote pleasure in their crinkling response to the pressure of his fingers; but his mind was almost entirely taken up with thoughts of Diana — her delight in auctions — her ingenuous excitement — her mounting colour and brilliant eyes — her inability to sit still or keep quiet — the library of Calvinist theology that she had once bought by mistake, the fourteen long-case clocks — and although he paid some mechanical attention to the preliminaries and to Pullings's early bids, his mind soon sank so deep that the clear vision of Diana, standing just inside the door at Christie's with her head held high and her mouth opening in an expression of vivid triumph did not fade until the auctioneer's hammer came down with a decided crack and Pullings gave him joy of his purchase.

'God love you, Doctor,' he said in a wondering tone, when the formalities were over and they were on deck again, 'to think you are the owner of *Surprise*!'

'It is a solemn thought,' replied Stephen. 'But I hope I shall not be her owner long. I hope I shall find Mr Aubrey happy and at large, ready to take her off my hands; though I love her dearly, so I do, as a floating home, an ark of refuge.'

'You, sir,' cried Pullings, laying his hand

on a belaying-pin. 'Leave those twiddling-lines alone.'

'I was only looking,' said the longshoreman.

'You may step over the brow as quick as you like,' said Pullings, and going to the side he called out to a wherry, 'Jospin, be a good chap and give your brother a hail. We must tow out to moorings before we lose all our standing rigging and the masts too. Lord, sir,' he said to Stephen, 'how I wish Bonden was here already, with his party. Even at moorings, out in the stream, I have only one pair of eyes.' He caught up a bucket and with wonderful dexterity he flung its water full on to some little boys on a raft made of stolen planks who were trying to prise some of the copper off the frigate's hull, under her bows. 'You whoreson little hellspawn buggers,' he called, 'next time I see you I shall have you taken up and hanged. No, sir, now the auctioneer's men are gone they look upon us as fair game. The sooner we are at moorings the better, and even then . . .'

'You mean to move away from the side, I collect? Away from the quay or wharf?'

'That's right, sir. Out into the middle or centre.'

'Then I shall step ashore now, by this convenient bridge or gangway; for were we in the middle I should have to go down into a boat, and I am not always quite at my ease, going down into a boat. You may have noticed it.'

'Not at all, sir, not at all,' said Pullings. 'Anyone can slip, just a little.'

'Besides, I must start back directly. Mr Lawrence may wish to call me as a witness on the third day, so there is not a moment to lose.'

The chaise lost not a moment: the weather was uniformly kind, and the elegant black and yellow machine ran steadily north throughout the rest of that day and all night, never lacking for horses at any stage on the road nor for zealous post-boys. It brought Stephen to St James's Street in time to breakfast, to call a barber to shave him and powder his wig, to put on a good black suit of clothes and a new neckcloth, and to step into a hackney-coach for the City with a quiet mind.

He was in good time and even when they were caught in an unmoving flood of vehicles this side of St Clement's he did not fret; nor, on reaching Guildhall at last, was he much concerned at finding the court full of lawyers arguing about a case whose nature he could not make out but which certainly had nothing to do with Jack Aubrey or the

Stock Exchange. He had always heard of the law's delays and for a while he supposed that Jack's case had been put back for some reason — that it would be heard later, perhaps in the afternoon. He sat there, contemplating Lord Quinborough, a heavy, glum, dissatisfied man whose thick, insensitive face had a wart on its left cheek; the judge had a loud, droning voice and he very often raised it, interrupting one counsel or another; Stephen had rarely seen so much self-complacency, hardness, and want of common feeling gathered together under a single wig. He also tried to make out the point at issue, at the same time keeping an eye lifted for Jack's solicitors, his counsel, or their clerks; but in time he grew uneasy — this case was obviously going to last a very, very long while —and tiptoeing to the door he asked an attendant 'was this the right place for Captain Aubrey's trial?'

'The Stock Exchange fraud? Why, it's all over — was over yesterday. They come up for sentence early next week, and won't they cop it? Oh no, not at all.'

Stephen did not know the City at all well; there were no hackney-coaches to be had, and as he hurried through the hurrying crowds in what he hoped was the direction of the Temple he seemed to pass the same church again and again. He also came to the gates of Bedlam twice. Presently his rapid walking took on the quality of a nightmare, but the fourth time he reached Love Lane — it was Love Lane that foxed him every time — he chanced upon an unemployed ticket-porter who led him to the river. Here he took a pair of oars, and the tide being in his favour the waterman brought him to the Temple stairs in less time than he had taken to reach Bedlam from Guildhall.

At Lawrence's chambers Stephen learnt that he was sick, confined to his bed, but that he had left word for Dr Maturin. The transcript of the trial was being written fair and would be ready tomorrow, but if Dr Maturin did not mind the risk of infection, Mr Lawrence would be happy to see him at home, in King's Bench Row.

'Conscientiously willing' would perhaps have been a more accurate expression, for as Lawrence heaved himself up in bed and pulled off his nightcap he looked perfectly wretched. His streaming eyes and nose, his obvious headache, his rasping throat, and his high degree of fever had a great deal to do with this, but he was also wretched as a lawyer and as a man.

'You heard the result, of course?' he said. 'Aubrey and all the defendants found guilty.

You will have the whole transcript to-morrow, so I shall only give you the main heads now.' He broke into a fit of coughing, said 'As far as I can recall them,' and began wheezing, gasping and sneezing again. 'Forgive me, Maturin, I am in a sad way — wits all far to seek. Pray pass me that stuff on the hob.' When he had drunk some he said 'Do you remember I told you to bring Aubrey's ideas of the law, or rather of the administration of justice, down to a less exalted pitch? Well, if you had spoken with the tongues of men and of angels you could not have done better than Quinborough and Pearce. It was butchery, Maturin, butchery. Long-drawn-out, cold, deliberate butchery. I have seen some pretty ugly political trials, but none to touch this; I had no idea that Government thought General Aubrey and his Radical friends so important or that they would go to such lengths to attack them, such lengths to obtain a conviction.' Lawrence went into another paroxysm, drank another draught, and clasping his head with both hands he begged Stephen's pardon. 'This will be a miserably disjointed account, I am afraid. As I told you, Pearce was for the prosecution — would-be handsome young fellow, smirking at the judge — very able speech nevertheless, I must admit, blackguarding

390

all the defendants. It was easy enough for him to make the stock-jobbers sound a pack of knaves and he fairly tore them to pieces: but you will see all that in the report. Aubrey is what matters to us. Pearce set about him in a way I had not expected, though perhaps I should have expected it if I had not been so dull-witted that day and if I had looked at the jury more attentively. Merchants, all of them, or money-men, and as heavy and commercial a set as you could wish; and it was the jurymen Pearce was addressing — he did not have to trouble about convincing the judge. Pearce had no lessons in patriotism to take from anyone and no man had a more sincere regard for the Navy than he: Captain Aubrey was a distinguished sailor — Pearce had not the least intention of denying it — Pearce was really sorry that his duty required him to prosecute such a man — should far rather see him on the poop of a frigate than in his present unhappy situation. But this distinguished career, this reasonably distinguished career, was not without its interruptions: there was the loss of no less than three ships of an aggregate value of I forget how many thousands, and several unfortunate courts-martial. Furthermore, although Pearce must not be understood as attempting to lessen these services in any way it must be pointed out that they were not entirely voluntary: Captain Aubrey had been paid for performing them, not only with very large sums of money, free quarters and free servants, but with splendid decorations, medals and ribbons. Oh Lord, Lord: pray give me those handkerchiefs.' He wheezed and wheezed and held dry cambric to his raw sore nose, and after a while he recovered breath and spirits enough to go on 'What I say now is not in due order: it is merely the gist of what he conveyed to the jury either by statement or evidence of cross-examination or reply. I protested at many of the statements and much of the wholly inadmissible evidence and sometimes even Quinborough was obliged to support me, but of course the harm was done — the impression was conveyed to the jurymen, whether it was unsupported statement, hearsay or improper inference, and it was no good telling those fellows to dismiss it from their minds. I resume. Pearce did not have to tell the gentlemen of the jury that physical courage, the natural endowment of every Briton, was a splendid virtue; it was one of the things that raised Britons so far above all other nations; but it did not necessarily bring every other virtue in its train. The gentlemen of the jury might think there was, to say the least, a want of delicacy, even of integrity, in a captain who received a Negro as an honoured guest in His Majesty's ship, the Negro being not only the fruit of the captain's criminal conversation with a black woman, but a Papistical clergyman into the bargain, and therefore totally opposed to His Majesty's supremacy. But of course Captain Aubrey might share his Radical connexions' views on Popery; he too might be all in favour of Catholic emancipation. Then there was the most distasteful question of sailing under false colours. It would be proved by extracts from his own log-books and by other evidence that Captain Aubrey had repeatedly sailed under false colours, and any attempt by the defence to deny it was doomed to ignominious failure. Pearce had nothing to say about false colours in war, except that to plain men, to straightforward city merchants, false colours had an ugly sound — the immortal Nelson did not bear down on the enemy at Trafalgar under false colours, he believed. But was there not a danger that this habit of sailing under false colours — and Captain Aubrey must have ordered them to be hoisted scores or even hundreds of times — might spread to civilian life?

That was the only reason that Pearce most reluctantly mentioned the subject. Was not this alleged Mr Palmer a mere extension of the same stratagem? Captain Aubrey had amassed a considerable fortune in prize-money, largely by tricks or rather stratagems of this kind; he had made some very hazardous speculations and cases now depending might sweep that fortune away entirely, together with everything he possessed. He is in the most urgent need of a large sum of money — he lands from the cartel at Dover — he shares a chaise with some unknown gentleman — and there are his false colours ready to hand! This so-called Mr Palmer is said to have deceived him — the whole fault lies upon poor Mr Palmer. But really, gentlemen, it will not do. The burden cannot be shifted on to the shoulders of a non-existent Mr Palmer: I call him non-existent, gentlemen, because it is a maxim of the law that de non apparentibus et non existentibus eadem est ratio. He is a figment of the conspirators' imagination, founded upon the innocent anonymous gentleman who happened to offer the Captain a seat in his carriage. The innocent anonymous gentleman can be shown to have had an existence, and my learned friends will most zealously call half a dozen ostlers and chambermaids to prove it, but there is not a scrap of evidence to connect him with the mythical Palmer or with this most disgraceful and dangerous conspiracy.'

'How did Jack Aubrey take all this?'

'He listened attentively at first, and passed me a few notes about the very general use of false colours at sea; but presently he seemed to detach himself — sat there grave and still, but elsewhere. Once, when Pearce was going on at a very high rate, Aubrey glanced at him, not with any anger but with an objective contempt that stopped him in his stride, for he caught the look full in the eye as he turned to make his point about warriors not necessarily making such good citizens as merchants. At this point a seaman in the back of the court shouted "Oh you infernal bugger" and had to be put out: whether or not Pearce's clerk had posted him there to show what a bad, dangerous crew sailors were I do not know, but it had a good effect on the jury and it enabled Pearce to get off dangerous ground and on to the usual platitudes about the dangers of Radical aims and connexions, anarchy, the Church and so on, and thence to an extraordinarily detailed and complex account of the conspirators' dealings on the

Stock Exchange the day after Aubrey's arrival in London. The only other time I saw Aubrey show any emotion was when his father's broker, who had turned King's evidence, swore that Aubrey had given them to understand that there was peace — not perhaps in so many words, but quite clearly nevertheless. He looked really dangerous then, and I saw his eye gleam when I roasted the fellow in cross-examination; but during the long, long speeches by the other lawyers, perpetually interrupted by the judge, he might have been gazing out to sea. Not that I looked at him very much, because this vile influenza was growing on me and I had to concentrate all my powers on the immediate questions before me. The lights had been lit hours before; their glare dazzled me so that I could hardly see my notes and their smell made me feel sick and faint. But still the prosecution witnesses came. I knew I was cross-examining badly, missing inconsistencies, confusing one set of figures with another and wasting my opportunities: these things have to be taken on the half-volley, you know. The other defence counsel were doing little better, but Pearce was still prancing away, as fresh as ever, with little private asides and simperings. Everything was going his way, and it stimulated him.'

'Will you take a sip of julep? You are painfully hoarse.'

'If you please. I was even worse then.' The poor man panted for a while like a dog, and then went on, 'Yet even Pearce ran out of witnesses in the end: he closed his case and we began groping about, thankfully gathering our papers. We had been there since nine in the morning and it was now about half past ten at night; there was no question but that we should adjourn. But then through a fit of sneezing I heard that old devil say we must go on. "I should wish to hear your opening," says he, "and get into the defendants' case, if I can; there are several gentlemen attending as witnesses who cannot, without the greatest public inconvenience, attend tomorrow." That was absolute nonsense and we protested. Serjeant Maule, for Cummings, said it was very hard to have the defendants' case heard so late and then for Pearce to be given a fresh day for his reply — we were forced to call a few witnesses ourselves, so he would have the right to speak again, alas, so having the last word before the summing-up.'

'There are strict rules in these matters, I find.'

'There were strict rules in the arena, too.

Every gladiator had to have a sword, oh yes; but if it was Caligula he was to fight with, the sword was made of lead. And a judge is an emperor in his own court. He made us go on. I remember listening to Maule, who spoke well to begin with, but then started rambling and repeating himself and muddling his figures, and as I listened I wondered what I could say to a jury that was two parts asleep and thoroughly disgusted with the whole thing. Maule was followed by Petty for two of the other defendants, and he spoke even worse, though at greater length: Quinborough dozed through most of it. When at last I got to my feet — but I will not go into it: it is too painful. I tried reason — no good — I tried emotion, victories, wounds, reputation — no good, and in any event I was scarcely audible and scarcely capable of consecutive thought. I did make my capital point of Aubrey's not having sold at the top of the market like the others, and I did produce my perfectly sincere ending: "It would be the most painful moment of my life if I should tonight find that the wreath of laurel which a life of danger and honour has planted round his brow should be for a moment blasted by your verdict." But that was no good either; the few waking jurymen stared like codfish on a slab. When I sat down, having wrecked my case, it was three o'clock in the morning. We had been sitting for eighteen hours, and after all Quinborough adjourned without having heard our witnesses.'

'Eighteen hours. Jesus, Mary, Joseph.'

'Yes, and we were there again at ten the next day. I was feeling so indifferent I could scarcely drag myself along or croak. However, the defence witnesses took up little time. Mine proved nothing more than Aubrey's splendid record, which was not really in question; and although Lord Melville spoke handsomely his words had little effect on the jurymen, few of whom knew that there was such a person as the First Lord. We should never have called them, because once they were done with Pearce began his reply, to which we could make no answer. It was a good reply: he had the exact measure of the jury, now quite awake and open to simple, repetitive argument. He first tore our speeches to rags, which I am afraid was no difficult task, and then he hammered home his points — Aubrey's need for money, his sudden perfect opportunity, the instant dealings after his arrival in London, dealings that ran into millions of money and that were indulged in by all concerned, and of course the obvious admission of guilt by those defendants who had run away. Then Lord Quinborough summed up; it took him three hours.'

'Is he the judge with a wart on the side of his face that I saw in the Guildhall this morning?'

'Yes.'

'Can he be an intelligent man, at all?'

'He *was* an intelligent man. You rarely come to be a judge without having been reasonably intelligent at one time. But like many others he has grown stupid on the bench, stupid and froward and overbearing and inordinately self-important. However, he did make an extraordinary effort this time, collecting all his faculties — he is, as you know, a roaring High Tory and the present chance of destroying Radicals was nectar to him — and although he was intolerably prosy and repetitious he did do all he wanted to do.' Another bout of coughing, sneezing and general distress seized upon Lawrence; when it was over, and when Stephen had propped him up against his smoothed pillows, he said in an almost voiceless whisper, 'I will not go into the details; you will read the report. But as far as Aubrey was concerned it was the most infamous summing-up I have ever heard. Quinborough assumed the guilt of all the defendants, lumped Aubrey in with the rest, passed over everything in his favour or touched upon it very lightly, with obvious scepticism, and emphasized every adverse point. He virtually told the jury to convict, and when they retired I wrote Aubrey a note, warning him to prepare for the worst. He nodded: he was perfectly self-possessed — grave, but in no way overwhelmed or dismayed. And he seemed equally unmoved when they came back in an hour or so with their verdict of guilty. He shook my hand and thanked me for my efforts; I could scarcely get a word out in reply. I shall see him again when he comes up for sentence on the twentieth.'

'What will the sentence be, do you suppose?'

'I hope, I *hope*, it will only be a fine.'

CHAPTER NINE

The morning drizzle was scarcely yet lightening in the east, but the nearby candle-factory had already started pouring out its nauseating smell and a damp group of wives, children, friends and servants had already gathered outside the gates of the Marshalsea.

A few minutes before the time for opening Sophie Aubrey came walking through the mud, high-perched on pattens. 'Why, Stephen,' she cried, 'here you are at last! What a pleasure to see you. But how early you are. And how wet,' she added, looking at him with large, startled eyes. 'Put your hat on at once: you must not get your head wet too, for Heaven's sake. Come and shelter under my umbrella: hold my arm.'

'I particularly wished to catch you before you went in to see Jack,' said Stephen. 'But in my hurry I mistook the hour. I have never been very clever at telling what's o'clock.'

The gates swung inwards with their usual

shriek and the people walked in, treading their habitual paths; but the debtors' side was open half an hour before the rest and Stephen led Sophie to the coffee-house, where they sat in a deserted corner.

'You look quite tired out, as well as wet. Give me your great-coat, Stephen.' She hung it on the back of a settle to drip. She said 'I am afraid you have not heard any good news, my dear,' but without waiting for an answer she called for 'coffee, hot and very strong, if you please, Mrs Goadby, some rolls, and two soft-boiled eggs for the gentleman'.

'Sure I have been travelling with barely a pause at all; I had hoped that hard labour would somehow earn an encouraging word, and indeed one great man did hint that the imprisonment might be remitted. But all the rest is black. Lawrence explains to me that a new trial is impossible: since all the so-called conspirators were included in the indictment and all were found guilty, they must all present themselves to make an appeal — it must be the whole body or nothing. It is a new rule of the court.'

'How I hate lawyers,' cried Sophie, her eyes growing dark.

'So much for the appeal; and as for the sentence, time and again I was told by the

403

men and women to whom I applied that "they could not alter the course of justice" . . .'

'Justice be damned,' said Sophie, in the very tone of her cousin Diana.

'And although to be sure that was exactly what I wanted them to do, I was even more concerned with altering the course of custom — I mean in preventing Jack's name from being struck off the list. If he is guilty, or rather if he is *found* guilty of an infamous crime, an officer's name is automatically struck off: it is not a matter of law but of custom and it has such a force that as Prince William assured me, speaking most earnestly and with tears in his eyes, neither he nor the First Lord could change it. Only the King or in this case the Regent has the power. He is in Scotland and in any event I am known to him only as his brother's friend; and he and his brother are on very bad terms at present. So I travelled down to Brighton and waited upon his wife.'

'His wife, Stephen?'

'She is usually known as Mrs Fitzherbert.'

'Are they indeed married? I thought she was a — a Roman Catholic.'

'Certainly they are married. The Pope himself wrote to tell her the ceremony was valid and that she was his canonical wife.

Charles Weld showed me the document — I knew him well, cousin to her first husband and at one time a priest in Spain. She received me very kindly, but she shook her head, said she had almost no influence now and even if she had, she doubted anything could be done. However, she did advise me to see Lady Hertford, and that is what I intend to do. But listen, Sophie, this appeal to the Regent cannot be made quickly, I find; if indeed it can usefully be made at all. In the meanwhile the *Surprise* has been bought. She is to be a private ship of war, and she now lies at Shelmerston with Tom Pullings in charge. He sends word that prime seamen by the score, many of them old shipmates, wish to embark if Jack commands her. If he will consent to do so, we can get away the moment all this is over, above all if there is to be no imprisonment. You must make him consent, my dear.'

'But why do you not ask him, Stephen? Why have you not told him all this?'

'Why,' said he, looking down at his eggs, 'in the first place there has been no time; I have been away. And then again there is a certain awkwardness, do you see? The role of deus ex machina is not one that I care for, at all. You would do it far better. If he raises the point, you will say that there is no obligation in the world: the one supplies the capital, the other the skill — I could not sail a ship across a horse-pond, nor attack a simple rowing-boat; and I should certainly never sail with any other captain. Pray tell him I hope to look in this evening to hear his good word. I must be away. God bless, now. Remember, you must not say privateer or corsair; you must say letter of marque, or private man-of-war.'

As Stephen approached Sir Joseph's door in Shepherd Market he saw Colonel Warren come out, step into a chariot that bowed under his weight, and drive off. He knew that Warren was the Horse Guards' new representative on the Committee, an unusually active, stirring, sharp-witted man; but he did not wish to be known to him, and he walked on for a few minutes. When he made his call he found his friend looking extremely grave. 'At this rate,' said Sir Joseph, 'I shall be suspecting Lord Liverpool and half the cabinet of high treason. There are some utterly inexplicable contradictions ... perhaps Cerberus himself has run mad ... how I wish this business were half as easily resolved as yours.' He opened a drawer and said 'Here are your letters of marque against France, Holland, the Italian and Ligurian Republics, the United States of America, vessels bearing the flag of Pappenburgh, and half a dozen others. I have had them ready for you since Wednesday.'

'God set a flower on your head, dear Blaine,' said Stephen. 'I am exceedingly grateful, and I should have looked in on Wednesday itself so I should, but it was two in the morning when I passed through London on my way to a town called Bury. I have been going to see every important man or woman in the kingdom who has the least kindness for me.'

'If you were travelling in Aubrey's favour, and I make no doubt you were, you might have saved your coach-hire. You can no longer bribe judges in this country, nor cause them to be bribed, nor persuaded, still less commanded. There is only one single exception, as I could have told you before you set out, and that is where the judge happens also to be a member of the cabinet, which is the case with Lord Quinborough; he is by definition responsive to the political wishes of his colleagues. Now your name has already been put forward as the ideal man for this entirely unofficial contact with Chile and possibly Peru to which administration attaches very great importance: it was represented that you were bilingual in Spanish, a tried and tested intelligence-agent in the ideal vessel with the ideal excuse for his presence in those waters, and that you would be a Catholic dealing with other Catholics, many of them Irish or half-Irish themselves — the younger O'Higgins, for example. These qualifications, together with that of a very large private fortune, were conclusive. The restricted gathering was delighted, and rubbed its collective hands. But a gentleman then observed that although you possessed all the virtues, you certainly would not sail unless the ship was commanded by Aubrey. So since the matter presses, I believe you may rest easy about the imprisonment.' Sir Joseph looked at the clock and said 'If you mean to be there for his appearance in court, you must hurry.'

'I do not,' said Stephen. 'It seems to me that onlookers are strangely out of place. But I have taken the liberty of desiring a message to be sent to me here.'

'Excellent,' said Sir Joseph. 'But I am afraid the sentence will shock you. Quinborough may not imprison, but he will jet out his venom in some other way. This was a very vile job, you know — the other men having bail so that they might walk off when they were found guilty — Aubrey alone held in prison. Of course there was the political side, the destruction of the Radicals, which was perfectly comprehensible in those whose political passions incline them that way; but there was some hidden malice as well, and this inveteracy against your friend . . .'

'I beg your pardon, sir,' said Mrs Barlow. 'A message for Dr Maturin.'

'Open it, I beg,' said Sir Joseph.

'Pillory,' said Stephen in a hard, cold voice. 'Fine and the pillory. *Shall pay the King a fine of two thousand five hundred pounds and be set in and upon the pillory opposite the Royal Exchange in the City of London for one hour between the hours of twelve at noon and two in the afternoon.*'

'I was afraid of it,' said Blaine after a long pause: and then 'Tell me, Maturin, have you ever seen a man pilloried in England?'

'I have not.'

'It can be a very bloody spectacle, on occasion. Oates was nearly killed; many people are maimed; and I once saw both a man's eyes put out by pelting. Since there is an evident personal malignance here, might you not be well advised to hire a guard of bruisers? Your thief-taker would know where to find them: he would recruit them for you.'

'I shall send to him at once: thank you for this warning, Blaine. Now tell me, what do you think of Lady Hertford?'

'Do you mean physically, or morally, or socially?'

'As a means for preventing Jack Aubrey's name being struck off the list. Mrs Fitzherbert advised me to apply to her.'

'Struck off he must necessarily be. That is the invariable rule. The real question is *restoration* to the list. It has been done, even with the former seniority, when officers have been dismissed the service for duels and that kind of thing, and occasionally for harmless false musters, though it generally takes a very long time and a great deal of influence. But in a case like this . . . Do you know the lady?'

'Only to bow to. But I understand that at present she is all-powerful with the Regent, and I am told that Andrew Wray is well with her. It occurred to me that with a proper introduction and a proper present I might perhaps induce her at least to start the matter moving in the royal mind.'

'It might conceivably answer. But at present the royal mind is in Scotland, displaying the full bulk of the royal form in a little cloth petticoat to his knees, a tartan cloak, particoloured stockings and a highland bonnet; and I rather fancy Lady Hertford is with him. If you like I will enquire and let you know.'

'That would be kind. In the meanwhile I shall call at Grosvenor Street on my way to the Marshalsea.'

'You know of course that between an odious woman and a clever showy coxcomb like Wray you are likely to lose both your present and your time?'

'Of course. Good day to you now, dear Blaine.'

Mr Wray was not at home when Dr Maturin called at Grosvenor Street, but Mrs Wray was: she heard him give his name at the door, came running down the stairs and seized both his hands. She was ordinarily rather a plain, thick, swarthy young woman but now she looked almost pretty: her face glowed and her eyes sparkled with generous indignation. She had already heard the news and she cried out 'Oh how unjust! Oh how wicked! The pillory for a naval officer — it is unthinkable. And he is so brave, so distinguished, so handsome. Come into my room.' She led him into a little boudoir all hung about with pictures of ships, some of them commanded by her father, but more commanded by Captain Aubrey in the days when Babbington served under him. 'And so tall. He used to take such kind notice of me when I was only an awkward lump of a girl, though my father was very hard on him sometimes. Charles thinks the whole world of him — Captain Babbington, I mean — and fairly worships him. And Dr Maturin,' she added in another tone and with a conscious look, 'Charles values your advice most amazingly: I am so glad. He put into the Downs last night.' Then resuming, 'But oh to think of his poor wife, standing there helpless while he is pelted — it is monstrous, monstrous. And the shame of it all, the hooting and the jeers, must kill him, sure.'

'As for that, ma'am, you are forgetting that he is innocent, which must do away with the bite of shame.'

'Of course, of course, he is innocent: that must make a vast great difference. Not that I should have cared if he had rigged the market ten times over: everybody does it. I know Mr Wray made a great deal at the same time. But oh, Dr Maturin, pray sit down. Where are my wits? What would Charles think of me? Pray take a glass of madeira.'

'Thank you, ma'am, but I must away. I am bound for the Marshalsea itself.'

'Then please, please give him my most respectful — no, most affectionate compliments, and to Mrs Aubrey my best love.

And if there is anything I can possibly do —
children, or looking after cats . . .'

As they came out of the boudoir the front
door opened. Two chairmen supported
Wray up the steps; two footmen took him
over with practised hands; and as they propelled him across the hall he turned his
blotched face towards Stephen and said

'*A beaten wife and a cuckold swain*
Have jointly cursed the marriage chain.'

At the Marshalsea Stephen found it difficult to make his way through the naval side
because of the number of sailors gathered
there, most of them talking at the same time
and all of them exceedingly angry. Even the
most gin-sodden and nearly demented still
retained a very high notion of the service,
and the idea of a sea-officer, a post-captain,
standing in the pillory was an intolerable
outrage, an insult to the whole Navy. Stephen was obliged to hear a petition read out
and to put his name to it before he could go
on. The prisoners had left the skittle-
ground below Jack's building empty, out of
deference to his feelings, which they would
scarcely have done if he had been sentenced
to be hanged; and Killick was sitting on the
bottom step, looking stunned, as though his

world had been destroyed.

As he went up the stairs, Stephen heard Jack's fiddle: it was a severe fugue, played with uncommon strength and austerity; and when, having waited for the full close, Stephen tapped and opened the door, he was met with a fierce, cold glare. 'I beg pardon, Jack,' he said, 'I thought you said Come in.'

'Oh,' cried Jack, his face relaxing, 'I took you for — I am very happy to see you, Stephen. Sit down: Sophie has just stepped out to buy some chops.' He collected himself, laid down his fiddle and bow, and turning his massive form squarely to Maturin he said, not without a certain constraint and formality, 'She told me about *Surprise*. I am exceedingly grateful for your offer and I should of course be delighted to command her as a private ship of war. But Stephen, I do not quite understand. Can you indeed fit her out, as well as buying her? For once I have paid my fine —'

'An iniquitous fine.'

'Aye, but whining will do no good. Once I have paid my fine and my losses on the market, I shall be of no use; and fitting out a ship for even a short cruise is far, far more costly than you can imagine.'

'Brother, I told you I had inherited from my godfather.'

'Yes. I remember you mentioned it when first we came home. But — forgive me for prying into your affairs, Stephen — I had imagined it was a little bequest for books, a mourning-ring, a keepsake, the usual kind of thing from one's godfather: and very handsome too I am sure.'

'It was in fact very much more than that, so very much more that we need not look attentively at each penny before we spend it. We shall carry on our private war in style.' Stephen stood up to peer out of the window at the evening sky, and now, looking back into the room, he saw Jack in the full north light, sitting as though for his portrait. He seemed broader than before, heavier, profoundly grave of course, and somewhat leonine; but beneath the unmoved gravity Stephen perceived a wound that was hardly affected by the news of the *Surprise*; and in the hope of easing it to some degree he added 'And in the strictest confidence, my dear, I may tell you that our war will not be entirely private either. You know something of my activities; and at intervals of harrying the enemy's commerce I may have errands of that kind to run.' Jack took the point; he expressed his pleasure with a polite inclination of his head and the appearance of a smile; and the pain remained unaffected.

Stephen continued, 'This damned spiteful pillory, brother. It is of no essential importance to an innocent man, but it is bound to be unpleasant, like a toothache: I have given you many a draught for the toothache, so I have, and here is one' — taking a small bottle from his pocket — 'that will make the pillory pass like little more than a dream: disagreeable, but only faintly disagreeable, and at a distance. I have often used it myself, with great effect.'

'Thankee, Stephen,' said Jack, setting the bottle on the mantelshelf. Stephen saw that he had no intention of taking it, and that the underlying pain was quite untouched. For to Jack Aubrey the fact of no longer belonging to the Navy counted more than a thousand pillories, the loss of fortune, loss of rank, and loss of future. It was in a way a loss of being, and to those who knew him well it gave his eyes, his whole face, the strangest look.

He still had this detached grey expression on the following Wednesday, as he stood in a bare dirty room on the south side of Cornhill waiting to be led out to the pillory.

The sheriff's men and the constables in charge of him were all clustered together at the window: they were intensely nervous and they kept up a continual flow of talk.

'It did ought to have been done days ago, right after the sentence. The news has had time to go down to the Land's End and up to John o' Groats.'

'And every fucking port in the kingdom: Chatham, Sheerness, Portsmouth, Plymouth . . .'

'Sweeting's Alley is quite blocked up.'

'So is Castle Alley, and more is coming in. They ought to have sent for the soldiers long ago.'

'We have four constables, four scavengers and one beadle in the ward. What can we do with such a crowd?'

'If we get out of this alive, I shall take my wife and children down to live the other side of Epping.'

'They keep pouring up from the river. There are the chaps from the press-tender itself, with their bloody cutlasses and bludgeons, Christ have mercy.'

'They are blocking each side of the Change with carts. God help us.'

'Why don't he give the word? Why don't Mr Essex give the word? They are growing outrageous down there. We shall all be scragged.'

Saint Paul's and the City churches had tolled twelve some five or ten minutes ago and the crowd in Cornhill was becoming impatient. 'Eight bells,' cried some. 'Eight bells, there. Turn the glass and strike the bell.'

'Bring him out, bring him out, bring him out and let's have a look at him,' shouted the leader of another group. He was the leader of a band hired by some disappointed stock-jobbers, and like his fellows he carried a bag of stones. Bonden turned sharp upon him and said 'What are you doing here, mate?'

'I've come to see the fun.'

'Then just you go and see the fun at Hockley in the Hole, that's where, cully. Because why? Because this is for seamen only, do you see. Seamen only, not landsmen.'

The man looked at Bonden, and at the many closed, dead-serious, lowering faces behind him; brown, tough, often earringed, often pigtailed; he looked at his own people, a pale and weedy crew, and with hardly a pause he said 'Well, I don't care. Have it your own way, sailor.'

Davis, a very big, ugly, dangerous man who had sailed with Jack in many commissions, had an even shorter way of dealing with Wray's gang of genuine bruisers, who stood out most surprisingly in their flash clothes and low-crowned hats among the now almost solid naval mass — most of the citizens, even the apprentices and the street-boys hawking pails of filth had withdrawn beyond the barrier or to neighbouring buildings. Davis, with his four uglier brothers and a dumb Negro bosun's mate, went straight to them and in a thick voice, choking with fury, said 'Bugger off.' He watched them go and then shouldered his brutal way through his shipmates to where Stephen was standing by the steps of the pillory with the few pugilists his thief-taker had managed to engage — men equally conspicuous. To them he said 'And you bugger off too. We mean you no harm, gents, but you bugger off too.' There was white spittle at his mouth and he was breathing very hard. Stephen nodded to his men and they sidled away towards St Michael's. As they reached the church its clock struck the quarter, and Mr Essex gave the word at last.

Jack was led out of the dark room into the strong light, and as they guided him up the steps he could see nothing for the glare. 'Your head here, sir, if you please,' said the sheriff's man in a low, nervous, conciliating voice, 'and your hands just here.'

The man was slowly fumbling with the bolt, hinge and staple, and as Jack stood there with his hands in the lower half-rounds, his sight cleared: he saw that the broad street was filled with silent, attentive men, some in long togs, some in shore-going rig, some in plain frocks, but all perfectly recognizable as seamen. And officers, by the dozen, by the score: midshipmen and officers. Babbington was there, immediately in front of the pillory, facing him with his hat off, and Pullings, Stephen of course, Mowett, Dundas . . . He nodded to them, with almost no change in his iron expression, and his eye moved on: Parker, Rowan, Williamson, Hervey . . . and men from long, long ago, men he could scarcely name, lieutenants and commanders putting their promotion at risk, midshipmen and master's mates their commissions, warrant-officers their advancement.

'The head a trifle forward, if you please, sir,' murmured the sheriff's man, and the upper half of the wooden frame came down, imprisoning his defenceless face. He heard the click of the bolt and then in the dead silence a strong voice cry 'Off hats'. With one movement hundreds of broad-brimmed tarpaulin-covered hats flew off and the cheering began, the fierce full-throated cheering he had so often heard in battle.

CHAPTER TEN

'It is understood, then,' said Mr Lowndes of the Foreign Office, 'that you proceed to no action at present, but that unless circumstances are extraordinarily favourable you confine yourself to making contacts in Valparaiso and Santiago; and that the aggregate prizes taken, less ten per cent, shall be deducted from the agreed daily subvention, and that there shall be no other claims on His Majesty's Government.'

'There is also half the fair wear and tear,' said Stephen. 'In a ship of such immense value, and in seas of such unparalleled turbulence, the fair wear and tear is reckoned at a hundred and seventy pounds a month, a hundred and seventy pounds a lunar month: I must insist upon this point; I must insist that it be specifically set down.'

'Very well,' said Mr Lowndes sulkily. He made a note and continued, 'Here you have a list of the notables and military men recommended by the Chilean Council for Liberation and by our own sources of information; and here you have the statement of what munitions and what sums of money the Council may provide. It is also understood that these sums and this material will invariably be assumed to emanate from the Council itself and in no way from His Majesty's Government. And since it is surely unnecessary for me to repeat that in the event of any unsuccessful conflict with the local authorities the whole undertaking will be disavowed and that you will receive no official support whatsoever, I believe that is all, apart from what Colonel Warren and Sir Joseph may have to add.'

'For my part,' said Colonel Warren, who was speaking not as a soldier but as a member of the Committee, to which all three belonged, 'I have only to give Dr Maturin the relevant codes and the names of the people with whom he may communicate. Perhaps you will check them, sir,' he added, passing the packet to Stephen.

'On the naval side there are these two documents,' said Sir Joseph, tapping them with his spectacles. 'A letter of exemption that will prevent the pressing of Dr Maturin's people, and another that will allow him to refit and obtain supplies at His Majesty's yards, paying by ninety-day bills on London at no more than prime cost.'

'In that case,' said Mr Lowndes, standing up, 'it only remains for me to wish Dr Maturin every success.'

'And a happy return — a very happy return,' said the huge colonel in his strange shrill voice, shaking Stephen by the hand with a kindly look.

Sir Joseph saw them to the street door, and as soon as it closed behind them he directed his voice down the back stairs and called out 'Mrs Barlow, you may dish up as soon as you please.'

'I am so sorry, Maturin,' he said, returning to the room, 'it was inhuman of Lowndes to go on so long. He might have been settling a treaty with a hostile power rather than — how I hope he did not destroy your appetite. Knowing that you people of the old faith are required to mortify your flesh today, I went down early and found some really fresh oysters, a couple of hen lobsters, and such a bold turbot! If he is overcooked I shall never forgive the Foreign Office, never as long as I live.' He poured two glasses of sherry. 'But I must say I did admire your tenacity about the financial side.'

'It is wealth that does it,' said Stephen.

'Ever since I had a great deal of money I have found that I much dislike being parted from it, particularly in a sharp or over-bearing manner. Whereas formerly I would meekly allow myself to be choused or bullied or put down, I now counter-attack with a confidence and an asperity that quite surprises me and that nearly always answers.' He raised his glass and said 'I drink to your complete and early success.'

'Thank you,' said Blaine. 'Warren and I believe we are fairly close behind our fox. It is very high treason indeed and only about twenty men are capable of committing it — I mean, are in a *position* to commit it. This twentieth man is very wary and cunning, but I think Warren, with all the resources at his disposal, will find him out. Warren is much more intelligent than you might suppose from his military face and his shape; he is a eunuch, you know, and a man without —'

'If you please, sir,' said Mrs Barlow severely, at the door, and Sir Joseph, blushing, led Stephen to the dining-room. 'What news of poor Aubrey?' he asked, as they sat down.

'He has all the hands he wants — has turned many away and has accepted others only on liking — and means to make a short cruise in the Bay for a month or so, to see how they shake down and whether any fail to give satisfaction. I am to join him on Saturday, taking the early coach tomorrow.'

'I am glad he is so fortunate with his crew: the cleverer men would of course come in droves to sail with such a captain, such a prize-taker. A wonderful change from having to rely on the receiving-ships! He does deserve some good luck after so much wretchedness. And yet, you know, that vile job did the ministry no good. Quinborough is perhaps the most unpopular man in the nation at present; he is hooted in the street, and the Radicals are clean forgotten in the general outcry against the sentence and the conduct of the trial. The town is full of praise for the officers and men at the Exchange and their cheering: Government completely mistook the feeling of the country. People enjoy seeing a short-weight baker pilloried, or a fraudulent stock-jobber, but they could not bear a naval officer being set up in the machine.'

'The seamen were indeed a glorious sight. I was astonished and delighted to see so many.'

'Government could scarcely have mismanaged the business worse. They delayed the execution of the sentence until the whole island was filled with indignation and until there happened to be a strong squadron in the Downs and several ships at the Nore, together with far more than usual in the Medway and the upper reaches of the Thames. All these ships present, to say nothing of the large floating population of seamen, at a time when tide and wind were perfect for bringing them up the river and taking them down again. Of course many officers came up and of course large parties were given leave — I am told that even the press-tender's crew appeared, on the pretence of looking for deserters. And now Quinborough and his friends are reduced to having pamphlets written to defend their conduct.'

The bold turbot came in, together with a bottle of Montrachet, and after a busy pause Stephen said 'I believe you may forgive Mr Lowndes after all.'

'A wordy animal,' said Sir Joseph, but without animosity; and then, 'Speaking of pamphlets, what did you think of your friend's? Of Mr Martin's?'

'Faith,' said Stephen, 'I have not read it. A packet came from the remote waste where he lives, the creature, just before I left for Bury. I saw from his note that all was well — a pretty wound and the stitches firm — so put it by to look into later. I imagine it is the paper on the True Weevils that he has been intending to write for some time.'

'Oh no, dear me no. Its title is *A statement of Certain Immoral Practices prevailing in the Royal Navy, together with some remarks upon Flogging and Impressment.*'

Stephen laid down his fork and his piece of bread. 'Is it very severe?' he asked.

'Scorpions ain't in it. He excepts the frigate *S* — under the honourable conduct of Captain A — from charges of whoredom, sodomy, and cruel capricious tyrannical punishment, but he comes down on the rest like a thousand of bricks. And on the system of recruiting. Happily for him he can afford to do so, since as I understand it he has married and settled down on his living in the country.'

'He has no living in the country or anywhere else. He meant to go on sailing with Aubrey and me as a naval chaplain.'

'Well, I am heartily sorry for it, he being such a capital entomologist and a friend of yours; for after this outburst, however moral, however true, he will never get another ship. He would have been far better advised to keep to his True Weevils, or even better his New World Cicindelidae. However, let us hope that his wife brought him a reasonable fortune, so that he may continue to indulge in the luxury of telling his betters of their faults. Cicindelidae, those glorious beetles! I have not yet arranged or even classed above half the collection you was so very kind as to bring me, though I often sit up with them till one in the morning. But oh, Maturin, I blush to admit it, seeing that he was the rarest of the rare — an awkward movement sent duodecimpunctatus to the ground, and an even unhappier lurch, trying to save him, set my foot square on his back. If you should happen to pass by the shores of the Orinoco, I should be infinitely obliged . . .'

Beetles, the Entomological Association, and the Royal Society carried them to their cheese, and when Mrs Barlow brought in the coffee she said 'Sir Joseph, I have put the gentleman's bones under his hat on the chair in the hall.'

'Oh yes,' said Blaine, 'Cuvier sent Banks a parcel of bones for you, and Banks, knowing you would be here today, gave them to me.'

'They are probably those of a solitaire,' said Stephen, palping the parcel as he took his leave. 'How very kind and thoughtful in Cuvier.'

He walked fast to Black's, hurried up-stairs to where all his possessions lay scattered abroad, waiting to be packed, and undid his packet. They were not the bones of a solitaire, far less those of a dodo, as he had half hoped, but a mixed set of commonplace storks, cranes, and possibly one brown pelican. The bones were loosely wrapped in a gannet's skin, reasonably well preserved but in no way extraordinary. Any naturalist's shop near the Jardin des Plantes could have supplied it. Yet it did not seem likely that anyone would have carried a witless joke so very far and Stephen began examining the bones one by one. Nothing there: but on the inside of the skin there was a message. It looked like a taxidermist's notes but in fact it read *Si la personne qui s'intéresse au pavillon de partance voudrait bien donner rendez-vous en laissant un mot chez Jules, traiteur à Frith Street, elle en aurait des nouvelles.*

'*Pavillon de partance,*' said Maturin aloud, frowning. He tried a number of recombinations but still it came out as *pavillon de partance;* and the more he repeated it the more it seemed to him that perhaps he had heard it long ago in France.

He walked down the stairs towards the library, still muttering; but at their foot he met the amiable Admiral Smyth. 'Good evening to you, sir,' he said. 'I was on my way to find a naval encyclopaedia, but now I may cut my journey short, I find. Pray what is meant by a *pavillon de partance?*'

'Why, Doctor,' said the Admiral, smiling benignly, 'you must often have seen it, I am sure — the blue flag with a white square in the middle that we hoist at the foretop-masthead to signify that we mean to sail directly. It is generally called the Blue Peter.'

'The Blue Peter! Oh, of course, of course. Thank you, Admiral — very many thanks indeed.'

'Not at all,' said the Admiral, chuckling. He carried on along the corridor while Stephen returned to his stairs and his room. There he tossed his three shirts off the elbow chair and sat down. His mind or perhaps his breast was filled with a tumult of emotions, some of them exquisitely painful. The series of incidents called up by the name of the flag and by the now comprehensible message had come back to him accurately and in great detail the moment Admiral Smyth gave his definition, yet now as he sat there staring at the blank window he went over the history again and again. The Blue Peter was a very large heart-shaped diamond, blue of course, that had belonged to Diana when she was in Paris earlier in the war, and it was an object that she delighted in, an object to which she was most passionately attached. She could live there perfectly well, since before she became a British subject again by marrying Stephen she was legally an American; and she was still there when Jack Aubrey's sloop the *Ariel* was wrecked on the Breton coast. Stephen was suspected of being an intelligence-agent and he and Jack, together with their companion Jagiello, an officer in the Swedish service, were taken to Paris and lodged in the Temple prison. It seemed likely that Stephen at least would be shot and Diana attempted to save him by bribing a minister's wife with the diamond, an act that very nearly sealed his fate by seeming to prove that he was an agent of great importance. They were in fact released, but for an entirely different reason: a body of influential men in Paris, headed by Talleyrand, were convinced that at this juncture Buonaparte could be put down and the war brought to an end if England would agree to a negotiated peace, and they needed an exceptional, well-introduced messenger to carry their proposals. Their agent, Duhamel, a senior member of one of the French intelligence services, put it to Stephen that he was the right man, and after a good deal of fencing Stephen agreed, his terms being the liberation of his companions and of Diana and the restitution of the diamond. The restitution of the diamond was politically impossible at such short notice, but it was promised at a later date. That was years ago, and there had been no word of the Blue Peter; indeed, so much had happened since then that the blaze of the great stone was now little more than the memory of a memory.

'It is an odd proposition,' he said, looking at the gannet's skin again, 'and not without its dangers.' He considered the possible disadvantages for a while — abduction, plain murder, and so on — and then said 'But all in all it is worth trying; and I can take the slow coach at noon. It will still get me there in time for Jack's holy tide, the tide that must on no account be missed.' He wrote a few lines stating that if the gentleman who had honoured him with the bones would present himself in the meadow at the end of the carriage-road in the Regent's park at half past eight o'clock tomorrow morning, Dr Maturin would be happy to meet him: Dr M begged that the gentleman might be unaccompanied and that he might carry a book in his hand. He took this down to the hall-porter, asked him to send a lad round to Frith Street, and returned to his packing.

His packing was slow, laborious, and inefficient; there were plenty of skilled hands in the club who would have done it for him, but the habit of secrecy had so grown upon him, had become so nearly instinctive, that he did not like strangers to see even his shirts unfolded. It was his sea-chest that gave him most trouble: it had two trays and a little inner chest or till, and time and again he filled the whole and forced down the lid, only to find that one of these three was lying on his bed or behind the door. Towards midnight he had the entirety closed and locked, and then he perceived that the pair of pocket-pistols he meant to take with him in the morning were in the lowest compartment of all.

'Life is not worth it,' he said, and went to bed with Martin's pamphlet, an accurate, well-informed statement of abuses in the service, and in the present circumstances perhaps the most impolitic essay ever written by a naval chaplain; for Mrs Martin had brought him no fortune whatsoever and he had no benefice nor any prospect of a benefice — he had relied entirely upon Jack Aubrey's patronage, Jack Aubrey's permanence.

One of the reasons there was so much

travelling between France and England was the presence of the Comte de Lille, the de jure King Louis XVIII, at Hartwell in Buckinghamshire. His advisers were constantly in touch with the various royalist groups, particularly those in Paris, and since some of Buonaparte's ministers thought it wise to insure against all eventualities they not only connived at this traffic but even sent emissaries of their own with messages that usually contained expressions of respect and good will but little else — nothing concrete. The number of these messengers rose and fell with Buonaparte's fortunes — there had been very few lately — and the figures provided the British intelligence services with a fairly accurate idea of the climate of informed opinion in Paris.

'It will probably be one of them,' said Stephen, as his coach carried him swiftly towards the Regent's park. Yet on the other hand, he reflected, the French intelligence services had very soon taken to slipping their own people in among these messengers, or if not their own people then those uneasy particoloured creatures the double or even triple agents, and conceivably the sender of the bones might be one of these. Obviously it was a man who knew that Stephen had been invited to Paris to address the Institut de France on the solitaire, a man who knew of his connexion with the Royal Society and of the interchange between Banks and Cuvier; but that was no really close identification. Thoroughly undesirable people might also know these things. 'I am glad I dug out my pistols,' he said. 'Though how I shall ever bring myself to face that chest again, I do not know.'

'Here we are, my lord,' said the driver. 'And an uncommon quick run it was.'

'So we are,' said Stephen, 'and so it was.'

Yet in spite of their quick run he was not first at the rendezvous. Leaning on the white rails at the end of the road and looking out over the grass that stretched away and away to the north, Stephen saw a solitary figure pacing to and fro with a book in his hand.

There was no sun, but the high pale sky sent down a strong diffused light and Stephen recognized the man almost at once. He smiled, ducked under the rail and walked out over the rough meadow towards the distant figure. Far to the west a flock of sheep were grazing, white on the vivid green: he passed a hare in her form, clapped close with her ears flat, persuaded she was invisible and so near he could have touched her, and at a suitable distance he called out

'Duhamel, I am happy to see you again,' taking off his hat as he did so.

Duhamel looked much older, much greyer, much more worn than when last they parted, but he returned Stephen's salute with equal cheerfulness and said that he too was delighted to see Maturin, adding that 'he hoped he saw him well'.

'I am truly sorry to have brought you to this remote spot,' said Stephen, 'but since I did not know who you were, it appeared to me that extreme discretion was best for all concerned. How clever of you to find it.'

'Oh, I know it well,' said Duhamel. 'I was shooting here last autumn with my English correspondent. Unhappily we had only borrowed guns and wretched dogs, but I shot four hares and he shot two and a pheasant. We must have seen thirty or forty. Hares, I mean, not pheasants.'

'You are fond of shooting, Duhamel?'

'Yes. Though I far prefer fishing. Sitting on the bank of a quiet stream and watching a float seems to me present happiness itself.' He paused, and went on 'I must apologise for communicating with you in such an improper fashion, but the last time I was in London I found your inn destroyed — I did not know any other direction, and I could scarcely carry this to the Admiralty without fear of compromising you.' He brought out a little packet of jeweller's cotton, opened it, and there in the strong light was the immediate blaze of the diamond, no longer a memory but actual, and far more brilliant, far bluer than Stephen's mental image, a most glorious thing, cold and heavy in his hand.

'Thank you,' he said, slipping it into his breeches pocket after a long moment's silent gaze, 'I am very much indebted to you, Duhamel.'

'It was the bargain,' said Duhamel. 'And there is only one man to thank, if thanks are due, and that is d'Anglars. You may call him a paederast if you choose, but he is the only man of his word I know among all that rotten bunch of self-seeking politicians. He insisted upon its return.'

'I hope in time to make my acknowledgements. So will the lady, I am sure,' said Stephen. 'Shall we walk back towards the town?' He had of course observed Duhamel's bitterness, but he took no notice of it until they had gone a considerable way in silence, when he began, 'Generally speaking questions are out of place in our calling, but may I ask whether it would be safe for you to come and drink a cup of coffee with me? There is a French pastry-cook in Marylebone who understands the making of coffee, a rare accomplishment in this island.'

'Oh, quite safe, I thank you. I am accredited to Monsieur de Lille. There are only three men in London — two men now — who know what I am. But I am afraid I must decline. I have a carriage waiting for me beyond that line of builder's waggons, and I must go on to Hartwell.'

'Then I shall have time to pack my chest and catch the slow coach quite easily,' reflected Stephen. But Duhamel went on in an altered voice, 'Our calling . . . Oh Maturin, do you not grow sick of the perpetual lies and duplicity, the perpetual bad faith? Not only directed against the enemy but against other organizations and within the same group.' Duhamel's face was greyer now and it twitched with the strength of his emotion. 'The struggle for power and political advantage and the falsity and betrayal right and left — shifting alliances — no faith or loyalty. There is a plan for sacrificing me, I know. My correspondent here in London, the man I was shooting with, *was* sacrificed: though that was only for money, whereas mine is to prove my chief's loyalty to the Emperor. You were going to be sacrificed in Brittany; and I could not have saved you, since it was Lucan's people who arranged

Madame de La Feuillade's affair. But as you did not go I suppose you know all about that.' With one accord they turned about and walked back over the grass. 'I am sick of it all,' said Duhamel. 'That is one of the reasons I am so glad to be finished with this particular mission so cleanly — something straight and clean at last.' He threw out his hands in a gesture of disgust and cried 'Listen, Maturin, I want to be shot of it all. I want to go to Canada — to Quebec. If you can arrange it I will give you the equivalent ten times over. Ten times the equivalent. I know something of your affairs and I give you my word that what I can tell you touches your organization and Captain Aubrey very closely.'

Stephen looked at him with pale, considering, objective eyes and after a moment he said 'I will endeavour to arrange it. I will let you know tomorrow. Where can we meet?'

'Oh anywhere. As I told you, there are only two men in London who know me.'

'Can you come to Black's, in St James's Street?'

'Opposite Button's?' asked Duhamel with a strange look — a glare of suspicion that faded almost at once. 'Yes, certainly. Would let us say six o'clock be convenient?'

'Certainly,' said Stephen. 'Until six

o'clock tomorrow, then.'

They parted on coming to the road, where Duhamel bore away westwards to regain his carriage and Stephen walked slowly south, keeping his eye lifted for a hackney-coach. He found one at last in a new-building crescent, scarcely visible for the masons' carts and flying dust, and drove to Durrant's hotel.

Here he asked for Captain Dundas and learnt without much surprise that he had gone out. 'Then I shall wait for him,' he said, and settled down for what might be a matter of hours, since notes miscarried and messages were forgotten, and even if they were not, the recipient rarely saw their urgency as clearly as the sender. It was indeed a matter of hours, but they did not drag excessively, because as usual there were many naval officers staying at the hotel and several who wished to show their kindness for Jack Aubrey came and sat with him for a while. The last of them, a fat, affable, spectacled post-captain called Hervey, was saying what a damned thing it was that the service should be deprived of such a fine seaman, with the heavy American frigates doing so well, when he broke off and said 'There is Heneage Dundas: he feels even more strongly than I do.'

'Come and eat your mutton with me, both of you,' said Dundas, coming over to them.

'Alas, I cannot,' said Hervey. 'I am engaged.' He peered at the clock in his poring way and sprang up, crying 'I am late, I am late already.'

'For my part, I should be happy,' said Stephen, which was true: he liked Dundas, he had missed his breakfast with that infernal sea-chest, and in spite of his anxious mind he was extremely hungry.

'You sail for the North American station quite soon, I believe?' he said, when they had reached their apple pie.

'On Monday, wind and weather permitting,' said Dundas. 'Tomorrow I must make my adieux.'

'Will you indulge me by walking into the smoking-room?' asked Stephen. But when they came to it he saw that there were too many people by far and he said 'The truth of the matter is that I wish to speak to you privately. May we go upstairs, do you think?'

Dundas led the way, gave him a chair and said 'I thought you had something on your mind.'

'I believe we may do Aubrey an essential service,' said Stephen. 'I have been talking to a man in whom I have great confidence. He wishes to go to Canada. In return for being taken there he will give me information of great value concerning Jack.' Replying to the doubt and dissatisfaction in Dundas's face he went on, 'In these blank bald words it sounds intolerably naive, even simple-minded, but I am bound by the confidential nature of so many aspects — I am unable to relate a whole host of details that would compel conviction. Yet at least I can show you this.' He brought out the Blue Peter from his pocket, unwrapped it and held it out in a beam of sunlight.

'What an astonishing great stone,' cried Dundas. 'Can it be a sapphire?'

'It is Diana's blue diamond,' said Stephen. 'She was in Paris, you remember, when Jack and I were imprisoned there, and her leaving it behind was connected with our escape. Its eventual return was promised however and the man I am speaking of brought it to me this morning, on his way to Hartwell. I tell you this so that you will understand at least one of the reasons that I rely on his word and that I take what he says very seriously. There was nothing to prevent him from keeping the stone, yet he handed it over straight away, without any conditions whatsoever.'

'It is an extraordinary great diamond,' said Dundas. 'I do not believe I have seen a finer outside the Tower. It must be worth a fortune.'

'That is what is so impressive: a man that means to go to the New World and start a new life and that hands over an eminently portable fortune is not one to speak lightly.'

'Do you know the reason for his wanting to go to Canada?'

'I would not ask you to take him if he were a common criminal escaping from the law. No, he is sick of his colleagues' bad faith, their dissensions and their dissimulation, and wishes to make a clean and sudden break.'

'He is a Frenchman, I collect, since he is going to Hartwell.'

'I am not sure. He may come from the Rhine provinces. But at all events he is not a Buonapartist, that I can absolutely guarantee.'

'Do you think a promise to take him on condition that his information proves useful to Jack would answer?'

'I do not.'

'No. I suppose not. Though proper flats we should look if . . .' Dundas walked up and down, considering for a while, and then said 'Well, I suppose we shall have to take him. I will write Butcher a note to receive him as my guest. Fortunately we have room and to spare — no master until we reach Halifax. Does he speak English?'

'Oh, very well. That is to say, very fluently. But he learnt it from a Scotch nursemaid and then a Scotch tutor, and it is the North British dialect that he speaks; it is neither very offensive nor incomprehensible — indeed, it has a certain wild archaic charm — and to any but the nicest ear it disguises the foreign accent entirely. He is a quiet, inoffensive gentleman, and is likely to keep his bed throughout the passage, being a most indifferent sailor.'

'So much the better. It is quite against the regulations, you know, he being a foreigner.'

'It is quite against the regulations to take young ladies to sea, foreign or home-bred, yet I believe I have known it done.'

'Well,' said Dundas, 'let us go downstairs and find pen and ink.'

Dr Maturin had all the next day to reflect upon what he had done and what he was doing. By all professional standards it was extraordinarily imprudent; and it was exceedingly unwise from a personal point of view, since he was compromising himself as deeply as possible and opening himself to very ugly accusations — his actions could be interpreted as criminal and they might in fact constitute crimes, capital crimes. He was relying solely on his instinct, and his instinct was by no means infallible. Sometimes it was affected by his wishes and before now it had deceived him very painfully. He reassured himself from time to time by looking at the splendid diamond in his pocket, like a talisman, and he spent the afternoon in the Covent Garden hummums, his sparse frame sweating in the hottest room until it could sweat no more.

'Is Duhamel a punctual man?' he asked himself, sitting in the vestibule at Black's, where he could command the entrance and the porter's desk. 'Does he pay strict attention to time?' Answer came there none until six had stopped striking, when Duhamel appeared on the steps, carrying a packet. Stephen stepped forward before Duhamel could ask for him and led him upstairs to the long room overlooking St James's Street. Duhamel looked greyer still, but his face was as impassive as usual and he appeared to be perfectly composed.

'I have arranged your passage to Halifax in the *Eurydice*,' said Stephen. 'You will have to be aboard before Monday, and you will travel as the captain's guest. He is a close friend of Captain Aubrey's. I have let it be understood that you are or have been to some degree attached to Hartwell, but I do most earnestly advise you to stay in your cabin on the plea of sea-sickness and to speak very little. Here is a note that will introduce you to the ship. You will see that I have retained the name of Duhamel.'

'Upon the whole I prefer it: one complication the less,' said Duhamel, taking the note. 'I am very grateful to you, Maturin: I believe you will not regret it.' He looked round the room. At the far end an aged member was poring over the Parliamentary Debates with a reading-glass.

'You may speak quite freely,' said Stephen. 'The gentleman is a bishop, an Anglican bishop; and he is deaf.'

'Ah, an Anglican bishop,' said Duhamel. 'Quite so. I am glad we are in this particular room' he added, looking out into the street. He collected himself and said 'How shall I begin my account? Names, names — that is one of the difficulties. I am not sure of the names of the three men I mean to tell you about. My correspondent here in London used the name of Palmer, but it was not his own and although he was a remarkably gifted agent in many ways he betrayed himself in this; he did not always respond at once or naturally to his nom de guerre. The name of the second man will be familiar to you: it is Wray, Andrew. For a considerable time I knew him as Mr *Grey*, but he is not a good agent and after a while, getting drunk, he gave himself away. He is not a good agent at all, and really, Maturin, I wonder you did not detect him in Malta.'

Stephen bowed his head as the light came flooding in, blinding humiliatingly obvious. 'I could hardly expect you to employ such a flashy, unreliable fellow,' he muttered.

'He is not without real abilities,' said Duhamel, 'but it is true, he is emotional and timid; he has no bottom and he would not only crack at the first severe interrogation but he is liable to betray himself without any interrogation at all. We should never have gone any distance with him if it had not been for his friend, the third man, whom I know only as Mr Smith, a very highly-placed man indeed — his reports were fairly worshipped in the rue Villars.'

'More highly-placed than Wray?'

'Oh yes. And of much greater force of mind: when you see them together it is like master and pupil. A hard man, too.' Duhamel looked at his watch. 'I must be brief,' he said. 'However, although Smith has great abilities and Wray enough to get himself a name, they are both poor, expensive, and given to very high play; and although they are both nominally and I believe genuinely volunteers they are both constantly asking for money. After the re-organization in the rue Villars, supplies were very much reduced. They sent appeal after appeal, each more pressing, but they were told that their recent information had been insufficient in quantity and quality, which was true. They replied that in another few weeks Sir Joseph Blaine would be finally disposed of, that they would then have full access to the Committee and that their information would be of the greatest possible value.' Duhamel looked at his watch once more and held it to his ear. 'In the meantime they mounted the Stock Exchange fraud.'

Although he felt Duhamel's piercing eye upon him, Stephen could not entirely conceal his emotion; his heart was beating so that he felt its pulsation strong in his throat, and then again he was most deeply shocked at his dull stupidity — the whole thing was so evident. He said, 'You seem preoccupied by the time.'

'Yes,' said Duhamel, shifting his chair nearer to the window. 'Of course, I am sorry that your friend was put to such distress, but apart from that, the objective observer must confess that the affair was neatly handled. You may say that given the exact knowledge of Captain Aubrey's movements and of his father's connexions, together with the possession of an agent as capable as Palmer, the thing was simple; but that would be shallow reasoning . . . Maturin, you will not be offended if perhaps I run out in a few minutes and return somewhat later?'

'Never in life,' said Stephen.

'At one time I thought they had succeeded entirely, and although of course they could not make much money without betraying themselves, they did clear enough for their most pressing debts.'

'That was when Wray paid what he owed me,' reflected Stephen, his shame renewed.

'But that did not suffice,' said Duhamel, 'and they made two other proposals: the first, that some surprisingly large bills should be negotiated on the northern market, and the second, that you should be handed over at Lorient. The proposal about the bills was either declined or withdrawn. I am not sure which; and you were not delivered. Lucan was extremely angry — he had gone down to Brittany himself — and he cut off even the monthly grant. They are now in a very bad way and they have prepared what they assert is an unusually valuable report.' Once again Duhamel looked at his watch. He went on, 'Palmer told me about the

Stock Exchange business in great detail when we were fishing in a stream not far from Hartwell. He was a man you would have liked, Maturin: he could make a kingfisher perch on his hand. He had all sorts of qualities. But that was the last time I ever saw him. A very large reward was offered — the chase became too hot — and so they killed him, in case he should be discovered or betrayed. They did not ship him away; they killed him or had him killed. That I could not possibly forgive. It was merely criminal.'

'Duhamel,' said Stephen in a low voice, moving his chair closer, so that it almost touched the glass of the window, 'can you give me any tangible, concrete proof?'

'No,' said Duhamel. 'Not at present. But I hope I shall be able to do so in five minutes' time.' He went on talking about Palmer, a man he had evidently loved dearly; but his words came somewhat at random. They stopped in mid-sentence: he caught up his packet, said 'Forgive me, Maturin. Watch, watch at the window,' and hurried from the room.

Stephen saw him appear on the pavement below, turn left, walk fast up towards Piccadilly, cross at great hazard among the carriages, and stroll down on the other side of the street towards St James's Park. Almost opposite Stephen's window, at the height of Button's club, he paused and looked at his watch again, as though he were waiting for someone. Stephen's eye ran down the street, and among the people walking up from the park and Whitehall he saw Wray and his taller, older friend Ledward, arm in arm. They disengaged themselves to take off their hats as Duhamel approached and all three stood there talking for a few moments: then Ledward gave Duhamel an envelope in exchange for the packet and they parted, the two going into Button's and Duhamel, not without a slight glance at Stephen's window, back towards Piccadilly.

Stephen ran downstairs, seized pen and paper at the porter's desk, wrote fast, and cried 'Charles, Charles, pray send a lad with this to Sir Joseph Blaine's in Shepherd Market haste post-haste — there is not a moment to be lost.'

'Why, sir,' said the hall-porter, smiling at him, 'never fret yourself about haste posthaste: here is Sir Joseph himself, coming up the steps, a-leaning on Colonel Warren's arm.'

We hope you have enjoyed this Large Print book. Other Thorndike Press or Chivers Press Large Print books are available at your library or directly from the publishers.

For more information about current and upcoming titles, please call or write, without obligation, to:

Thorndike Press
295 Kennedy Memorial Drive
Waterville, ME 04901
Tel. (800) 223-1244

OR

Chivers Press Limited
Windsor Bridge Road
Bath BA2 3AX
England
Tel. (0225) 335336

All our Large Print titles are designed for easy reading, and all our books are made to last.

NM2

NM2 MAR 04	18. AUG 08.	
18 JUN 2004	13. OCT 08.	
28 OCT 2004	11. DEC 08,	
15 MAR 2005	12. OCT 09.	
4 JUN 2005	04. 09	
-9 DEC 2005		
20 JUN 2006	04. JAN 10.	
30. NOV		
14. MAY 07		
08. NOV 07 07.		
20. DEC 07.		
10. APR 08.		
MM2 4/08		
21. JUL 08.		

F O'BRIAN   LARGE PRINT

C

The reverse of the medal

L 5/9

The Reverse
of the Medal

PATRICK O'BRIAN

Thorndike Press • Chivers Press
Waterville, Maine USA   Bath, England

This Large Print edition is published by Thorndike Press, USA and by Chivers Press, England.

Published in 2002 in the U.S. by arrangement with W. W. Norton & Company Inc.

Published in 2002 in the U.K. by arrangement with HarperCollins Publishers Ltd.

U.S. Hardcover 0-7862-1931-9 (Famous Authors Series)
U.K. Hardcover 0-7540-1798-2 (Windsor Large Print)
U.K. Softcover 0-7540-9182-1 (Paragon Large Print)

The text of this Large Print edition is unabridged.
Other aspects of the book may vary from the original edition.

Cover design by Thorndike Press Staff.

Set in 16 pt. Plantin.

Printed in the United States on permanent paper.

British Library Cataloguing-in-Publication Data available

Library of Congress Cataloging-in-Publication Data

O'Brian, Patrick, 1914–
    The reverse of the medal / Patrick O'Brian.
      p. cm.
    ISBN 0-7862-1931-9 (lg. print : hc : alk. paper)
    1. Aubrey, Jack (Fictitious character) — Fiction.
    2. Maturin, Stephen (Fictitious character) — Fiction.
    3. Great Britain — History, Naval — 19th century —
    Fiction. 4. London (England) — Fiction. 5. Criminals —
    Fiction. 6. Large type books. I. Title.
    PR6029.B55 R48 2002
    823′.914—dc21   2001054088